The Girl With No Name

Diney Costeloe is the bestselling author of *The Throwaway Children*, *The Runaway Family*, *The Lost Soldier* and *The Sisters of St Croix*. She divides her time between Somerset and West Cork.

Also by Diney Costeloe

The Throwaway Children

The Lost Soldier

The Runaway Family

The Sisters of St Croix

DINEY COSTELOE

The Girl With No Name

9 7 5 3 1 2 4 6 8

A catalogue record for this book is available
from the British Library.

ISBN (HB) 9781784970055
ISBN (XTPB) 9781784970062
ISBN (E) 9781784970048

Typeset by e-type, Aintree, Liverpool

Printed and bound in Germany by GGP
Media GmbH, Pössneck

Head of Zeus Ltd
Clerkenwell House
45–47 Clerkenwell Green
London EC1R 0HT

WWW.HEADOFZEUS.COM

*To all those who were evacuated and to those who
opened their homes and took them in.*

Prologue

Hanau, Germany, 9 November 1938

'Jews out! Jews out! Jews out!' The chanting grew ever nearer and was accompanied by bangs and crashes and cries of terror. The Becker family huddled in their kitchen with the lights off and all the curtains in the apartment drawn against the night and against the terrifying sounds from the street below. Their apartment was on the first floor of the building. Once Franz Becker had had his surgery on the ground floor, but that had long since gone, taken over by a neighbour when the new laws forbade Franz from practising as a doctor. But the house and the apartment were marked. Marta pushed her children, Lisa and Martin, into the small broom cupboard, and saying, 'Lisa, you have to! Be brave!' she closed the door firmly on Lisa's frightened eyes. She knew that her daughter was terrified of being shut in small places, she always had been, but it was for her own safety and Marta had to be strong for them all.

As the baying crowd passed along the street, Marta crept under the kitchen table. Bricks were hurled through the windows and shards of glass showered down on the table where she crouched, curled into a ball in an effort to protect herself from the flying splinters. The sound of excited chanting moved on, but even as Marta crept from beneath the table and was opening the broom cupboard, there was the sound of boots on the staircase and the door to the apartment was kicked open. Two storm troopers burst in, one holding a pistol, the other armed with a long wooden club. They

I

were followed by a man from the Gestapo, tall and sinister in his trade-mark long, dark coat and trilby hat. He paused in the doorway looking round.

'I can't believe that filthy Jews are still living in an apartment like this when there are so many true Germans without proper homes.' His tone was one of disgust as his eyes ran over the woman and two children cowering in the kitchen. 'Where is your husband?' he demanded. 'Where is he hiding?'

'He's not here,' faltered Marta. 'He's… he's out… looking after a patient.'

'Find him,' the Gestapo officer snapped out the order. 'He has no patients!' The two storm troopers jumped to obey and crashed their way round the flat, tipping up beds, pulling at curtains, opening cupboard doors, until one said, 'Nobody here, sir.'

The Gestapo man looked angry and turning to Marta, he said, 'We will find him. Pack one case and then out! Take your Jew-spawn with you and be gone… before I come back!' With that all three men stamped back down the stairs.

When they'd gone, Marta sank down on to a chair and buried her head in her hands. Thank God Franz had indeed been visiting a patient, a young Jewish mother about to give birth, and thank God that in the gloom of the darkened room, neither the storm troopers nor the Gestapo officer had realised that Martin was blind. For the moment her two men were safe, but not, she knew, for long.

What should they do? Her brain seemed numb and she had to force herself to think. If they stayed put the Gestapo would almost certainly be back, looking for Franz and checking to be sure she and her children had left the apartment; but if they went now they would be out on the streets where a frenzied mob was still chanting, still setting fires, smashing windows, and beating up anyone fool enough to protest.

'Mutti,' whispered Lisa, 'where's Papa?'

'I don't know, Lisa,' replied her mother. It was the truth. Franz could be anywhere, just not, she prayed, in the clutches of the mob outside.

'What are we going to do, Mother?' asked Martin quietly.

'I'm going to pack a case now, before they come back looking for us, then if they do, we can simply walk out into the street and we shall have some things to keep us going.'

'It's not safe to stay here,' Martin said.

'It's not safe out on the streets either,' replied his mother. 'We're not safe anywhere, but for the moment I think it's better to stay here. If they see us walking through the dark, carrying a case, they'll simply grab it and beat us up. For the moment it sounds as if they've moved on.' She went cautiously to the window and keeping well behind the curtain, peered out into the grey of dawn. There were a few shadows moving about in the street below, dark silhouettes against the red-orange glow of fire, blazing through the synagogue at the end of the street and the rabbi's house beyond. The sky itself seemed on fire and Marta wondered why their home had been spared. Probably because a good 'German' family would like to live in it. For whatever reason, she decided, it might give them shelter for another hour or two yet. To venture out into the street now with two children, one of them blind, would be suicidal, Marta realised, but they should prepare for flight.

Lisa watched as her mother pulled out the biggest case they had and began to fill it with some clothes for each of them. In the pocket of a skirt, she slipped the pearl necklace Lisa knew Papa had given her on their wedding day and a ring that had been her grandmother's.

'Fetch the flour jar,' Mutti said, and when Lisa brought it to her, she plunged her hand into the flour and pulled out the roll of Reichsmarks that had been hidden there.

'Put these in your knickers,' she said to a startled Lisa and turned her attention back to the suitcase.

Outside, the chanting and the sound of smashing glass continued, but further off; the crowd was turning its attention elsewhere. Martin sat on a chair, his head in his hands, listening. He could see nothing and his blindness made him even more frightened. The room had been turned over and he no longer knew where the furniture was. If he moved he knew he'd fall over.

'Where shall we go, Mother?' he asked.

'To Aunt Trudi's,' replied Marta firmly, though she really had no idea where. 'I'm sure Papa will come and find us there, if ...' she hesitated, biting back the words, 'if they haven't caught him' and saying instead, 'if he can.'

The three of them spent the early hours sitting, waiting. Gradually the children nodded off into uneasy sleep, but Marta remained wide awake. There was no point in her trying to sleep, indeed, Marta knew it would be foolish. She needed to be alert in case the Gestapo man returned. Outside she could still hear shouts and as daylight filled the sky she went once again to the window to look out. What she saw made her gasp. Was this really the street in which she lived? It was strewn with glass, the wood of smashed doors and broken furniture. The windows of the two houses opposite gaped back at her, a few jagged shards still clinging to the frames, the front door of one lay flat on the ground, that of the other hung crazily from one hinge. The houses on either side seemed undamaged and Marta realised with a jolt that they belonged to two of her non-Jewish neighbours. There were not many non-Jews living in the area, but as far as she could see their homes had remained untouched. None of the houses showed a light, but she could see Frau Klein in the road outside her house, picking through the contents of her home which lay trampled in the gutter.

It's time to move, she thought. About to turn back to wake the children, she caught a movement in the shadows at the entrance of an alley a little further down the street. Someone was there. As she watched she saw that it was Franz, peering anxiously round the corner. She raised her hand to wave, but even as she did so, two men stepped out of a doorway and confronted him. Franz turned to run, but a third man was behind him, swinging a wooden baton, and without a cry Franz crumpled to the ground. Two of the men grabbed him by the feet and dragged him, his head banging against the cobbles, unceremoniously up the road and round the corner.

Marta crammed her hand into her mouth to stop herself from crying out and stared at the place where Franz had stood. The third man, still standing there, glanced up towards the window. Though Marta was sure he couldn't see her concealed by the heavy velvet of the curtain, he fixed his eyes on her window and smiled, before turning away and following his companions, and Franz, out of sight.

With renewed panic she crossed the room and shook the children. 'Wake up,' she said, 'it's time to go.'

'Go where?' asked Lisa sleepily, the events of the night momentarily forgotten.

'To Aunt Trudi's, now. Before they come back. Come on, both of you. There's no time to be lost.' She could only pray that her sister Trudi's apartment had not been wrecked as well, that the madness had been localised.

The two children dressed quickly and at their mother's insistence put on two sets of underwear, two jerseys and thick woollen stockings. She wanted them to wear as many clothes as possible, for she knew they could well lose their precious suitcase if they were seen carrying it in the street.

'And these,' she said, handing them their winter coats. It would be cold outside at this time on a November morning. 'Hats, scarves and gloves too,' she insisted as she donned her own winter clothes, 'and your winter boots.'

Moments later they were ready to leave. The suitcase was heavy. Marta had crammed it as full as she could, for she knew that they wouldn't be coming back to this apartment for a long time... if ever.

'Hold Martin's hand,' Marta instructed her daughter, 'and don't let go whatever happens, understand?'

'Yes, Mutti,' replied the girl and taking hold of her brother she said, 'Don't let go of me, Martin.'

'My stick,' Martin cried in alarm, 'I need my stick.'

'No,' snapped his mother. 'No stick. We can't let them know that you're blind. Put your hand here.' She took his hand and put it on the handle of the case. 'You have to help me with this. I'll carry it with you, but they may not realise that I'm leading you with it.' With a final glance round the apartment that had been her home for more than fifteen years, she said quietly, 'We're going to walk downstairs and then out into the street. Stay together, but if we do get separated, go to Aunt Trudi's house.'

Chapter One

London, 1939

When Naomi Federman read an advertisement in the *Evening Standard* asking for people to become foster parents to refugee children from Germany, it gave her pause and she began to consider the idea. She showed it to her husband, Dan, when he got home that evening.

'It's something we could do, don't you think?' she said. 'We've got room here for a child.'

Dan knew that there was a space in Naomi's life that she'd always hoped would be filled by children of their own, but there had been none, and now that she was past thirty-five, he knew, too, that she'd given up hope of having a family. Her suggestion of fostering a refugee child might, he thought, help fill the void.

'Right-ho, love,' he said. 'If that's what you want to do, we'll find out about it.'

They went to Bloomsbury House where the arrival of Jewish refugee children from Germany was being co-ordinated and their offer was accepted.

'We'd really love a baby or a toddler,' Naomi said hesitantly to the woman behind the desk who was taking down their details.

'I'm afraid we can't possibly guarantee that,' she replied. 'We're never quite sure who is coming in on the trains these days. Most of the children, those whose names we've been given, have already been paired with families, but there are sometimes children we aren't expecting, those who've been pushed on to the train at the last minute. Those are the ones who'll need families when they get here.' She smiled up at the Federmans. 'Generous people like you, ready to take them in and give them a home.'

'We quite understand,' Daniel said. 'We're happy to provide a home for any child who needs one, aren't we, love?' And Naomi had nodded.

So, one afternoon in July, they found themselves at Liverpool Street station, waiting for the arrival of their new child. There was a group of other prospective foster parents waiting in a large hall at the station. Many of them had already been assigned children, knew their names and ages, but the people at Bloomsbury House had contacted the Federmans just yesterday and told them there was an unexpected child on this train due from Frankfurt and asked them to come to the station.

The sight of a line of children straggling wearily into the hall tugged at Naomi's heart. Each wore a label, each carried one small suitcase, all were tired and pale, grubby and frightened. Several were tearful at the end of the long journey, already homesick, arriving in an alien country where everything looked different and they couldn't understand what was being said to them.

A woman, who introduced herself as Mrs Carter and who spoke German, had come from Bloomsbury House. With quiet efficiency she had introduced the arrivals to their new families, checking off their names and addresses on her list. Gradually they left the hall, foster mothers leading their new charges by the hand, foster fathers carrying suitcases, out into the sprawl of London to begin their new lives.

At last there was only one child left, a girl of about thirteen, small for her age, with tangled brown hair and smudges of dirt on her face. She stood forlorn, her case at her feet, and unshed tears gleaming in her brown eyes. She had been a last-minute addition to the fleeing children and had no sponsor.

Mrs Carter crossed over to her and said with a smile, 'Now then, who've we got here? What's your name, my dear?'

'Lisa Becker,' came the whispered reply.

'Well, Lisa, we're very pleased to see you. We didn't know you were on the train until it arrived in Holland, but we're very glad you were. Where do you come from?'

'Hanau.'

Hanau. Not the first from there, Mrs Carter thought sadly, but all she said was, 'Well, you're safe in London now. Did they give you a letter to give me when you arrived?'

Lisa nodded and feeling in her pocket, handed over an envelope. Mrs Carter opened it quickly and perused the contents.

She turned to the Federmans and reverting to English said, 'Her name is Lieselotte Becker, aged thirteen, and she's come from Hanau, which is a town not far from Frankfurt. She is Jewish, but according to this letter, not observant.' She glanced at Naomi. 'Are you?'

Naomi shook her head. Her father had been Jewish, but her family had not followed the Jewish laws of daily living. 'No,' she said.

Mrs Carter nodded. 'Well, Lieselotte follows no dietary rules, so you have no worries there, she can eat whatever you do.'

Naomi looked at the girl, waiting fearfully in the now-empty hall. With her grubby face and straggly hair, she was not an attractive prospective daughter, but they had promised to give a refugee child a home and Lieselotte was such a child.

Mrs Carter turned back to her. 'Lieselotte,' she said, 'these are the kind people who you're going to live with. Mr and Mrs Federman. You'll be going home with them now and that's where you'll be living. You must write to your parents to let them know that you've arrived and give them the address.'

Lisa looked at the couple standing, waiting. The man was small with a wiry frame. He wore rather baggy, dark trousers and a checked jacket over a collarless shirt. His hair, showing from under the flat cap that perched on his head, was touched with grey, but his eyes were a deep blue, laughter lines etched at the corners. He was smiling at her now, his eyes crinkling as he did so.

So different from Papa, Lisa thought, as a picture of her father in his neat suit, collar and tie, flashed before her, but he has a kind face.

His wife was only a little shorter than he and built on far more generous lines. Her hair, a dark blonde, was caught up at the back of her head, she was wearing a blue cotton frock that strained a little across her ample bosom, and her arms, emerging from cotton sleeves, looked strong and capable. She was smiling too, but her eyes, a sharp, light grey, were noting Lisa's travel-worn state and somehow Lisa felt she was being assessed and found wanting. She hung back, waiting for Mrs Carter to speak again. How was she going to talk to this couple once German-speaking Mrs Carter had gone? she wondered, an edge of panic rising through her. But Mrs Carter said nothing, it was the woman who addressed her next.

'Hallo, Lieselotte,' she said. 'Welcome to London.'

Lisa stared at her uncomprehendingly until Mrs Carter translated, then she spoke one of the few English sentences she had learned and said, 'Good day, madam.' She pointed to herself and added, 'Lisa. *Bitte*, Lisa.'

'It's a diminutive of her name,' explained Mrs Carter to Naomi's look of enquiry. She smiled. 'And a lot easier to say. I think you should call her Lisa. By the way,' she added, 'how would you like Lisa to address you?'

The Federmans looked at each other. The husband shrugged, but his wife suggested tentatively, 'Aunt Naomi and Uncle Dan?'

'Perfect,' agreed Mrs Carter cheerfully, and reverting again to German explained this to Lisa.

Before they left the station Mrs Carter noted Lisa's details on her clipboard and then shaking the Federmans by the hand, she sent them all home.

With Dan carrying the suitcase, they left the station and boarded a bus, climbing the stairs to its upper deck. Lisa had never seen a double-decker bus before and was pleased they had gone upstairs.

'There you are... Liesel... Lisa,' Dan said, stumbling a little over her unfamiliar name, 'you can see a bit of London on our way home.' He waved an expansive hand at the window and what lay beyond. As the bus wove its way through the city Lisa, wide-eyed, peered out of the window at her first sight of London. All was bustle and rush. She had never seen such busy streets; buses, cars, lorries, taxis, seemed to be coming from every direction, horns hooting, engines roaring. People thronged the pavements, in and out of shops and offices, disappearing into the jumble of narrow streets that twisted away from the main road. Would she ever, Lisa wondered, dare venture out into streets such as these?

Naomi and Daniel sat in the seat behind her and spoke in low voices.

'Not quite what we'd hoped for,' Dan said cautiously.

'No,' Naomi agreed, 'but we couldn't leave her, could we?'

'Course not, love,' Dan said with some relief in his voice. He knew that Naomi had set her heart on a much younger child. 'She'll be fine.'

'This way,' Dan said when they got off the bus. 'Not far now.' Carrying Lisa's case he strode ahead, leaving Naomi and Lisa to follow him, threading their way through the web of streets that spread beyond the main road. They were lined with houses, some set back in pairs behind a tiny front garden, but most of them flat-faced terraced houses which opened directly on to the pavement, each identical to its neighbour like a row of cut-out paper dolls. To Lisa the roads all looked the same and as they took first one turning and then another, she wondered how on earth she was going to find her way through this maze another time.

Aunt Naomi was chatting to her, even though it was perfectly clear that Lisa couldn't understand a word she was saying. And then they were there, after one final turn they entered yet another street, looking to Lisa identical to all the others.

Uncle Dan had waited for them on the corner and when they caught up with him he pointed at a street name, high up on a wall. 'Kemble Street,' he said. 'Kemble Street. We live in Kemble Street.' He looked expectantly at Lisa and when she didn't say anything he said, 'Kemble Street,' and touched her with his pointed finger. 'You,' he said, 'you say, "I live in Kemble Street."'

Once she had realised what he wanted of her, Lisa made a valiant effort to repeat the name and a stammering, 'I live in Kemple Street,' earned her a warm smile of approval.

'Good!' Dan said. 'Good girl!'

Lisa recognised the word 'good', so like the German '*gut*', and for the first time since she had met her foster parents, they saw her smile, and her pale face was transformed.

They walked a little way along the street and then stopped outside one of the small terrace houses. It had a green door with the number 65 painted on it.

'Here we are,' Dan said. 'Number sixty-five. This is where we live, Lisa. Sixty-five Kemble Street.' He unlocked the front door and led the way inside. Lisa followed him into a narrow hallway with a room to the left, a passageway to the back of the house and immediately in front of her, a steep staircase to the floor above. Dan put down the suitcase and said, 'Welcome to your new home, Lisa.'

'I'll show Lisa where she's going to sleep,' Naomi said, 'you put the kettle on, Dan, and we'll all have a cuppa. This way, Lisa.' Naomi picked up the case and beckoning Lisa to follow her, led the way upstairs. At the top of the stairs she pointed to a door and then to herself saying, 'Our bedroom.' She opened a second door to show a tiny bathroom and then a third, gesturing Lisa to go in. 'Your room, Lisa.'

Lisa went in and looked about her. It was a small room furnished with a bed, a chest of drawers and a chair. The bed was covered with a floral quilt and on the chest there was a china bowl and a jug patterned with roses. On one wall was a mirror and on another was a picture of a horse pulling a plough.

Naomi put the suitcase on the bed. 'Why don't you unpack your things and then come down to the kitchen.' And when Lisa looked at her uncomprehendingly, she pulled open the drawers and then pointed to the suitcase, miming unpacking.

Lisa nodded and Naomi gave her a smile and went back downstairs.

Left alone, Lisa went to the window and looked out. Below her was an untidy yard bounded by wooden fences, with identical yards on either side. Beyond was what looked like an alleyway and the backs of the houses crowding along the next street. She turned back to the bed and opened her case. It held all she now possessed in the world. Her mother had packed what few clothes she had and

had managed to buy her a new coat for the coming winter, but she was wearing her only pair of shoes. Tears flooded her eyes as she looked at the clothes so carefully mended and folded by Mutti. What was Mutti doing now? Where was Papa, had he come home yet? How was Martin coping living in an unfamiliar, cramped apartment? Had he learned his way around the furniture? She picked up the photo of them, taken in happier days, all smiling at the camera. Her family. It was the only photograph she had of them. She put it into her pocket and with a determined effort blew her nose and began to put her clothes into the open drawers. When the case was empty she pushed it under the bed and sat down. Here she was, in London, in a tiny house, with people she didn't know and all she wanted to do was go home, back to Hanau; to be with her family, no matter how difficult life there was becoming. Tears trickled down her cheeks. She felt entirely bereft and alone and she wanted to howl.

Papa had thought they were safe. He was a well-known doctor in the town, his practice flourishing. The fact that his mother happened to be Jewish had never concerned him. They were fully assimilated and he considered himself, first and foremost, a German. He had been an army doctor in the Great War and had received a medal for his service. But now that counted for nothing. His mother was a Jew, so he was a Jew. He was no longer allowed to treat anyone but Jews; his former colleagues treated him as if he had the plague and when he had gone to the aid of one of his pregnant patients who was in early labour, he had been arrested by the Gestapo and had disappeared. On the now notorious 'Kristallnacht' they had been turned out of their home, left to find shelter wherever they could while another, Aryan, doctor who'd already taken over the surgery, now took the apartment above it. They had taken temporary refuge with Mutti's sister Trudi and her family, but their apartment was small and crowded and it was almost impossible to house so many, particularly a blind child, so they'd had to move on. Marta had found two rooms in an old tenement building on the edge of the town and there they had managed to stay. Martin, Lisa's blind older brother, had gradually learned to find his way about and for a short while some sort of normality had returned. Except there was no Papa. He hadn't been released, he had simply disappeared and so Marta had decided that she must try and get her children to safety. Lisa's name had been added to the list of Jewish children waiting for places on one of the Kindertransport trains to take them to safety, out of the country.

'I don't want to go,' Lisa had pleaded, but her mother was insistent.

'If a place comes up, darling, you're going. I need to know you're safe.'

'But what about Martin?'

'They won't take Martin,' her mother said bitterly. 'They won't even put his name on the list; blind children are too much trouble.'

The days and weeks had passed. There had been no news of Papa, despite every effort her mother made to find out what had happened to him, where he had been taken. Lisa got her passport, but she had not been given a place on the train. She was relieved. She didn't want to go and she hoped against hope that she wouldn't be chosen. Then suddenly, one afternoon, a man came to the apartment and said there was a place on the train leaving Frankfurt the next day. Someone was not going after all. There was room for Lisa if she had her passport and wanted to go. She didn't want to go, but her mother was determined that she should and began to pack. The next day Lisa had bid a tearful farewell to Martin and then gone to the station with her mother.

'The war is coming,' Mutti had said. 'I can't leave Germany without your father and Martin can't leave without me. As soon as you get to London, you must send me your address and we can write to each other, but if the war comes and you can't write directly, you can try to get letters to us through your father's cousin Nikolaus, in Switzerland.' She pressed a folded sheet of paper into Lisa's hand. 'Here's his address in Zurich, and we'll write to you the same way. If we can, we'll go to him. It may be possible, because Switzerland will surely stay neutral.'

Lisa looked at the paper now, Nikolaus Becker's name and address. Would Papa ever come home, she wondered. And if he did, would the three of them be allowed to leave Germany, to go to Zurich?

She looked round the bleak little room that was now hers. She was here, she must make the best of it, but it wasn't going to be easy. She got to her feet and went into the little bathroom that jutted out, a precarious afterthought, on the back of the house. She splashed cold water on her face and then determined to pull herself together, she went downstairs.

Chapter Two

'She'll be fine,' Dan had said. It was an optimistic remark, but neither he nor Naomi knew just how optimistic. It was far more difficult being a foster parent than Naomi had expected; being responsible for a child who wasn't yours, needing to keep her safe so that, one day perhaps, she could be reunited with her parents. When she and Daniel had offered themselves she hadn't realised how heavy the responsibility would feel.

The early weeks had not been easy on either side. Lisa was desperately homesick and unable to explain her fears and her emotions to her new parents. She spoke only a few words of English and the Federmans spoke absolutely no German. Everything was strange to Lisa, and with no children of their own, Naomi and Dan were at a loss as to how they might deal with a thirteen-year-old girl, who looked at the world through wide, frightened eyes and often cried herself to sleep.

'I'm beginning to wonder what we've taken on,' Naomi sighed to Dan one evening when Lisa had been with them for a week. 'The poor kid is so homesick and I can't communicate with her except by signs and the odd word or two. I tried to give her a hug today when she was looking very down, but she pulled away and ran out of the room. I don't know what to do, I feel so helpless.'

Dan pulled her into his arms and held her close. 'You're doing the best you can, love. You can't do more. We just have to take each day as it comes and when her English improves we'll be able to talk to her properly. Till then, well, we have to be patient and try and understand how she must be feeling, dumped on us, complete strangers, and away from everyone and everything she knows and loves.'

Naomi returned his hug. 'You're a wise man, Daniel Federman,' she murmured. 'I don't deserve you, but I'm glad you're mine.'

It did indeed take patience and goodwill on both sides, but with a great deal of sign language they managed to communicate enough to get by.

Soon after Lisa had arrived, Mary James, Naomi's oldest friend, looked in for a cup of tea one afternoon. She and her husband Tom kept the Duke of Wellington pub on the corner. It was Dan's local and the four of them had been friends since their school days, growing up in the area, building their lives in the familiarity of their London streets. When Naomi and Dan had decided to offer themselves as foster parents to a refugee child, Mary had, Naomi knew, suggested to Tom that they should do the same, but Tom had refused. He'd been in the last war, he said, and he'd seen enough bloody Germans to last him a lifetime and he wasn't bloody going to have one in his house.

Mary had said no more about it, but when Lisa arrived in Kemble Street, she had taken pains to get to know her. On her first visit, she'd brought an English–German dictionary with her. 'Found this on a stall down the market,' she told Naomi. 'Thought it might be useful!'

Naomi gave her a hug. 'You're a saviour! Look, Lisa!' She held out the dictionary. When Lisa saw what it was she gave Mary a huge beam and said carefully, 'Thank you, madam.'

Mary smiled back at her and said, 'I hope it helps you.'

It certainly did. The dictionary was well-used. Left on the mantelshelf in the kitchen, it was there to hand when anyone was at a loss for a word in either language.

After that, Aunt Mary, as Lisa was instructed to call her, often dropped in to see how the girl was getting on and Lisa found herself looking forward to her visits. Mary seemed to understand how lost and lonely she must feel, a child in a foreign country, living with strangers and with war fever building around her.

It was indeed a time of national tension. War was coming, everyone knew that now, it was only a matter of when. The country had been preparing for months and Lisa was soon involved in some of the preparations. Naomi took her to the local distribution centre to have a gas mask fitted. People were queuing up to get their masks which were laid out on tables ready for trial. Harassed-looking volunteers dealt with each person in turn, finding the right mask and explaining how it should be put on. Lisa watched, wide-eyed, as Naomi was fitted with hers, not at all liking what she saw. Then it was her turn. The woman picked up a mask and, pressing it firmly against Lisa's face, told her to push her chin forward into it and then adjusted the straps, so that it fitted snugly round her head. Lisa hated it. She hated the smell of the rubber, the touch of it on her skin, but more she hated having her face enclosed, feeling that she couldn't breathe.

'Just breathe normally,' the woman said. But Lisa couldn't, she fought for breath as a bubble of panic rose in her chest, threatening to suffocate her, and she ripped the mask from her face, gasping for air.

Naomi tried to encourage her to put it back on again, but she refused. She couldn't explain her panic, all she could say was, 'No! No! No!'

'She's a refugee,' Naomi explained. 'She doesn't speak English.'

'Well,' snapped the weary volunteer, 'that won't stop her getting gassed, now will it? Never mind,' she glanced back at the queue of people waiting, 'it was a good enough fit. Just take it home with you and get her to practise wearing it, so she gets used to it. Instructions are in the lid.' She handed them the two gas masks in their cardboard cases and turned to the next in the queue.

Another day they went to the street market and Naomi managed to buy the end of a roll of black material so they could make blackout curtains. Together they sat in the front room and covered the wooden frames Uncle Dan had made to fit each window.

'Good thing our windows ain't big,' Naomi remarked as they stretched the scant fabric across the frames and stitched it into place. 'We was lucky to get this much.' Black material was in great demand and she knew she had been extremely lucky to find any at all. Lisa liked to sew and helping Naomi with the blackout brought her a little closer to her foster mother. Naomi could see that Lisa had been well taught. Her stitches were neat and even and she worked quickly.

'Good, Lisa,' she said. 'That's very good. You sew beautifully.' She was rewarded with a shy smile and Lisa's first unprompted words. 'My mother do me this.'

Building on this effort, Naomi said, 'Your mother taught you. That's good, Lisa, very good!' They exchanged smiles and another link was forged between them. The next evening, when Naomi was listening to the wireless and darning one of Dan's socks, Lisa leaned across and took another from the mending basket, neatly darning the hole which had appeared in the heel.

Number sixty-five Kemble Street had no garden, nowhere to put one of the Anderson shelters that the government were providing, and though there was a public air raid shelter at the far end of Hope Street, the thought of running there through a raid in the dark of night and being crushed in among so many was frightening, so Dan decided to fix up the old vegetable cellar as a shelter.

'Is it deep enough?' Naomi asked anxiously.

'Should be,' Dan reassured her, 'unless we get a direct hit.'

'So, shouldn't we go to the Hope Street shelter?' persisted Naomi.

'That wouldn't survive a direct hit either,' he told her. 'We're just as well here.' He brought down a couple of sagging armchairs and an old mattress with blankets and pillows, so they could sleep if the raid was a long one, keeping them there all night. There was a rickety table and on a shelf along one wall were some candles, stuck into the tops of beer bottles, matches, some bottles of water and biscuits in a tin.

When Lisa saw the cellar shelter she was terrified. She hated small spaces and being shut in. She had never liked closed doors, always leaving her bedroom door open, and the idea of being underground, actually under the house, filled her with horror. The cellar was a dark, cramped space, with no window and no electric light. The low ceiling and the grey stone walls pressed in on her, the dank musty air smothering her so that she could hardly breathe. She froze at the top of the steps and only allowed herself to be taken down, holding firmly to Dan's hand. He had lighted some of the candles and the light flickered in the draught from the door.

'Not shut door,' she had begged. 'Not shut door.'

'No.' He spoke reassuringly, knowing that she understood few of his words and hoping his tone would calm her. 'Not today anyway. Only if there's a raid.' He recognised her panic and said soothingly, 'We won't be down here much, me duck, only if there's an air raid,' and with that he led her back upstairs to the kitchen.

'She's claustrophobic,' he told Naomi later. 'We're going to have trouble getting her down into that cellar when the siren goes.'

Always pragmatic, Naomi said, 'We'll face that when the time comes. We ain't at war yet, thank God.'

War fever was in the air though and it was only three weeks later that, listening to the wireless, they heard the grim news that Hitler had invaded Poland. Naomi and Lisa had come home from the market weighed down with groceries: tins of meat and vegetables, soup and sardines, iron rations to be squirrelled away for future use. Everyone was stocking up against the expected scarcities. Londoners knew they would be Hitler's prime target and they were preparing themselves.

'I saw some kiddies being taken to the railway station today,' Naomi told Dan. 'Dreadful it was. They was all lined up with labels on their coats, being taken away from home to goodness knows where.' She looked across at him and added softly, 'Just like poor Lisa.'

'Better than staying here in London and being bombed to death,' Dan said.

'S'pose so,' Naomi reluctantly agreed, 'but heart-breaking for their mums.' Secretly, she'd often wondered how Lisa's mother could bear to send her daughter so far away, all alone; it wasn't natural, she'd thought. But now, she realised, London mothers were doing exactly the same thing. Sending their children off into the unknown, with no idea of where they'd gone or who would be looking after them. It took brave women with deep love for their children to do that. And for the first time she was glad that she had no children to send. Then she thought of Lisa.

'D'you think we ought to be sending Lisa away to the country, too?' she asked Dan.

He shook his head. 'Don't know. Be a bit much for her, wouldn't it? She's only just got here, poor kid.'

'Perhaps I ought to go and ask that Mrs Carter, at Bloomsbury House. What d'you think?'

'You could, I suppose. See what she thinks is best.'

Naomi nodded. 'Yes,' she said, 'I think I will. Don't want Lisa to escape from the Nazis only to be bombed by them here.'

She went to Bloomsbury House the next day and had less than two minutes of a very harassed Mrs Carter's time.

'I can't do anything for her at present,' she said. 'The best thing is to keep her with you for the moment and get her into a school as soon as possible. If the school is then evacuated, well, she can go with them.'

So Lisa stayed on with the Federmans in their little house in Kemble Street, never realising how close she'd come to being put on yet another train, with a label on her coat.

On 3 September, that fateful Sunday morning, she and her foster parents listened in silence to Mr Chamberlain's broadcast.

'This morning the British Ambassador in Berlin handed the German government a final note, stating that unless we heard from them by eleven o'clock that they were prepared at once to withdraw their troops from Poland, a state of war would exist between us.' The prime minister's speech was slow and sombre and the sound of it filled Lisa with fear. 'I have to tell you now that no such undertaking has been received and that consequently this country is at war with Germany.'

Lisa had only understood very few words in the whole broadcast, but 'war' and 'Germany' were among them and she could see the horrified look on Aunt Naomi's face and the weary resignation on Uncle Dan's.

'Here we go again,' he said, 'so much for "peace in our time"!'

At war with Germany, the words echoed in Lisa's head. Mutti, Papa and Martin are still trapped there, she thought, as she fought to keep the tears of desolation and despair from flooding down her cheeks. I'll never see them again.

Lisa had written home to tell her mother that she had arrived safely in London and to give her the Federmans' address. She had received one letter back.

Aunt Naomi handed her the envelope one morning, saying, 'This is for you, Lisa. Looks like a letter from home.'

Lisa had almost snatched it from her, and muttering, 'Thank you, thank you,' had retired to her bedroom to open it. Tearing the envelope open she found the letter written on a sheet of paper torn from an exercise book. There, suddenly dear to her, was her mother's familiar handwriting.

My darling,

I was so pleased to hear that you have arrived safely and are now living with such kind people. Please thank Mr and Mrs Federman for me and remember to be a good girl. They are so generous to take you into their home and look after you, you must be sure to show how grateful you are and behave like the loving and thoughtful girl I know you are. We are well here. You'll be glad to hear Papa is home again now and though he hasn't been very well, he is getting better.

We all miss you very much, but are so relieved to know that you're safe. Remember you can write to Cousin Nikolaus, he would love to hear from you.

Write again soon, darling, as we are longing to hear about your new life in London, about your school and the friends you have made, indeed everything that's happened to you since you got on the train.

We all send our love and Martin says to tell you that he's looking after us very well.

All our love,

Mutti

Tears filled Lisa's eyes as she read and reread the letter, savouring the news it brought. Couched in such general terms that nothing in it might be construed as seditious or dangerous should it be intercepted and read, it still told Lisa much of what she wanted to know.

Papa was home again. The Gestapo, or whoever had been holding him – her mother had been careful not to say – had finally let him go. Perhaps now that he was home, they'd be able to leave Germany, perhaps go to Cousin Nikolaus in Switzerland. Surely now he was with them they could try. Surely it wasn't too late.

Though the letter made Lisa ache with homesickness, at least she had news of them all. She kept it under her pillow, often reading it again before she went to sleep, kissing the paper her mother had touched. That and the photograph, which she carried everywhere, were her last precious links with home.

As they sat in the kitchen that Sunday morning and Uncle Dan and Aunt Naomi pondered Mr Chamberlain's words, Lisa fingered the picture in her pocket of her family, now trapped by the declaration of war.

'Thank God you're too old to go this time,' Naomi was saying.

Daniel, ten years older than she, had, as a seventeen-year-old lad, spent several months in the Flanders trenches. He had not been wounded but his health had been broken and ever since then he'd had a weak chest, on occasion wheezing and fighting for breath. Privately, Naomi thought his general weakness could be the reason that there had been no babies, but she would never have said so. She loved him dearly and if no babies was the price she must pay for marrying her Dan, then so be it. At least he didn't have to go to war again.

'They said it was the war to end all wars,' murmured Naomi, 'and that was only twenty years ago!'

'Reckon it'll be a different sort of war this time,' Dan said, 'air raids and the like.'

'Like in Spain, you mean?' Naomi asked fearfully. She, like everyone else, had been horrified to see the newsreel films of the bombing in the Spanish civil war which had been shown at the cinema.

'That,' said Dan dismissively, 'that was just 'itler practising. You'll see.'

At that moment an air raid siren began to wail. Lisa started to her feet with a cry of alarm. It was only a test, but the sound of its swooping howl made all three of them realise that it wouldn't be long before they heard it again and next time it would truly be warning of an attack.

Chapter Three

It was the beginning of the new school year, but many schools had already been evacuated from London. Some parents had decided not to send their children away and these children were gathered together in several area schools. There was one not far from Kemble Street and following Mrs Carter's advice, Naomi went to see Miss Hammond, the headmistress. She explained Lisa's background and asked for a place. The head had been happy to accept her.

'The children here will be a mixed bunch,' she explained, 'coming from all different places. Your Lisa certainly needs to be with other children. She'll soon settle into her life here if it's governed by a regular routine. Bring her along. She'll be fine, you'll see.'

Thus it was that a few days later Naomi took an extremely reluctant Lisa to Francis Drake Secondary, leading her across the playground and in through the front door of the big, old Victorian building. Its brick walls were heavily overlaid with grime, so that it was almost impossible to see what colour they might once have been. The building was close to the railings that divided it from the road and was bounded on its other three sides by a tarmacked playground and a high stone wall. Grubby rectangular windows stared out across this play area to the street beyond and the whole place had a bleak and forbidding air.

Lisa hung back a little as they walked to the main entrance, watched with interest by the children already gathered in the playground waiting for the morning bell.

'Don't worry, Lisa,' Naomi said encouragingly, 'I've already been to see the headmistress, so she's expecting you.'

In the entrance hall they were greeted by someone who introduced herself as Miss Barker, the school secretary.

'I'll take you up to Miss Hammond,' she said. 'Please follow me.'
She led them up a flight of stairs and along a short passage. She
knocked on the door at the end and then opened it for them to enter.

Miss Hammond was sitting at her desk, but she immediately stood
up and came forward to greet them with a cheerful 'Good morning.'

'Good morning, Miss Hammond,' Naomi said. 'This is Lieselotte
Becker, the child I spoke to you about? She's just arrived from
Germany and she doesn't speak much English.' She turned to Lisa.
'Lisa, this is Miss Hammond.'

Without prompting, Lisa made a small curtsy and said, 'Good
morning, Miss Hammond.' Her accent was heavy, but she spoke the
few words she knew with care.

Miss Hammond smiled and replied, 'Good morning, Lisa. No
need to curtsy.'

Lisa looked at Naomi for guidance and Naomi made a small
curtsy and then with a cutting motion of her hand said, firmly, 'No,
Lisa.'

Lisa coloured and took a step backwards, but Miss Hammond
ignored her retreat and said to Naomi, 'I'll take her from here. We'll
soon have her settled in. Will you meet her after school to take her
home?'

'Just for today to be sure she remembers the way,' agreed Naomi.
'She's thirteen, she's not going to want me to meet her from school
every day.' She put her hand on Lisa's arm. 'I'm going now, Lisa,' she
said, 'but I'll come back at three o'clock.' She pointed to her watch
and held up three fingers. 'Come back at three!' And with that she
gave Lisa a quick smile and left.

'Now, Lieselotte,' said Miss Hammond walking to the door,
'come with me.' She led the way back downstairs and along a corridor off which opened several classrooms. The doors were
glass-panelled and in each room they passed, Lisa could see desks
set out in rows facing a blackboard. Miss Hammond opened the
door to the fourth room and pointing to the number 4 screwed to
the door, said, 'Room Four,' before she led the way in.

A small, thin woman was sitting at the teacher's desk, a pile of exercise books in front of her. She looked up as they came in and immediately got to her feet, smiling. She had a narrow face, made even narrower by the way her grey hair was plaited and coiled about her ears. A pair of round, wire spectacles perched on her nose through which her eyes, a faded blue, looked with interest at the newcomer.

'Good morning, Miss May,' said the head. 'This is Lieselotte Becker, a refugee from Germany. She is being fostered by Mr and Mrs Federman and will be joining your class.' She turned to Lisa. 'This is Miss May, Lieselotte. Say good morning.'

Remembering not to curtsy, Lisa dutifully said, 'Good morning, Miss May,' and both women looked at her with approval.

Good, Miss Hammond thought, she learns quickly. She'll do. 'I'm afraid Lieselotte has very little English yet,' she said. 'I suggest you put her beside Hilda Lang, that'll help. Otherwise you'll have to cope. I'll introduce her to the school at assembly.' With that Miss Hammond nodded and returned to her office, leaving them to it.

'Well, Lieselotte, you can sit here.' Miss May pointed to a desk right at the front.

Lisa went towards it before turning back and, pointing to herself said, 'Lisa. Better Lisa.'

'Lisa,' repeated Miss May. 'That's much easier. Lieselotte *is* a bit of a mouthful, isn't it? Lisa it shall be.'

Lisa looked at her questioningly, recognising only her own name, but Miss May gestured that she should sit and at that moment a bell rang and children began to come in from the playground. The swell of chatter as they came into the classroom died away as they looked with interest at the new girl sitting in the front desk.

'Be quick and sit down,' Miss May told them briskly and with a clatter of chairs they took their places. Miss May opened the register in front of her and began taking the roll, each child answering 'Present' when his or her name was called. Lisa's name was added to the end of the roll and she echoed the word she'd heard the others use. 'Pleasant.'

This was greeted with a gale of laughter, causing her cheeks to flood with colour, but the laughter stopped abruptly as Miss May said sharply, 'Enough!' She looked round the room at nearly forty children who looked back, expectantly.

'As you see, we have a new girl joining us today,' Miss May said. 'Her name is Lisa Becker and she comes from Germany.'

This was greeted by a hiss from somewhere at the back of the class. Miss May ignored this interruption and continued, 'Lisa's had to leave her home and her family to escape from the Nazis. She's come here to be safe ...'

'Till they start bombing,' muttered someone.

Miss May continued unperturbed. 'Lisa doesn't speak English yet, but I'm sure she'll learn very quickly if we all help her.'

'We don't want no Germans here,' said a boy sitting behind Lisa. He kicked the back of her chair and Miss May snapped, 'Stand up, Roger Davis!' The boy pushed his chair back noisily and slowly got to his feet.

'I'm ashamed of you, Roger,' Miss May said, 'and we'll have no more talk like that.'

Still crimson-faced, Lisa kept her eyes firmly to the front, ignoring Roger standing behind her. She didn't know what he'd said, but she knew the tone of voice, she'd been hearing it for months back home in Hanau. It said, 'We don't want you here. You're not one of us.'

At that moment another bell rang. Without prompting the children got up and made a tidy line by the door.

'Hilda,' Miss May called. One of the girls left the line and came back. 'You're to look after Lisa until she's settled in. Make sure she knows what to do and where to be, all right?'

'Yes, miss.' The girl pulled at Lisa's arm, drawing her in at the back of the line. 'Come on, we're all going to assembly now. Just watch me and you'll see what to do.' Lisa stared at her in astonishment. Hilda had spoken to her in fluent German.

'No German after today, Hilda,' Miss May warned her. 'Only English in school unless I specifically ask you to tell Lisa something important. She has to learn English as quickly as she can and you can help her.'

The line of children walked smartly along the passage into the school hall. They stood in neat rows facing a platform at one end, the youngest children at the front through to the oldest at the back. Lisa stood next to Hilda, watching and waiting. When the whole school was assembled, Miss Hammond walked in and mounted the platform.

'Good morning, everyone!'

'Good morning, Miss Hammond! Good morning, everyone!' came the chorused reply.

Assembly followed its normal passage, much of which was incomprehensible to Lisa, freeing her to follow her own thoughts. How amazing it was, she thought, that the girl beside her, Hilda, could speak German. Was she German too? Had she escaped on a train?

Before she dismissed the school back to the classrooms and the daily round of lessons, Miss Hammond said, 'Today we have a new girl joining us. Her name is Lieselotte Becker, and she's come all the way from Germany, by herself, which is a very brave thing to do. She doesn't speak English yet, though I'm sure she will before very long, and she doesn't know anybody, so I want you to make her feel welcome here.'

Her words were greeted with a murmur from the assembled children and she quelled it instantly with the lift of her hand. 'Let us hope,' she said, 'that none of you will ever have to flee from your home and family to escape persecution.'

'Just the bombing,' said a voice loud enough to be heard, but quiet enough to be unidentified, and there was a ripple of laughter.

Miss Hammond ignored the comment and simply said, 'School dismiss.'

When they returned to the classroom, Miss May moved Hilda to the desk next to Lisa, and pretended not to notice when she spoke to Lisa in German, but the other children noticed.

At break time they all went out into the playground. It was a sunny day and most of the girls gathered in groups chatting. Some of the younger ones played hopscotch on a grid painted on the tarmac or took turns to turn the rope for a skipping game; the boys, seemingly more energetic, played tag, let off steam kicking a football about or scuffled in a suddenly erupting playground scrap. Hilda led Lisa to a bench at the far end of the yard, away from the more exuberant games, and they sat down together in the warm September sun.

'Where are you from, then?' she asked.

'Hanau, near Frankfurt,' Lisa replied.

'Your parents come too?'

'No.' Tears welled up in Lisa's eyes and she blinked hard to dispel them. 'I came on the train. They would only take children, one from each family. My brother, Martin, couldn't come. He's still at home with my mother.' Her voice broke on a sob as she said, 'I wish I was, too.' She pulled out a handkerchief and blew her nose. 'My dad was taken by the Gestapo. He didn't come back, not for ages, and now Mum says he's ill.' Determined not to break down completely in front of this stranger and even more in front of the other children, some of whom were covertly watching her, Lisa blew her nose again and changed the subject. 'What about you? How come you speak German?'

'My mum's German. She met my dad when he was working in Berlin. He's English. My brother Peter and me was born in Berlin, but we're Jewish, so when Hitler began to make laws against the Jews, we come home here. We're safe here.' She looked at Lisa with interest. 'You Jewish?'

'Yes, well, no, not really. Grandma is and that's enough over there.'

At the end of school the two girls crossed the playground to the gate where Aunt Naomi was waiting and Lisa took Hilda over to meet her.

'I'm looking after Lisa at school,' Hilda said. 'I can tell her stuff in German if she don't understand.'

'Oh, that's marvellous.' There was great relief in Naomi's voice. 'Poor Lisa, she can't understand us and we can't understand her and it's very difficult for everyone.' She smiled at Hilda. 'What's your name?'

'Hilda Lang, well Hildegarde really, but,' she gave a rueful smile, 'it doesn't do to have a German name just now, does it?'

When Hilda got home that evening, she told her mother about the new girl who had come to school.

'She's come on the train all the way from Frankfurt, Mum, by herself, and the Gestapo took her dad.'

Esther Lang felt the familiar stab of fear, though she tried hard not to let her daughter see it. As a German Jew herself, the very mention of the Gestapo instilled terror. Her own parents were still living in Berlin in circumstances she could not imagine. They had been turned out of their home some months earlier and had moved in with Esther's younger sister, Elsa, and her family. As far as Esther knew they were still all crammed into that tiny apartment, but she didn't know for certain and since the declaration of war, all communication between them had ceased. Her heart went out to the child who had come all that way, seeking safety in London. A child alone.

Esther had married Max, Hilda's father, in the twenties when he'd been sent by his firm to work in Berlin. Hildegarde and her brother, Peter, had both been born there, but with the rise of Hitler and with anti-Semitism rife, the family had returned to London, where they had settled and Esther had become naturalised British. Both children were bilingual, as both parents knew how useful it was to know another language, but English was the language of the household.

'Well, I hope you'll help her all you can, darling,' said her mother. 'I don't think she's going to have a very easy time of it.' She thought for a moment and then said, 'Where did you say she was living?'

'With some people called Federman over in Kemble Street.'

'Is she now? I think I met them once, at Anthony Stein's bar mitzvah. Perhaps I should pay them a call.'

True to her word, a few days later Esther walked the mile or so to Kemble Street to introduce herself as Hilda's mother. Naomi invited her in and they spent a pleasant half-hour, each discovering what she could about the other.

'It's good of your Hilda to help Lisa out at school,' Naomi said.

'It's very difficult for her, speaking so little English. Dan and I do our best, of course, we talk to her all the time, trying to teach her, but she can't tell us anything about the things that matter to her, about her home and her family.'

Esther had heard a little about Lisa's background, but she didn't repeat it, that was for Lisa when she was able. Instead she said, 'I was wondering if Lisa might like to come back with Hilda to our house after school sometimes. Playing with Hilda and her brother might be one of the quickest ways to help her learn English.'

'Oh, Mrs Lang,' Naomi said, 'I think that would be a marvellous idea. Are you sure?'

'Of course,' replied Esther. 'She's a brave child and needs all the help she can get. Please ask her if she'd like to come and if she agrees, Hilda will bring her home after school, tomorrow.'

That evening Naomi sat Lisa down and said, 'Hilda's mother asks you to go to Hilda's house after school. Would you like to go?'

'Go to Hilda?'

'Yes, after school.'

'Not sleep?'

'No, sleep here. I will come for you.'

Lisa's face broke into a broad beam. 'Yes, Aunt Naomi, I go.'

From then on Lisa went home with Hilda after school most days. Esther forbade them to converse in German.

'This is to help Lisa learn English,' she reminded them. 'While she is here with us we will all only speak English. You, too, Peter,' she said to her son. 'No cheating when you're playing outside!'

Lisa loved going to Hilda's house. The Langs were more affluent than the Federmans and though their home in Grove Avenue was only a mile or so from Kemble Street, it was quite different; much larger with a garden at the back where Max Lang was growing vegetables. The windows were wide and the house light and airy. The autumn sunlight flooded into the kitchen in the afternoon where the children sat up to the table to have their tea and it was always warm. Esther Lang sat them at the kitchen table to do their homework, giving Lisa a helping hand when she thought it was all getting too difficult.

'You're always welcome here,' Esther told her one day as she was leaving to return to Kemble Street. 'Any time you want some company your own age, just come round. Don't wait to be asked.'

Lisa was soon accepted by the other children who lived nearby as a friend of Hilda's. Her English improved by leaps and bounds, Hilda teaching her the words she needed, albeit with an East London accent and vocabulary. They became firm friends, and because the Langs lived only a few streets away, Naomi was happy enough for Lisa to spend much of her time at their house.

'Far better she has someone to play with,' she said to Dan, 'than come home to an empty house and me.'

'I think you're right,' Dan agreed. 'Once she can talk to us properly, we'll all feel much more comfortable.'

Lisa was a quick learner and though nothing like fluent, she soon understood a good deal of what was being said and could make herself understood in return.

Life at school, however, was not easy. Despite Miss Hammond's admonition, there was still a significant group of children who did not make her welcome, who regarded her as the enemy and were ready to gang up on her. Roger Davis and his cronies, egged on by their peers, would surround Lisa, pressing in on her, and pretend to touch her before leaping backwards shouting, 'Lisa's got the measles! German measles! Don't catch her germs! Dirty German germs!' They clasped their throats and made 'dying' groans before collapsing dramatically to the ground.

Lisa would push her way free of them, but within moments they'd be back. On occasion she hit out at them, once punching one of Roger's sidekicks in the face and making his nose bleed. They backed off for a while, but they were soon back, always lying in wait for her, always out of sight of the teacher on playground duty. Hilda, unable to do anything and recognising she would be in for the same treatment if she tried, stayed well clear.

'Don't say nothing at home, though,' she warned Lisa. 'If you split on them and your Aunt Naomi come down here and complained, things'd only get worse. They'll get tired of it in the end and find someone else to pick on.'

Lisa knew she was right. They weren't hurting her physically, they were only shouting abuse at her and she was used to that. It had happened all the time in Hanau. But she longed to fight back, to give as good as she got.

It all ended quite suddenly. Roger's gang cornered her on her way home from school one day. It was the first time she'd been waylaid outside the school yard. They backed her up against a wall, shooting out their arms in Nazi salutes, shouting, *'Heil Hitler!'*

'Go away! Go away!' she screamed. 'I hate you! I hate you. You're all Nazis!'

They roared with laughter at her fury, posturing and prancing, but blocking her way so that she had no escape. She swung a punch at Albert, the boy whose nose she'd made bleed before, but he was ready for her this time and caught her arm, gripping it tightly, easily holding her off.

'Hey, Rog,' he jeered, 'we got a wild cat here. Teach her a lesson, shall we? German bitch!' The others crowed their delight, but their cheers were short-lived. Suddenly, from round the corner, someone erupted into the middle of them, his fists flying, his elbows crashing sideways and his feet, in heavy leather boots, kicking shins and stamping on toes. Taken completely by surprise, the gang found themselves on the ground, nursing bruises, bleeding noses, cut eyebrows and aching heads. Roger, turning to make a fight of it, was slammed against the wall and then spun round, his arm jerked up painfully behind his back, so that he cried out.

Lisa, as surprised as her tormentors by this sudden attack, cowered back, but when she saw that Roger was held in an arm-lock and his cronies were edging away, she stepped forward to stand beside her saviour. To her surprise her spoke to her in German.

'I've seen this scum picking on you before,' he said, 'just say the word and I'll break his arm.'

'No don't,' Lisa said, 'it'll just make more trouble for me. Just scare him so badly that he never comes near me again, him or his mates.'

'You sure?' He jerked Roger's arm suddenly and Roger gave a yelp of pain. 'Well, if you say so.'

The boy, for a boy he still was, looked disappointed, but with a swift movement he spun Roger round and backed him up against the wall. 'She say I not break your arm. I wish to, she say no. You not go near this girl or her friend again.' He spoke the careful English of one who was still learning. 'You understand me?' When Roger didn't answer immediately he punched him in the stomach and Roger doubled up. 'You understand me?' he said again and Roger managed to croak 'Yes,' thus avoiding another punch.

'If you touch girl again, I will come to you. Understand?'

'Yes.'

'Good.' The boy let him go, tossing him aside like a rag doll.

Roger picked himself up from the ground and scuttled away to find his mates. But seeing Roger so totally defeated, they had all melted away.

Lisa looked at the boy left standing beside her. He wasn't much taller than she, but wiry and strong. His clothes were old and patched, his thin legs thrust into heavy workman's boots. He had dark hair, cropped short, and brown eyes set above a prominent nose and wide mouth. He grinned at her and she saw he had a front tooth missing.

'That's him sorted,' he said, 'shouldn't have no more bother with him.' Again he spoke in German and Lisa answered him in the same.

'Thanks for coming to my rescue.'

'It's OK. Saw him pestering you in the school yard, but couldn't do nothing about it there. Too many people about. Might have got messy!'

'Are you at my school?' Lisa asked. 'I haven't seen you.'

'Only just come,' replied the boy. 'Heinrich Schwarz at your service,' and he gave a funny little bow, 'now called Harry Black.'

'I'm Lisa, Lisa Becker. Where do you come from? Did you come on one of the trains?'

'Same one as you,' Harry replied. 'I saw you at the station at Frankfurt and in London, too.'

'Did you?' Lisa was amazed. 'And you recognised me at school?'

'Saw them picking on you and when I realised why, I remembered you on the train.'

Lisa shook her head in disbelief. 'Well,' she said, 'I'm very glad you did.'

'You with a foster family round here?'

'Yeah, some people called Federman.'

'All right, are they?'

'They're OK. They're kind to me and try and help me with things. It's getting easier now I speak some English. What about you? You with foster parents, too?'

'No, not now,' Harry said flatly. 'Foster parents and me didn't get on, so I left.'

Lisa stared at him in amazement. 'You mean you just walked out?'

'Not quite. They complained to the Bloomsbury people and I got moved. Live in a hostel now in Stoke Newington. Much better. Can come and go as I like.'

'But you come to school?'

'Part of the deal,' Harry said. 'I get to live in the hostel, but I have to go to school till they find me a job.'

'A job?'

'Yeah, I'm fifteen next month. Got to earn my keep, haven't I?'

Lisa looked at him again. He didn't look fifteen. In some ways he looked younger – he was small for fifteen – but in others he looked older. There was a sort of worldliness in his expression, an air of being able to look after himself. His missing tooth suggested that he was no stranger to a fight and she knew he was ready with his fists.

'Where did you learn to fight like that?' she asked. 'All four of them, by yourself!'

Harry sniffed dismissively. 'Them? They ain't nothing.' His expression hardened. 'Nothing like the Hanau Hitler Youth. Had to handle yourself against that lot.'

'Hanau?' Lisa pounced on the name. 'You come from Hanau? Really? So do I.' Tears filled her eyes as she looked at Harry, Harry was a boy from another life, someone from home, who remembered 'before'.

'Hey,' Harry said anxiously, 'don't start blubbing on me!'

'I'm not,' protested Lisa, blinking hard. 'Just can't believe you come from home.'

'Not home any more,' said Harry. 'I ain't never going back there.'

'What about your... parents... family?' Lisa asked hesitantly.

'None left,' replied Harry, and his tone made it clear there was no more to be said. Abruptly he changed the subject and asked, 'Who's that girl you go round with? With her all the time.'

'That's Hilda,' Lisa said and explained how Hilda and her family had been helping her learn English.

'She's all right then, is she?'

'Yeah, we're good mates. I often go there after school.'

'But not today. Which gave that scum their chance.'

'Yeah, suppose so.' Lisa looked round a little anxiously. 'I better go, Aunt Naomi will be wondering where I am.'

'I'll walk with you,' Harry said, 'till I get to my bus stop.'

Together they set off down the street, watched from a distance by Roger. He knew better than to go near Lisa again. His mates were waiting in the next street and as he joined them he said dismissively, 'Another Nazi Jew-boy.'

'Not sure he can be both,' said Albert, his second in command. 'The Nazis is killing the Jews, ain't they?'

Roger glowered at him. 'Pity they didn't get that one, then, before he came here to bother us!'

'Yeah, you're right there,' grinned Albert, and Roger knew that despite his ignominious defeat at the hands of the new German boy, his authority over his own gang was still intact.

'Come on,' he said, setting off in the opposite direction, 'we got better things to do than muck about with shit like them.'

Harry watched Lisa walk away as he waited for his bus. She's a plucky little thing, he thought as she turned, once, to wave. Them buggers have been tormenting her for weeks and she's put up with it. Threw a punch at one of them boys, showed some spunk, that did.

For the next week or so he kept an eye on her at school. Roger and his cronies ignored him entirely, ostentatiously turning their backs if he came anywhere near them, but he saw that they didn't go near Lisa either.

Under Harry's protection life at school became much easier for Lisa. No one molested her in the playground and she was gradually accepted by the other girls in her class, joining in their games. They teased her about her English, laughing when she got words wrong, but it was good-natured teasing and her English continued to improve. She still went home with Hilda sometimes after school and always felt comfortable in the Langs' house. Esther was determined to include her in the family. She knew what it was like suddenly to be transplanted to a new country and, kind as she knew the Federmans were, they had no children. She wondered if they should suggest that Lisa come to live with them, but Max told her quite firmly that she shouldn't interfere.

'The child is settled with them now,' he said. 'Far better that she and Hilda stay friends at school and she visits.' Esther wasn't sure she agreed, but she bowed to her husband's decision.

On occasion Hilda went home with Lisa. Naomi was keen to return the hospitality, but they were neither of them as comfortable together in the Federmans' little house. Lisa felt that Hilda was judging them and she felt oddly protective of her foster parents. She had grown fond of them over the months, of Uncle Dan particularly, and she didn't want Hilda to think they were beneath her.

On other days Harry would wait for her in the road beyond the gate and walk with her to the end of Kemble Street. At first Lisa thought it was because Roger and co might resume their bullying, but she soon realised that it was because Harry was lonely. He wanted the company of someone who had come from the nightmare that was Germany and understood the fear which had ruled their lives for so long. Sometimes they would wander into the park and sit chatting on a bench. If no one was near they spoke German; it was a relief to be able to express themselves freely without struggling for the words they needed, but they were careful to stick to English if they might be overheard. Roger and his mates weren't the only ones; anti-German feeling was, understandably, strong.

At first they said little of their lives 'before', but gradually they began to speak of those they had left behind. Lisa told Harry about her parents and Martin, able at last to tell of what had happened to them to someone who understood. Harry found himself opening up to Lisa as he had to no one else; because she had lived through it all too, she understood, and a special bond was forged between them.

Like Lisa's, Harry's father had been arrested on Kristallnacht, leaving the young Heinrich to try and look after his invalid mother. They had no money and no way of making any. Harry had taken to the streets, earning a few pfennigs wherever he could, doing the dirty jobs that were the province of Jews: cleaning the gutters, scrubbing the daubed graffiti, *Juden Raus*, from walls and windows so that the new German owners would no longer be reminded that Jews had once inhabited their homes. Other times he stole from market stalls, occasionally from the offertory box in the local church, but always on the lookout for the Hitler Youth who delighted in tormenting any hapless Jew happening to cross their paths. He had become a tough street kid, a feral animal, fighting hard and dirty to defend himself against those marauding gangs. Then one day his mother received a postcard telling her that her husband, Ezra Schwarz, had died of a fever in prison. No further explanation was given. Harry was filled with fury, angry at everyone and everything; his mother seemed to give up and simply faded away. Within a month she, too, was dead, and Harry was left an orphan.

'So what did you do then?' asked Lisa.

'Hanau was too hot for Jews by then, so I got myself to Frankfurt. There was still a Jewish community there. They put me in an orphanage and then on the train, so here I am and here I'll stay.'

Like Lisa, he hadn't been evacuated when war with Germany had once again burst upon England; that day, they were both too newly arrived, already refugees with nowhere further to run.

Lisa didn't take Harry home to meet Aunt Naomi and Uncle Dan. She knew, instinctively, that Aunt Naomi in particular wouldn't approve of him. Though they, too, lived in a tough area, Aunt Naomi had very high standards. Her house, though small, was spotless, her doorstep scrubbed, her windows bright. Lisa was never allowed to go to school in anything but clean and pressed clothes and the food on the table, though plain, was always well-cooked. Even on their small income, Aunt Naomi managed to keep her little family well fed. She definitely wouldn't approve of a street urchin like Harry in his scruffy clothes and workman's boots. Secretly, Lisa knew that her own mother wouldn't approve of him either. Back in Hanau their paths would never have crossed; their families came from entirely different social strata, but here Harry was special, Lisa's private link with home, and so she didn't even mention him in Kemble Street.

Hilda knew about him of course, she'd heard how Harry had come to Lisa's rescue, but she didn't like him. She felt he wasn't the sort of person someone like her should know and was surprised when Lisa continued to be friends with him. Part of it was jealousy; Lisa was *her* friend, it was *she* who had helped Lisa to learn English, it was *her* mother who had invited Lisa to come home with her at any time and Hilda resented Harry's intrusion. For his part, Harry considered Hilda a snobby little madam. She lived in a posh house and he knew she looked down her nose at him. Well, let her. He didn't care.

Their mutual antipathy kept them apart, but Lisa drew strength from each of them.

Chapter Four

The expected air raids had not happened. There was one a few days after the declaration of war. The siren wailed its warning into the early-morning sky and the Federmans insisted that Lisa should take shelter with them in the cellar. As before, she had frozen in the doorway, looking down into the underground room, and Dan almost had to drag her down the steps.

'Come on, Lisa, me duck,' he said encouragingly. 'We have to go down. It won't be for long.'

Naomi, coming in behind them, had pulled the door closed and the draught from the closure had snuffed the candle, engulfing them for a moment in total darkness. Lisa began to scream in terror. Remembering her earlier fear, Dan held her close, his arms wrapped round her, his voice soothing, 'It's all right, me duck, you're all right,' but she had remained rigid against him, her breath coming in ragged bursts, until Naomi had struck a match and lit the candles stuck in their beer bottles, the only light they had. The raid lasted two hours and Lisa sat stiff with fear throughout. In the flickering candlelight the stone walls seemed to move, closing in round her, the ceiling pressing down.

I'm buried alive, she thought wretchedly as the minutes dragged by. I'd rather be upstairs in the house and take my chance with the bombs. She gripped her hands together so hard that her fingernails dug into her palms.

Watching her, Dan and Naomi spoke softly to each other.

'D'you think she's going to be like this every time there's a raid?' Naomi wondered.

'Let's hope not,' said Dan. 'P'raps she'll get used to it. She's ter-rified, poor kid.'

When the all-clear finally sounded Lisa leaped from the chair and ran up the stairs, bursting the door open, and was out into the fresh morning air before Dan or Naomi had even got to their feet.

'I don't know what to do with her,' Naomi confided to Mary later in the day. 'She's really afraid of being shut in. We could all go to the public shelter in Hope Street, but Dan thinks that would be worse.'

'Difficult for you,' Mary mused. 'Don't know what to suggest. Do you have to shut the door? Silly question, of course you do.'

'Not sure it would help anyway,' said Naomi. 'If only we could discuss it with her properly, perhaps find out what's behind it.'

They all waited in fear for the next warning, but it didn't come. The days turned into weeks and there was no sign of the Luftwaffe. Everyone began to relax a little, except perhaps the air raid wardens. The blackout was severely enforced and the wardens patrolled the streets as soon as darkness fell, banging on any door where a dan-gerous shaft of light leaked past badly fitting curtains or blinds. Everyone still carried a gas mask in its box slung over the shoulder and at school there were regular gas mask drills. Lisa still hated hers, but she'd learned how to put it on correctly and by taking steady, deep breaths managed to breathe through the filter without panicking.

'I hate these things,' she said to Harry on the way home one day.

'Better'an being gassed,' Harry said, who had no problem wearing his.

'I know, but I can't breathe and it makes me panicky.'

Harry, seeing the fear in her eyes at the thought of the mask, changed the subject and said, 'Not coming back to school after Christmas. Got a job.'

'What job?'

'Errand boy.'

'Errand boy?'

'Don't say it like that. It's a job, OK? I get paid for it. Working for a bloke what runs a market stall, delivering stuff.'

'What sort of stuff?' asked Lisa, intrigued.

Harry just tapped the side of his nose and grinned. 'Just stuff,' he said. 'He gets it for people, stuff they want.'

'Black market?' cried Lisa.

'Ssh!' Harry hissed, looking round anxiously. 'Course not. It's all legit.'

But he knew it wasn't. The previous Saturday, he'd been caught nicking a packet of Woodbines from one of the stalls in Petticoat Lane. He'd been grabbed by the ear by a big bloke with ginger hair, who held him in a painfully tight grip and dragged him over to the Black Bull, the pub his boss, Mikey Sharp, used as his headquarters.

'Caught this blighter pinchin' from your barrow,' he said, giving Harry such a shove that he fell on to the floor at Mikey's feet.

'Did you now?' Mikey looked down at Harry with interest. 'You been stealin' from me, sunshine?'

'Only Woodbines,' quavered Harry. 'Only ten.'

'Only Woodbines,' repeated Mikey as if considering the offence. 'Only ten? What'd happen if everyone thought they could half-inch fags off my barrow? Where would I be then, eh?'

'Dunno, sir,' Harry said miserably.

'No, nor do I,' Mikey said. 'Reckon you'll have to pay for them somehow. Got any money, have you?'

Thankful that he'd left the few coins he did have back at the hostel, Harry said, 'No, sir.' It might mean he was in for a beating, but he was used to those; far better than having what little cash he had, taken from him.

'So how you gonna pay me, then?'

'Could work for you,' suggested Harry, feeling suddenly brave. 'Do jobs for you an' that.'

Mikey had looked at him speculatively for a moment. 'You're not English, are you?' he said. 'What's your name?'

'Harry Black an' I am English, now.'

'Now?' Mikey raised an eyebrow. 'What was you before?'

'A refugee.'

'From?'

Harry thought fast. Don't say Germany, he thought, this bloke might kill you for that. 'From Hitler,' he said.

'I suppose that means we're on the same side,' Mikey said with a laugh. The man who'd caught Harry laughed, too. Harry didn't. He didn't know if he was supposed to. He just stayed where he was, sitting on the floor, and waited.

'I reckon you're German,' Mikey said and waited for Harry's nod before saying, 'but not a bleedin' Nazi.'

Harry shook his head vigorously. 'No! Not Nazi!'

'Good,' Mikey said. 'Well, sunshine, that's all right, as long as you behave. I could make use of a lad like you. Speak German, do you?'

Harry nodded.

'Course you do. Even that might prove useful.' Mikey turned to the other man. 'OK, Ginger, back to the barrow. I reckon half my stuff'll have gone missing while you've been pratting about in here. Go on, out!'

'Yes, boss.' And the man hurried from the room.

'So what is your name... when it ain't Harry Black?'

'Heinrich Schwarz.'

'Hmm. Just like to know who it really is who's working for me. And that's what you wanna do, is it? Work for me?'

Harry nodded.

'Well then, Harry, get up and listen to me. If I catch you nickin' stuff from me or from any of my stalls ever again, you'll wish you'd never been born. Understand that, do you?'

Though scared, Harry had nodded again. 'Yes, sir.' It would be a risk, working for a man like Mikey, but anything was better than going back to that school.

He grinned at Lisa. 'Anyway,' he went on, 'I'm a working man now and I won't be coming back to that school no more, not after Christmas.'

'So I won't see you,' Lisa said.

'Course you will,' Harry assured her, 'just not at school, but you tell me if that little shit Roger touches you again when I'm not there and I'll come and break his neck for him.'

'He won't,' Lisa said. 'He leaves me alone, now.'

'Yeah, well if he doesn't, you just let me know,' Harry said darkly. 'Tell you what,' his mind darting forward to the next thing, 'tell you what, tomorrow we could go up west. What d'you think?'

'Up west?' replied Lisa uncertainly. 'What do you mean?'

'Up to the West End. Look at Buckingham Palace and Trafalgar Square. See the shops and that.'

'Aunt Naomi would never let me.'

'Then don't ask her,' came Harry's reply. 'We'll just go.'

Lisa thought about it. It was tempting. She had hardly been out of Shoreditch since she'd arrived and she did want to see the famous parts of London, the places she'd heard about before she came.

'I could say I was going round Hilda's, I suppose,' she said thoughtfully.

'Yeah, say that,' grinned Harry. 'She won't know.'

''S all right as long as she don't come looking for me.'

'Why would she?'

'All right for you.' Lisa jabbed him in the ribs. 'You can just walk out of your hostel and no one asks where you're going. Aunt Naomi doesn't let me go far. Always wants to know where I'm going, and who with.' She glanced sideways at Harry. His dark, curly hair was unruly and needed cutting. He had a graze across his cheek and a streak of mud under his chin. He was always muddy or bloody, or both, Lisa thought. Always in a scrap or a scrape. 'She wouldn't approve of you!'

'Why ever not?' Harry cried. 'What's the matter with me?'

'Nothing,' Lisa said with a grin, 'but she likes to keep me close. She lets me go to Hilda's house, she knows Hilda's parents, but she doesn't know you.'

'Then just say you're going there. Come on, Lisa, let's have a bit of a lark.'

They'd reached the end of Kemble Street now and Harry stopped on the corner. 'See you tomorrow morning,' he said as if it had all been agreed. 'Meet you in the park.'

'Don't know when I'll be able to get there,' Lisa said, knowing as she spoke that she was giving in.

'I'll wait,' said Harry.

'See you then, but I'm not going on the Tube. Not going underground!'

'No, OK,' Harry agreed easily. 'We can go on the bus.'

'You got money for the bus?'

It was Harry's turn to grin. 'Don't worry about that,' he said. 'I can get some.'

Lisa ran the last hundred yards home. The evening air was bitter; they had lingered too long and she wanted to get into the warm. She found Mary and Naomi sharing a pot of tea in the kitchen and flopped down at the table beside them. The kitchen was the warmest room in the house, but even so, with the fire as yet unlit in the grate, it was December-cold.

'Tea, love?' Naomi said, looking at Lisa's chilly face. 'You look freezing.'

'Yes, please, Aunt Naomi.'

Naomi poured her a cup, topping up her own and Mary's. She gave a half glance to a letter leaning against the clock on the mantelpiece. A letter for Lisa.

After the declaration of war Lisa knew that she couldn't write directly to her family any more and as her mother had told her, she'd written to them care of Nikolaus Becker's Zurich address. There had been no reply and she wasn't even sure if her letter had reached Cousin Nikolaus. She wrote again, this time to the man himself, asking if he had received the letter to forward. It was some time before Nikolaus wrote back to say that he had sent the letter on, but had heard nothing back.

Lisa had been clinging to the hope that Cousin Nikolaus would have definite news of them all. She ached to hear from them, to know for certain that they were all right, to know if they were still living in Hanau, in the same small apartment she'd left five months earlier.

'D'you think they're OK?' she'd asked Harry one afternoon, longing for reassurance to bolster her hope.

Harry shrugged. 'I don't know, do I?' Then, seeing his answer had upset her he said, 'They're probably OK if they keep their heads down, don't draw attention to theirselves. Nazis'll have other things to think about now, won't they? Being at war with everyone, Poland, England, France. They won't have no time to worry about a few Jews still scratching a living in a small town. Stands to reason.'

'Suppose you're right.' Lisa was eager to accept this; the alternative was too awful to contemplate. She liked to be able to think of her parents and Martin being strong for each other. She wrote to them again care of Cousin Nikolaus, hoping that the letter might get through and they'd know she was thinking about them.

Now, as she drank her tea, safe in the Kemble Street kitchen, she was about to get her answer.

That morning, after she had left for school, a letter had plopped on to the mat; a letter with Swiss stamps and addressed to Lisa in neat, pointed handwriting. Naomi picked it up and looked at it.

Is this the letter from her parents that she's been longing for? she wondered as she put it up on the kitchen mantelpiece. I do hope so, it's so hard for her to have no news at all.

She and Dan knew Lisa had written again and there had been no reply, but neither of them dared mention it, for fear of reopening a partially healed wound.

The morning passed slowly and Naomi was constantly aware of the thick envelope, propped against the clock, waiting, bringing who knew what news of Lisa's family. She wished Dan was at home, so they'd both be there when Lisa got in from school, but Dan was out driving his taxi and wouldn't be back until the evening, when it would be too late. Should she hide the letter until Dan got home? she wondered. Keep it for a couple of days until they were all three together?

I'll go and see Mary, Naomi thought. See what she thinks.

She hurried down the road to the Duke of Wellington and found Mary serving the lunchtime customers in the public bar.

'I just don't know what to do,' Naomi told her. 'There's this letter from Switzerland come for Lisa. On the back is the name "Becker" and an address in Zurich. I think Lisa has relations there, so I'm hoping it'll be good news about her family, but Dan isn't home and in case it isn't...'

'In case it isn't, I'll come round before she gets home from school,' Mary said with a smile. 'Don't worry, I'll be there. We shut at two and Tom and Betsy can manage the clearing up.'

So, here they were, the three of them, sharing a pot of tea in the kitchen, Lisa cradling the cup in her hands to warm them as she drank the hot tea in tiny sips.

Now was the time. Naomi reached the letter down from the mantelpiece and laid it on the table, saying, 'This came for you this morning, Lisa.'

For a long moment Lisa looked at it, then she put down her cup and picking up the envelope, turned it over.

'Cousin Nikolaus in Zurich,' she said and put it down again.

'Aren't you going to open it?' Naomi asked.

'Maybe when you're alone,' suggested Mary quietly.

Lisa picked the letter up again. It was thick and squashy. What could be inside it? A letter from her mother? Surely that must be it. She slid her finger under the flap and pulled out the contents. Another, smaller envelope fell on to the table, wrapped in a single sheet of paper. Lisa looked at the second envelope, addressed in Cousin Nikolaus's spiky writing to her parents' address in Hanau. It had been opened and stamped on the back in smudged black letters were the words GONE AWAY. Inside was the letter she had sent to her parents weeks ago. The colour drained from her face and she dropped the letter back on to the table. Mary and Naomi looked at her with concern as she buried her head in her hands.

'What is it?' Mary asked gently.

'I send letter to my family,' Lisa said flatly. 'It comes back.' She scanned the note from Cousin Nikolaus which had come with it.

Dear Lisa,
I forwarded the letter to your parents, but it has since come back to me marked as you see, 'Gone Away'. I'm afraid I do not know where they have gone and have no way of finding out. I hope you are well with your London family. If I hear more I will write again.
Nikolaus Becker

Pain flooded through her, the pain of despair. Fighting a lump in her throat, she managed to say, 'He says he has no news of my family. They are lost. Now I have no one.' With that she scooped up both letters and ran from the room, upstairs to her bedroom.

Naomi and Mary looked at each other in dismay. 'Poor child,' Naomi said softly. 'Poor, poor child. As she says, now she has no one.'

'She has you,' replied Mary firmly. 'You and Dan. You're her family now. Her parents.'

'Poor substitute for her own mum and dad,' Naomi sighed.

'But alive and well and the ones to take care of her from now on,' Mary answered briskly.

'I suppose...' Naomi said, adding, 'I wish Dan was here.'

'He'll be back before long,' Mary said, 'and in the meantime I think you should go up to her. She needs you.'

Naomi nodded and got to her feet. Quietly, she went upstairs, pausing outside Lisa's room. She could hear the girl sobbing and hesitated. Should she leave her alone to come to terms with her loss, or should she go in and try to offer comfort? She looked back downstairs and saw Mary at the bottom, gesticulating her into the room. She turned again and, tapping on the door gently, pushed it open and went in.

Lisa was sitting on her bed, clutching the letters, tears streaming down her cheeks. Naomi said nothing, simply crossed the room and kneeling down beside her, gathered her into her arms. She had become very fond of her foster daughter in the few months since she'd been with them and now she was probably the only mother the child had. Neither of them moved, Naomi holding her close, Lisa clinging to her, sobs racking her body.

When at last the sobs subsided and she pulled free, Naomi pulled her hankie from her pocket and Lisa blew her nose. 'It says "Gone away".' She pointed to the smudged black ink on the envelope. 'Where would they go? Not to Cousin Nikolaus. He don't know where.'

'They may just have had to move house,' suggested Naomi, 'to a new address.'

'If they went they would tell Cousin Nikolaus. He is, how you say? He is between us in Zurich.'

'Well, they may have written,' Naomi said, trying to sound encouraging. 'He may not have had their letter yet.'

She stood up and taking Lisa by the hand helped her to her feet. 'Come on, me duck,' she said, 'we have to make Uncle Dan some tea.'

When they got down to the kitchen, it was getting dark outside and Mary had disappeared.

'She's gone back to the Duke, I expect,' Naomi said as she wrestled the blackout screen into place before turning on the light. Bending down she put a match to the ready-laid fire and immediately the room was more cheerful. 'After all, it's nearly opening time. Tom will be needing her.'

'She very kind,' Lisa said with a glance at the dictionary still perched in readiness on the mantelpiece. 'He not like me.'

'Who? Tom? Course he likes you.'

'No, I meet him in the street and he turn away with bad face.'

'Expect he was going somewhere in a hurry,' said Naomi. 'Never saw you.' But in her heart she knew Lisa was right. Tom had been taken prisoner by the Germans in the last war and had nearly starved to death in one of their POW camps before being released. She knew only too well that Tom hated anything and everything German. She had seen him scowl at Lisa and it'd made her angry. Lisa was only a child and had nothing to do with what was happening in Germany. She was a victim of this war as he had been a victim of the last.

It was with great relief that Naomi saw Dan coming in the front door that evening. She had managed to calm Lisa down, settling her by the kitchen fire with the mending basket while she herself peeled some potatoes. She knew that Lisa had to be kept occupied so that she didn't brood on the news she'd received, but she, herself, needed Dan's company and his solid reassuring presence.

'Now then,' he said as he quickly closed the door behind him against escaping light. 'Hive of industry going on here.' He kissed his wife on the cheek and patted Lisa on hers. 'You mending the potatoes in my socks again?' he asked. 'Glad of that cos me feet was getting cold.' He turned back to his wife. 'Any tea on the go, love?'

Naomi set the kettle to boil and put out a clean cup and saucer. Dan settled himself in his chair and looking across at Lisa said, 'Had a good day, Lisa?' It was a question he asked every evening when he got in. It had become almost a game as Lisa searched for the right words to tell him of her day, but this evening she did not look up and smile, she kept her head bent, apparently concentrating on her mending.

'Lisa's had some bad news today, Dan,' Naomi said softly. 'Her letter to her parents has been returned "Gone away". She don't know where they've gone and her cousin don't know neither. As you see she's very upset.'

Dan reached over and rested his hand on Lisa's. 'I'm very sorry to hear that, duck,' he said, 'but whatever happens, we're here, Aunt Naomi and me. We ain't yer mum and dad, we know that, but you do have us.' Lisa dropped the sock she'd been darning and grasped his fingers. Looking at both her foster parents watching her anxiously, she remembered her mother's admonition to be a good and grateful girl and though the tears were welling once again in her eyes she mustered a tremulous smile.

'Thank you for your kindness,' she said. 'I thank you and my mother thank you also.' Her careful English sounded a little stilted, but the Federmans knew it came from the heart and Dan felt tears prick his own eyes as he gave her an awkward hug and damned himself for being soft.

Chapter Five

Lisa didn't sleep well that night. She was haunted by dreams of the Gestapo raid and woke in a cold sweat, certain that the man in the long black coat was coming up the stairs to find her. Once she was awake, she couldn't go back to sleep. She tossed and turned, still hearing Nazis on the stairs. Determined not to wake Aunt Naomi and Uncle Dan, she stifled the sobs that rose in her throat. They had both tried to keep her spirits up all evening, but it had been almost impossible to respond. When it began to get light Lisa finally gave up trying to sleep and, easing the blackout screen from the window, she sat looking out into the street, watching the colour creep back into the houses opposite. And as she sat there, she made up her mind. She would meet Harry in the park later and she would go with him 'up west'. She'd tell Naomi that she was going to Hilda's, but she knew it wasn't Hilda she wanted or needed, it was Harry, because he knew what their life had been 'before'. He had lost his family to the Nazis. He would know how she felt. No one who hadn't lived in fear of the Nazis could begin to imagine what it was like, day after day, never knowing if the Gestapo would come and take you away. Seeing them striding the streets, their arrogant sneers directed at you simply because you had a Jewish parent. So many had fled, but her father had left it too late. She needed to be with Harry, doing something different, something daring, something to obliterate, if only for a few hours, the desperate loneliness that was consuming her.

She was already downstairs when Naomi appeared in the kitchen to prepare breakfast.

'Oh, well done, Lisa, I see the kettle's on. Lay the table, can you?' And Lisa laid out plates and cutlery while Naomi busied herself at the stove.

'Aunt Naomi, I go to Hilda today, please?'

Naomi looked round and smiled. 'If they've asked you,' she replied.

'Oh, yes,' Lisa lied. 'To go for whole day.'

'Then certainly you can,' Naomi said. It's a good idea, she thought as she scrambled eggs and made toast, it'll give Lisa something to do, help take her mind off her letter.

Feeling a little guilty at having lied to Aunt Naomi but determined to go, Lisa set off to meet Harry in the park. He was waiting on a bench tossing pebbles into the pond.

'Knew you'd come,' he said with a grin, but his grin faded when he saw her pale face.

'Hey, kid,' he said, 'what's up?'

Lisa flopped down beside him on the bench. 'Had a letter,' she said.

'From your family?'

'No, they're not there any more,' she answered, her voice breaking on a sob.

Harry listened as she told him what Cousin Nikolaus had written. When she finally came to a stop he stood up and, taking her hand, hauled her to her feet.

'We still got each other,' he said, 'us orphans. You and me. So, let's go up west and see what it's all about.'

Lisa wasn't sure what reaction she'd expected from Harry, but it wasn't quite that.

'Up west? Today?'

'You got to make your own life now,' he said. 'I learned that the hard way, too. Got to look after number one. We ain't kids no more. So, we get on with it. And today we're going up west to see the sights. Come on, Lisa, today's going to be special.'

Still uncertain, Lisa allowed him to drag her along to the bus stop outside the park gates.

'We can get the bus from here,' he said and within minutes he had his hand out, hailing a number 22. 'Follow me.' He led the way up the stairs to the very front of the bus. They sat side by side looking down on the London streets as Lisa had on her way from Liverpool Street. They were still busy, but Lisa had got used to them and she looked out with interest.

'You get a good view from up here,' she said as she peered through the window. 'I'm glad we came upstairs.'

'Best to be upstairs,' Harry agreed. 'You'll see.'

'You got the money for the fare?' she asked him softly.

'Nope, but it don't matter, you'll see.'

About two stops later the conductor appeared at the top of the stairs and gradually made his way along the gangway, taking money and issuing tickets until her reached them.

'Fares please,' he said.

Harry looked up at him and then felt in his pocket. He got to his feet and felt in the other pocket, then shook his head. 'My money,' he said in his heavily accented English. 'Where is my money? It is lost!' He made a great show of feeling through his empty pockets, but the conductor wasn't deceived.

'Off!' he roared. 'Down them stairs and off!'

'Yes, yes, we go. So sorry!' Harry's accent was still heavy and he grabbed Lisa by the hand, hurrying her along the gangway and down the stairs. The conductor rang the bell and when the bus pulled into the next stop Harry and Lisa jumped off. As it drew away again, leaving them on the pavement, Harry said, 'There you go! Easy!'

'Harry, haven't you any money?' asked Lisa.

'Not to spend on bus fares,' replied Harry, cheerfully. 'Come on, here's the next bus.' And he stuck out his hand again.

It took them six buses before they were disgorged into Piccadilly Circus, but Harry's system worked and once Lisa knew what was happening, she simply followed his lead, giggling as they were turfed off the buses by the angry conductors.

It was a beautiful December morning, with a clear blue sky and pale winter sun, but the air was bitterly cold. Lisa shivered despite the winter coat her mother had managed to buy for her before she left. Harry, with only a jacket to keep him warm, seemed impervious to the cold, simply standing, taking in everything around him, the bustle, the traffic, the noise.

It was the Saturday before Christmas and people were hurrying along the pavements, in and out of shops finishing their Christmas shopping. Despite the war, everyone was determined that Hitler shouldn't stop the usual celebrations. There might be fewer things in the shops and more unusual presents to be bought, but if you simply glanced at the pre-Christmas streets, you might well think everything was normal. Of course it wasn't; it was all too clear that the country was at war. Uniformed servicemen, home on a few days' Christmas leave, were among the shoppers laden with parcels. Everyone carried a gas mask, slung over the shoulder, signs directed people to public air raid shelters and a huge sign across the front of Swan and Edgar's urged everyone to DIG FOR VICTORY!

In the middle of Piccadilly Circus, where Eros should have stood, brave atop a fountain, there was a strange, sandbagged cone. Eros had been removed for his own protection and his fountain boarded and sandbagged. Around the base of the cone was a banner cautioning: *Keep them Happy! Keep them Safe! Christmas Treat Fund.*

Christmas was nearly here, but it would be an entirely different Christmas. For many children it would be a Christmas away from home; children who'd been evacuated for fear of the bombing. There had been none and parents were beginning to bring their children home again, something the government was anxious to discourage. Even so, too many families would be apart this Christmas and the Treat Fund had been established to distribute extra treats to those children who were spending Christmas without their parents.

Harry and Lisa stood at the side of the road, watching the traffic driving round the sandbagged fountain, awed by the perpetual busyness of the famous Piccadilly Circus.

'You wouldn't think there was a war on,' Lisa said, 'not really. Look at all that traffic.' Petrol was rationed, she knew that, because Uncle Dan had only a limited amount for his taxi, but there seemed no fewer vehicles on the road here. Horns hooted, men shouted, engines roared, a man on a bike wove his way through the congestion.

High above them were huge advertisements for Bovril, Coca-Cola and Wrigley's gum, things that were now almost impossible to come by, still advertised on great signs; and ticking away the minutes of that busy Saturday morning was the famous Guinness clock. Above it all floated huge barrage balloons, silver whales wallowing in the ice-blue sky.

'D'you think them balloons'll stop the bombers coming in?' Lisa wondered as she looked up at them.

'If they come in low they will,' Harry said. 'None today, anyway.'

'P'raps they won't come at all,' said Lisa hopefully.

'Oh, they'll come,' Harry assured her. 'Hitler ain't going to say "Thanks for Poland, now I'll stay put," is he?' He turned and began walking towards Piccadilly.

'Shall we go in the shops?' asked Lisa. She longed to go inside one of the tall, gracious buildings and see what they had on display. She moved towards Swan and Edgar, pausing outside to peer in at the window.

'OK,' Harry sighed, 'not for long, mind.'

They went inside and wandered through the different departments looking at all the goods displayed. Lisa wished she had some money. She would have liked to buy something for Aunt Naomi and Uncle Dan.

Harry was quickly bored with window shopping and edged them back out into the street. 'Come on,' he urged, 'let's go this way. P'raps get something to eat.'

He strode along Piccadilly with Lisa almost having to run to keep up with him.

'What's the hurry?' she panted. 'Slow down.'

Harry did slow down, eventually, and when he did he pulled a silk scarf out of his pocket and knotted it about his neck. 'You were right,' he said with a grin. 'They had some good stuff in there.'

'Harry! You stole it!' cried Lisa.

'They had plenty more to sell, they can spare this one for me...' he reached into his pocket again, 'and this for you.' He handed her a string of blue beads. 'Happy Christmas!'

It was a day to remember. They continued to walk up Piccadilly, pausing outside the Ritz to watch the wealthy going in for lunch. Ladies wrapped in furs on the arm of officers in uniform, sleek gentlemen in camel-hair coats handing their ladies out of taxis.

'Toffs,' said Harry dismissively. 'Snobby toffs. Just like the Nazis.'

Comfortable in the anonymity of the crowded streets, Harry had been speaking in German. As he spoke a hand dropped on his shoulder, holding him in a vice-like grip.

'You should be careful what you say, young guttersnipe.' A tall man dressed in immaculately tailored civilian clothes towered over him and was addressing him in German. 'You should be careful what you say about people who've taken you in and given you a home.'

'You don't know nothing about me,' Harry answered with more bravado than he felt.

'I know that you're a refugee, young man. Speaking German; but anyone would know it. Just look at you! Look at your clothes! Ungrateful street kids like you should be sent back where you came from.' The fingers tightened their grip on Harry's shoulder, making him yelp with pain.

'You let him go!' shrieked Lisa. 'He ain't done nothing to hurt you.'

'Well, little madam, you're another of them! Out to pick our pockets, were you? Thieving?' He eyed Harry's silk neckerchief with suspicion. 'I should get out of here pretty damn quick if I were you, before I call the police.'

At this moment the commissionaire stepped forward and said, 'Is there some problem, Sir Edward?'

'No, just some rude German children making nuisances of themselves.' Sir Edward Marshway let go of Harry's shoulder and, giving him a cuff round the ear that sent him staggering off the pavement, turned and walked into the hotel.

'You kids better scarper,' hissed the commissionaire. 'Go on! Get lost.'

Harry picked himself up and the two of them edged away.

'Typical Teddy Marshway,' drawled a woman's voice. 'Likes to forget his mother was German.' She had been speaking English, but both children understood most of what she'd said and turned round.

A tall lady, wearing a black fur coat with a matching fur hat perched on her smooth fair hair, had paused beside them.

'Take no notice of him,' she said, seeing them turn. 'He's always been a bully.' She reached into her handbag and extracted a florin. 'Here,' she said, holding it out, 'expect you could use this. Happy Christmas.'

Harry snatched the coin and stuffed it in his pocket with a muttered, 'Thanks, miss,' and then grabbing Lisa's hand, he set off up the road, leaving the disapproving commissionaire to open the door to the lady, saying, 'Good day, Lady Meldon.'

Further along the road, Harry paused for breath and said, 'One day I'm going to walk into that hotel and the bloke on the door is going to hold the door open for me.'

By mid-afternoon they had walked themselves to a standstill. They had found their way through Green Park to the top of The Mall and had stared up at the sandbagged front of Buckingham Palace.

'D'you think the king's at home?' Lisa wondered. 'I'd like to see the king.'

'Not if he's got any sense,' Harry replied. 'He don't have to stay in London, do he? He's got palaces all over the place.'

They kept walking and finally reached Trafalgar Square where they looked up at Nelson on his column, standing tall and proud against the sky.

'Don't rate much for his chances if the bombing really starts,' said Harry. 'They've boarded up the bottom, look, but that won't be any good against a bomb.'

They wandered round the square, admiring the lions, and then sat on the steps of the National Gallery and shared a pie from a stall and a rather tired-looking chocolate bar Harry had in his pocket. The fountains weren't playing but even so they were impressed with it all.

The day was clouding over and it was now very cold. The clouds, grey above them, seemed laden with snow and Lisa looked up at them anxiously. As she did so, she caught sight of the clock on the steeple of St Martin-in-the-Fields and saw the time.

'Harry!' she cried, grabbing his hand. 'It's nearly four o'clock!'

'So?'

'So I have to get back. Before it's dark. Aunt Naomi will wonder where I am. She might go looking for me at Hilda's!'

'OK.' Harry still sounded not in the least worried. 'Come on then, let's find a bus.'

'We haven't time to keep changing buses,' Lisa told him. 'We have to pay the bus fare.'

'Waste of money,' Harry said.

'But, Harry, we can use the money that lady gave us.'

'You can if you like,' said Harry. He gave her a sixpence from his pocket and flagged down a Shoreditch bus.

'Aren't you coming with me?' asked Lisa apprehensively.

'Oh, all right,' Harry said with a sigh, 'but I ain't paying no fare.'

They scrambled on to the bus and headed up the stairs. When the conductor came, Lisa paid her fare, but Harry, having been through his 'no money' routine was put off at the next stop and so it was that Lisa found her way back to Kemble Street alone. It was almost dark and bitterly cold. Flakes of snow, drifting down from the leaden sky, were already laying a cold carpet on the freezing ground. As she approached number sixty-five she saw Uncle Dan coming up the street towards her.

'Lisa!' he cried. 'Thank God! Where on earth have you been? Your Aunt Naomi has been frantic with worry.'

Lisa knew that if she'd been returning from Hilda's house she'd have been coming from the opposite direction, but she said it anyway. 'I was at Hilda's.'

'No, you wasn't,' Dan said angrily, 'cos Naomi went round to bring you home when it started to snow. The Langs ain't seen you and weren't expecting to.' He gripped her wrist. 'So, where've you been then? You been out all day and we been out looking for you.'

Lisa had never seen Uncle Dan angry and tears sprang to her eyes. She let him pull her indoors and found Naomi and Mary in the kitchen. Both women leaped to their feet and Naomi grabbed Lisa and hugged her close.

'Lisa, where've you been? I've been so worried.' Feeling strong arms around her, Lisa's pent-up tears flooded down her cheeks. She clung to her foster mother and cried; cried for her family, cried because Dan was angry with her, cried because Harry had left her on the bus, cried because Naomi was holding her, cried because she couldn't stop.

'There, there,' Naomi soothed as she held the child tightly till the sobs died away, 'it's all right. You're safely home. As long as you're safe. But, Lisa, you're freezing cold. Here, come to the fire and get warm.' Naomi pulled a chair to the fireside and Lisa sank gratefully into it. Mary went to the stove and set some milk to heat. When it was hot she filled a cup and handed it to Lisa.

'There you are, get that down you. You'll soon warm up.'

Lisa cradled the cup in her chilly hands and sipped the milk, feeling it course down inside her, warm and comforting. Clearly they were all waiting for some sort of explanation. Lisa didn't want to tell them about Harry, Harry was her secret and one that she hugged to herself, so she settled for a half-truth.

'After I have the letter from Cousin Nikolaus I need time to be alone. I walk a little and then I take a bus. When I get off I am lost.'

'And you've been wandering about all day?' Dan sounded incredulous.

'I look at places,' Lisa said. 'I see Trafalgar Square with Nelson.'

'Gracious, child, you've been miles!' exclaimed Naomi.

'I ask for bus to Shoreditch and a lady told me the number and gave me the money.'

'Well, you're safe home at last.' Mary entered the conversation for the first time. She had realised that they were getting a very edited version of Lisa's day, but she was also aware, more than Naomi and Dan seemed to be, that Lisa had needed the day on her own to help her come to terms with the disappearance of her family. It would, Mary knew, take a long time for the desolation that had engulfed Lisa to lessen and it would always be there within her, like a faded bruise that doesn't hurt unless you press it.

'I'd better go,' Mary said. 'We'll be opening up soon and Tom will be wondering where I've got to.' She got to her feet and reached down to give Lisa a hug before letting herself out.

Naomi said to Dan, 'You'd better go and tell the Langs that she's home safe and sound. They'll be worrying, too.' Dan nodded and, putting his coat back on, went out into the night.

'You must be very hungry, Lisa,' Naomi said, happier to deal with the practicalities of life. 'I've got fish for tea and I'll make some chips. Would you like that?'

'Yes, please, Aunt Naomi,' Lisa replied and watched as her foster mother prepared the meal.

That evening, when Lisa had gone to bed, Naomi said, 'Where do you think she got to then?'

Dan shrugged. 'I don't know.'

'I was worried sick,' Naomi admitted. 'I couldn't bear it if anything happened to her now.'

'Nor could I,' agreed Dan. 'We're her family now and we're lucky to have her.'

Chapter Six

Lisa settled back to school after the Christmas holidays. She missed Harry, who had started his job as an errand boy, but her friendship with Hilda was strengthened with his departure. Several children who had been evacuated in September had returned home when the expected bombing had not happened. The numbers at the school increased. New classes were formed and after consultation with Miss May, Miss Hammond made sure that Hilda and Lisa were left together while Roger and his cronies were placed in a parallel class. She knew that being German in a London school at this time was not easy for Lisa and that Roger in particular had been making life difficult for her.

Just occasionally Lisa would find Harry was waiting for her round the corner after school. He had changed, suddenly far more grown up than he had been, no longer a boy, but a streetwise youth with a knowing look on his sharp-featured face. He always seemed to have money in his pocket and would often bring Lisa a bar of chocolate.

'Well, I got wages now, ain't I?' he replied when Lisa remarked on this. 'All right, are you?' he always asked. 'No more trouble with them Nazis?'

'No, they leave me alone now. Other, younger kids to bully.'

'Well, you just let me know.'

He told her very little about his new job, though she asked him what he had to do.

'Just take messages for my boss, mostly,' he replied vaguely. 'Parcels and that, deliveries, you know.'

'But what do you deliver?'

'Stuff the boss wants delivered, of course,' snapped Harry. 'He's got a supply business. I don't know what he wants delivered, do I? I just do what I'm told and he pays my wages.'

'You still at the hostel?'

'Yeah, for now. May have to move soon. They need the space for younger boys, them still at school.'

Together they would walk towards Kemble Street, passing the park, where there was now a sandbagged anti-aircraft installation, above which two barrage balloons tugged at their moorings. War was all around them and yet left them strangely unaffected. No bombs, no gas, no invasion, but high awareness of the possible 'enemy within'.

Esther Lang had warned both her children and Lisa not to speak German anywhere they might be overheard.

'There's so much talk of a "fifth column",' she said, 'you know, German spies who may have infiltrated themselves into English life, people will be very suspicious if they hear you speaking German. English only from now on.'

Harry knew, too, that speaking German was asking for trouble.

'Never going to speak it again,' he told Lisa. 'Not my lingo. I'm English now. Heinrich Schwarz don't exist no more, just plain Harry Black.'

Lisa agreed with him and unless they were entirely alone, they spoke only English together. Even so there was still the bond between them; they had known what it was like 'before'. Lisa had written to Cousin Nikolaus again, but had received no reply and Harry was her only link with her previous life.

War was sweeping through Europe both on land and at sea. British troops had been sent as an expeditionary force to support France and Belgium. Despite the valour of the Royal Navy, British merchant ships bringing much-needed food to Britain were being sunk by the German U-boats. Rationing was introduced in January, of butter, sugar and bacon, and Naomi took all three ration books to be registered at the local shops.

Life at home with the Federmans had settled into a comfortable routine, Lisa going happily enough to school each day. Naomi had started work in a nearby clothing factory where they made service uniforms. She spent most of her days sitting at a sewing machine, putting sleeves into uniform jackets for the army. It was very boring work, but she enjoyed the company of the other girls and the cama-raderie within the workshop and it pleased her that she was doing valuable war work. Dan had agreed that she should take the job, though he didn't really approve of his wife going out to work.

'It's a poor show if I can't keep my own wife,' he said when she told him what she wanted to do.

'You know I wouldn't if there wasn't a war on,' she replied, 'but I want to do my bit like everybody else, don't I? Everyone has to do something.'

'I know, girlie, and I'm proud of you! But just while the war's on, eh?'

Uncle Dan was out with his taxi. As a cabbie at the outbreak of war, his livelihood had been restricted by the immediate introduction of petrol rationing. However, the government, realising that taxis were an important form of transport, allowed the cabbies three gallons a day, so he was still able to ply his trade. As petrol rationing bit harder, more and more people were giving up their cars, putting them up on blocks; public transport of all sorts was needed and he was just able to make a living.

He was pleased that he still had his cab. Other taxis had been requisitioned to be converted into fire engines or ambulances.

'Cabs are built strong, see,' Dan explained to Naomi. 'Old Malcolm, you remember Old Malcom?' Naomi nodded. 'Well, he's had his took away and they've stuck a ladder on the roof and put hoses in the luggage space. Part of the fire brigade now!'

'But what about Malcolm?' Naomi asked. 'Does he still drive it?'

'No, he's too old. A specially trained bloke does now. Some of the other drivers still do, cos they have the Knowledge. They know quick ways to get to places, specially if the roads get blocked, so they've been trained as auxiliary firemen, then they can drive their cabs.'

Naomi came home at the end of each day tired and stiff, so Lisa always helped make the family tea in the evening. When she got home from school she would peel potatoes or prepare vegetables and when Naomi got in the two of them would work companionably in the kitchen, often listening to the wireless.

Lisa's English had come on by leaps and bounds and she could now hold a proper conversation and with extra help from Miss May, she was learning to read and write English too. One evening Dan came home with the *Daily Mirror*. He sat down at the kitchen table and spread it out in front of him.

'Now then, Lisa, me duck,' he said. 'You come and read the paper to me.'

'I can't,' Lisa said in dismay, 'it's too hard.'

'No it's not,' Dan insisted. 'Come on, girl, sit here by me and we'll do it together.'

Reluctantly Lisa drew up a chair and looked at the paper. Dan chose a short article about the importance of carrying gas masks and hesitantly Lisa began to decipher it. It was slow going, but with much reference to the dog-eared dictionary which still sat on the mantelpiece, together they worked their way through to the end.

Dan was full of praise and Lisa was delighted that she had managed to read so much of it on her own. From then on, if Dan got home early in the evening, they would choose an article in the paper and read it together. Gradually Lisa realised that she was beginning to think in English and though she still had to resort to the dictionary to find the words she needed, it was far less often.

She took on the family's mending as her particular chore and often sat by the fire in the evenings listening to the popular programmes on the wireless as she darned Dan's socks, mended tears and sewed on buttons. Lisa liked sewing and she was pleased to be able to do something that really helped Naomi. Ever since her day out with Harry, when she'd been so late home, her relationship with Aunt Naomi and Uncle Dan had changed. She missed her own parents and Martin with an almost physical ache, but she knew that, though they never put their feelings into words, Naomi and Dan had grown fond of her and she returned that affection and felt secure within it.

The cold, wet spring finally gave way to a warm May. More rationing had been imposed and the news from Europe was getting blacker and blacker. The Nazi war machine was roaring its way through Belgium, driving into the Netherlands and attacking France. Everything fell before it and by the last week in May the British Expeditionary force was cut off from the main French army and hemmed in at the port of Dunkirk. The British government decided to try and rescue as many of their fated army as possible and an armada of over eight hundred ships, large and small, set off for the coast of France. For nine days the navy, fishermen and many volunteer sailors repeatedly crossed the channel to pluck the stranded soldiers from the harbour and the beaches of Dunkirk.

The Federmans and Lisa followed the news of the evacuation on the wireless. The whole country seemed to hold its breath as, under almost continuous German artillery fire and Luftwaffe attacks, more and more soldiers scrambled aboard the rescue ships and made it to the safety of the English shore. The French held the Germans at bay, allowing over three hundred thousand troops to be saved, and it wasn't until 4 June that the Germans hoisted the swastika over the devastated port.

Sitting beside the wireless like millions of others, Lisa and her foster parents listened as Mr Churchill broadcast to the nation, promising that whatever the state of war in large tracts of Europe, Britain would fight to the end. 'We shall defend our island, whatever the cost may be, we shall fight on the beaches, we shall fight on the landing grounds, we shall fight in the fields, and in the streets... We shall never surrender.'

His words were echoed on the front page of the *Daily Mirror* the next morning under the headline WE NEVER SURRENDER. Lisa pored over the paper when Dan brought it home, reading of what was being called 'the miracle of Dunkirk'.

'Will the Nazis come here now?' she asked Dan, fearfully.

'If they do, me duck, they'll get a bloody nose,' he replied stoutly. 'You heard what Winston said last night, didn't you? We got our boys out, and some of them Frenchies and Belgies, too. We live to fight another day, but I reckon we'll all be in the front line now.'

Dan was right. The war had come to them, all of them. France surrendered and Hitler turned his attention to Britain. He was determined to break the morale of the English before he invaded and the Nazis took over the country as they were doing everywhere else. What Mr Churchill was to describe as the Battle of Britain was on and the long-expected air raids began as the Luftwaffe filled the skies. The RAF flew unending sorties against the waves of bombers who had come to drop death and destruction on the airfields, trying to gain supremacy in the air by destroying the RAF on the ground. Time and again the marauders were driven back from the coasts and chased out to sea, and Hitler's plan to destroy the RAF and take supremacy in the sky failed. It was then that he turned his attention to the cities, determined to undermine the morale of the general population with continual night-time raids and, as Dan had predicted, everyone became part of the front line.

The first wave of bombers descended on London at the end of June. The air raid sirens rent the air at about one in the morning. Lisa awoke with a jolt as the wail of the siren continued, warning everyone to go to the shelters.

Naomi hurried into Lisa's room. 'Come on,' she said briskly. 'Bring your gas mask and down to the cellar.' She waited as Lisa put her dressing gown on over her pyjamas and then took her hand and together they went downstairs to the kitchen.

'It'll be all right, me duck,' Dan assured her as she paused in fear at the top of the steps. 'I've lit the candles, it won't be dark.'

Taking her hand, he led Lisa down into the cellar where the candles he'd lighted gave a warm glow to the cramped space. Naomi stayed up in the kitchen just long enough to boil a kettle and fill a vacuum flask.

'I'll make us some cocoa,' she said, as she came down with the hot water, a bottle of milk and a tin of cocoa. 'We'll have a midnight feast.'

Together they sat in the candlelit room and drank cocoa and ate biscuits from the tin. They heard nothing from above, no drone of planes or blast of bombs.

'P'raps they saw them off before they got here,' suggested Dan.

At last the all-clear sounded and the little family went upstairs again.

'You're a brave girl, Lisa,' Dan said. 'Not easy for you down there, I know, but you got spunk and you coped.'

'Spunk?' queried Lisa.

'Courage,' said Dan giving her a hug. 'You're a brave girl.'

There were no more raids on London for several weeks, but the dogfights continued over the English Channel, and the coastal towns and the Channel Islands were badly bombed. Every morning Lisa woke with relief that they hadn't had to spend another night in the cellar. At school they had air raid drills which she hated, but Hitler seemed to be leaving London alone for now.

London, however, had long ago made its preparations for the onslaught it knew must come. Air raid warden posts were strengthened, wardens trained. So far most of their duties had been to patrol the streets, but now they knew they would soon be put to a far greater test. Sand and water were stored at strategic places ready to deal with incendiary bombs before the fire should take hold. Volunteers manned the first aid posts. Anti-aircraft placements lay sandbagged, concealed under camouflage netting; searchlights deployed ready to scour the night skies for enemy planes, pinning them in a shaft of light as targets for the gunners.

'How do the planes find where to come in the dark?' wondered Lisa.

'All the buggers will have to do is follow the Thames,' Dan replied. 'Simply follow the river and there we are.'

'Daniel!' Naomi scolded. 'Language!' She turned to Lisa. 'Don't use that word,' she warned, 'it's very rude.'

'D'you know what "buggers" is?' Lisa asked Harry, when he met her from school a few days later.

'Buggers?' Harry shook his head.

'It's very rude,' Lisa told him.

'Then I'll find out,' he promised.

They were walking back towards Kemble Street and when they reached the corner outside the Duke of Wellington, they paused. Harry never went nearer to Lisa's home and as they were about to part Mary came hurrying out of the pub, almost cannoning into them.

'Lisa!' she cried in surprise. 'Sorry, I didn't see you.' She then looked at Harry with interest. 'Hallo,' she said, 'who's this?'

Harry returned her look but said nothing, leaving Lisa to say in some confusion, 'Oh, just a friend from school. Bye, Harry, see you tomorrow.'

Harry took the hint and with a brief, 'Bye, Lisa,' turned and sauntered away.

Mary watched him go, undeceived. Clearly Harry was no school boy, but for the moment she said nothing more than, 'Had a good day?'

'Yes,' Lisa replied, pleased that Mary asked no more questions. 'We read a book, *Great Expectations*. It is difficult for me, but I like very much.'

'Dickens? No, he's not easy! Well done, Lisa.'

'There is an old lady who wears her wedding gown,' Lisa explained. 'It is a little strange, but a good story, I think.'

Later that evening Mary slipped away from the pub and went to see Naomi. It was late and Lisa had gone to bed. Dan was out with the volunteer firemen and Naomi was dozing in her chair.

'Who's the lad that Lisa's going round with?' Mary asked when they were settled with a pot of tea between them.

Naomi looked up, startled. 'What lad?'

'I saw them together today,' Mary said. 'Lisa said he's a friend from school, but I don't think he is. He looked too old and he was pretty scruffy. There was something about him... I don't know what, really, just something I didn't quite trust. She said his name was Harry.'

'She's never mentioned anyone called Harry,' said Naomi. 'She don't seem to have many friends at all, just Hilda Lang. She goes round there quite a lot.'

'Are you sure that's where she goes? She wasn't there that time she got lost.'

'She wasn't with this Harry either,' pointed out Naomi, 'she was on her own.'

'She was on her own when Dan found her.'

They left the subject there, but Naomi gave it great thought when Mary had gone and decided to tackle Lisa about the mystery boy.

'We need to know who she's going about with,' she said to Dan. 'This boy doesn't sound very suitable and she's only just fourteen.'

The next morning Naomi said casually, 'Lisa, don't forget any of your friends from school are welcome here if you want to ask them.'

Knowing what was behind the suggestion, Lisa reddened, but she said, 'Thank you, Aunt Naomi, I'll ask Hilda today.'

'I wasn't just thinking of Hilda,' Naomi said, 'I thought there might be someone else.'

Lisa smiled and, taking the bull by the horns, answered, 'Did Aunt Mary tell you she saw me with Harry? He's just a boy from school. He lives this way somewhere and sometimes we walk home together. I don't want him to come home here.'

Naomi found herself smiling at Lisa's easy use of the word 'home'. She loved the fact that Lisa regarded their home as hers. So, she asked nothing further about Harry.

Chapter Seven

It was during the summer holidays that the Luftwaffe finally turned their attention to London. The sirens wailed the alarm on several August nights and occasionally during the day.

One day when Lisa was supposed to be round at Hilda's house for the day, she left early and met up with Harry. Together they went to Petticoat Lane market, wandering through the narrow streets crowded with all the people out to find a bargain. Lisa hadn't liked being in such a large and pushy crowd, but Harry, in his element among the market stalls, took her hand and led her from stall to stall, fingering the clothes, peering at the strange array of goods offered for sale, listening to the patter of the stallholders.

Lisa suddenly realised they had stayed too long and said, 'Harry, it's late, I got to go.'

'Shall we go up west again on Saturday?' Harry suggested as they left the market and headed back to Kemble Street.

'You mean tomorrow?'

'No, I got to work tomorrow. Next week. I got money this time.'

'Wonder where from?' murmured Lisa.

'Come on, Lisa, let's do it. We did it before.'

'Yes, and I got into real trouble for it.'

'Did you?' Harry didn't sound particularly interested. 'I didn't know that.'

'You didn't ask,' snapped Lisa.

'Say you're going round Hilda's.'

'It's not that easy, Harry.'

'I'll wait for you in the park, Saturday. Next Saturday, right?' He seemed to take her acquiescence for granted and, with a wave of his hand and a quick 'See you then,' he was gone.

Lisa scurried through the streets knowing she was late and that Aunt Naomi would be worried. The trouble was, Aunt Naomi always worried and it seemed to Lisa that she was often the cause. When she'd said as much to Hilda one day she'd been overheard by Hilda's mother.

'Of course she worries about you,' Esther scolded. 'She's looking after you for your parents. It's a big responsibility.'

'I haven't got any parents,' Lisa said flatly. 'They're dead.'

'No, Lisa,' Esther said more gently. 'You don't know that for sure and you must never give up hope. My parents are in Berlin and I haven't heard from them either, but we have to remember that they can't write to us from Germany, can they? We have to keep hoping.'

Lisa had been keeping a tiny flame of hope alive in her heart, but Harry thought she was silly.

'You have to accept that they're gone, Lisa,' he said. 'Same as mine have.'

'I know you're right,' she said. But, secretly, she still harboured the hope.

As she hurried home now the air was suddenly rent by the swooping wail of the air raid siren, the normal afternoon sounds of the streets drowned in its agonised howl. For a moment Lisa paused, peering up into the August sky. Silver barrage balloons swung in the breeze, tugging at their tethers, bulbous grey whales shifting against the clear blue of the sky, but there were no planes in sight. Was it a false alarm? she wondered. Perhaps it was, for although they happened occasionally, daylight raids were rare. But then she heard, through the wailing of the siren, the distant sound of anti-aircraft fire and the faint but insistent drone of engines, planes as yet unseen but roaring relentlessly as they homed in on their target. People were hurrying to the public shelter at the end of the street, but nothing would have induced Lisa to join them and take refuge there. Being shut in, especially with a crowd of other people, was her worst nightmare. She wasn't far from home. She'd have to go down into the cellar; that was bad enough, but better than the public shelter.

As she turned into the little street with its flat-faced terraced houses opening directly on to the pavement, she saw Aunt Naomi, standing at the front door of sixty-five, looking anxiously up and down the road. Catching sight of Lisa, she waved at her frantically, shrieking her name, though her voice was lost in the sound of the siren, and Lisa began running again.

'Where have you been, Lisa?' Naomi cried as she pulled her indoors. 'You're late! You could have been caught in the street!' Her fear made her angry and she said, 'Go down to the cellar.'

Lisa opened the cellar door but waited at the top of the stone steps, listening to the continuing wail of the siren outside and wondering where Uncle Dan was, wishing he was there with them.

Aunt Naomi snatched the kettle off the hob and filled a vacuum flask with hot water. 'Come on, Lisa,' she said, 'we must go down,' and she led the way into the comparative safety of the underground room. Naomi usually had time to fill her thermos, as she had today, and she kept some of the precious tea ration in a small jar, so that they could have a hot drink.

Lisa and Naomi sat in the candlelit cellar listening to the drone of aircraft overhead, the boom of the anti-aircraft battery in the park not three streets away and the crump and thud of falling bombs. The house seemed to be shaking above them and they held hands for mutual comfort.

Lisa wondered if Harry had got back to the hostel before the raid. She knew they had a shelter there, so he should be all right. Naomi was worrying about Dan. He was out with his taxi when the siren had gone off and a surprise daylight raid like this would have caught him, like so many others, unawares.

One very loud explosion made the whole house shake and groan above them, and they clutched each other in terror at the sounds of destruction nearby. 'That one was close,' cried Naomi. 'Oh God, I hope Dan's all right.'

'He'll have taken shelter somewhere.' Lisa tried to sound reassuring, but her own fear made her voice shaky. She hoped he was safe, as well.

It was more than an hour and a half before the all-clear sounded and Lisa and Naomi could emerge into the kitchen. Naomi looked in dismay at the broken glass on the kitchen floor. The window sagged inwards, still criss-crossed with strips of black tape as a defence against bomb blast, but the tumblers which had been on the draining board and two vases at either end of the mantelpiece lay in smithereens on the lino. The front door had been blown open and hung askew on one bent hinge.

Outside there was the sound of shouting, voices echoing down the street as people came out of shelters to view the damage the Luftwaffe had left in its wake. There was immediate activity further along the road and Naomi and Lisa went outside to see what had happened.

'Oh, God,' Naomi cried, rushing down the street in distress, 'the Duke's been hit.' Lisa followed her to join the crowd gathering outside the pub. There was a crater in the road and the roof of the Duke of Wellington hung unsupported over a collapsed wall.

Leon Hardman, the air raid warden, had taken charge and was urging people to stand back and stay clear. 'That roof could come down at any moment,' he shouted. 'Keep right back.' Even as he shouted, a shower of tiles clattered down, smashing on the pavement below, and everyone drew back, looking up anxiously at the crumbling roof.

But it was something else that caught Naomi's eye, a flash of orange, a flicker of red. Flames. She gave a shriek of panic. 'The Duke's on fire!' she screamed. 'The Duke's on fire!' Smoke began to seep out through a broken window.

'Where's Mary and Tom?' someone called. 'Are they inside?'

With another bellow of 'Stand back! Stay back!' Leon Hardman made a dash for the door of what had once been the public bar. Its glass panel was gone and he peered through the small opening into the room beyond.

He could see Mary lying on the floor, her arm flung out and her face turned away. There were already flames on the stairs to the floor above and smoke was swirling through the room. Leon flung his weight against the door, but it wouldn't budge, the shifting of the wall had left it wedged.

'Mary's inside!' he yelled. 'Get an axe! Call the fire brigade! Get some water!' Again he drove his shoulder against the resistant door. Someone dashed off to the wardens' post to summon help and to find an axe, but at that moment a man hurtled round the corner, erupting through the crowd and flinging himself towards the door.

'Where's Mary?' he shrieked as he ran. 'Is Mary inside?' He thrust Leon aside and flung himself against the unyielding door.

'It's jammed,' yelled Leon. 'Tom, it's jammed. They're getting an axe.'

Tom gave a roar of rage and set off round the building. With a glance up at the overhanging roof, he clambered up and over the rubbled remains of its supporting wall and appeared inside the bar. Smoke was now pouring from the damaged building and the crackle of the burgeoning flames was clearly heard by those outside in the street. Another shower of tiles from the roof caused the watching crowd to step back again. With an anxious upward glance, Leon followed Tom over the ruined wall and together the two men managed to lift the prostrate Mary and drag her towards the door. Outside, two more men were trying to break it down, while other neighbours had organised a bucket chain, but the water thrown through a smashed window hardly reached the fire and the only way out for the two men and the unconscious Mary was back over the remains of the wall.

At that moment an insistent clanging announced the arrival of a fire engine. Firemen leapt from their machine. Immediately taking in the situation and hearing there were folks inside, two of them grabbed axes from the cab and attacked the jammed front door. Moments later the door disintegrated and they were through the billowing smoke and inside the building, grasping Mary and carrying her out into the street. A third man had followed them through the door and now grabbed Tom and Leon, pulling them coughing and gasping from the burning pub.

'Where's Mary?' cried Tom as soon as he could breathe. 'Where's my Mary?' He ran to where the rescuing firemen had laid her on the pavement. One was on his knees beside her, giving her artificial respiration.

Lisa, standing with Naomi in the group across the street, watched in horrified fascination as the man, kneeling beside Mary, frantically pumped her chest. She could see Mary's face was deathly white, and the tears sprang to Lisa's eyes. Mary was Naomi's best friend and had always been particularly kind to Lisa, somehow understanding, where others had not, how lost and lonely she felt being sent away from her family to an alien country, to live with strangers.

'Mary! Mary!' Tom was crying as he dropped to his knees beside her still figure. 'Mary, it's me, Tom! Speak to me, Mary! Open your eyes. Please open your eyes!' His voice rose in desperation, but a fireman laid a hand on his shoulder.

'Sorry, mate. There's nothing we can do. She's gone.'

Tom gave a bellow of pain and gathered his lifeless wife into his arms, burying his face in her hair, before suddenly raising his head again and looking round him wildly. 'Fuck you, Hitler!' he shouted. 'Fuck all Germans! The only good German's a dead German!' His eyes came to rest on Lisa, pale and frightened beside Naomi, and with a look of vicious hatred he said, 'You fucking Germans killed my Mary,' he snarled, 'and you *all* deserve to die. Every fucking one of you!'

Lisa blenched at the hatred blazing at her and Naomi, grabbing her hand, pulled her away. There was a murmur among the assembled crowd as it parted to let them through. Tears streamed down Lisa's face now and Naomi put her arms around her, holding her close.

'But I hate Hitler as much as he does,' Lisa sobbed.

'I know, pet,' soothed Naomi, 'but he's just lost his wife to the Luftwaffe, and he's not thinking straight. He doesn't blame you!'

But Lisa knew he did, and in some way, she did herself.

No one else seemed to have been killed or injured in the raid. The Duke continued to burn, but once the firemen got a hose attached to a nearby hydrant, a powerful jet of water began to bring it under control. The sour smell from the sodden, blackened pub filled the air as the firemen continued to damp it down and check that the surrounding buildings were not smouldering, about to erupt into flame.

Mary's body was removed on a stretcher, followed by a white-faced Tom, and now that the drama was over, the crowd of onlookers began to drift away to assess the damage to their own homes.

Daniel had been out in his cab when the sirens wailed their warnings. He was taking an RAF officer to the Air Ministry.

'Drop me off as planned, please, cabby,' the officer said calmly. 'They won't be here yet and there's a shelter just round the corner.'

Dan did as he was asked, knowing the squadron leader was right. The sirens sounded as soon as enemy aircraft were detected, sometimes, as in a daylight raid like this, well before they reached the coast. He decided not to abandon his cab and take shelter. No, Dan decided, he would park the taxi in its usual place beneath the railway arch and then go to the fire station where he was a volunteer fireman. Naomi had hated him being out on the streets during a raid, but Dan was determined.

'I can't just sit in our cellar all the time when I could be out there watching for fires and helping to put them out. They'll be dropping more and more incendiaries and unless we all do our bit, London will burn to the ground.' He'd smiled across at her. 'Don't worry, girlie, I'll look after myself. You look after you and Lisa, eh?'

Gradually, over the months since they had collected Lisa from Liverpool Street, Dan had become very fond of his foster daughter. Like Naomi he wished they had children, and he'd been happy enough to give a refugee child a home, but it had surprised him how quickly, despite her early difficulties, Lisa had become an integral part of their lives. He admired the spunk she'd shown when going to her new school when she spoke no English, and the way she always stood up for herself, facing down the bullies. She had an independent streak which was sometimes difficult to live with, but she also showed a dependence on him, asking him questions, paying attention to his answers, which he found endearing.

The siren continued its lament and the streets were crowded with people, hurriedly making for the shelter of the Underground. As he drove the two miles to his garage, he watched them pouring into the

Tube stations and he gave a grim smile. Hitler won't get any of these this time, he thought.

He parked the cab and then hurried to the fire station.

'Need a spotter on that warehouse roof,' the chief, John Anderson, told him briskly. 'Get yourself up there and keep your eyes peeled.'

'Right-ho, chief! On my way.'

Someone was always sent up to the roof of the nearby warehouse. Filled with paint, it would burn like an inferno if a fire took hold. Spotters were needed to deal with the fire before it could spread and alert the fire brigade if necessary.

Dan puffed his way up the metal staircase, his lungs bursting by the time he got to the top. The fifteen months he'd spent in the trenches of Flanders had taken their toll and any real exertion left him gasping painfully. But fire-watching was something he could do. He couldn't fight again, that was for younger men, and how young they all looked to Dan these days, scarcely more than boys, but he could still do his bit to defend his home.

When he reached the roof he could see the jumble of streets laid out below him. The river shimmered in the late-afternoon sun, a gleaming trail for the incoming aircraft, leading them to the docks, the factories and the warehouses of London. All prime targets for the Luftwaffe.

His mate, Arthur, was already in position, binoculars in hand, scanning the sky to the south-east.

'Here they come,' Arthur said, the quietness of his voice belying his fear. 'And our boys, too.'

Black dots, far away against the blue of the sky, grew bigger, an angry swarm of lethal machines, hell-bent on destruction. But the invaders certainly weren't having it all their own way. RAF Fighter Command were up there too, diving in among the enemy bombers, machine guns blazing, harrying them, coming out of the sun to swoop and kill. Some of the Germans forced their way through the defending planes, unloading their bombs on the docks and the surrounding areas, before high-tailing it back the way they had come.

Anti-aircraft batteries strafed the sky, and they saw one bomber spiralling down, a plume of smoke streaming behind it as it spun to the ground, out of control. and exploded above the river in a ball of fire.

'Got 'im!' said Arthur with bitter satisfaction. 'That's one bugger that won't be coming back!'

Many of the bombs were incendiaries, and the two men could see flame flowering in every direction.

Overhead, the German planes having unleashed devastation on the city below, beat a hasty retreat, chased all the way to the coast by the valiant fighter planes. Smoke and dust filled the air, a pall of grey hanging over the streets. Fires blossomed angry red below, but miraculously the warehouse had not been hit. The all-clear sounded and Dan and Arthur made one final sweep with the binoculars and having noted fires below in the next street hurried down to direct the firefighters to those and to join in their fight.

It was some time before the fires in their area were under control. Dan and Arthur and other volunteer firemen dealt with small fires which had broken out in the narrow streets and on waste ground, leaving the more serious fires to the regular and auxiliary fire services.

'Hear that Kemble Street took a hit,' one man said as he shovelled sand on to a patch of burning weeds. He looked across at Dan. 'You live that way, don't you?'

Dan had gone pale. 'Kemble Street? You sure?'

'Called in from the ARP post earlier. Pub on fire.'

Arthur looked up. 'Better go straight home, Dan,' he said, 'we can cope here now!'

Dan hesitated for a moment, then with a quick word of thanks darted off along the street, heading for home.

Lisa and Naomi had just got back when he appeared round the corner, his face red from running, his breath ragged. When he saw them he stopped, flopping forward to ease the pain in his chest.

'Thank God you're all right!' he gasped as he pulled Naomi to him. 'They said the street was hit.'

Naomi returned his hug, holding him close, her arms tight around him.

'We're all right,' she said, and reached out to include Lisa in her embrace, 'both of us. It's the Duke what's been hit.' Her voice trembled as she said, 'Mary was inside. She's dead.'

'Mary?' echoed Dan. 'Does Tom know?'

'Yes, he was there when they got her out. As you can imagine, he's in a dreadful state.' She didn't mention Tom's reaction when he'd seen Lisa in the crowd, she'd tell him later when Lisa wasn't there. 'They took her away on a stretcher. Tom went too.'

Dan looked shaken at the news. He tried to imagine what Tom must be going through, but he couldn't... If it had been his Naomi... He turned towards the house and saw the blast-damaged door, hanging on its single hinge. It had been close for her, too.

'Much damage inside?' he asked, trying to sound normal.

Naomi shook her head. 'Some broken glass, that's all, I think. We was lucky. We heard the explosion, me and Lisa, in the cellar. It must have been the blast from the Duke what...' Her voice trailed off.

She led the way back into the house and between them they set about clearing up the mess. Sweeping up the broken glass, tears brimmed her eyes as she had a sudden vision of poor Mary, lying pale and broken in the road; killed in her own home. They had been friends since their school days and for as long as Naomi could remember, Mary had been part of her life. She couldn't yet believe that Mary would never again wander in through the front door with a cheerful call of, 'Kettle on, Naomi?' Dear Mary, who despite Tom's antipathy, had taken the trouble to get to know Lisa, showing her great kindness.

'You finish peeling them spuds,' Naomi said to Lisa now, knowing that she, too, was upset and needed to be doing something, however mundane.

Without a word, Lisa turned to the sink and picking up the kitchen knife lying on the draining board, began peeling the potatoes Naomi had left when the siren had sounded. How long ago? It seemed to Lisa that it was a lifetime, a time when Mary was still alive.

'Did you look upstairs?' Dan asked when he had nailed a blanket over the gaping front door.

'No,' answered Naomi. 'We went straight out into the street.'

'I'll have a look.'

He went through the little house, checking for more damage. The window of the tiny front parlour wasn't broken though there was a crack right across one corner, but a bedroom window upstairs lay in pieces on the floor.

When the kitchen had been set to rights, glass swept away, the broken windows boarded up, Naomi made a pot of tea and they all flopped down round the kitchen table.

'We'll have to check the blackout again,' Dan said. 'May not fit closely with the window blown in. You can help me, Lisa. I'll put it up, you can go outside and see if there's any light getting out.'

Later, when Lisa had gone to bed, Dan and Naomi sat in the kitchen together.

'I just can't believe she's gone,' sobbed Naomi, at last giving way to her grief. She had held herself together for Lisa's sake. The child had lost another person she was fond of and Naomi had known that she must be strong for her. 'And I had such good news to tell her,' Naomi said on a sob.

'News?' asked Dan, hoping to divert her thoughts from Mary. 'What was you going to tell her?'

'I was going to tell you first, of course,' Naomi said, grasping his hand. Despite her tears and the sadness and the terror of that dreadful day, a new light of happiness glowed in her eyes.

'Well?' prompted Dan. 'What news?'

'You're going to be a father.'

'What?' asked Dan feebly.

'You're going to be a father. I'm going to have a baby. Dr Marshall confirmed it today. I'm nearly four months gone.'

Dan stared at her in mute amazement for a moment before he eventually said, 'Are you sure? I mean, why didn't you tell me?'

'Didn't want to get your hopes up – or mine for that matter,' beamed Naomi, 'not till it was confirmed.'

'When's it due?'

'January.'

'January!' he echoed. 'I'm going to be a dad in January.'

Dan still couldn't believe what she was telling him. They'd given up all thoughts of children of their own. 'Aren't you too old? I mean...' he stammered as he saw the look on her face at this remark, 'I mean, well, I thought...'

'I'm only thirty-nine. It's old for a first baby, but Dr Marshall says everything seems to be going fine. I'm fit and healthy and lots of women my age have babies. And Dr Marshall says it's probably due to Lisa being here. We've been so busy worrying about her, we've stopped worrying about babies and relaxed. Think about it, Dan, our own baby!'

'I am thinking about it,' Dan said, 'and I'm thrilled to bits, girlie, but it'll take a bit of getting used to.'

'I just wish Mary had known,' said Naomi sadly.

'P'raps she does,' Dan said.

'D'you really think so?' Naomi's face brightened.

'I don't know, do I? Maybe she does. More important, what's Lisa going to say?'

'I don't know. I hope she'll be pleased with the idea of a brother or sister. But we don't have to tell her yet. It's early days. Let's just keep it to ourselves for now, shall we. Our secret.'

'Whatever you want, girlie,' said Dan. 'Whatever you want.'

Chapter Eight

The death of Mary and the destruction of the Duke weighed heavily on Kemble Street. There was an air of sadness, but with an underlying anger that Hitler had finally burst in upon their corner of the world. The rubble was cleared away, the overhanging roof pulled down and the doors boarded up. The Duke of Wellington, the social centre of the area, would be closed from now on.

The air raid warnings continued, often with two or three a night. At first they all trooped down to the cellar, but with so many broken nights Dan finally agreed, to Lisa's immense relief, that they not go down until they heard the planes overhead and the sound of gunfire.

Mary and Dan went to Mary's funeral. Lisa stayed at home; they all knew that Tom would not want her there.

'It'll be a difficult day for him, pet,' Naomi said. 'It's not your fault.'

It was this that decided her to go and meet Harry the next Saturday. She hadn't been going to go, but now she needed to be with someone the same as she, someone else who was an outsider.

Saying she was going to Hilda's, Lisa set off for the park. Harry was sitting on his usual bench, waiting for her.

'Knew you'd come,' he said by way of greeting.

'Needed to get away,' Lisa said and flopping down beside him told him about Mary.

'Well, she ain't the first and she won't be the last,' Harry said dismissively.

'Harry! How can you say that?' cried Lisa.

'Cos it's true. Something you got to get used to, Lisa. *You* know that. We had some bombs, yeah, but Hitler's blitz ain't started yet. Lots more people are going to die before he's done.'

'You sound as if you don't care,' Lisa said bitterly.

'How can I care?' demanded Harry. 'It's all too big for me to care about. I can only care about me.'

'And me?'

'Yeah, and you. Come on, Lisa, let's go up west and forget it all for a bit. I got money and we'll go to a caff and eat sausages and chips.'

This time when they took the bus Harry felt in the depths of his pocket and produced money for the fares, so they were able to travel all the way to Trafalgar Square without having to get off. They spent the morning exploring the small streets around Soho and Leicester Square and then, as he'd promised, Harry treated them to a sausage and chips. Lisa had never been to a café to eat before and she sat at the table in the window watching all the people coming and going in the street outside.

'This is lovely,' she said, 'eating in a proper restaurant, like grown-ups.' Then she looked anxiously at Harry. 'You have got the money, haven't you, Harry?'

'Of course!' Harry looked affronted. 'Told you I had, didn't I?'

By the middle of the afternoon Lisa knew she had to go home. She had been asked to Hilda's for tea and she was determined to get there in time. She'd told Naomi she was going to Hilda's, and she wanted to make it true.

'I got to go, Harry,' she said when they'd finished eating. 'I got to go to Hilda's like I told Aunt Naomi.'

'OK.' Harry shrugged. 'I got to stay up here.'

'What do you mean?'

'I got to see someone,' Harry said. 'I'll put you on the bus.'

'Aren't you coming with me?'

'No, I told you, I got to see someone up here. Don't worry,' he said with exaggerated patience. 'I'll give you the bus money.'

He waited with her at the bus stop and waved as she looked back at him through the window, before disappearing into the crowds on the street.

The bus was quite full and Lisa was pleased to get a seat inside. She paid the fare and sat back to enjoy the journey. Her enjoyment was short-lived. Suddenly the air was rent by the blast of air raid sirens.

'Bloody Wailing Winnie off again!' groaned the man sitting next to her. The bus continued its way along the road for another few minutes and then it pulled up.

'Everybody off,' shouted the conductor. 'We ain't going no further till them Nazis has gone home.'

People began to clamber off the bus, heading for the public shelters. Many of them hurried down the stairs into the Underground. Lisa, standing for a moment on the pavement, didn't know what to do. All around her people were hurrying to find shelter, the continuing sirens encouraging them to be quick, and even as she stood there she heard the thunderous roar of hundreds of planes in the sky above her.

'Come on, love,' cried a woman, catching her by the arm and pulling her towards the Tube station, 'got to get under cover.'

But as they reached the entrance and Lisa saw the people thronging the stairs leading down, she knew she couldn't go in there. With a sharp tug she pulled herself free and began to run. She didn't know where she was running to, but nothing would have induced her to go into the Underground. Somehow it felt safer to be running than standing still staring up at the bombers overhead.

And then the bombs started to fall; the whistle through the air followed by the boom of the explosion. Even as she ran, fires began to blossom in nearby buildings. Firemen and volunteers rushed to each red and orange glow to douse it with sand or water to prevent it from taking hold.

Lisa continued to run, ducking into doorways, cowering against the buildings as the intensity of the raid increased. The noise of the planes, the crump of the bombs and the thunder of the anti-aircraft guns were deafening, an all-enveloping din which intensified the chaos around her. She was completely disorientated, veering from one side of the street to another looking for shelter. She had no idea of the way to the nearest shelter, nor the way back to the Underground station. There were other people in the streets, the air raid wardens, firemen and first aid volunteers, but they were all intent on dealing with and trying to contain the damage caused by the bombs. No one seemed to see the young girl whirled about by the turmoil and confusion. There was no respite as wave after wave of enemy aircraft filled the skies. Harried by the fighters of the RAF, dogfights developed among the clouds, but the bombers continued dropping their deadly load on a London already on fire.

Lisa was shaking with fear, her arms about her head as she curled in a ball in a shop doorway.

'Christ, child!' cried a voice. 'What are you doing out here?' Someone reached into the doorway and hauled her to her feet. 'There's a shelter this way. Come on!' Holding her firmly he hustled her along the road towards the concrete shelter little more than a hundred yards away. Lisa allowed herself to be dragged along, her legs too weak with fear to support her properly.

Above them there was a swish and a whistle. The man grabbed her into his arms as if to shield her with his body and then there was an almighty explosion and a building only a couple of hundred yards behind them disintegrated, folding in on itself with a crash that reverberated along the narrow street, bringing with it a thick cloud of dust. The man and Lisa collapsed on to the pavement and neither of them moved again.

It was soon after four o'clock that Saturday afternoon. Dan had just got home when the air raid sirens began their lament. He grabbed Naomi and said, 'Down into the cellar, girlie, there's two of you to save now.'

'Where's Lisa?' Naomi cried.

'Don't you fret about her,' Dan said firmly. 'She's round Hilda's and they've got an Anderson in their garden. Lisa will be OK.'

'Come down with me,' begged Naomi. 'The baby needs a dad as well, you know.'

'I know that, but I have to gotta out. I'm needed at the fire post. Can't let the others down, can I?' He led his wife down the steps into the cellar, made sure that she had a torch and lit the candles. By now they could hear the drone of the aircraft above and the anti-aircraft fire from the battery in the park.

'It's a big raid,' quavered Naomi. 'Don't leave me, Dan.'

'Must, girl. Big raid is all the more reason for me to get out there. It'll be all hands to the pump for this one.' He pulled Naomi into his arms and whispered, 'Keep Junior safe for me, there's a good girl, and don't you come out again till you hear that all-clear, promise?' She nodded and very gently he put her from him and with a blown kiss went back up the stairs, closing the cellar door behind him.

As soon as he got outside he realised just how immense the raid was. Looking up he could see planes in every direction, heavy bombers lumbering across the sky, and even as he watched, the bombs they carried began cascading downward. The siren continued to shriek, and everywhere people were dashing towards the nearest shelter. Dan hurried through the emptying streets to the fire post where he was a volunteer.

'Christ almighty,' the chief was shouting as he arrived, 'they've sent the whole fucking Luftwaffe this time!' Some of the planes passed on overhead, flying to targets further along the river. Others, their cargo discharged, were beating a hasty retreat, harried by the RAF fighter pilots. But the bombers had not come alone. Determined to make it to London and set the city ablaze, they had come with fighter escorts to protect them and the battle for the air was fierce and furious. Anti-aircraft batteries all over the city were pounding away at the enemy planes and the noise was ear-splitting and unceasing. Orders were shouted and the fire crews and valiant volunteers rushed from place to place as the news of fire and destruction came in from the wardens' posts.

Dan worked in a team of three, with Arthur and another, younger man, George. Together they moved swiftly to deal with outbreaks of fire, caused by incendiary bombs which fizzed into action the moment they landed. Their task was to contain these with sand and a limited supply of water before they burst into red-hot flame, consuming everything they touched. The raid seemed to go on for ever. Dan was soon exhausted, but there was no respite. As soon as one fire was extinguished they were dealing with another, shovelling sand and working the stirrup pump. The sky across the city was glowing red, thick smoke billowed above them and still the bombers came. It wasn't till nearly two hours after the sirens had warned of the raid that they sounded the all-clear. London was still ablaze and when Dan and his team were sent up on the warehouse roof to spot still-burning fires they had the first sight of the devastation which the Luftwaffe had wrought. All across the city fires were burning out of control. Many buildings had been blasted to the ground, others stood in partial defiance, roofs and walls blown away, interiors exposed. People emerging from shelters were faced with an unbelievable scene of destruction.

Even when the all-clear had been sounded there was no rest for the firefighters. Dan was desperate to know that Naomi was all right, but he couldn't leave his team to go and find out. They all worked as before, trying to contain the fires, heaving sand buckets and pushing water carts to wherever they were needed. After a couple of hours the chief called a halt and sent them to get something to eat.

'Just fifteen minutes,' warned the chief. 'We all need a break and we'll go in turn. Your lot first, Arthur, and as soon as you're back, Tony and his lot'll go.'

'No time to go home,' Arthur said. 'Let's see if the Dog and Duck's open.'

They hurried down the rubble-strewn street and found to their astonishment that the pub was, indeed, open. There was no hot food, but the barmaid was furiously making sandwiches. Arthur's lot weren't the only crews coming in to refuel.

They flopped down at a table and wolfed down a stack of cheese sandwiches, washed down with pints of beer.

'Come on,' Dan said after ten minutes. 'If I don't get up again now, I shan't get up again at all!'

They all dragged themselves to their feet and just as they walked out into the street, the air raid sirens went off again.

'Bloody hell!' exclaimed George. 'Don't them bleedin' things ever give over?'

'May be a false alarm,' Arthur suggested hopefully.

But it wasn't and they soon knew it wasn't as the sound of gunfire could be heard in the distance. Moments later the drone of the invaders was in the air. Having left themselves a beacon that couldn't be quenched, the Germans were back. Squadrons of bombers thundered towards London and apart from the RAF fighters which defied them in the air, there was nothing that Londoners could do but wait for the bombardment to begin again. It wasn't until four-thirty the next morning that the all-clear sounded. The long-awaited 'blitzkrieg' had begun.

Naomi had been in a state of near panic ever since Dan had left in the afternoon. Sitting in the cellar alone was terrifying. She could hear bombs falling, but where? Were they as near as they sounded, or was the sound just magnified as it echoed along the narrow streets, channelled between the rows of houses? Was the street above her still a street at all, or had it been flattened? Our house is still standing, she told herself fiercely, so probably the others are too. The bombs she'd heard must have been further away. It was far more frightening, she decided, not to know, to be unable to see what was going on up above; to be stuck in the cellar by herself where at any moment the house might collapse on top of her, burying her in its ruins where she would die alone. She was tempted to go back upstairs and watch the raid – at least she'd know what was happening outside – but she'd promised Dan that she'd stay in the cellar until the all-clear sounded and so she gritted her teeth and kept her promise. More than once there was a shriek, a whistle, a swish, followed by an explosion making the house rock on its foundations.

'Where are you, Dan?' she shrieked as another explosion shook the house. 'Why aren't you here with me? I can't do this alone!'

She thought of him out there in the middle of this nightmare and a wave of panic flooded through her. How could anyone survive in the streets in a raid as fierce as this?

'Oh, Dan,' she cried, 'where are you? I need you! And Lisa? Where are you, Lisa? I wish you were here! I wish I could see you! I wish we were all together!'

The continuous pounding of the anti-aircraft battery in the park was deafening and Naomi crammed her hands over her ears as if that might block out the sounds from above. It didn't, and shaking with fear she curled up in a ball on the mattress, burying her head under a pillow.

When at last the all-clear sounded she was still shaking, her head singing with the noise long after it had actually stopped. She crept up the stairs to the kitchen, opened the front door cautiously and looked along the road, dreading what she might see. Smoke filled the air and there was a halo of orange across the sky. Fire flickered at the end of the street as shadowy figures moved about trying to subdue it. People were emerging from their houses and from the public shelter on the corner of Hope Street. She could see air raid warden, Leon Hardman, coming along the pavement assessing possible bomb damage as he passed each house. He smiled wearily as he reached her.

'You all right?' he asked. 'Dan with you?'

'No,' replied Naomi. 'He's out fire-watching. What's burning down there?' She pointed to the blaze of red and orange at the end of the road. She could hear the crackle of the flames as they leaped and danced amid the billowing smoke.

'The Duke,' said Leon. 'The rest of it's come down. Not a hit, probably blast from another bomb further over. It's just a heap of rubble now. The road's blocked and there's two more fires the other end of Hope Street. You go back inside, Mrs F, fewer people on the streets the better. It's not safe, what with the fire and the unstable buildings. We'll be better able to see in the morning.' He moved on to continue his inspection of the houses in his patch, pausing occasionally to speak to Naomi's neighbours as he went.

The Duke had really gone! Naomi could hardly believe it. It had stood on that corner all her life. It had been the centre of a community, her own dad's watering hole, and now there was nothing left, it had been reduced to a pile of blackened stones.

Thank God Tom's already moved in with his sister in Bow, Naomi thought. At least the bombers haven't got him, too.

She stood for a moment or two longer, peering along the road, hoping to see Lisa emerging from the gloom.

Don't be silly, she told herself. The Langs would never let her venture out into the streets so soon after such destruction. And as for Dan, she had no idea when he'd get home. The whole sky was red with fire, the clouds of smoke pink, underlit by the flames. Dan and all the firemen in London would have their work cut out to quench so many fires. She didn't allow herself to think that he might not come home. He'd survived the Great War, surely he'd survive here at home in London. She knew the whereabouts of neither Lisa nor Dan and there was nothing she could do about either of them except wait, wait until they were able to come home again. And so, following the air raid warden's advice, she turned back to the house. As she reached the front door she heard the forlorn cry of a baby, little Jonathan Doig, three doors up the road. Her hand flew to her own stomach as if to check that her own baby was still there. How terrifying, she thought, to have to keep a small baby safe in a raid like the one they'd just endured. Thank goodness her precious babe was still safe inside her. While she lived, he or she was safe.

Back in the house, Naomi needed something to do, so she prepared vegetables for the evening meal. Potatoes to peel, onions to slice, ready to make bangers and mash for their tea. She'd managed to get hold of some sausages, not yet rationed with the other meat, and looked forward to surprising Dan with one of his favourite meals. He would be starving when he finally came home, and Lisa, of course, if she came home tonight, would be hungry too. She switched the wireless on for company and tuned to the light programme, hoping it would be *ITMA*, or one of the other comedy programmes to raise her spirits; perhaps even some dance music. There was music, but it was soon interrupted by Alvar Lidell reading the news, the news she already knew first-hand, that London had been hit by hundreds of Luftwaffe bombers and the dreaded 'Blitz' had begun. Naomi turned him off.

Time concertinaed and it seemed only moments later that the sirens sounded their eerie warning once more.

'Not again!' wailed Naomi. Surely they couldn't be back again so soon. But it appeared they could and she heard the sound of the anti-aircraft guns in the distance. She considered making a dash for the Hope Street shelter so that at least she wouldn't have to sit the raid out on her own, imagining the worst, but even as she gathered up her coat there was a loud explosion not far away, and she gave up the idea. To go out into the street now would be suicidal. She filled the vacuum flask, picked up her torch and went back down into the cellar. It was almost dark outside now and she had to put on the torch to light the candles. As she struck a match she had a sudden vision of the leaping flames at the end of the street. Suppose the house was hit? Suppose the candles were knocked to the ground and the cellar caught fire? She'd be trapped. Naomi blew out the match and, using the torch, crept across to the mattress. For the second time that day, she pulled the blanket over her head, put her fingers in her ears and waited, alone and this time in the dark, for the din outside to cease and the all-clear to sound. She waited another eight hours. Despite her fear and the battle raging in the sky outside she drifted in and out of sleep, an unrestful sleep, full of fear and the nightmares it bred. When after an eternity the siren sounded the all-clear, she was stiff and cold and miserable. She climbed the stairs to discover the damage left in the bombers' wake. She found that their repaired front door had been blown askew again, but other-wise the house was still standing. She still had a home. Others in the street had not been so lucky. Further up the road two houses had suffered severe damage where an incendiary bomb had caught hold. Even now firemen were struggling to contain the blaze and the owners, Mr and Mrs Goldman, an elderly couple emerging from the Hope Street shelter, had to be restrained from trying to go inside to save some of their possessions.

Naomi turned away in despair. How would any of them survive more attacks like these? She went back indoors to wait. She wanted to cry, but she was beyond tears. All she wanted was for Dan to come home, Dan and Lisa.

Dan got back to Kemble Street in a state of exhaustion. He had never felt so tired. He and his team had laboured through the night, using reserves of energy that they never knew they had. As he turned into Kemble Street he looked along the line of houses. Two on the opposite side of the road had sustained some damage, their blackened frontage and burned-out roofs evidence of an incendiary device. Another had lost its chimney, which had crashed through the roof leaving a gaping hole. Otherwise they were all there. No real gaps in the terrace and his heart gave a leap of happiness. Naomi must be all right and the miracle baby which was growing inside her would be too. Now that he'd got used to the idea that he was really and truly going to be a father, Dan was more excited by the idea than he would have thought possible.

Can't let Naomi stay at risk if there's more raids like this, he thought as he hurried towards his home. She and Lisa'll have to go to the country. Can't risk losing them and the baby. But, as he reached number sixty-five and pushed the front door open, he knew it would be a hard task to make her leave him and go to safety alone.

When Naomi heard the front door scrape open and saw Dan coming in, his hair black with soot, his face streaked black, she gave a shriek of delight and flung herself into his arms.

'Thank God, thank God,' she cried. 'You're safe, oh, Dan, you're safe.'

Dan held her close, his face against her cheek, which was wet with tears of relief. 'It's all right, girlie,' he soothed. 'I'm back and you're safe, that's all that matters now. Where's Lisa?'

Naomi's courage finally failed and she burst into tears. 'Oh, Dan, I don't know. She didn't come home after the first raid so I think she must have stayed with Hilda. Probably Mrs Lang didn't think it was safe for her to come home by herself through all the chaos. There were some loud explosions and Leon Hardman said there's fires and damage and danger everywhere. They probably made her wait until it was daylight. It's a good thing she didn't try and come home, she might have been caught in the second raid. Oh, Dan! How could they come twice in one night like that?'

'To try and frighten us to death,' said Dan. 'But it ain't going to work!'

'I *was* frightened, Dan.'

'I know, girl, I know. But we ain't going to let the buggers win, so we got to be brave.'

Naomi hugged him again. 'At least you're home,' she said. 'You must be exhausted.'

'Bit tired,' he admitted.

'And hungry?'

'I'll have something when I wake up!'

'And Lisa?'

'Don't worry about her,' he soothed. 'I'll just have an hour's shut-eye and when it's daylight I'll go round and fetch her.'

Together they went upstairs and instantly Dan fell into a sleep of total exhaustion.

Naomi lay awake listening to her husband's regular breathing beside her. Though she was tired and despite Dan's reassurance, she was worried sick about Lisa. Why hadn't she come home? Dan was probably right about her staying with the Langs in their shelter during the first raid, but surely she could have come home before the second wave came in. What would she, Naomi, have done if Hilda had been with them instead of the other way around? Would she have kept her with them until all the planes had gone? Kept her until it was daylight? She heaved a loud sigh. Yes, she probably would. And with this thought she curled up against Dan's back and finally drifted off to sleep.

Chapter Nine

As the first wave of raiders were driven off, Mark Davenham and Andy Drew, air raid wardens in the Clerkenwell area, were patrolling their sector searching out damaged buildings, checking for fires and more importantly casualties who might have been caught in the street when the raid began. They passed a half-demolished office building, the whole front of which had crumbled into the road.

'What a mess,' Andy said, edging towards the exposed offices.

'Watch it!' admonished Mark, 'the rest of that could come down at any time.'

Standing back from the ruins, Andy cupped his hands together and called, 'Anyone there? Anyone inside?'

There was no reply, but together the two wardens called again. 'Anyone in this building?'

It was dark inside, no fire to be seen and, as far as they could tell, no people either. But they made a note to call it in so it could be thoroughly checked by the rescue service.

'Unlikely anyone would have been in an office at five o'clock on a Saturday afternoon,' Mark said.

'True,' Andy agreed, 'but people have been working some funny hours lately, so you never know.' But calling once more he was answered by silence.

They continued down the road. There was more damage to the nearby buildings, broken glass from shattered windows, an occasional door, a porch collapsed on to the pavement, but it was mainly a commercial area and as far as they could tell no one had been in the buildings when the bombers struck. As they reached the corner something in Mark's peripheral vision caught his eye. Half hidden in the doorway of an undamaged building was... something. He grabbed Andy's arm and pointed.

'Look, what's that?'

They went over to investigate and discovered them, two bodies, a man lying, wide-eyed and staring, with his arm wrapped round an unmoving child.

Mark knelt down beside them. He could see that the man was dead, but the child lay face down, inert, seemingly not breathing.

Holding his own breath he reached forward and pressed his fingers to the child's neck. 'Pulse!' he cried. 'Faint pulse.' He looked up at Andy. 'Get an ambulance, Andy. I'll stay here with her. We might save this one.'

'On my way!' Andy raced off down the road to the nearby wardens' post to summon an ambulance.

Mark sat down on the pavement and reached out to hold the child's cold hand. 'Hang on tight, brave girl,' he murmured. 'Help's coming. I promise help's coming. Just hold on.'

There was no reaction from the child and he felt again for the pulse. It was still there, but faint, no more than a flutter. Mark knew that help would come, but he had no idea when. After such a raid the ambulance service would be stretched to breaking point. As he sat there, there was a rumble and crash behind him and, spinning round, he saw the remains of the office building disintegrate in a boiling cloud of dust, leaving a gap like a broken tooth in the row of buildings that lined the street. He tried to shield the child from the worst of the dust with his body, but he dared not move her. Suppose she had spinal injuries that he could make more serious? For the next half-hour he looked continually for some sign that help was coming. Surely Andy had got back to the post and phoned in the news of the casualty. Of course he had, it was simply that there were so many calls on the ambulance service they hadn't got to him and his little girl yet. The dead man lay beside them and, unnerved by his staring eyes, Mark leaned over and closed them. He had been trained as a warden since he'd volunteered in October

1939, but he'd never yet had to deal with an actual dead body, indeed, he'd never seen anyone dead before. Mark was only twenty-three, but his asthma had, so far, kept him out of the services. The continuing dust combined with the smoke from more distant fires combined to make breathing difficult for him and he was coughing and fighting for breath when the ambulance, in the form of an adapted taxi, finally arrived. Two ambulancemen jumped out. One look told them not to bother with the man still lying with his arm across the girl.

'What we got here, mate?' one asked Mark.

'The child's still alive, but I don't know how bad. She was partly shielded by this bloke, I think. They must have been caught out in the open when the bomb fell on that.' He jerked his thumb at the ruined offices down the street.

'Identity?'

'Don't know,' answered Mark, 'haven't dared move her in case of doing more damage.'

'Good, let's have a look.' The man knelt down beside her and gently felt for the pulse, then very carefully he began to examine her. 'She's out cold,' he said, 'and this is what's done the damage.' He lifted her hair to display a bleeding wound on the side of her head. 'She's broken her arm, too, probably when she fell.

'Help me turn her, Mike,' he said to his partner and together they turned her on to her back so that he could continue his examination.

'She's a mass of bruises,' he said. 'If the blast killed her dad, she's lucky to be alive. He probably saved her life.'

'Reckon he's her dad?' asked Mark.

'Seems likely. See if he's got any identity docs.'

Mark turned to the dead man and gingerly turned him over, slipping a hand into his jacket pocket. Inside was his national identity card naming him as Peter Smith aged fifty from Harrogate in Yorkshire.

'He was a long way from home, poor bugger,' remarked Mike. 'Wrong day to visit London, eh, Jack.'

'Any identity docs on the kid?' Jack asked.

Mike looked in the pocket of Lisa's dress but all it contained was a photograph.

'No, nothing. Typical kid going out without her identity card.'

'Well, let's get her to the hospital,' said Jack. 'They can do a thorough check and patch her up there.' He removed her gas mask, which was still looped round her neck. He reached back into the taxi and grabbed a label on which he wrote *? Smith from Harrogate* before he tied it to her ankle. They hauled a stretcher out of the converted back of the taxi and, gently lifting her on to it, slid it back inside.

'What about Mr Smith?' Mark asked, looking down at the dead man still on the pavement.

'We got to deal with the living first, mate,' the ambulance driver told him. 'Report his whereabouts and name back at the wardens' post and he'll get picked up.' He gave a brief wave of his hand and the taxi disappeared, taking its casualty to hospital.

Mark stood looking down at Peter Smith. It didn't seem right simply to walk away and leave him, but the ambulance driver was right, it was the living that needed his help now. He bent down and straightened the man out, so that he lay as if asleep.

'You did your best, mate,' he said. 'At least you saved your little girl.' He bowed his head for a moment and then set off, jogging back to the wardens' post to report on what they'd found so far and perhaps continue his rounds with Andy. Surely there must be vital work for them to do.

It was beginning to get dark but the sky glowed an orange arc above him. So many fires, he thought as he ran back. So much destruction. The firefighters must be flat out. As soon as he reached the post he logged in the body of Peter Smith, registering name and position, and then the chief warden dispatched him with Andy to search another sector. They had only been out a quarter of an hour when the sirens started wailing again.

'Christ!' exclaimed Andy. 'Are the fuckers back already?'

They were, and the two wardens began their now familiar routine, shepherding those who had returned to the streets back to the shelters and checking that there was no one who needed assistance to get there. They watched for lights showing, but as Mark said, 'Pointless really, the whole bloody town's a bonfire.'

By the early hours of the morning much of the city of London was aflame and many buildings, large and small, had been destroyed or damaged. The building that had sheltered Peter Smith had been torched by an incendiary, the heat so intense that when the firemen finally put out the blaze there was nothing left to find. Only Mark Davenham's record of Peter Smith's resting place survived to say that he'd ever been there.

The child, however, had made it to the hospital just before the second raid had burst upon them. She was carried in through Casualty and a nurse checking the label on her ankle, logged her in as *? Smith, Harrogate.*

Casualty was ordered chaos. Injured and disorientated people had flooded in. The worst cases were dealt with first, the less serious had to wait. The unconscious child was wheeled into a cubicle where she had to wait for a doctor to come and examine her. Her coat was bloodstained and a nurse cut it away to release her broken arm. When a doctor was able to examine her, he was concerned by her head wound and the fact that she hadn't regained consciousness. Assessing her level of consciousness he shone a pencil torch into her eyes and watched the pupil shrink.

'Still unconscious, but stable,' he said. 'Don't think there's a bleed, but you can never be quite sure. Clean, stitch and bandage that wound and then regular monitoring. I think it's just a bad concussion and she'll come round in her own good time. Keep her in the recovery position for now in case she's sick when she does.'

A commotion outside claimed his attention and he headed for the door, saying as he did so, 'Keep her as quiet as possible and check her every half-hour. Once that arm's in plaster we'll get her up to the children's ward and have her closely monitored for the next twenty-four hours. If there are no complications, we can take further decisions about her then.'

She was moved into a small side ward where a nurse dealt with the head wound, and there she waited for her arm to be set before she was sent upstairs to the ward.

As darkness fell and the sirens warned of another raid, all the walking patients were hurried down into the hospital basement. Those who could not be moved were protected as far as possible where they lay.

With the sound of the siren a nurse hurried into the side ward and placed a cradle over the girl which she covered with a mattress, intended to protect her from any flying glass or debris should the hospital take a hit. She took the child's pulse which continued with a steady beat and then, satisfied that her patient was comfortable she moved on to the next bed where an elderly woman lay, her leg broken when she'd fallen in the rush to get into a shelter. She, too, was unable to be moved to the basement and the nurse took the same precautions, saying as she did so, 'Don't you worry now, Mrs...' she glanced at the name card on the bed, 'Mrs Dean. This'll protect you if necessary. You just lie still and see if you can get some sleep. That's the best thing for you till we can deal with that leg of yours.'

'Sleep, nurse?' moaned the old woman. 'You got to be joking! What, with the pain in me leg and them Huns making that racket out there, a body'd never get to sleep.'

'Well, you just try, anyway,' smiled the nurse encouragingly. 'The aspirin the doctor gave you will help with the pain and I'll be back to see you in a little while.'

Good as her word Nurse Carlton came back to the ward twenty minutes later to find Mrs Dean snoring gently and the condition of the child unchanged. She looked at the label still tied to the child's ankle and wondered how they knew her surname but not her Christian name. If the raid hadn't started, she knew that the doctor would have set the broken arm while the child was still unconscious, sparing her the pain, but with all hell let loose outside and more patients already flooding in, there was no way he could begin that procedure now. She kept the necessary checks on the child and though she still remained unconscious she seemed to rest more easily as the night went on, despite the clamour of the raid outside.

It was just as the all-clear began to sound that she was summoned back into the side ward by a bell-ringing Mrs Dean. As she came into the room, she realised why. The child in the other bed had regained consciousness and was lying under the protective cradle screaming, with piercing, terrified screams. Nurse Carlton rushed to the bedside and lifted the mattress and the cradle away to reveal the girl, wide-eyed and staring, her mouth open in an almost continuous scream.

'Can't you shut her up, nurse?' demanded Mrs Dean. 'That noise is doing my head in.'

Nurse Carlton ignored her, giving her full attention to the panicking child. 'It's all right, pet, it's all right,' she soothed, taking the girl's hand and stroking it. 'You're all right. You're in hospital. You got caught in a raid, but you're safe now. You're safe now.'

Gradually the girl calmed down and her screams stopped, but her eyes stared wildly about her and her hand gripped the nurse's in a ferocious grasp. She had stopped screaming but she was muttering something unintelligible. Nurse Carlton leaned forward, trying to catch what she was saying, but she couldn't understand the words.

'What's she talking about?' demanded Mrs Dean. 'She's talking German, she is. She a Jerry? Jerries shouldn't be allowed in here!'

'Of course she's not a Jerry,' snapped the nurse, 'she's a child and she's concussed. She was caught out in the raid and has a bad head wound. She's disorientated. I'm going to get the doctor now.' She eased her hand from the girl's grip and left the room. She was soon back with a doctor, who gave the child an injection so that she relaxed and drifted off to sleep again.

'It was a nasty head wound,' he said. 'We'll set the arm now and then send her up to children's.'

Half an hour later the still-sedated child was moved on to a trolley ready to go to the children's ward.

'Children's says it's got no beds,' the porter told the nurse. 'We got to take her up to Women's Medical.' He glanced at the name card still attached to the child's ankle. 'Smith?' he said. 'What's her first name?'

'We don't know,' replied the nurse. 'She was brought in off the street but had no identity card. All we know is her name is Smith and she comes from Harrogate.'

The porter shrugged. 'Be difficult to find her family after this lot. Where's Harrow-gate then? Harrow's where that posh school is, ain't it?'

'Harrogate,' said the nurse. 'It's a place in Yorkshire.'

'What the hell was the kid doing down here, then?' wondered the porter. 'Thought we'd sent all the London kids up there!'

'We don't know,' replied the nurse, briskly. 'Now, can you get her upstairs so she can be looked after?'

'Yeah, all right, I'm going, ain't I?' grumbled the man and began pushing the trolley towards the lift.

It was some time later that the girl surfaced once more. This time there were no panicked screams, she just lay there and looked about her. Nurse Sherwood went to her bedside and took her hand.

'Hallo, love,' she said. 'You awake now? That's good.' She smiled down at her patient, but the child did not return her smile, simply stared blankly up at her, her face pale under the bandage round her head. Her arm, in its clean white plaster, lay outside the bed covers, but she made no effort to move it.

Nurse took her pulse and her temperature, both of which were a little high and having noted these on the chart, she said, 'I'll go and tell Sister that you're awake.'

Back at the ward desk she spoke to Ward Sister Miller. 'The child is awake now, Sister, but she isn't responding to me when I speak to her.'

'What do we know about her?' Sister Miller asked.

'Very little,' replied the nurse. 'The notes that came up with her simply said her surname, "Smith", and that she was from Harrogate. When we undressed her and put her to bed we found a snap of a family, presumably hers, in her skirt pocket and she was wearing a necklace of blue beads, but no other form of identification.'

'So we don't know her Christian name?'

'No. She did mumble something as we made her comfortable, but I couldn't make out what she was saying. She has a head injury, so she may still be concussed.'

'I'll call Dr Greaves to come and take a look at her when he can and in the meantime I'll come over and see her.'

Once she had spoken to the doctor, Sister Miller went over to the child's bed and pulling up a chair, sat down beside her.

'Hallo,' she said. 'I'm Sister Miller and I'm going to look after you while you're here in my ward.'

The girl gave no sign that she'd heard, but continued to stare into space with unfocused eyes.

'I've told you my name,' said the sister. 'Can you tell me yours?'

The girl said nothing, just closed her eyes and seemingly slipped back into sleep.

When the doctor came he examined her again, checking her eyes carefully. 'Her arm isn't a problem,' he said, 'that was a simple fracture of the radius, but I don't like the way she's drifting in and out of consciousness. Keep a close watch on her, check every hour and call me immediately if there's any deterioration.'

The nurses kept a strict watch on the child and the next time she woke up, she took a little liquid food and seemed much more aware of her surroundings. Still she didn't speak and it was only when the sirens yet again gave warning of impending attack did she try to communicate with those about her. Nurse Sherwood was covering her patients with cradles, mattresses and blankets in the now practised attempt to shield them from shattered glass and falling masonry, but when she got to the girl's bed she met with complete refusal.

'Nein! Nein!' cried the child, her eyes once again wide with fear. 'No! No!'

Surprised at both her vehemence and her use of two languages but delighted she had spoken at all, Nurse Sherwood put down the cradle and despite the continued warning from the siren, sat down beside the bed.

'Don't you want me to cover you and keep you safe?' she asked. Her words were greeted with a vigorous shaking of the head.

'If the hospital is damaged, these,' she pointed to the cradle and the blankets now piled on the floor, 'could save you from being cut or bruised.'

'Please, not shut in,' came the reply. The girl's voice was shaky, her use of English odd, her accent alien, but there was no doubt that she meant what she was saying as she repeated, 'Please, not shut in.'

There was no time to argue, other patients in the ward needed their protection too, so Nurse Sherwood smiled down at the frightened face and said, 'All right, I'll leave you as you are.' With speedy efficiency she covered the other patients where they lay in their beds before going back to Sister Miller to report her conversation with the unknown girl.

'She doesn't seem afraid of the siren,' she explained, 'just of being "shut in" as she calls it. Maybe she's claustrophobic. What should I do?'

'Have you seen to the other patients, nurse?'

'Yes, they're all done.'

'Let's have another go, then.'

The two nurses walked over to the unprotected bed. The girl was lying with her eyes closed, but as soon as she heard their approach she opened them and was sitting up to protest.

'Please, not shut in!' she said firmly.

Sister Miller took her hand. 'It's all right, dear, we're not going to shut you in.' The girl relaxed visibly and lay back against her pillow.

The sister sat down beside the bed. Outside, a fierce anti-aircraft bombardment had begun and the now familiar drone of aeroplanes filled the sky, but ignoring these, Sister Miller took the child's hand and said gently, 'Can you tell me your name, dear?'

The girl shook her head, confused, as if she were trying to shake her brain into some sort of order.

'You're in hospital now, because you were caught out in an air raid. You've had a bump on the head and broken your arm. But we don't know who you are.'

The girl listened, but again shook her head.

'We know your last name is Smith,' went on the sister encouragingly, 'and we know you come from Harrogate, in Yorkshire, but we don't know your Christian name. What shall we call you?'

'I don't know.'

'You don't know your name?'

'I don't know it,' replied the girl, adding with an edge of panic in her voice, 'Who am I, please?' The sound of explosions not far away drowned out anything else that she had been going to say and the two nurses, called to the aid of other patients, left her lying in her bed, wide-eyed and afraid, as the raiders did their best to annihilate the world outside.

Chapter Ten

Dan and Naomi slept for an hour, but their underlying anxiety for Lisa woke them again soon after the sun rose. Naomi slipped out of bed and went down to the kitchen to make them a pot of tea, managing to squeeze something approximately tea-coloured out of the already twice-used tea leaves. She took the cups back upstairs and found Dan still sitting up in bed.

She handed him the tea and then went to the window to take down the blackout screens.

Outside, the street was just coming to life again. The damage to the houses opposite, homes of long-standing neighbours, looked far worse by daylight. One, belonging to an elderly couple called Goldman, was little more than a ruin, its brickwork blackened, shattered windows staring sightlessly across the road, the roof burned out, charred beams pointing to the sky, accusing fingers daring the bombers to come back. The house next to it had fared a little better. Its roof sagging and its windows and doors blown out, it was uninhabitable, but its walls still stood, defiant, in the morning sun.

'Poor Shirley Newman,' Naomi said with a cry. 'She's quite bombed out; and she's all on her own cos her husband's away at sea. What'll she do now, I wonder? And the Goldmans, too. I saw them last night, trying to save some of their stuff. The firemen wouldn't let them go in.'

'They was quite right,' said Dan. 'If they had gone in, some poor firefighter would have had to risk his life just to pull 'em out again.'

'You can understand it, though,' Naomi said. 'It's their home. Only last week she was telling me they've lived there for over forty years.' She opened the window and leaned out, looking further along the road to the third damaged house, belonging to the Drake family. Its chimney had crashed through the roof but it had not caught fire.

'I think they was all in the Hope Street shelter,' she said as she shut the window and turned back to Dan. 'Don't think there were any casualties in our street.'

Dan downed the last of his tea and got out of bed. 'Now it's daylight I'll get round to the Langs' and fetch Lisa,' he said as he pulled his shirt over his head. 'Want to get our girl back as soon as we can, don't we?'

'I'll come too,' Naomi said, throwing on her dress and searching for her shoes.

Five minutes later they were on their way along the road, heading for the Langs' house in Grove Avenue. As they reached the end of Kemble Street they paused for a moment to look at the heap of stones and debris that had once been the Duke of Wellington.

'Can't believe it's really gone,' said Naomi.

'Had to happen,' Dan said. 'Couldn't stay like it was. If the blast hadn't finished the job last night, the demolition squad would've been round in a couple of days. Just thank God no one was inside this time.'

They continued through the battered and blistered streets where exhausted firemen were still damping down the last of the fires or shovelling sand on to still-glowing embers. They passed the Hope Street shelter, the brick shelter built to serve the surrounding area. It was empty now and a volunteer was sweeping it out, brushing away the detritus left by those who'd been crammed into it for most of the night. All around there was the evidence of the night's bombardment, broken windows, flattened doors, heaps of rubble, smoky dust filling the air.

'Glad Lisa didn't try and come home through this lot,' Dan said as he gave Naomi his hand to help her over a pile of bricks. 'Glad they kept her there.'

'Yes,' agree Naomi. 'I was thinking last night, I'd have done the same if Hilda had been with us.'

It took far longer than usual to reach Grove Avenue. Several streets were closed off with unstable buildings threatening the pavements or because of craters in the road. In one a fractured water main was flooding the thoroughfare and in another a ruptured gas main burned merrily in the early-morning light. Everywhere labouring workmen struggled to clear away the ravages of the raids and make the area safe once more. People were doing what they could to repair the damage to their homes; men and women too, already up ladders, nailing tarpaulins across torn roofs, boarding up broken windows, mending hanging doors. Hitler had given them all a bashing last night, but they weren't giving in. As Dan had said the night before, they were determined not to let the buggers win!

At last they turned the corner and stepped into Grove Avenue, but what they saw brought them up short. The street was almost empty, but the damage that it had sustained was enormous. Halfway along there was a gaping chasm between the houses. Two houses were no longer there. Not just damaged or burnt out, but pulverised to nothing from the direct hit of high-explosive bombs. The houses on either side leaned drunkenly towards the gap between them, their walls, blackened from now-extinguished fires, yawning open to reveal the rooms within. Dan and Naomi simply stood and stared.

'Which house was theirs?' whispered Naomi.

'Thirty-four, weren't it?' replied Dan.

'But which is thirty-four?'

'Much further down, I think,' answered Dan. 'Come on, let's have a look,' and taking her hand, he led Naomi into the ruins of the street.

'Road closed, mate,' called a voice and a man in ARP uniform came out of one of the houses towards them. 'Buildings too dangerous.'

'But we're looking for our daughter,' Naomi croaked. 'She was staying here last night.'

'Probably in the shelter in Madison Road,' said the man. He pointed back the way they'd come. 'Next street on the left. The wardens' post's there. You can ask the bloke on duty.'

'Which is number thirty-four?' asked Naomi. 'She was staying at number thirty-four.'

The warden's expression changed. 'Thirty-four, you say?'

'Yes,' answered Dan. His cheeks grew pale as he could already read the answer in the man's face. He looked again at the gap where two houses should have stood. There was nothing left of either of them. The warden looked in the same direction.

'Sorry, mate, no survivors there. Whole family gone.'

'Gone?' Naomi had yet to take in the import of what she was being told. 'Gone where?'

'Direct hit, nothing left of them. No survivors.'

Naomi's head spun and Dan clutched her in his arms as she sagged towards him in a dead faint. Together the two men managed to get her into the house from which the warden had emerged.

'This is my house,' he said as he pushed open the front door. 'Doris,' he called, 'lady here fainted.'

His wife bustled out of her kitchen and pushed open the door of her front room. 'In here,' she instructed, 'bring the poor dear in here.'

The two men laid Naomi on a settee and Doris produced a blanket which she laid across Naomi's prostrate form.

'Joe, what happened?' she asked her husband.

'She thinks her daughter was staying in number thirty-four.'

'Oh my God,' breathed the woman. 'That was the Langs' house.'

'That's the one,' murmured Dan. 'She was visiting her friend Hilda when the sirens went. We thought she'd stayed in their shelter with them. We wasn't surprised when she didn't come home after the first raid. Would have been stupid to walk through them streets when it was getting dark. We thought she'd stayed with them for safety.'

'She probably did,' replied Joe. 'The Langs' house went in the second raid.'

'But weren't they in the shelter?' demanded Dan. 'Why weren't they? Surely they'd have taken shelter.'

'No, no sign of anyone in the Anderson, what's left of it. We looked straight away.'

'But they did have one?'

'Oh yes, most houses in this street have them, but they don't all use them.'

'But that's crazy!' exploded Dan.

'Agree with you, mate,' replied Joe, 'but I can't force them.'

'Are you sure that they were actually in the house? Perhaps they took shelter somewhere else. You said there was a shelter in Madison Road? Perhaps they went there to be safer.'

Joe glanced across at Naomi who under Doris's ministrations was coming round.

'It was a direct hit,' he whispered again, 'and there are... remains. Definitely, both adults and children. Sorry, mate.'

It was some time later, with the assistance of Joe, that Dan got Naomi home again. She walked, supported on both sides by the two men, through the crumbling streets, back to Kemble Street.

'We don't know for sure that she was in that house,' Naomi said when she was finally back in her own home. 'Perhaps she was on her way home and she sheltered in one of the public shelters.'

'Doesn't seem likely,' Dan said cautiously. 'If she'd done that, girl, she'd have come home by now.'

While Doris was giving Naomi some hot tea, Dan had gone back out into the street with Joe. Together they had approached the gaping crater left by the bomb. There was little left to see.

'You sure the bodies you found were in thirty-four?' Dan asked. 'I mean, two houses have gone. P'raps the bodies belonged to the folk who lived next door.'

'No, afraid not.' Joe spoke gently. 'They was all in the Madison Road shelter. After the first raid they decided to go there. Wanted to be with other people. They're being looked after in the rescue centre.'

'So their house was empty.'

'Yup, far as we know.'

'And the bodies were in the other one.'

'What we could see of them.'

'But they were identified?'

''Fraid there weren't much left to identify. The blood wag— the ambulance came and took what there was. Obliterated, they'd been.

Sorry, mate, but I reckon they won't dig any more for this one. They'll bring in the dozers and flatten it.'

'Just leave them there?' Dan was horrified.

'Depends on what else has to be done. After raids like these they have to deal with stuff quick. Have to think of public health and all that, don't they?'

Joe was very matter-of-fact and his very steadiness helped Dan to stay calm for Naomi. Neither of them went to work that day. The loss of Lisa was too heart-breaking.

'You say that the warden says the Langs' house went in the second raid,' Naomi said sobbing. 'If I'd gone round there and fetched Lisa after the first raid, 'stead of cowering here at home, I could have saved her, couldn't I? If I'd've gone round there straight away she'd be here with us now.'

'Darling girl, you don't know that,' Dan said, trying to reassure her.

'Course I do,' cried Naomi. 'The house weren't bombed till the night-time raid. That bloke said it. D'you think they didn't go into the shelter cos Lisa wouldn't?' she went on miserably. 'Maybe she wouldn't go into the shelter and they all stayed out to keep her company. Oh, Dan, I shoulda gone and fetched her home.'

Dan didn't know what to say to comfort her. If Joe was right – and there was no reason to suppose he wasn't – then, yes, if Naomi had gone looking for Lisa she might still be alive, but she hadn't and there was nothing any of them could do about that.

'Maybe,' he said, 'but listen, Naomi, if you had gone round, you might have been caught in the house, too, and I'd have lost all three of you.' It was precious little comfort he could offer, but it was the best he could do. The baby was still safe and that meant everything to both of them.

Naomi's recourse was to lose herself in hard work. She went through the house, cleaning windows and polishing surfaces within an inch of their lives. Dust from outside had been forced in through the open door and it lay, a thick coating, on all the furniture. She scrubbed the bath and toilet, she swept the landing and the stairs. Cleaning numbed her brain and numbness was what she needed. When she reached Lisa's room she stripped the bed and remade it with clean sheets. She laid out a clean towel and polished all the furniture.

They could be wrong, she told herself. They could be wrong and Lisa could still be out there somewhere. Her room'll be ready for her when she gets back. Tucked into the pillowcase she found the letter from Lisa's mother. She spread it out on the chest of drawers and looked at it. She couldn't read a word of it, of course, but she knew what it was and refolding it carefully she laid it on top of the chest, so it would be the first thing Lisa saw when she came home.

While Naomi was cleaning the house Dan fixed the front door as best he could, before going across the road to see what he could do for their neighbours. The elderly Goldmans had borrowed a handcart and were loading it with all they could rescue from their burned-out home.

'Going to the wife's sister for a few days, till we can find somewhere else,' Jeremiah Goldman said. 'Her son's coming round to fetch this lot. We'll put it in her garage.' Dan helped them load the cart and then watched as they trailed off down the street, following their nephew to the illusory safety of another house.

A little later that day there was a knock at the door and when Dan opened it he found Shirley Newman from the other damaged house along the street.

'Hallo, Mrs N,' he said. 'Anything we can do for you?' He glanced out over her shoulder at the remains of her home and knew there was little. 'Come on in. Naomi's in the kitchen. We was just going to have a cuppa.'

Mrs Newman followed him into the kitchen and Naomi, who had just sat down for the first time since she'd started to clean the house, jumped to her feet again.

'Shirley!' she cried. 'So sorry. So very sorry.' She didn't know what else to say and her neighbour simply shook her head and said, 'I got my life. I was in the shelter.'

'What you going to do now?' Naomi asked.

Shirley shrugged. 'Dunno, do I? Nowhere to go 'cept the rescue centre, but they ain't got much room, not today after all that last night.'

'You can stay here the night,' Naomi said impulsively. 'We don't mind, do we, Dan?'

'No, course not,' Dan said, though less than enthusiastically. If you once let a neighbour into your house, even for a night, who knew how long they would stay or how you were going to get rid of them later on?

'I got to go to the fire post in a while,' he added. 'If you're sleeping here, Mrs N, you two can keep each other company while I'm out. And if there's a raid, you both go down in that cellar and don't you dare come out again till the all-clear goes. Right?'

They promised and with a feeling of relief Dan left them together in the house. He had been wondering how he was going to be able to leave Naomi after such a dreadful thirty-six hours. As he walked along he thought about poor Lisa. She'd come here to be safe and now she'd been killed in a raid. Hitler's long arm had taken her here in London where he'd failed at home in Germany. The irony of it made Dan's heart ache. Poor, brave little Lisa. She was just in the wrong place at the wrong time. It was no good Naomi blaming herself for it, though she would for some time to come, he knew that.

It's no more Naomi's fault than the man in the moon's, Dan thought, but convincing her of that is going to be a very difficult job. Perhaps if I'd been here it might have been different. P'raps I'd've gone and fetched Lisa home.

But Dan knew his place wasn't staying safe at home when raids were at their height and so he wasn't going to blame himself for what might have been; but he knew he would long mourn the refugee child they'd taken in, the brave girl who'd become their own.

The siren went as he reached his post and from then on he had no time for further thoughts, indeed no time to think about anything but fires and putting them out. The Luftwaffe were back and it was, literally, all hands to the pump.

Chapter Eleven

Harry had still been in the West End that Saturday afternoon when the raiders struck. He had been to Soho Square to meet a man called Dave Dickett, who was doing business with Harry's boss, Mikey Sharp.

'Tell him I'll take any fags he can get,' Mikey had said. 'Tell 'im to bring 'em down the lock-up, Tuesday.' Mikey was more than ready to take a consignment of cigarettes that had been stolen from a lorry earlier in the week, but he was far too fly to be seen meeting with a known thief. Let the lad do the talking. No one would take any notice of a scruffy lad up west on a Saturday afternoon.

Harry had just left the meet when the sirens began to sound. Bloody Moaning Minnie's off again, he thought as he looked up. The sky above was clear and blue, the sun still warm, but already he could hear the sound of ack-ack and the ever-increasing thunder of hundreds of planes. Then they were there, a swarm of locusts, flying in formation, filling the sky so that it darkened with their number.

'Off the street, lad,' shouted a warden as he hurried to clear his sector. 'Into the shelter with you!' He pointed back into the square.

Harry didn't need telling twice. He ran back to the square, thrusting through the people who were crowding in off the streets, flooding out of shops, pubs and clubs, pushing their way down into the shelter. The underground area was soon packed, people jostling and shoving, trying to find somewhere to sit.

No wonder Lisa don't like going into these places, Harry thought as he forced himself through to a place against the wall. He hoped she'd got to safety somewhere. She might even have got as far as Hilda's and be safe in their shelter. There was a hubbub of noise within the shelter, but it couldn't drown the thunder of the raid outside. Someone started singing; others joined in and for a while there was a feeling of camaraderie. Everyone in the shelter was in the same boat, and together they'd see it through. When at last, some two hours later, the all-clear sounded, the push to escape from the crush and the foetid smell of the shelter into the fresh air was almost as great as the push to take cover had been. Camaraderie forgotten, they flooded back into the square.

Once outside, Harry looked about him. He could see little damage in the immediate area, but smoke filled the air and the sky burned orange. Everywhere people were exclaiming their relief at being safely through the raid, many returning to the buildings they had left, others hurrying away to discover the fate of their own homes elsewhere. Harry set off to walk back to the hostel. It was a long walk, but there seemed to be no buses and he was loath to take the Tube, even if he found one running. He'd had enough of being underground for the time being.

He reached the hostel just as the second warning began to sound. He had passed through areas where there had been considerable damage and he spared another thought for Lisa travelling by herself on the bus.

She'll be all right, he told himself. She'll have sheltered somewhere and be on her way back home now. I'll go round the school on Monday, he thought, see how she's doing.

The warden at the hostel was hurrying its inmates into the nearby shelter and Harry, pressed in among them, had to spend the rest of the night cheek by jowl with the other boys who lived with him.

Next morning he set out to find Mikey Sharp to report back on his meeting with Dave Dickett. As he headed towards Petticoat Lane he was shocked by the amount of damage he saw. Buildings destroyed or burned out. Fires still burning. The East End of London had been badly bombed as the raiders aimed for the docks, warehouses and any shipping lying in the port of London. When he'd been crushed in the shelter near the hostel he'd told himself 'never again'. He'd risk being above ground, take his chances with the bombs, but now, as he hurried through the streets and saw the havoc they'd caused, he wasn't so sure.

He found his boss with two of his henchmen in a back room at the Black Bull just off Middlesex Street. Harry waited nervously for Mikey to notice him. The other two men left the room and Mikey finally gave his attention to Harry.

'Well, kid, did Dickett turn up?'

'Oh, yes, Mr Sharp,' Harry said. 'He coming Tuesday like you said bringing—'

'The merchandise,' interrupted Mikey.

'Right and say he might have something else you like to see.'

Mikey raised an eyebrow. 'Did he now? And what was that?'

Harry looked round to be sure he wasn't being overheard and said, 'Whisky. Had some crates he'd "lib... librated" or somethink.'

'I see. So what's he going to do about that?'

'I tell him to bring on Tuesday,' Harry said.

'Did you now?' Mikey gave a brief smile. 'Aren't you the bright lad?' He pulled a roll of notes from his pocket and peeled off a pound. 'Here you go,' he said, handing it to Harry. 'Shove off now. Be back at the lock-up Tuesday. I'll need you to unload.'

That evening the Luftwaffe were back, bombing the docks and the surrounding area. The raiders seemed to come from all directions, guided by some of the still smouldering fires, but this time they certainly didn't have it all their own way and fewer than the previous day got past the south coast defences. But come they did, flinging themselves against the barrage of anti-aircraft fire. Their bombs hurtled, whining, to earth, exploding into lethal fragments as they obliterated warehouses, stores, homes, people.

Searchlights directed their powerful beams up through the darkness, criss-crossing the sky as they attempted to pin marauding planes in their beams, targets for the anti-aircraft gunners below. Shells exploded in the night sky, bursting round the enemy planes, brilliant flashes of orange and white, driving them away. Several bombers were shot down in flames, spiralling downward with a shriek of destruction before, still carrying their lethal load, they exploded in a display of pyrotechnics, fireballs that lit the sky for miles round as they hit the ground below.

Dan and his team scrambled from place to place, dousing small fires, calling the regular firemen to the big ones. Around them buildings crumbled and fell, showers of bricks from collapsing walls thundered down into the streets below. The noise was deafening and they had to bellow at each other to make themselves heard. There was no respite and the volunteers laboured as hard and as long as the men in the regular services. Everyone knew that it was up to each man to give his utmost to help save the city.

Naomi and Shirley crouched together in the cellar of number sixty-five. They could hear the crashes, booms and bangs, some distant, some frighteningly close.

'How long can they keep this up?' cried Naomi as another blast shook the house.

'How long can we put up with it?' said Shirley unsteadily. 'There ain't going to be nothing left of London soon.'

'That's what Hitler wants,' said Naomi. 'Dan says he's trying to terrify us so's we sue for peace.'

'He's took my home,' said Shirley, sounding braver than she felt, 'but we ain't going to let him march in here.'

'He's taken my Lisa,' Naomi said, and so saying, her iron grip on her emotions crumbled and she burst into tears.

'Tell me,' Shirley said, reaching for her hands. 'Tell me what's happened to her.'

So, sitting in the torch-lit cellar, Naomi told Shirley all about Lisa, where she'd come from, how difficult it had been to start with and finally what had happened to her the previous night.

Shirley had known that the Federmans were fostering a child, but though she'd seen Lisa about, she hadn't got to know her. Hearing about her now, she wished she had made more effort to be friendly.

'You don't know she's dead,' she said when Naomi had finished. 'You don't know she was in that house when it was hit.'

'They found bodies,' Naomi said, adding with a gulp, 'bits of bodies. Adults and children.'

'Still might not be Lisa,' said Shirley. 'You said there was children living there anyway. Could be them.'

'I'm sure it was them as well,' Naomi said bitterly. 'But Lisa must've been there, where else can she be?'

'Have you checked all the rescue centres? The hospitals? Talked to all the local air raid wardens?'

'No, we haven't,' sighed Naomi. 'There's no point. She was in that house and the warden round there said it was a direct hit. Everyone was killed, there was almost nothing left to find.'

'Well,' said Shirley, 'if it was my kid, I'd be round all the hospitals and centres before I'd be sure I'd lost her. If she's been injured or sommat, they may not know who she is.'

The idea gave Naomi a flicker of hope. 'You're right,' she said. 'That's what I'll do first thing in the morning. Oh, Shirley, I'm so glad you're here with me. Last night I was here all by myself and I was so frightened.'

'I was in the Hope Street, ' Shirley said, 'and it was scary enough in there, too. I feel safer here.'

Naomi poured them some cocoa from her flask and they drank it as they listened to the war going on in the world outside. It was still scary, but at least they had each other for company, to talk to.

Shirley spoke about her husband, Derek, who was in the merchant navy. 'Trouble is,' she said, 'they're as much a target as the warships and they don't have no guns. He wrote to me last time he was in Liverpool, but that was ten days ago. He could be anywhere now.'

Naomi talked about Dan, pouring out her worries about him being above ground during these dreadful raids, and before she knew it she had confided their secret, that she was expecting.

'Oh, Naomi, that's so exciting,' Shirley enthused. 'But that means you have to be extra careful now.'

'Yeah, I know. But what sort of a world am I bringing a baby into? Poor little mite'll being bombed from the moment it's born.'

'Not if you get out of London,' said Shirley. 'That's what I'd do if I had a kid on the way. Can't risk it being killed before it's born, can you? What does your Dan say?'

'I don't know,' Naomi said, 'we haven't talked about it.'

'Well, you should,' said Shirley in her forthright way. 'Specially now these raids is getting worse. You need to get out into the country somewhere Hitler don't know about.'

When the all-clear sounded the two women went back upstairs. As before, they peered out into the street, but could see no activity that suggested there was any more destruction nearby. There was smoke in the air and the sky was still on fire, but Kemble Street seemed to have escaped any further damage.

'Come on,' Naomi said. 'Better try and get some sleep. Tomorrow's going to be a busy day.'

'What about your Dan?'

'He'll be home soon as he can,' Naomi replied. ''Spect he's still going flat out with them fires out there.' She longed to hear him opening the front door, but now she had re-established control of her emotions she wasn't going to let go again. She would go upstairs to bed and wait for him there.

She found blankets and a pillow for Shirley and when she'd made her comfortable on the old couch in the front room, Naomi went upstairs. She looked into Lisa's room. She could have offered Shirley Lisa's bed, but somehow she couldn't bring herself to do it. Until she had done everything she could to find Lisa, until she knew for certain that she wasn't coming back, she didn't want anyone else sleeping there.

Dan came home with the dawn, his face black, his eyes red-rimmed. He crept upstairs and crawled into bed beside Naomi. She gathered him into her arms and on the instant he plunged into the depths of slumber. Naomi lay beside him, her brain churning as the events of the day flooded through her mind. Be positive, she told herself. Shirley could be right. And Naomi began to plan her search for Lisa in the morning. School, rescue centres, hospitals. She would visit them all.

I won't go in to work, she decided. They can do without me for another day. I'll tell them why later.

She thought, too, of what Shirley had said about getting out of London. She knew that many expectant mothers had left the cities when war had first been declared, but lots of them had returned when the expected bombing hadn't happened. Now the much-feared Blitz had indeed begun, would they go again? Should she go? How could she go and leave Dan to face the bombing on his own? Could she bear to be without him for weeks at a time? But then, Shirley was without her Derek, away at sea. Thousands of women were living without their menfolk. Why should she be any different? She should be protecting the baby. Her most important duty was to her unborn child. But to be without Dan, when Dan was exposed to the Blitz, not even safe in the cellar, but out on the streets, unprotected… Her heart contracted with love and fear at the very thought of it.

Finally she, too, drifted off to sleep and awoke only when she heard someone downstairs in the kitchen. For a moment she couldn't think who it was. Dan was still fast asleep beside her. Then she remembered Shirley. It must be her. And she slid out of bed, threw on her dressing gown and went downstairs to see.

'Couldn't sleep no more,' Shirley said, 'so I come in to make a drink.'

'I couldn't sleep neither,' Naomi said and poured herself some tea from the pot Shirley had made.

'When I've had this,' Shirley said, lifting her cup, 'I'll be off round the rescue centre to see if they can find me somewhere to live, temporary like.'

'You can stay here for a bit,' Naomi offered. 'I was glad you was here last night through the raid.'

'Thanks, and I will if I have to, but it'll be better if they find me somewhere more permanent, like.' As soon as she'd drunk her tea she slipped out of the house and was gone.

When Dan came down he looked round. 'Where's Shirley?'

'Gone. May be back later. You going out in the cab today?'

'Yes, have to,' replied Dan as he ate the piece of toast she'd made for him. 'Can't afford to miss another day, can I? What about you?'

'No, I ain't going to work today. I'm going round the school. They was supposed to start the new term today. Maybe some of the kids might have seen her.'

'Naomi—' began Dan, but she cut him off.

'Don't say it!' she said sharply. 'I'm going to look for her, Dan. After the school I'm going round the hospitals, see if she's been taken to one of them. She *could* have been,' she said firmly when he was about to interrupt again. 'Then I'll go to the rescue centres. Maybe they found her and are looking after her. She could still be alive, Dan. She mightn't have been in that house.'

Dan looked across at her with a reluctant smile. He didn't think she had a hope in hell of finding Lisa, but he admired her determination to try. 'You do that, girl,' he said, 'but please, darlin', don't get your hopes up.'

Dan left the house and went to the railway arches where he and several other cabbies kept their taxis. He hadn't been there for two days and was dreading what he might find. If the cab had been destroyed in one of the raids, then apart from Naomi's paltry wage, their source of income was gone. When he reached the arches he found several of his mates there as well. All were relieved to see their cabs parked where they had left them, still undamaged.

'May have problems finding a way through the streets today,' said Jim Tucker. 'The damage is something fierce, specially round the docks.'

'Had to detour round Milton Road,' said Bert Halford. 'Unexploded bomb!'

'Think I'll head up west,' Dan said. 'Usually pick up a fare round Whitehall.' The cabbies drove their taxis out from the shelter of the arches and set out to do a day's work. The night's bombing was over and, unbowed by the German air force, they were back in business.

Naomi cleared away the breakfast things and then put on her coat and went out. She'd chosen the school as her first port of call. Walking the route Lisa would have taken, she kept an eye out for any children she might know, but she recognised none. When she reached the school gates she looked into the playground. There were a few children arriving, but not the usual crowd waiting for the bell. Where are they all? she wondered. She very soon had her answer. When she asked to see Miss Hammond she was taken straight into the head's office.

Miss Hammond looked pale and exhausted. 'What can I do for you?' she asked wearily. 'There's no school today, we're sending them all home again, so if you've come to say Lisa won't be coming, don't worry. Nor will anyone else. Not today.'

Naomi's heart sank. 'No,' she murmured, 'I wasn't coming to say that. I was coming to ask you if you'd seen Lisa. She's been missing since Saturday afternoon.'

If possible, Miss Hammond went even paler. 'Not Lisa, too?' she whispered. 'I just heard that Hilda and Peter Lang and their parents were killed on Saturday night.'

Naomi drew a deep breath. 'We think Lisa might have been with them.'

'At the Langs'?'

'We don't know. It's what I'm trying to find out. She was supposed to be round their house on Saturday, but maybe...' Naomi's voice broke on a sob, 'we thought maybe she'd been on her way home and had sheltered somewhere.'

'Perhaps she has,' Miss Hammond said. 'Have you tried asking at the hospitals?'

'Doing the rounds straight after here.' Naomi blew her nose. 'Just thought I'd ask here first... case any of the other kids had seen her, or she'd been with someone else.'

'I'll ask around, Mrs Federman, and if I hear anything about her, I promise you'll be the first to know. We've cancelled school for today; we're trying to organise evacuation again for those that want it. London isn't safe, and you can be sure there's more of this to come. We can't risk losing any more children.'

Naomi left the school and set out to try the local hospitals. She knew there were several hospitals in the area and if she'd been injured somewhere, Lisa could have been taken to any of them. She was determined to visit every one.

At each one she went first to the Casualty department and spoke to the receptionist on the desk. Casualty was still hectic, with more victims of the bombing still coming in, some to be patched up and sent home again, others to stay in for more serious treatment.

The receptionists were all extremely busy dealing with the continuing influx of patients, but in each case they made time to look at the register to see if the name Lisa Becker was there.

'Sorry, dear,' said the woman behind the desk at Bart's. 'No one of that name been treated here.'

'She's only just turned fourteen,' Naomi explained. 'I just wondered if she'd been brought in, you know, without anyone knowing who she was.'

'No unknown teenage girls brought in on Saturday,' said the woman firmly. 'Sorry, I can't help you.'

'Could I speak to someone who was here at the time?' Naomi asked.

'Madam,' the receptionist's voice became brusque, 'you have no idea of the chaos we had here on Saturday night and it's little better now. If the child's name is not in the book as having been treated, then she wasn't treated here.' She looked over Naomi's shoulder and called, 'Next!'

It was the same at the London Hospital. 'No, afraid not, no one of that name brought here.'

'Any girls of about fourteen?' asked Naomi desperately. 'You might not have her name.'

'No, the only child we had in on Saturday who was unidentified at first turned out to be called Smith and came from Harrogate. Sorry. Try King's College...'

'Try Guy's...'

'Try St Thomas's...'

Naomi trailed from one to another, across the river and back again, but no one had any knowledge of a fourteen-year-old girl by the name of Lisa Becker. Nowhere was there an unidentified child patient. Everywhere the hospitals were under immense pressure, trying to treat those who had been injured, those who were suffering from shock and those who were simply ill and in need of care.

She got back to Kemble Street in the late afternoon, worn out and miserable. She had found no trace of Lisa and she was beginning to accept that she must have been in Grove Avenue when the bombs fell. Determined not to give up quite yet, she made herself a sandwich and set out to visit the three local rescue centres.

The first was not far from Grove Avenue. Mrs Barber, a harassed WVS volunteer, was struggling to find shelter for all those whose homes were no longer habitable. No, she had not seen a fourteen-year-old girl wandering about on her own, lost.

'Sorry, my dear,' she said, dashing untidy hair out of her eyes. 'I've a list of everyone who's been here yesterday and today, where they came from and where I've managed to place them, but there's no Lisa Becker. Try the Kingsland Road centre. It's much bigger than this one.'

It was the same both in Kingsland Road and Shoreditch High Street. No one had heard of Lisa nor any unidentified girl. With a leaden heart, Naomi went back to Kemble Street.

Chapter Twelve

Clutching his pound note, Harry had made a quick exit from the back room at the Black Bull. Truth to tell, he was afraid of Mikey Sharp, though he didn't like to admit as much to himself. He liked to think it was a great thing to work for a man like Mikey, a man of the world who knows what's what, a man in charge, *The Man*! Ever since that first day, Harry had been a runner for Mikey Sharp. He carried messages, delivered parcels, loaded and unloaded lorries and vans and did anything else that Mikey told him to. Harry was a child of the streets, a city-rat, and Mikey recognised something of his younger self in the boy. He was smart, fast on his feet and despite his small stature, he could handle himself in a fight. Yes, he had an eye to the main chance, but didn't everyone? Hadn't it been just that which had got Mikey to where he was now? Cock of the walk?

Harry made himself very useful to Mikey, but he never forgot that the moment his usefulness ceased, or if he made an error of some kind, Mikey wouldn't hesitate to dispose of him, possibly permanently.

He'd soon found his way about the streets of East London, learning the alleyways and back doubles, able to outrun and evade anyone who might want to catch or question him about what he was up to. Working for Mikey he was never short of money, but he knew that he was walking a thin line and if he were caught while on a job somewhere there'd be no cavalry coming to his rescue. Mikey would disown him.

He was aware he'd taken a risk, telling that Dickett bloke to bring the whisky with him on Tuesday. Mikey might not have wanted it and simply having it in the same van as the fags could have posed a problem. Still, Harry thought as he was leaving the market to head towards Lisa's school, Mikey had seemed OK about it and instead of the usual ten bob for a job, he'd given him a whole pound! As he passed a stall selling cheap jewellery he paused. He remembered how pleased Lisa had been with the necklace from Swan and Edgar he'd given her just before Christmas. There was no way he could 'borrow' anything from any of the stalls or barrows in Petticoat Lane – for a start he didn't know which were actually run by Mikey – but with a whole pound in his pocket, Harry thought he'd buy something for Lisa, to make up for having left her to find her own way home on Saturday. He chose a bracelet of blue beads, thinking they were the same colour as the necklace. He handed over a florin for it and there was no change. Expensive, he thought, but worth it for Lisa.

When he reached the school he was surprised to find it apparently closed. Despite it being nearly dinner time, there were no children in the playground, no children in the street on their way home to their dinner. He stood outside the gates and watched for a while, but no one came or went. Where were they all? The place seemed deserted. He was about to go when he saw Miss May coming out of the front door. She was carrying a basket and her handbag and was clearly leaving for the day.

As she emerged into the street Harry stepped out in front of her, barring her way. She stopped, surprised, and then said, 'Harry Black, isn't it? You left at Christmas. I hardly recognised you.'

'Is school closed?' Harry asked by way of response. 'Isn't it term again yet?'

'Yes, it should have started today,' said Miss May, 'but with all the bombing, well, things are changing here.'

'So where is everyone?'

'At home, I suppose. Sorry, young man, but I can't discuss school matters with you.' Then she added, 'What are you doing here, anyway?'

'Oh, nothing. Just looking for friends still at school.'

'Well, I'm sorry, there's no one here. Now, if you'll just let me pass...'

Harry stood aside and watched as she hurried along the street and into the butcher's.

Wonder if Lisa's at home, Harry thought and turned his steps to Kemble Street. As he came to the corner where the pub now lay in ruins, he looked along the road and saw a woman, coming from the other direction, go into a house halfway along. Was that Lisa's house? Harry thought it was. He'd watched her go into a house about there before now. He felt the bracelet in his pocket and decided to go and see if she was at home.

Perhaps, he thought, if I walk past the house a couple of times, Lisa'll see me and come out.

He strolled up the road, passing the house on the opposite side. Yes, the one the woman had gone into was number sixty-five. He glanced across, but the front room windows were still blacked out. Even if Lisa was in there she'd be at the back, not sitting in the front room in the dark. He had just passed the second time when the woman came out of the house again, slamming the front door behind her. She strode off down the street without a glance in Harry's direction. Harry waited for several minutes in case she came back and then went up to the front door. He gave it a push, but it wouldn't open. Surely the woman would have left it on the latch if someone was still in the house. He gave a quick glance up and down the street. There was no one in sight. The two houses almost opposite were derelict and burnt out, so he risked it. He bent down and, pushing open the letter box, peered through. He couldn't see much, just the edge of the staircase and a passage leading to the back of the house.

He banged on the door and when there was no response he called through the letter box. 'Lisa! Lisa? It's me, Harry. Are you in there, Lisa? I got something for you.' The house remained silent. It was obviously empty.

Where is she? Harry wondered. Now he'd got her a present he wanted to give it to her.

Hilda's! he thought. That's where she'll be, round Hilda's house. He decided to go round there and wait for her to come out, then they could walk back to Kemble Street together. He wouldn't knock on the door or anything, he'd just wait for her, like he did outside school sometimes.

He set off down the road, back the way he'd come. He knew where Hilda lived. He'd followed the girls home from school on one occasion just to find out. Now he headed for Grove Avenue, determined to see Lisa before he went back to the hostel.

As Dan and Naomi had before him, he turned the corner into Grove Avenue and came to an abrupt halt. There was a yawning chasm where two houses had been completely destroyed and one, he was sure, was Hilda's. He stared at the sagging houses on either side of the gap, both unstable, both open to the elements. The front door of one of them stood out, a brave royal blue. He remembered that door; he'd admired the colour and it was the house next to Hilda's.

They've been bombed out, he thought with a jolt. So where've they gone?

At that moment the door of the house behind him opened and a man in ARP uniform came out.

'Can I help you?' he asked. 'I'm the local warden. Are you looking for somebody?'

'I... I'm friend of Langs,' Harry said uncertainly. 'That is their house? The one bombed? Are they OK? Where they gone to?'

'A friend of the Langs?' The warden looked him up and down. He didn't look the sort of youngster who'd have been friendly with the Lang family.

'I was at school with Hilda,' Harry said, sensing the man's reluctance to tell him anything. 'I came to see how she is...'

'I see.' The warden's attitude softened a little. 'Well, I'm sorry to tell you that they took a direct hit. No survivors.'

Harry stared at him incredulously. 'You mean they're dead?'

'I'm afraid so, son,' replied the warden. 'The whole family, and another friend. Perhaps you knew her too, Lisa someone?'

Harry felt the whole world swing round him. 'Lisa?' he whispered. 'Lisa?'

'Afraid so. Sorry to have to break the news to you sudden, like this. Her poor parents was here yesterday, looking for her. Broke my heart to have to tell them, an' all. She'd spent the day with the Langs and was in the house when the raid came.'

'Did they... did you find bodies? Lisa's body?'

'There weren't much to find,' the warden said soberly. 'They took what there was away first thing yesterday. Bulldozer's coming in any day. Have to take down them other two houses. They ain't safe, neither.' He looked hard at Harry's face, completely drained of colour and said, 'You all right, mate?'

Harry gulped hard. 'Will be,' he said. 'Will be soon, just shock, you know?' He gave one last look at the bomb site and then turned and walked away.

Once he was out of sight of the still-inquisitive warden, Harry broke into a run. He ran to the park, to the bench where he and Lisa always met. It was warm and sunny; the park looked as it always had, except for the sandbagged gun emplacement at the far end. The trees were dressed in their autumn finery, yellow and orange and gold. The ducks still quacked on the pond, children still played on the swings and slid down the slide, watched by their mothers.

How can all this be going on as if nothing has happened? thought Harry fiercely. How can the world simply go on as if nothing had happened?

He remembered the time when the Duke had first been bombed, when Lisa's friend Mary had died. What had he said then? Something like 'she ain't the first and she won't be the last'. Lisa had accused him of not caring, and she'd been right, but he'd promised he'd care about her. He'd tempted fate, he'd said lots more were going to die, but not Lisa, brave Lisa from Hanau.

He thought of the way he'd put her on the bus to go home by herself and felt himself go cold. If he'd gone with her she might not have gone to Hilda's, she might have stayed with him till it was time to go home. No, the raid came too early, but if he *had* stayed with her he would have taken her into a shelter somewhere. He'd have kept her safe. Except he couldn't have stayed with her. He had to meet that Dickett bloke for Mikey. He knew he wouldn't have dared go back to Mikey and say, 'Sorry, couldn't make the meet, had to take a girl home instead.' Take a girl home! That sounded as if she was his girlfriend, which would be worse. No, there was no way he could have missed the meeting with Dickett. Mikey's business had to come before anything else, or there'd be major trouble.

He sat on in the park, thinking about what he could or couldn't have done, and then he suddenly remembered that the warden bloke had said there was little left to find. What if Lisa hadn't gone to Hilda's? After all, he, Harry, knew that she hadn't been there the whole day like she was meant to be. Suppose she hadn't gone there at all? For a moment hope sparked, only to be doused again with cold common sense. If she hadn't gone to Hilda's, where had she gone?

But as he gave this even more thought he realised that he had to tell Lisa's foster parents that Lisa had been with him for much of the day and, just possibly, hadn't been in the Langs' house when it was hit. They would know where else she might go. Decision taken, he jumped to his feet and set off for Kemble Street, afraid if he lingered and thought about it some more, he might not go.

It was creeping towards dusk as he approached the house. No lights were showing, but he assumed the blackout was in place and hoped they were at home. He walked straight up to the front door and listened. He could hear the wireless on inside and so, taking his courage in his hands, he knocked loudly.

The wireless was turned down and a woman's voice called, 'Who is it?' Harry drew a deep breath and called back, 'Harry Black. I'm friend of Lisa's.'

Immediately the door was flung open and the shadow of a woman was outlined against the deeper darkness of inside.

'Come in, quickly,' she cried. 'Do you know where she is? Is she with you? Oh, thank God, thank God.'

Harry passed into the house and as soon as the door was shut the woman put on the light.

'Who did you say you were? Oh, come in. Come into the kitchen and tell me where she is.'

Harry followed her into the kitchen where a man and another woman were sitting at the table.

'He's a friend of Lisa's,' she cried.

The man jumped to his feet. 'Are you saying you know where Lisa is?' he demanded.

Harry looked at their expectant faces and slowly shook his head. The man sank back into his chair and the woman let out a cry of despair. The second woman took her hand and led her back to the chair where she'd been sitting.

'Who are you?' asked the man.

'Mr Federman, Mrs Federman.' Harry looked at them as they nodded. 'I don't know where Lisa is, I wish I did.'

'You said you were a friend,' said Dan.

'I was... I am. From Hanau, the same as Lisa. Same train. Met her at school. Lisa chased by some Nazis...'

'Nazis? Here in England?'

'Fascist boys,' Harry said. 'Hit her because she's German. Teachers didn't see. But I see.'

'So what happened?'

'You can see I'm a Jew. So can the Hitler Youth, so I learned to fight. These Nazi boys... I grab the gang leader and I beat him. I said I'll break his arm but Lisa said "No!" I said if they touch her again or shout names, I will come back and next time I *will* break their arms. They all ran away.'

'And it worked?'

'Yes, it worked. And after that Lisa and me are friends.'

'But we know nothing about you. Why didn't she tell us about you?'

Harry shrugged. 'Dunno. Her secret.'

'So, why have you come here now?' asked Dan, still wondering if he could believe all this youth was saying.

'Because Lisa not at Hilda's house on Saturday. Up west with me.'

'What? Up west? Where?'

'To West End.'

'Why? No, never mind that. Where is she now?'

'Dunno. She left West End on a bus to come home. Today I hear Hilda's house is bombed. Everyone killed. But maybe Lisa wasn't in Hilda's house. Maybe she was still on bus when the bombers came.'

'Was she going to Hilda's when she left you?' asked Naomi, speaking for the first time since Harry had begun his story.

'She said yes. She wanted not to tell you lies. She told you she was going to Hilda, so she must go there, but not all day. Perhaps not there when raid comes.' Harry was vehement now. '*Must* be still on bus.'

'No, I'm afraid not,' Dan said. 'The house wasn't bombed until the second raid. She must have gone there as she planned. She didn't come home here. We think she stayed there...' his voice quavered, 'to be safe.'

Harry's shoulders slumped. He had been so sure that Lisa must have been somewhere else. 'May be hurt somewhere?' he suggested, but Naomi shook her head.

'I've been round all the hospitals. No one's heard of her. She ain't in any of them.'

For a moment the room was silent, but the silence was suddenly rent by the howl of the air raid siren.

Dan stood up. 'Better go,' he said. 'You all go down in the cellar.'

The two women got slowly to their feet, but Harry looked at Dan. 'Not to shelter?' he asked.

'No, firefighting,' said Dan, and put on his coat.

'I come,' Harry said. 'Fight fires.'

Dan gave him a sharp look and then said, 'Come on then, we always need runners.' He reached over and kissed Naomi hard before saying, 'In the cellar till the all-clear. OK?'

Shirley and Naomi promised and Dan and Harry left the house together, heading out into the hostilities of the night.

Chapter Thirteen

'She seems to have lost her memory, doctor,' said Sister Miller as they discussed the child in the corner bed. 'Her surname is Smith, we know that much, and the note that came with her from Casualty says that she's from Harrogate, though I'm not sure how we know. She was brought in by ambulance after the first raid on Saturday and that was the information the driver passed on.'

'How has she been since she came round properly?' asked Dr Greaves.

'Physically better, both her head and her arm are healing, but she has no memory. She doesn't remember her name and as far as I can tell she doesn't remember anything else either. She speaks English, but I'm sure it's not her first language. At times she lapses into German.' She looked across at the corner bed, hidden behind drawn curtains. 'It's why we've put her over there. It upsets the other patients if she starts to speak in German. She's very withdrawn,' she went on. 'All she says is, "I don't know my name." I'm really worried about her.'

'I see,' said the doctor. 'Well, let's go and have another look at her.'

'Good morning, young lady,' he said cheerfully when he reached her bedside. 'And how are we today?'

The girl looked up at him. She was pale, her eyes huge in her pinched face. 'I don't know my name,' she whispered.

'So I hear,' he replied. 'The trouble is, you've had a nasty bang on the head, and just for now your memory isn't working. It often happens after a bang on the head. Nothing to worry about. It'll all come back to you soon, you'll see.'

'But I don't know who I am,' insisted the girl. 'I haven't got a name.'

'We know part of your name,' Sister Miller said with a smile. 'Your surname is Smith. Tell you what,' she said with sudden inspiration, 'would you like to borrow my Christian name for now? It's Charlotte. How about you being Charlotte, just till you remember your own name? Would you like that?'

The girl looked a little doubtful, but nodded and answered, 'Yes, please.'

'Charlotte you are then,' smiled the sister. 'So, Charlotte, I'll be back to see you in a minute or two.'

'Good idea, that,' said Dr Greaves when they had left her. 'Gives you something to call her and gives her some sort of real identity. Probably won't be long before she remembers who she is. It's the brain's way of dealing with the trauma she's been through. Simply blocks it out until it's in a position to cope with it.' He glanced back at the curtained bed in the corner. 'The next problem,' he went on, 'is going to be what do we do with her? She can't stay here much longer. She's got over the concussion physically, her head wound is healing nicely and her broken arm is plastered and on the mend. Did you know St Thomas's was bombed last night?' Sister Miller shook her head. She hadn't heard that piece of news.

'So, you see,' he continued, 'beds are at an even greater premium. She's taking up a bed we need for someone else.'

'I know.' Sister Miller looked worried. 'I do understand that, but we can't just discharge her without finding somewhere for her to go until her people can be found.'

'Better talk to the almoner,' advised the doctor. 'She's the one to deal with situations like this. Now, who's next?'

Sister Miller spoke to Mrs Barnett, the almoner, later that day. 'Dr Greaves says that the girl known as Charlotte Smith in my ward must be discharged as soon as possible. The trouble is, we don't really know who she is. Somebody Smith from Harrogate.'

'Must be hundreds of Smiths in Harrogate,' said Mrs Barnett, wearily. She was a woman in her fifties, but looked older. Her normal workload had increased a hundredfold since war had broken out and like so many others, tested to the limit, she was exhausted. 'Not going to be easy to find her people, but we can try.'

'I've been wondering,' said the sister cautiously, 'I've been wondering if the child is half German? Perhaps through her mother, as her surname is Smith.'

The almoner looked surprised. 'What makes you think that?'

'Well,' replied the sister, 'she certainly speaks German as well as English. While she was still confused and talking to herself she almost always spoke in German, but if you speak to her in English, then she answers in English. She has some sort of accent, but maybe that's because she comes from up north. I'm not good at accents.'

'I see,' said Mrs Barnett. 'Well, I suppose that might make it easier to trace her family. If we can get in touch with the authorities in Harrogate, they may be able to find a Smith family with a German mother.' She sighed. 'Trouble is, everything's completely chaotic everywhere, it'll take some time.'

'Yes, I can see that,' sighed Sister Miller. 'So what can you do for her in the meantime?'

'Find a place in a children's home if I can,' came the reply, 'but it won't be easy. The number of displaced children is growing. Well now, who shall I list her as, I wonder?'

'She's known as Charlotte Smith here,' Sister Miller reminded her.

'Fair enough,' said Mrs Barnett. 'That'll do for now.' She closed the notebook in which she'd written down all the information they had and got to her feet. 'I'll see what I can do.'

She came back the next day and taking Sister Miller aside said, 'I've found a place that'll take her. It's called St Michael's. It's a children's home in Streatham.'

'But that's near Croydon Airport!' cried the sister in dismay. 'That's a definite target for the bombers.'

'I know,' sighed the almoner, 'it's not ideal, but at present it's the only place I can find with space for her. They're a sort of staging post. They don't usually keep the children for long. They give them a home until they can be found something more permanent, so there's quite a quick turnover. That's why they've got a place free. When can she be discharged?'

'As soon as she has somewhere to go.'

'Then I'll come for her this afternoon,' said Mrs Barnett. 'St Michael's won't keep the place for long.'

'I'll get the doctor to sign the discharge papers when he comes round,' promised the sister. 'Should be about lunchtime. I should think you could take her any time after three.'

When the almoner had gone, Sister Miller went over to the corner bed and drawing up a chair sat down beside the girl, beside Charlotte Smith.

'Hallo, Charlotte,' she said gently. 'How are you feeling?'

'All right,' came the non-committal reply.

'That's good,' said the sister cheerfully, 'because we're going to let you out of here today. Dr Greaves says you're well enough to go home.'

'But I haven't got a home!' The cry was one of sheer panic. 'I don't know who I am and I don't know where I live!'

'I know, dear, I know,' soothed the sister. 'But you see you can't stay here. We need the bed you're in for someone else. Don't worry,' she continued before Charlotte could interrupt, 'we've found you somewhere to go until we can find your family.'

'Where?' Charlotte looked suspicious.

'It's called St Michael's and it's a children's home. So you'll be with other children.'

'I don't want to go there,' wailed Charlotte.

'I'm afraid you have no choice,' said Sister Miller firmly. 'You have to move on from here, and that's where there's a place for you. We're still trying to find your family, but because you come from so far away, it isn't going to be quick or easy. Mrs Barnett, the almoner, is doing her best, but it may take some time.'

The girl said nothing but her look was mutinous.

'And who knows,' went on Sister Miller, 'it won't be long before you get your memory back. You'll find you begin to remember bits and pieces; your name, perhaps your address. Then finding your family will be easy.'

'I have been trying to remember,' Charlotte said. 'I've tried very hard.'

'I know you have, my dear, but it doesn't always work like that. Perhaps it'd be better if you *didn't* try so hard. Just let the information float up to the front of your brain.'

When Mrs Barnett arrived later that afternoon she brought clothes for Charlotte. Her own had been ruined in the blast. She had no luggage to take with her except her gas mask, which had come with her in the ambulance, a blue bead necklace and the photograph of the family group they had found in her pocket.

'We've looked at this with her a lot,' Sister Miller said as she showed it to the almoner, 'and talked to her about the people in it, but though we presume that it's her family, she doesn't recognise anyone.'

She handed the picture to Charlotte and said, 'Keep this safe, dear, it's very important. I'm sure it's a picture of your parents and your brother.'

They went to Streatham by taxi. When they got into the cab, Charlotte felt it was familiar; that she'd been in one before, but where? When?

St Michael's was a large, three-storey redbrick house, set back from the road. Its gateposts, now bereft of their iron gates, led on to a circular drive. The taxi turned in and deposited them at the front door. Mrs Barnett told the driver to wait and, marching up the steps, rang the bell. Moments later they were inside and being greeted by the home's superintendent, Miss Caroline Morrison.

She was a tall, slender woman, with dark auburn hair that stood in a halo around her head. Her eyes, a dark velvet brown, were warm and twinkled when she smiled.

'Hallo, Charlotte,' she said. 'Welcome to St Michael's. I'm Miss Morrison and I'm the superintendent here, which means I'm in charge, but we're all here to look after you.'

Mrs Barnett handed over some papers and then she went back out to the waiting taxi. Her job had been done and Charlotte was on her own.

Miss Morrison took her upstairs to the first landing. 'Girls on this floor,' she said, 'and boys on the top.' She opened the door to a small bedroom painted light green. It had a window through which the afternoon sun was streaming, making the room bright and cheerful. There were three beds, all neatly made and covered in green and white counterpanes, with a locker beside each. 'This is where you'll be sleeping and that's your bed.' Miss Morrison pointed to the one in the middle. 'You'll meet your room-mates, Clare and Molly, when they get back from school. In the meantime we must get you sorted out with some more clothes. Mrs Barnett told me you only have what you're wearing. You can leave your gas mask on your bed for now. Come along, I'll show you round.'

Charlotte followed Miss Morrison along the passage.

'Bathroom there,' Miss Morrison waved a hand at a closed door, 'lavatories there,' another wave, then on past two more bedrooms to a room at the end. 'This is Matron's room,' she said as she knocked on the door. 'And here's Matron.'

Matron was a small woman with iron-grey hair cut short and hooked behind her ears. She wore a blue uniform with a white apron and looked, to Charlotte, very like one of the nurses from the hospital. She was standing at a table, sorting laundry into piles, but as they came in she looked up and smiled.

'Hallo,' she said. 'Who's this?'

She knew perfectly well who it was. They had been told about Charlotte Smith at the morning staff meeting.

'She's a child who was brought in off the street after a raid,' Miss Morrison had told them. 'We know almost nothing about her except that the ambulance crew said she was found with a man named Peter Smith who came from Harrogate. He was dead, but seemed to be protecting her with his body and is presumed to be her father.'

'So, what's *her* name?' asked the matron.

'That we don't know. The child has amnesia. She remembers nothing, not her name nor why she was in London or who she was with. The only other clue we have is that when she first came round she was speaking German.'

'German!' exclaimed Mrs Downs, the cook.

'Yes. It could well be she's nothing to do with this Peter Smith from Harrogate. We don't *know* that he was her father. She could be a refugee, or she might be the child of a mixed marriage and have a German mother.'

'All sounds very odd to me,' said Mrs Downs.

'It's certainly a difficult situation both for us and for her,' agreed Miss Morrison. 'They had to call her something and apparently the ward sister offered her own Christian name, Charlotte. The child seems to have accepted that, so at present she's known as Charlotte Smith.'

Miss Morrison looked across at the two main members of her staff and said, 'I think the poor child is in a very fragile state and we're going to have to tread extremely carefully with her when she gets here. There is also the question of her status. The only firm information we've had from the hospital almoner is that she is bilingual. It was she who suggested Charlotte might have a German mother,' Miss Morrison explained, 'but I think it's more likely that she's a refugee. However, as we don't know and as she's been passed to us as Charlotte Smith, that's what she'll be known as here. If nothing more is found out about her family she'll become a ward of court.'

They moved on to discuss the air raid warning drill which the superintendent insisted was practised every few days. The population of St Michael's was very fluid with children coming and moving on, sometimes after only a few days, so it was vital that they all knew what to do when the sirens went, where to go, without panic, to take shelter.

Now Matron, looking at the whey-faced girl standing behind Miss Morrison, knew the superintendent had been right. She was a traumatised child who would need firm but gentle care.

'This is Charlotte Smith,' replied Miss Morrison. 'She's just arrived and we've come to find her some clothes.'

'Welcome to St Michael's, Charlotte. I'm Mrs Burton, but everyone just calls me Matron.' She waved a hand at the room. 'This is my room and this is where you can find me if you want me. This is where you come if you're not well, or you need me for anything. The door's always open. And,' she went on, 'it's also where we keep the extra clothes.'

'I'll leave you in Matron's capable hands,' Miss Morrison said to Charlotte. 'She'll bring you downstairs when she's got you sorted.'

'Now then,' said Matron when Miss Morrison disappeared, 'let's have a look.' She threw open a large cupboard and began to rummage through the clothes inside. She pulled out a dark green winter coat and held it up against Charlotte. 'Looks about right,' she said. 'Try it on and see.'

The coat was, indeed, a pretty good fit and before long Charlotte had been equipped with some underclothes, pyjamas, a warm skirt, two blouses and a red cardigan. 'That should be enough for now,' Matron said, handing her the pile of clothes. 'Let's go and put them away in your room and then I'll take you down to meet the others. They'll be coming back from school any moment.'

Charlotte put her new clothes into the locker by her bed and then followed Matron down the stairs and into a large living room.

'This is the common room,' Matron said. 'This is where you all come to do your homework and relax in the evenings. See, there's a wireless which we have on after supper, and there are some books over there if you like reading.'

Charlotte looked round. The room was homely, if a little shab-bily furnished. There was a radiator along one wall and it felt warm and welcoming.

'The dining room is next door,' Matron said. 'We all eat together, of course, and we help Mrs Downs, our cook, with the washing up afterwards.'

At that moment there was the sound of voices and the bang of a door and several girls erupted into the room. They stopped short when they saw Charlotte.

'Ah, girls, you're back,' said Matron. 'Good. This is Charlotte who's coming to live with us. She's in your room, Molly, so you look after her and make sure she knows what we do. Tea in about ten minutes and then we're having another air raid drill, so make sure you have your gas masks with you.'

Molly came over to Charlotte. 'Hallo,' she said. 'You been bombed out too?'

Charlotte shook her head. 'No... I mean, I don't know.'

Molly stared at her. 'What d'you mean you don't know?'

'Cos I don't,' snapped Charlotte. 'I can't remember.'

'All right, keep your hair on,' Molly said. 'I only asked.'

Ten minutes later a bell rang and the children all moved into the dining room. There were two long tables each laid with eleven places, five on either side and one on the end. When they were all in their places Miss Morrison introduced Charlotte.

'We're pleased that Charlotte has come to stay with us for a while. I expect you all remember how worried you felt when you first came here, so I know you'll make her welcome. I just have to tell you that poor Charlotte has had a bang on the head and it's made her lose her memory for the moment. It'll come back very soon, but in the meantime you must remember that she can't!' She then said grace and there was a buzz of chatter as they all sat down to cauliflower cheese followed by stewed apple.

Charlotte didn't say much during the meal. She was conscious of the covert glances the other children gave her, but she didn't want to talk to any of them. She simply sat next to Molly, ate her food, drank her milk and waited for it to be over.

After tea they were all called back into the common room for the air raid drill.

'In a minute you're all to go up to your bedrooms and lie on your beds,' said Miss Morrison. 'Make sure your gas masks are on top of your lockers, so you can grab them quickly.'

There was a muttering from some of the children, but she hushed them with a lift of her hand. 'I know you all think you know what to do,' she said, 'but we have a new girl among us who doesn't and I'd like to remind you boys that you're to come down the stairs in an orderly way, with no pushing, like last night.'

There was a murmur of 'Yes, miss,' before Miss Morrison continued. 'Good. Now, when Matron rings the bell you get out of bed, put your coats on over your pyjamas, pick up your gas masks and come downstairs. We go out through the kitchen door, still without any pushing, and into the shelter. There is enough room for every-one, so when you're inside, you simply sit down and wait until we're sure everyone is accounted for.'

The drill went as she'd explained until Charlotte reached the door of the shelter. She stopped, causing the other children to back up behind her.

'Come along,' called Miss Morrison from behind. 'Straight inside, please.' But when Charlotte didn't move she came forward to see what the hold-up was. She found Charlotte standing, as if frozen, outside the shelter, her face a mask of fear. Gently she took her hand and pulled her aside to allow the other children to go in. Then when everyone was inside, she said, 'We have to go in, Charlotte. We have to go in to be safe. Look, it's not dark inside.' She eased the child through the door. The shelter was lit with elec-tric light. Two bulbs hung down from the ceiling, lighting the shelter with a yellowish glow. Mattresses were spread out across the floor and the children were all sitting on them, looking expec-tantly at the door.

'Move up, Clare,' Miss Morrison said to the girl nearest the door. 'Make room for Charlotte.'

Charlotte sat down on the mattress, but she remained stiff, with fear in every line of her body. Clare reached over and took her hand and Charlotte gripped hers in return as if her life depended on it.

The door was pulled shut behind them and then Miss Morrison took a roll-call to be sure everyone was safely in the shelter.

'One of us will have to bring Charlotte down separately,' Miss Morrison said to the matron when the drill was over and the chil-dren were back in the common room. 'There's some deep-seated fear here that can't be dismissed. I suggest you and Mrs Downs take the rest of them on in as usual, I'll gather up Charlotte as they come downstairs and bring her with me. I'll keep her near the door.'

Her plan was put into action less than two hours later when the sirens blared and the children had to leave their beds and trek out to the shelter, to spend the rest of the night sleeping on the mattresses, wrapped in their coats with blankets spread over them. Charlotte was still afraid to enter the shelter, but with gentle pressure and encouragement from Miss Morrison, she was finally persuaded to go inside and the door was closed behind her.

The raids continued, night after night, and Miss Morrison realised it was becoming gradually easier to get Charlotte into the shelter. She was always first out when the all-clear sounded, but that didn't matter.

Miss Morrison had given some thought to the question of who Charlotte could be. Since she had arrived she had started at the local school, going with the other children. It was found that her reading and writing were behind the others, but that she had an excellent grasp of maths.

'The more I see of her,' Miss Morrison said to Matron, 'the more certain I am that she's a refugee. I think I'll try an experiment.'

Matron looked startled. 'What sort of experiment?'

'My brother, George, speaks German,' said Miss Morrison. 'I'm wondering if he spoke to her in German, it might trigger her memory.'

'Worth a try, I suppose,' agreed Matron.

That evening Miss Morrison phoned George, who was home on a week's leave, and explained the situation.

'I just wondered,' she said, 'if you'd come and talk to her. Speak to her in German.'

'Well, I will if you think it'd help, Caro, but I'm afraid my German's pretty rusty these days.'

'But you can speak it,' his sister persisted. 'Will you try?'

'All right,' sighed George. 'When shall I come?'

'At the weekend? Or one afternoon when she gets home from school.'

'My leave's up on Friday,' he said, 'so I'll come tomorrow afternoon.'

Next day, when they all got home from school, he was waiting in Miss Morrison's sitting room. The superintendent collected Charlotte from the common room and took her in to meet him. Charlotte came into the room a little nervously, wondering if she'd done something wrong, but Miss Morrison smiled as she led her forward and said, 'Nothing to worry about, Charlotte, there's just someone I'd like you to meet. This is George. Sit down and have a chat, I'll be back in a minute or two.'

Charlotte looked at the man enquiringly and said, 'Good afternoon.'

George replied, hesitantly at first, in reasonable German. 'Hallo, Charlotte,' he said. 'Why don't you sit here so we can talk?' He waved at an armchair on the opposite side of the fireplace. Charlotte sat down, perching on the edge of the chair as if ready for flight.

'That's better,' George said with a smile. 'How was school today?'

'All right.' Though he had addressed her in German Charlotte replied in English.

'That's good. Can you understand my German? It's not very good, I'm afraid.'

'I understand you,' said the girl, 'but why do you speak to me in German?'

'I thought perhaps you might be more comfortable speaking German,' George answered. 'We know you can. You've lost your memory at the moment, haven't you? I just thought it might help you to remember.'

'I hit my head,' said Charlotte. 'They tell me I was caught in the street in a raid, but I don't remember. They say it is because I hit my head. They tell me I shall remember soon, but I don't.' She looked up at him and with quivering lips, said, 'I don't know who I am.'

'I know,' George said gently. 'It must be awful for you, but it will all come back to you in time.'

'Don't think I did any good at all,' he reported later. 'She didn't speak any German to me, though she clearly understood what I was saying.'

His sister sighed. 'Oh well, it was worth a try. Thanks for coming, George.' She walked with him to the front door. 'When do you have to leave?'

'Friday morning.'

'Where are you going this time?'

George gave her a rueful smile. 'Caro, you know better than to ask.'

'Will I see you again before you leave?'

'Doubt it. Off down to Somerset to see Avril before I go.'

'Are you? How lovely. Give her my love.'

'I will.' He gave her a hug and she held on to him for a moment.

'Look after yourself,' she said, 'wherever you're going.'

He kissed her cheek and said, 'You too, Caro.'

Chapter Fourteen

Dan took Harry to the fire station and introduced him to the chief, John Anderson, who gave a brief nod. 'Can always use another runner,' he said. 'You stay with Arthur and his team. They'll send you back to me with any news, all right, lad?'

'Yes, OK. I'll run with messages.'

'Good. Know your way about round here, do you?'

'Yes.'

'Where'd'you find him?' the chief asked Dan.

'Just a lad who wanted to help,' said Dan. 'Thought we could use him.' And he hurried off without further explanation. Within half an hour the sirens were sounding and all the firefighters were soon at full stretch. Harry started with Arthur's team, but as he ran back to the station to warn of a blaze near the wharf, he was sent on other errands, pushing a water cart, shovelling sand, and Dan hardly saw him again. As always the work went on long after the steady blast of the all-clear and Harry and Dan were there until Anderson sent them home.

'You did well, lad,' he said, clapping Harry on the back.

'I'll come again tomorrow,' Harry said.

'Good, we'll need you.'

No one was under the illusion that the bombing would stop in the foreseeable future, and it was this general expectation and acceptance of more raids that made them somehow easier to deal with.

Harry walked back with Dan, leaving him just before Kemble Street to head back to the hostel. After his night among the firefighters, Harry was determined to be out with them during future raids. He felt he was taking a bash at Hitler out there in the streets, his natural habitat; better still, he wasn't crushed in the air raid shelter with the other boys, being treated like a child.

'Where d'you live, son?' asked Dan as they paused at the street corner.

'A hostel in Stoke Newington.'

'That's miles from here,' Dan said in surprise. 'You want to doss down at our place?'

It was Harry's turn to look surprised. 'Sleep in your house?'

'Just for tonight,' Dan said.

'Yes, please.'

They walked back to the house and Dan showed Harry the mattress in the cellar. 'You'll be safe enough down here, lad,' he said, lighting a candle. 'Just don't burn the place down, all right?'

Dan climbed the stairs wearily and crept into the bedroom where Naomi was lying awake in the darkness, waiting for him.

'Put the lad in the cellar for the night,' he said. 'Too far for him to go home.'

'Shirley's still in the front room,' Naomi told him.

'Guessed she would be,' said Dan, heaving himself into bed. Within moments he was fast asleep.

Naomi lay beside him. She needed to talk to him; she and Shirley had hatched a plan, but it could wait until the morning. She needed Dan to be in the right mood. Her thoughts turned to the boy now sleeping in the cellar. Why had Lisa kept him a secret? Was he, she wondered, the boy Mary had seen with Lisa some months ago? Lisa had said it was just a friend from school who lived nearby, but now Naomi was almost certain that it must have been this scruffy youth called Harry.

Downstairs in the cellar, the scruffy youth was also lying awake, thinking about Lisa. She was dead, he knew that now. She would never wear the bracelet he still had in his pocket. She would never grin at him as they met in the park, or giggle as they cheated another bus conductor of his fare. Harry lay in the dark, the candle carefully snuffed out, and for the first time since he'd heard of his father's death, the tears slid down his cheeks. He hadn't cried for his mother, she had given up and wanted to be dead. He had accepted her death with stony resignation, but now, lying here in this chilly cellar, he was crying; crying for the girl who'd been so brave. He'd promised he cared about her and now he found that he did, more than he'd have dreamed possible, and he'd lost her.

'Be back tonight, if you like,' he said to Dan in the morning. 'To go fire-watching with you.'

'Be pleased to have you, lad,' Dan said, and they headed off in different directions: Dan to pick up his cab from under the railway arches, Harry to go back to the hostel.

But that evening, when the sirens sounded, Harry did not return.

When he'd finally walked into the hostel that morning, he was greeted by Mr Pate, the warden.

'Ah, there you are, Heinrich.'

Harry glowered at him. He had told Mr Pate months ago that he now went by the name of Harry Black, not Heinrich Schwarz, but it was as Heinrich Schwarz he'd come to the hostel and been registered and Mr Pate was not a man to accept any changes that didn't come from the authorities and come in triplicate.

'Yes, Mr Pate,' he retorted, 'I am here.'

'I'm afraid I must ask you to stay within the hostel until further notice,' said Mr Pate.

'You mean I can't go out at all?' Harry stared at him.

'Exactly,' agreed Mr Pate, looking relieved.

'Why? Why can't I? What about my job?' demanded Harry. 'I have to go out.'

'I'm afraid the police want to talk to you.'

'Me?' Harry's mind was racing. Why did the police want him? Was it something to do with Mikey? Had he been seen with the Dickett bloke? What could have gone wrong?

'They'll tell you,' Mr Pate assured him. 'They're coming back. Please go to your room and wait for them there.'

Harry went to his room as instructed, but he had no plans to wait for the police. He must get over to the Black Bull and warn

Mikey that something was up. He couldn't stay here now and he certainly couldn't come back. Quickly he gathered his few possessions together and stuffed them into the small case he'd brought from Germany. His money, which had been hidden in a slit he'd made in the thin mattress on his bed, he put into the pocket of his trousers. He'd learned the hard way in Hanau: never keep your money in your coat pocket. If someone grabs you, you can wriggle free of your coat, leaving it in your captor's hands as you break away. It had happened once when he'd been cornered by two Hitler Youth boys. Harry had put up a good fight and escaped, minus his jacket but also minus the money in its inside pocket. Now he had everything that he owned with him, all he had to do was slip out of the hostel without being seen. Mr Pate would be in his office near the front door, but there was always the way out the back, through the kitchen into the yard and over the wall.

Very quietly he opened his door. All was quiet. Most of the inmates of the hostel were younger and at school. He could hear one of the cleaning ladies singing as she scrubbed the kitchen floor. He'd have to get past her without arousing suspicion. Difficult, he decided, when he was carrying a suitcase. Perhaps better to try the front door after all. He edged along the hallway and peered round the corner. There was Mr Pate, sitting at the desk in his office with the door wide open. Could he sneak past without him noticing? Then he saw the chain. The front door was shut and its chain, usually only put on last thing at night, was across the door. Not difficult to open, but impossible simply to make a dash for it. Harry turned back, out of sight.

Better going out through the back door, he thought; after all, what can an old charwoman do to stop me?

As he moved quietly to the kitchen door he heard the front doorbell ring and then voices. No time to be cautious now! Harry burst through into the kitchen and tripping over the charwoman's bucket of water fell flat on his face in a puddle of dirty water. He scrambled to his feet, still clutching his case, and made for the back door. It, too, was locked, but it was the work of only a moment to turn the key and fling it open. As he fled across the yard he could hear the woman shouting behind him and heavy-booted feet in hot pursuit. Tossing the case up and over the wall, he launched himself upward, grabbing for the coping, but it was just too high. Again he jumped and the second time managed to get hold of a jutting piece of stone and haul himself up. Behind him a policemen dashed out through the back door and made a grab for his feet. Harry kicked out, catching the man in the eye before managing to swing himself clear and drop down into the alley on the other side. As he landed he wrenched his ankle and a shaft of pain shot up through his leg. He gasped and clutched the wall for balance, but before he could snatch up his case and limp away into the lanes of London, a hand gripped his arm and a voice said, 'Going somewhere, was we?'

The uniformed policeman towered over him, his grip on Harry's arm like a vice. Harry tried to pull free, but the cop was too strong. Moments later a second officer appeared in the alley and snapped a pair of handcuffs on to Harry's wrists. They picked up his suitcase and led him, hobbling, back to the front of the hostel where Mr Pate hovered, looking anxious.

'Ah, you got him, Constable. Well done. That's good.' He turned on Harry. 'That was very stupid, Heinrich,' he said. 'Did you really think I was going to let you walk out of here? You're an enemy alien.'

Harry stared at him incredulously. He was well aware that a great many male refugees had been interned after the fall of France, when the whole country was panicking about spies and fifth columnists, but he'd never even been interviewed. As a boy of under sixteen he wasn't considered likely to have been sent as a spy by the Führer. He'd only been fourteen when he'd arrived at Liverpool Street station and was clearly no threat to anyone.

'Enemy alien? You're joking me!'

'Heinrich Schwarz, by order of His Majesty's government you are to be interned as an enemy alien for the duration of hostilities,' intoned one of the policemen.

'Not Heinrich Schwarz,' pleaded Harry in desperation, his English beginning to desert him. 'Harry Black, fire-watcher's runner. There last night. Ask down at the docks.'

It wasn't the right thing to say. Until now the constable holding him had had some sympathy for him. Surely a scruffy kid like this wasn't an enemy. But now he said he'd been at the docks, well who knows what he'd been doing down there… Fire-watching, he said, but he could just as easily have been fire-*raising*. An enemy alien indeed!

'Sorry, lad,' his partner was saying, 'but whatever you've been doing, you got to come along with us.' He turned to Mr Pate. 'You got all his documents ready, have you?'

'Oh, yes, officer.' Mr Pate rushed back into his office and scooped up a file from his desk. 'Everything here and in order. Passport, immigration papers, ration book, school report. Job information…'

'What my boss say when I don't come?' demanded Harry. He felt he could mention his job again now that he knew the police were not there because of anything to do with Mikey Sharp.

'He's got his own ID card, of course,' Mr Pate went on as if he hadn't spoken. 'All you need, I think.'

One of the policemen took the file and walking either side of Harry they led him out into the road. As they marched him along to the police station in the next street, people watched curiously, wondering what the young lad had been doing. Scruffy-looking bloke he was, clearly been up to no good.

Later that afternoon the news reached Mikey Sharp that Harry Black had been arrested by the police. Mikey swore vociferously, wondering what the lad had been doing, his mind racing as he tried to decide which, if any, of his deals might be at risk. Later still, he was able to heave a sigh of relief when another of his sources told him that Harry had been arrested as an enemy alien. His arrest had nothing to do with Mikey or any of his various businesses and Harry Black was erased from his mind. He'd ceased to exist.

Naomi had been plucking up courage to speak to Dan about herself and the baby. The Luftwaffe had put in an appearance every night since that first fateful Saturday. Dan was out on the streets until the small hours, while still trying to make a living from his taxi. As a volunteer he was not obliged to turn out every time the sirens went off, he was not a paid fireman or auxiliary, he went because he felt he must, but as the raids continued he became more and more worried about Naomi left at home in the cellar. She now had Shirley for company, but even so, he knew only too well if the house received a direct hit as the Langs' had, she could be killed outright, or buried alive in the cellar. Each of them hovered round the subject they both had been considering, neither wanting to broach it.

'I'll speak to him this evening before he goes out,' Naomi had promised Shirley.

'Well, you'd better,' said Shirley firmly. 'Cos if you don't soon I'll be going without you. There's nothing here for me now and I ain't staying for Hitler's pleasure. I'm off! I'll keep out the way while you tell him, but you got to tell him tonight, or I'll be gone.'

So, when Dan came in from his day at the wheel, he found Naomi on her own in the kitchen.

'We got to talk,' she said, almost as soon as he was through the door. She was dreading the conversation and knew if she didn't launch into it straight away she'd put it off again.

'So we have, girlie,' he agreed. 'But a cuppa first, eh?'

Naomi poured him the tea and a cup for herself and they sat either side of the table, sipping it, each waiting for the right moment to speak.

Finally Naomi said, 'Dan, I been thinking...'

'Yeah? What about?'

'About me and the baby.'

'So've I,' said Dan, and it was he who took the plunge. 'I think you should be getting out of London and quick. This bombing ain't going to stop and you need to be out of it, you and the baby.'

Naomi could have cried with relief. She didn't want to go, but if they both agreed she ought to, it would be a great weight off her mind.

'I don't want to go,' she said, 'but...'

'You're going,' Dan told her. 'I been thinking about it ever since... the bombing started.'

'But what about you?' Naomi asked. 'Will you come with me? The baby wants a father, too, you know.'

'Naomi, love, you know I can't. I have to do my bit here in London.'

'You did "your bit", as you call it, in the last war,' Naomi said bitterly. 'Ain't that enough?'

'No, girl, it ain't, and you know it ain't.'

It was as Naomi had feared. Dan wouldn't leave London with her, but difficult as she would find it and much as she would hate it without him, she wasn't going to change her mind.

'I knew you'd say that really,' she admitted, 'so I've got a plan.'

Dan, who'd only considered the first hurdle, that of getting Naomi to agree to go, hadn't thought of how it would all be achieved, but Naomi was more than a step ahead.

'Shirley's got a cousin, Maud. She lives up in Suffolk in a little village. Shirley's going to stay with her and she says I can go too. There's room for both of us.'

Dan stared at her. 'I see you got it all sorted,' he grunted.

'No,' Naomi snapped, 'I ain't said I'm going yet, but Shirley can't wait to go. Her house here has gone, she's nothing to keep her and her cousin has offered her a home.'

'And you?'

'Shirley told her cousin that we'd given her a place to stay when she had nowhere else, and she wants to do the same for me and the baby.'

'It's all very quick,' Dan said a little sulkily.

'It might be the difference between being the quick or the dead!' retorted Naomi, suddenly cross. She had plucked up the courage to broach the subject and though Dan had got in first, and agreed, he didn't seem keen on the plans she had made. Having decided to go, she wanted to leave quickly, before the Luftwaffe intervened and made it too late.

'Of course,' Dan said sheepishly, 'you're right. I'm just being stupid. It's just, well... I'm being stupid.'

Naomi went over to him and enveloped him in a hug. 'No, darling Dan, you could never be that. I don't want to leave you, you know that, but my first thought has to be for the baby. If something happens to me it won't ever be born. I can feel it moving inside now and I know he, or she, is a real person. I have to protect them.'

'It's not just the baby,' Dan reminded her as he returned her hug. 'I want you to be safe, too. When will you go?'

'Shirley's going tomorrow,' Naomi said.

Dan felt as if something had hit him in the chest. Tomorrow! So soon! But he forced a smile to his lips and said, 'Then I think you should go with her. I could come and see you in a week or so, just to see you settled in.'

It was decided. They both hated the idea, but they agreed it was the right thing to do. Shirley came back in and as they ate their tea together, Dan asked where her cousin Maud lived.

'Just over the Suffolk border,' she replied. 'A place called Feneton. Train direct from Liverpool Street. Don't take long to get there.'

By the time the sirens were howling it was decided. The two women would leave for Feneton tomorrow.

'I'll try and ring my cousin tomorrow and tell her we're both coming,' Shirley said.

'She's on the telephone?' Dan sounded surprised.

'Yes. Don't worry, I'll give you the number and you'll be able to talk to Naomi and hear how she's getting on.'

Dan was on the doorstep, but there was no sign of Harry, despite his promise to come firefighting again.

'Perhaps he'll be there already,' suggested Naomi as she hugged Dan tight and kissed him goodbye.

'Doubt it,' said Dan. 'He'd've been here by now if he was coming. Bit of a fly-by-night, if you ask me.' He turned back before he doused the hall light so he could open the front door. 'Down to the cellar with you. I'll be back as soon as I can.'

It was another broken night with two alerts. The drone of the bombers overhead forced Naomi and Shirley back down into the cellar.

'If I hadn't decided to come with you already,' Naomi said, 'I certainly would've after tonight.'

'An' I'd've gone without you if you hadn't,' Shirley replied, as she instinctively ducked at the crump of a distant bomb. 'I've had enough of this!'

'All I want is unbroken sleep,' cried Naomi. 'I'm so tired!'

Once she'd made her decision to go earlier that day, she'd been to the factory and seen the boss.

'I'm pregnant,' she told him. 'I'm being evacuated.'

He'd looked her up and down as if assessing the truth of the statement, but the sight of her expanded waistline convinced him and all he said was, 'Oh well, we need more babies now, I suppose.'

When she got home again she went into Lisa's bedroom and closed the door. It was cold and miserable. Suddenly she pulled Lisa's case out from under her bed and opening the drawers packed everything into it. The last thing she put in was the letter. This time she realised that the photo of Lisa's family wasn't there. She must have had it with her when she died, thought Naomi. So in a funny way they were all together at the end. She closed the case and carried it down to the cellar.

Shirley saw her coming down the stairs and said, 'What's that?'

'It's Lisa's things,' replied Naomi. 'I'm going to put them in the cellar. They'll be safer there if... they'll be safer there.'

'What you keeping them for?' Shirley asked.

'This war has to end some day and when it does, who knows, Lisa's family might come looking for her.'

'I thought you said they was dead.'

'We don't know where they are, but I know there's a cousin in Switzerland and if they don't come to find her, well, I'll send it all back to him.'

'Suit yourself,' Shirley said, her tone making it clear that she thought it all a waste of time. 'I'd have thought some kiddie round here could have made use of them clothes.'

Naomi didn't answer. She knew Shirley was probably right, but even so she went down the steps and put Lisa's case at the far end of the cellar, against the outside wall. She stood for a moment looking at it and then abruptly turned on her heel and went back up to the kitchen.

When Dan got home, once again in the early hours, he found Naomi sitting up in bed waiting for him. Though he was dog-tired, they didn't sleep, but lay in each other's arms savouring every

moment together, each realising that they didn't know when they'd
be together like this again.

'You will be careful, won't you?' Naomi begged him. 'I know
you think you have to go out every night, that London needs you
and perhaps it does, but you won't forget that I need you too, will
you, Danny?'

Dan drew her even closer, burying his face in her hair. 'You're
everything to me, girl,' he murmured. 'It's only because I love you
so much that I can bear to let you go.'

The morning dawned, dull and grey. A cold wind had sprung up,
driving away the lingering smoke of night-time fires. Naomi put the
last of her things in a suitcase, together with the few tiny baby
clothes she'd managed to buy in the market, all carefully folded.
Dan went and fetched the taxi and the two women climbed into the
back of it.

'Have you really got enough petrol to spare?' worried Naomi.

'Enough to take my wife and her friend to Liverpool Street
station,' Dan replied. 'And,' he went on, 'I can probably pick up a
fare from there.' He had been thinking of the last time they had been
to Liverpool Street to collect Lisa and was determined that Naomi
wasn't going to face that recollection alone.

As they drove through the streets Naomi was horrified at the
devastation. She knew, of course, who didn't, that the Blitz had been
battering London relentlessly for weeks, but she hadn't ventured out
of her own area and the reality and extent of the destruction was
brought home to her for the first time. Buildings blown apart, their
contents still clinging to sloping floors, craters in the road causing
traffic to divert round them, one street closed where an unexploded
bomb lay, threatening, lethal; another where a fire, reignited by the
freshening wind, swept through the ruins of somebody's home.

'How will we ever survive all this?' she cried out in dismay. 'How
can we bear it?'

'We can, because we must,' Dan answered firmly. 'Just keep on
saying "We ain't going to let the buggers win!"'

They reached the station and Naomi and Shirley clambered out
of the cab. Dan put their luggage on the pavement. Shirley had little

more than a capacious handbag in which she had stowed the few clothes she had managed to buy since the fire. Almost everything else she'd owned had gone up in flames with her house. She and Dan had crept into the burned-out shell of her home and she had managed to retrieve a few precious items the fire had not consumed, but as she left for Feneton her world was packed into a bag she could carry over her shoulder.

Dan walked with them, carrying Naomi's case as they went to the ticket office and then to the platform. There wasn't a train for Feneton for another half-hour. Naomi turned to him and said, 'Go now, Dan. I ain't any good at goodbyes.'

He put down her case and gathered her into his arms. 'Look after yourself, girlie,' he said gruffly. 'Look after yourself and the little 'un.'

'I will,' promised Naomi, her voice breaking on a sob. 'And you, Danny. We need you safe.' And for a long moment they clung together.

'Don't you worry about me,' Dan said as he let her go. 'I'll be up to see you, soon as I can.' He laid a hand on Shirley's shoulder. 'Thanks for taking her with you,' he said. 'Good luck!' and then without a backward glance he strode away.

The two women sat down on a bench and waited for their train. Naomi dashed away her tears, determined to be brave. All around her the world was falling apart, people were being killed, losing their loved ones, losing their homes. Why should she be any different? She was travelling to a place of safety, she was carrying a much-wanted baby within her, she was luckier than many who had lost everything.

As she looked round the station Lisa's face floated into her mind and she forced it down again. She couldn't cope with Lisa's death, not yet, and until she could she wouldn't allow it to confront her.

Chapter Fifteen

The raids continued night after night. There wasn't a single night that the children at St Michael's spent entirely in their beds. Each morning the new day would have to be faced and they would set off for school, often tired and bleary-eyed.

Charlotte had settled fairly well into the home. In a strange way she found the regular routine of the home comforting. She lived within its framework and had the security of knowing exactly what she was supposed to be doing and when. School was the same; the day was organised and broken into manageable sections by bells and break times. She was happy enough living with children who were also lost in some way. Molly, she learned, had been bombed out of her home in August when a bomber, driven back by the fighters, emptied its bomb bay over New Cross. None of her family had been killed but their home had become uninhabitable and the family dispersed among friends and relations. Molly, as the eldest child, was the one who had been placed at St Michael's. Clare had been living with her grandmother. She didn't remember her mother who had died when she was two and her father, in the navy, had been lost at sea. When her grandmother had been knocked down by a car in the blackout and killed, Clare, left alone in war-torn London, had been taken into St Michael's. Every child had a story to tell and Charlotte began to realise that she wasn't the only one living with loss.

'At least you know who you are,' she said despondently to Clare one evening as they sat together in the common room doing their homework. 'I can't remember anything before I woke up in hospital. Not my name. Not my home. Not my family.'

'I know, but at least you've got a photo of them,' Clare reminded her.

'I've got a photo of... people. I don't know them.'

'Surely they must be your parents and your brother.'

'Maybe,' sighed Charlotte. 'I hope I remember soon. It's so stupid I can remember my tables but not my name!'

'Come on,' Clare said, anxious to change to a happier subject. 'I think I've learned the poem now. Will you hear me?' And for the next twenty minutes they recited the poem they been set to learn for homework.

Miss Morrison saw the budding friendship and was pleased. She still hoped that as she relaxed into her new surroundings, Charlotte would gradually recover her memory. Perhaps friendship with Clare, another courageous child, would aid that recovery.

It was one night in early November that everything was to change. The siren started its dismal wail and the children, practised into normality now, filed down the stairs and out to the shelter in the back garden. As had been established over the nightly exodus, Clare took Charlotte's hand as they approached the shelter and gently led her inside. Miss Morrison allowed herself a weary smile as she saw the two girls sit down together on one of the mattresses. As the raid gathered force outside, she encouraged them all to lie down and try to go back to sleep. Obediently they curled up on the mattresses, but then came a tremendous crash somewhere close, shaking the shelter to its foundations. Everyone was jolted awake and little Polly Elliott, one of the younger girls, began to cry. Matron reached over and pulled her on to her lap, cuddling her against her shoulder and murmuring soothingly into her hair. Since there was little chance of anyone going back to sleep now, Miss Morrison started singing. One or two of the children joined in and before long they were all singing 'My Bonnie Lies Over the Ocean' and 'Old MacDonald Had a Farm'. The noise of the raid filled the world outside, but within the shelter they continued to sing. When at last they seemed to have run out of songs, a quiet voice began to sing a new song. No one joined in; the words were unintelligible. Charlotte was singing, and she was singing in German. *Grün, grün, grün sind alle meine Kleider.* They all turned to stare at her, but no one interrupted. Miss Morrison listened, fascinated. Clearly this song was coming from the recesses of Charlotte's closed mind and Miss Morrison wondered if this was the breakthrough they'd been waiting for. When at last the song died away, she said, 'That was lovely, Charlotte. Thank you.'

When the all-clear finally sounded and they emerged from the shelter, they found a world utterly changed. St Michael's itself was still standing, but several houses in the street were on fire and two of them had been partially destroyed, leaving leaning walls, gaping windows and dangerously lop-sided roofs.

Miss Morrison hurried the children inside and sent them back to bed for a couple of hours' sleep before they had to get up to face the new day, but she called the two other live-in staff to her sitting room for a meeting. She had been thinking hard as she been sitting with her fifteen children in the brick shelter, listening to the destruction of the world above, and she had made some decisions.

'We're in the front line here,' she began without preamble. 'We're within a few miles of Croydon airport and that's a definite target for the bombers. We have to move the children somewhere safer. Any of those bombs could have hit us and we'd all have been killed.'

'You say move the children,' said Matron, 'but where? If they had anywhere else to go they wouldn't be here.'

'I realise that,' Miss Morrison said, 'but they're in particular danger here and we have to get them moved somewhere. Now, I've had an idea which I hope will work. The best thing for them all would be to be evacuated to the country.'

'Fair enough,' agreed Mrs Downs, 'but where? The government-sponsored evacuation seems to have finished. People are leaving of their own accord, of course, going to stay with people they know outside the towns, but who do we know who'd accept fifteen children all of a sudden?'

'My sister, Avril,' replied Miss Morrison.

'Your sister?' Matron echoed. 'Where does she live? Has she got room for fifteen evacuees?'

'She lives in Wynsdown, a village in Somerset, where her husband is the vicar. I'm sure if I ask her she'll be able to find families prepared to take children who've been made homeless by the Blitz.'

'It's a big thing to ask,' remarked Mrs Downs doubtfully.

'I know,' agreed Miss Morrison, 'but I'm going to phone her this morning and ask if she can. I don't think she'll turn me down.'

When the children had left for school, Miss Morrison got on to trunks and managed to put a call through to her sister in Wynsdown. Avril Swanson answered.

'St Mark's Vicarage. Good morning.'

'Av? It's Caro.'

'Caro?' The delight at hearing her sister's voice sounded in Avril's. 'Where are you? Are you coming down to see us? Do say you are!'

'No, afraid not,' answered Caro. 'Look, I've only got three minutes. Can I send you the children from St Michael's?'

'What? Can you what?'

'We were nearly bombed out last night, Av. Houses all round us have been damaged and I need to get the children out of London, away from the Blitz. It's been every night since September.'

'Yes, we've heard how bad it is,' Avril said.

'I'm sure you have,' replied her sister, 'but until you've actually lived through these raids, you can have no idea of just how bad. Half the street was destroyed last night. It's a miracle St Michael's is still standing. I have to get these children away, Avril, and I thought you might be able to help. There are only fifteen of them.'

'Only!' cried Avril. 'Where am I going to put fifteen children, Caro? I know the vicarage is big, but it's not that big!'

'I didn't mean just you,' Caroline said with a shaky laugh. 'I hoped you'd be able to spread them round the village.'

'I can try, I suppose,' said Avril. 'We had some evacuees when war broke out, but almost all of them went back home before the first Christmas. Not sure how happy people here will be to have another lot descend on them.'

'Would they be happier if fifteen kids were obliterated by high-explosive bombs, or incinerated by incendiaries?'

'Don't, Caro,' cried Avril. 'Of course not, but I'll have to talk to David before I give you an answer. I'll try to ring you back later.'

Caroline Morrison sighed. Her three minutes were almost up. 'All right,' she said, 'but don't leave it too late, Av, or I shall be in the shelter with fifteen children, in the middle of an air raid.'

As she put down the receiver, Miss Morrison began to plan for the evacuation. She was sure Avril and her husband, David, would find places for her charges, but it might take time and after last night's raid, she wasn't sure how much time they'd got.

In Somerset, Avril Swanson put the phone down. She stared out of the kitchen window at the garden beyond. Gone were the lawn and herbaceous borders that had been her delight when they'd first come to the parish. Now there were neat rows of winter vegetables, beyond which was the hen house and its wire-fenced run. The vicarage was digging for victory and keeping chickens.

I should go out and feed them, she thought, we're certainly going to need more eggs. The thought made her laugh out loud. If there was to be an influx of fifteen London children, they were going to need a darn sight more than extra eggs!

Wynsdown was a small village crouched on the Mendip Hills. Its cottages and one or two larger houses radiated out from a small village green. This was definitely the centre of village life. The church and vicarage stood on one side with the tiny church hall close by; the pub, the Magpie, faced them from across the green and on a third side were the low stone buildings of the village school. The post office and general store, standing either side of the Magpie, completed the hub. The bus to Cheddar came through, morning and evening, to take people to work, but most of the families in Wynsdown were employed on the land. Children from outlying farms came to the village school, sometimes hitching a lift on a tractor, but more often walking the two or three miles from home and back again in the afternoon.

Avril loved it here. She had thought she'd feel cut off when they first moved, it was so far and so different from the sort of town where, until now, she'd spent her life, but it wasn't long before she knew that this was where she felt at home. She loved the feeling of community and of being an integral part of it. David, as the vicar, soon got to know most of his parishioners and had been tentatively welcomed as a younger replacement for the retiring vicar, Gerald Parker. He had been careful to institute any changes slowly, gradually bringing in new ideas, but without antagonising the inhabitants who had lived there all their lives and regarded anything 'new-fangled' with suspicion. The Swansons had been here for four years now and were accepted by most as part of the village. When the previous batch of evacuees had descended on Wynsdown, they had found homes for all the children, though many had now returned to the cities when the expected bombing didn't materialise.

Can we do it again? Avril wondered as she went out into the garden, basking in the pale winter sunshine, to feed her hens. It all looked so peaceful; no sign of the destruction being faced elsewhere. Could they go through all the upheaval again? She gave a sigh and, as she'd promised Caro, went in search of her husband to discuss the idea with him.

She found him in the church talking to Marjorie Bellinger, the squire's wife. The squire, Major Peter Bellinger, had served in Flanders in the Great War and, anxious to do something positive for the war effort, was working hard to ensure that every inch of his land was productive. Marjorie was a stalwart of the church, organising the flower rota, church cleaning and parish magazine deliveries. She was a tall woman in her late fifties, with permed grey hair and serious grey eyes. Conscious of her position in the village as wife of the squire, with its attendant responsibilities, she was always ready to step forward to take a lead in village affairs. Their son, Felix, was a pilot in the RAF, flying with Fighter Command. They, more than anyone in Wynsdown, knew the horrors of the Blitz, fearing for their son each and every night. She was cleaning the brass now, rubbing energetically at the memorial tablet for those from the village who had given their lives in the last war, as she discussed the idea of a Christmas Bazaar with David.

'If we give people enough warning, vicar...' she was saying, but broke off when Avril came running into the church.

They both looked up in surprise and David said, 'My dear, you look flustered. Something happened?'

'Just had Caro on the phone from London.'

'That's nice,' said David, 'is she coming to see us?'

'She wants to send fifteen children from St Michael's down here, to us!'

'Fifteen!' exclaimed Marjorie.

'That's what *I* said,' replied Avril, 'but she says there was a dreadful air raid last night and they were lucky not to be bombed out. She says the children *have* to be moved.'

'Where does she think we're going to put them?' wondered the squire's wife.

'Let's go back to the vicarage for a cup of tea,' suggested the vicar, 'and work it out.'

They walked out into the winter sunshine and across the church-yard to the vicarage gate. It was hard to imagine the Blitz bursting upon them every night for weeks as it had in London. They had heard the occasional plane fly over, but usually too high for them to identify, and so far their nights had remained undisturbed.

'I suppose we'd better reconvene the evacuation committee,' Avril said as they sat round the large scrubbed table in the vicarage kitchen.

Since the outbreak of war this room had become the heart of the house. A large kitchen with a scullery on the side, it looked out over the vicarage garden. The old, solid-fuel range provided an oasis of warmth in the otherwise unheated, sprawling vicarage. David had brought two armchairs in from the chilly drawing room and it had become the place where they ate their meals, sat in the evening listening to the wireless, discussed the worries of the parish and talked through the events of each day. David had his study for seeing parishioners and dealing with parish matters, but very often he brought those, too, into the warm kitchen. It was to the kitchen that they naturally repaired when there were problems to be solved.

'I suppose we'd better,' agreed David. 'We need everyone on board for this.'

'So we're going to say we'll have them?' asked Avril.

David treated her to his gentle smile. 'Of course we are. You ring Caroline back and tell her to sort out her end.' He turned to Marjorie. 'Have you the list of those who offered homes last time?'

'I'm sure I have somewhere, but I think you're right, we need to reinstate the committee, so that everyone feels involved. Finding places for fifteen extra children shouldn't be beyond us, but it'll need careful handling.'

'I'll call a meeting for this evening,' Avril said. 'I'll contact everyone and ask them to come here and we can make proper plans.'

Good as her word, within the hour Avril had rung those committee members who were on the phone and had bicycled to visit those who were not.

'Fifteen! That's a lot,' said Nancy Bright, the postmistress. Nancy was the fount of all village news and Avril had gone to her first, knowing there was no quicker way of disseminating the information than by telling her.

'We're having a meeting of the committee this evening, so if you could come over to the vicarage at seven...'

Andrew Fox, who ran the village general store, said at once he could be there. 'Not surprised your sister wants those kiddies out of London,' he said.

She caught Michael Hampton, the headmaster of the village school, in the lunch hour. 'What you're telling me is that I've got to find space for another fifteen children in the school,' he sighed. But she could see the light of zeal in his eyes and knew he would rise to the challenge and achieve it somehow.

'Maybe not all of them,' she pointed out. 'Some of them will surely be old enough to go down to Cheddar Secondary.'

That evening they all met at the vicarage. Once again they sat round the kitchen table and Marjorie Bellinger produced the list of families who had offered foster care to the first batch of evacuees.

'Of course, some of those children are still here,' she said. 'The Tates still have the Morgan twins, Daphne Cooper is still with Mrs Harper and of course there are the Cleggs.'

There was a groan round the table as they all contemplated the Clegg family. They had arrived soon after war was declared, an expectant mother, Sheila, and four children under eight. They had been housed in a farm cottage belonging to the Bellingers on the manor estate. Having come from Manchester, they were unused to country life and never stopped complaining to the Bellingers about what they considered the shortcomings of the cottage. There were three bedrooms and a kitchen. The privy was in the garden and baths had to be taken in front of the fire. Marjorie doubted if it had been any different where they had come from, but Mrs Clegg assured her that she wasn't used to such primitive conditions. The new baby had arrived, a boy named Eustace, delivered by Dr Masters, and all six still continued to live in the cottage. Mr Clegg had turned up for a weekend several months ago to admire his new son, and Mrs Clegg was now expecting again.

'Let's hope there aren't any more like them,' said Nancy Bright in heart-felt tones.

'Not the children's fault,' Michael Hampton pointed out gently. 'Difficult start in life with a feckless mother and an absent father. The children are not at all bad, all things considered. Young Edwin's quite bright, if you'll pardon the pun, Nancy,' he added with a sideways glance at her.

'I've spoken to my sister again,' Avril told them, bringing them back to the matter in hand. 'She's given me a list of names, so we know who to expect. There are seven boys and eight girls. There are two sets of siblings. One family called Dawson, Paul aged eleven and his two sisters, Frances who's eight and Valerie who's five. I thought we might have them here with us. We've got the room and it means we can keep them together.'

'That sounds fine,' said Marjorie. 'Everyone agreed with that?' She made a note of the names and where they were going on her pad. 'Who are the other family?'

'Jack and Diane Payne. Jack is ten and Diane eight.'

'We could have them,' offered Rose Merton. She and her sister lived together in a small house on the village green. Their father had been the village doctor until he had died ten years earlier and they had stayed on in the village where they had lived most of their lives. 'Violet and I have room for two.'

'All the rest are individuals, but of course if some families are willing to have two that would be a great help.'

'When do they get here?' asked Rose.

'Not sure yet,' replied Avril, 'but I promise I'll let you know as soon as I do.'

By the end of the meeting they had made a list of possible foster homes and tried to match them up with the children on Avril's list. Michael Hampton had the names and ages of the children so that he could decide how he was going to accommodate them at the school.

'I haven't mentioned any of this to Martha Mason yet,' he said. 'I'll discuss it with her at school tomorrow, now that I know exactly who's coming.'

'There is one last thing,' Avril said. 'I should mention Charlotte Smith, she's about fourteen. At least, Charlotte Smith is the name she goes by...'

'What do you mean "the name she goes by"?' asked Nancy.

'The unfortunate child was picked up unconscious in the street after an air raid. She was with another casualty, a man named Peter Smith, from Harrogate. He was dead, but they rushed the girl to hospital and she survived. However, she has amnesia. She has no recollection of the raid and no memory of her life before it. They think the man may have been her father, but they don't really know. She's been given the name Charlotte because, well, she needed a name. My sister, Caroline, just wanted to warn us that this loss of memory is an added problem the poor girl has to contend with. Most of the time she seems to be coping all right, but she does have the occasional panic attack, so we must be prepared for that.'

Caroline had also told Avril that Charlotte was almost certainly half German.

'She speaks English pretty well, Av, but lapses into German when she's under any pressure. We think maybe her mother's German and she's been brought up bilingual. The other possibility is that she's a refugee, but until we know her real name it's virtually impossible to trace her family.'

'Poor child,' Avril said. 'How desperately sad. Let's hope when she's away from all the bombing, her memory'll come back.'

'That's what I'm hoping,' Caroline said, 'but I just thought I'd warn you.'

Avril had decided not to share this second piece of information with the committee yet. It wasn't definite that Charlotte was German and it wouldn't be fair to the child if it turned out not to be true and the whole village supposed she was. She knew that if it were mentioned now, it would, without doubt, be round the village first thing in the morning. Nancy, with the best will in the world, couldn't keep a secret. A secret to Nancy was something you told only one person at a time and then, of course, in complete confidence.

They all got up to leave in a bustle of finding coats and torches to light their way home. Outside, the darkness was complete, the blackout as strictly enforced here as in the towns. David switched off the lights, opened the front door and with a continued mutter of conversation, the evacuation committee disappeared into the night.

When they'd all gone Avril and David flopped down in their chairs in the warmth of the kitchen.

'Well, that didn't go too badly,' Avril said with a sigh of relief. 'Now all we have to do is approach those families and see if they'll take in the evacuees.'

'I'm sure you and Marjorie between you will be able to persuade them,' David said. 'But shouldn't we be having that child, Charlotte, here with us?'

'I would have liked to, but I think we have to take the Dawson children ourselves. It's so important that families stay together and nowhere else has room for all three.'

'You're probably right,' David agreed. 'Come on, old thing,' he said affectionately, pulling her to her feet. 'Bed. You look completely bushed.'

Avril followed him up the stairs, saying as she did so, 'I know Caro's right. We need to get those children out of London.'

'And we will,' David said. 'Now stop worrying. It'll all be fine.'

Chapter Sixteen

In London Caroline was doing her best to cut through any red tape which might prevent the speedy evacuation of her children. She went to the local authority who had legal responsibility for St Michael's and spoke to a rather unhelpful woman named, according to the sign on her desk, Miss Ruth Miles.

'I'm not sure we can simply allow you to remove these children to the country,' she said. 'There's the question of permission from their families.'

'I'm afraid several of the children concerned have no family,' Caroline pointed out. 'Three of them are orphans, another has no knowledge of her family, and several have been bombed out already which is why they're with us in the first place.' She fixed Miss Miles with a resolute stare. 'I can see no possible reason why they should not be moved to a safer environment. Or would you prefer to leave them where they are and risk their lives for even longer during this bloody awful Blitz?'

'There's no need for language like that, Miss Morrison,' scowled Miss Miles.

Caroline tried to rein in her temper. It would be hopeless if she lost Miss Miles's goodwill. 'I'm sorry,' she said, 'but as you can imagine I'm under quite a strain keeping these children safe and it's beginning to tell.' She forced herself to smile. 'What I'm trying to explain, Miss Miles, is that St Michael's is very close to Croydon airport. We seem to be on the direct flight path for the German bombers targeting the airport. All round us last night houses were demolished, burned out or at least rendered uninhabitable.

It is a miracle to me that so far our building has remained undamaged, but seriously, I don't think it will be long before St Michael's is destroyed as well. So, you can see why I need to get these children moved.'

'I'll have to speak to Mr Carver,' Miss Miles said. Though unwilling to admit it, she was probably not senior enough to make such a decision herself. 'Please wait here.'

Caroline Morrison waited… and waited, and was just about to go through the door Miss Miles had used when she returned, followed by a middle-aged man she introduced as 'Mr Carver, who deals with children's homes'.

'Now, Miss Morrison,' he said, 'what is it you want to do?'

So Caroline drew a deep breath and went through the whole thing again.

'I see,' Mr Carver said slowly when she'd finished. 'And you say you have somewhere definite to send these children?'

'Yes, indeed,' she replied, feeling that perhaps now they were actually getting somewhere. 'An offer of foster homes for fifteen children at Wynsdown in Somerset.'

'And what do you know of these places?' he enquired.

'My brother-in-law is the vicar of Wynsdown, David Swanson. It is he and his evacuation committee who have found homes for the children.'

This seemed to silence Mr Carver for a moment. Then he said, 'You do realise that we shan't be able to close St Michael's. Even if we send these children away, we shall have to use you to house others when necessary.'

'So, I had to accept that, in return for permission to evacuate the children down to you,' Caroline told Avril that evening on the phone. 'I have to keep the place open, so that more children can be put at risk even if we've managed to save the present inmates!' She sighed. 'I suppose they have a point. There are always going to be children who need a home, and St Michael's will certainly be needed again.' She gave a wry laugh. 'Unless the Luftwaffe gives up and goes home.'

'So, when will they come?' Avril asked. 'Will you bring them yourself? It'd be lovely if you could, just to give us a chance to see you for a couple of days.'

'It's a nice idea,' Caroline said. 'I'll have to sort out all the travel arrangements and let you know, but I hope to have them on the train tomorrow, or the next day at the latest.'

'We'll be ready,' Avril promised, hoping as she said it that they really would.

The day after the committee meeting, she and Marjorie Bellinger visited the homes of those who had offered to foster evacuees last time.

'Not just bringing them up from the station and putting them in the village hall, like last time, then?' Mrs Marston stood, arms folded, in the doorway, not inviting her callers inside.

Avril treated her to her best smile and said, 'Trying to be a bit better organised this time, Mrs Marston. We know the names and ages of the children coming this time, so we know how many places we have to find.'

'You agreed to take a child last time,' put in Marjorie, 'so we were hoping you'd offer to take another.'

'Not if it's another guttersnipe like the last one,' snapped Mrs Marston. 'Nightmare he was, with his swearing and shouting and turning his nose up at decent, well-cooked food. Always in trouble, he was, here and at school. My Charlie had to take a strap to him on more than one occasion. Don't want another one like that, thank you very much.' She stepped back and began to shut the door, but Avril, with great determination, put her foot in the door so that it wouldn't close.

'Not a boy, Mrs Marston, but perhaps a girl? There are several girls looking for a home.'

'You take your foot out of my door, Mrs Swanson, and I'll think about it. Don't think my Charlie'll be too keen.'

Avril removed her foot and Mrs Marston shut the door firmly in their faces.

'Not sure I want them to foster a child if that's the way they treat them,' remarked Avril as they walked away.

'I do remember the child concerned,' said Marjorie. 'He wasn't easy. I think we were all glad when his father came and took him back to London.'

They continued their enquiries, speaking to each person whom they thought might take on a child. Several felt much the same as Mrs Marston.

'Of course, we did have one last time, but it wasn't really a success. She cried every night and kept us all awake.'

'London kids don't understand the country, do they. Wouldn't drink milk cos it came from our cow, they said it was dirty cos it didn't turn up in a bottle.'

'We had that lad, Bert, but he didn't get on with our Tommy. Always fighting, they were. We were glad when his mum came for him at Christmas.'

'Wouldn't mind a girl,' Janet Tewson in School Lane Cottages said. She was the mother of ten-year-old twin boys and though she'd hoped for a daughter, none had appeared.

'There are two who are good friends,' Avril told her. 'Charlotte and Clare. They'd like to stay together. Perhaps you could have them both.'

'Not sure about two,' said Mrs Tewson, doubtfully. 'How old are they?'

'Fourteen,' replied Avril, consulting her sheet. No one knew how old Charlotte was, of course, but it was an educated guess on Caroline's part.

'Too old,' came the reply and then, 'Any little girls?'

'Two,' said Avril. 'I expect they'd like to stay together, as well.'

'How old?'

'Polly's six and Jane's seven.'

'I'll take the younger one. Polly did you say?'

'Thank you, Mrs Tewson,' Marjorie said. 'That's very kind of you.'

'When're they coming, then?' asked Mrs Tewson.

'Tomorrow or the next day. We'll let you know as soon as we know for sure.'

'She'll have a ration book, won't she?' demanded Janet Tewson, already wondering not only if she'd done the right thing but what her husband, Frank, would say when he got home from the bank in Cheddar.

'Certainly,' Marjorie assured her and wrote down Polly's name against the Tewsons.

Gradually they found homes for all the children on their list, until there was only Charlotte left. Several times they had tried to place her with Clare as Caroline had suggested.

'If you can keep them together, Av, do try. As I told you, Charlotte has extra problems but she and Clare have palled up and she seems much calmer now.'

No one wanted to take on two teenage girls and there were only a few homes where Avril thought she would be comfortable, but none of these was available.

Marjorie herself had agreed to take two of the older boys, Fred Moore and Malcolm Flint, both aged thirteen. She knew Peter would prefer to have boys in the house.

'Know what to do with boys,' he said when she talked to him about fostering. He agreed she could take on two if they were boys and so she'd marked their name against the two oldest, knowing they'd be the hardest to place.

'It's getting late,' Marjorie said, looking at her watch. 'I must get back. I'll have a think and see if I can think of someone else who might help.'

'Thank you for all your help, Marjorie. I think if the worst comes to the worst we'll have to squeeze her into the vicarage. It would be easier if she were a boy; still, I expect we can manage something.'

Marjorie headed off to the manor and Avril turned her steps towards the village green and home. As she reached the vicarage gate she heard someone call her name and paused. Looking round she saw Edith Everard walking towards her.

'I hear you're looking for foster homes,' Miss Everard said without preamble. 'I'll take a girl.'

'That's very good of you,' said Avril in surprise.

She hardly knew Miss Everard. She was not a church-goer and she kept herself very much to herself. She lived alone in a small house on the edge of the village, coming in only occasionally to buy food at the village shop. Avril had seen her catch the bus to Cheddar some mornings and thought she did some sort of work for the Red Cross, but what it was Avril didn't know. When they had arrived in Wynsdown, David had visited every home in the parish, including Miss Everard's, but she had given him short shrift.

'I don't believe in God,' she said. 'And I don't go to church.'

David had smiled. 'Never mind,' he'd replied. 'God believes in you.'

'Then he's more of a fool than even I thought he would be,' she retorted. 'I'm sure you mean well, vicar, but please don't bother me again.'

'As you wish,' David answered, 'but if you ever change your mind or there's anything I can do for you, do please ask me.' He'd held out his hand and grudgingly, Edith Everard had shaken it.

'I could visit her,' Avril had volunteered, 'if you think it would help.'

'No, dear,' David said. 'I don't think it would. Better to leave her alone and see what happens. We can't force ourselves on her and I think that's what she's afraid of.'

'We're looking for a place for a girl called Charlotte,' Avril said. 'She's about fourteen, and—'

'She'll do,' said Miss Everard. 'When does she come?'

Avril told her she'd let her know and the two women parted.

When she told David that they'd managed to find places for every child he was delighted. 'Well done, old thing,' he said. 'Can't have been easy.'

'The strangest thing is,' Avril told him, 'that we hadn't found anywhere for Charlotte, you know, the girl who's lost her memory. Well, your Miss Everard accosted me on the green just now and offered to have her. She was the only one we hadn't managed to place so I was delighted. I thought we were going to have to squeeze her in here.'

'Well, that's good,' David agreed. 'You know, I expect Miss Everard is quite lonely. She'll probably be pleased to have Charlotte's company, even if she doesn't admit it.'

That evening Caroline rang again. 'The day after tomorrow,' she said. 'We'll be coming by train to Cheddar. Can you meet us there?'

'You said "we",' cried Avril. 'Are you really coming down too?'

'Yes, just to bring them, then I'll have to get back.'

'But you stay the night first?'

'Yes, thanks, Avril, of course I will. Can't wait to see you.'

When Avril contacted Marjorie the next day she told her that she had now placed Charlotte, so that every child coming would have a place to go.

'Where is she going?' asked Marjorie.

'Believe it or not, to Miss Everard.'

'To Edith Everard?' Marjorie sounded less than overjoyed. 'Is that a good idea?'

'Why wouldn't it be?' asked Avril in surprise.

'Well, she's not a very...' Marjorie searched for the right word, 'sociable person.'

'Maybe not,' answered Avril testily, 'but she offered without being asked and I said yes.'

'Well, I'm sure it'll work out all right,' Marjorie said. 'Now tell me the arrangements.'

Avril contacted all the foster parents and told them their new charges would be arriving the next afternoon. 'They're coming on the train to Cheddar,' she said, 'and we'll bring them up to Wynsdown on the school bus. They'll only have had a sandwich on their journey down, so they'll need supper when they get here. If you could rustle up something for the first evening, you'll have their ration books after that.'

Avril spent the next day preparing the vicarage for its new inhabitants. She spring-cleaned the two unused bedrooms, moving a portable electric fire from room to room, trying to warm them. She made up beds with clean sheets, looked out towels and hung blankets over the windows as blackout curtains.

She bought some corned beef from Andrew Fox and made a corned beef hash with potatoes from the crop she'd stored in the garage and picked some winter cabbage from the garden.

'I hope they'll like it,' she said doubtfully to David when he came in at lunchtime for a sandwich and some soup.

'Course they will,' he assured her. 'What? Not like your famous corned beef hash?'

'Silly ass,' Avril said affectionately. 'Eat your sandwich.'

'You going to Cheddar to meet the train?' David asked.

'Of course. I've asked Sam to wait with the school bus for the extra children, and we'll all come up here together.'

'Will you all fit in?'

'It'll be bit of a squash,' admitted Avril, 'but Sam says we'll manage.'

After lunch Avril rode her bicycle through the lanes into Cheddar gorge, speeding down to the village below. She went to the school where she found Sam the bus driver sitting in his bus on the main road.

'As soon as they get here I'll bring them along to the bus,' she promised.

'Don't worry,' he said, 'I'll wait. I've explained to the parents in the other villages, so they know we might be late today.'

Avril rode on to the station and there she waited impatiently on the platform for the train that would bring, not only the evacuees, but her beloved sister. At last she saw a puff of smoke wafting into the sky and then she saw it, the train emerging from the cutting, chuffing and wheezing under the bridge and into the station with a whoosh of steam and a squeal of brakes.

As soon as it stopped doors began to open and Caroline jumped down on to the platform. She waved to Avril, but her attention was taken up by the children she'd brought with her.

'Out you get,' she cried, 'and stand over there so I can make sure we've got everyone.' The children piled out on to the platform. The older children carried two cases each, one of their own and another belonging to a younger child.

Caroline did a quick head count and when she was sure she hadn't left anyone on the train, she waved to the guard. 'Got them all!' she called. He blew his whistle and the train drew out of the station, leaving them all wreathed in steam.

Avril ran over to Caroline and gave her a hug. 'Oh, Caro,' she cried, 'it's so good to see you.'

Caroline returned her hug and then said, 'Right. Where to now?'

Avril led them out of the station and along the road to where the bus was waiting. There were several children already sitting in the bus, ready to go home.

'Are we all going to get in there?' Caroline asked doubtfully.

'No problem, miss,' said Sam and he stuck his head in through the door. 'Now then, you kids, squash up there and make room for this lot.'

With a good deal of grumbling the children moved up to make room and eventually everyone was aboard. The last thing to be hoisted on board was Avril's bike and once that was safely in, Sam started the engine and the bus chugged its way up the hill towards the higher Mendip villages.

Avril and Caroline sat in the front and at first there was a strange silence behind them as the children assessed each other. Then the noise began to grow until they could hardly hear each other. Sam raised his voice above it all.

'That's enough noise from you lot,' he bellowed. 'Shut it!' And for a very short while there was quiet again. They reached the first village and several children got out, leaving more space. The remaining children immediately spread out.

'Don't want to sit next to them vaccies,' Avril heard someone say, and looking round was surprised to see it was Stephen Morgan, one of the original 'vaccies'.

When they reached Wynsdown the bus pulled up as usual on the village green and all the children scrambled out. Caroline assembled her group, who were looking nervously about them, and under Avril's guidance led them into the church hall.

There, already waiting, were most of the people who had agreed to foster a child.

Avril had her list with her and as Caroline called a child's name, she called the parent.

Marjorie was there and led her two boys away to the manor. Janet Tewson took Polly Elliott's hand and picking up her suitcase, led her across the green to her new home in School Lane.

At last there were only the Dawson children and Charlotte left standing in the hall. 'You're staying with us,' Avril told the Dawsons. She turned to Charlotte. 'You'll be staying with Miss Everard,' she said. 'She'll be here as soon as she can, but the evening bus from Cheddar doesn't get in for another half an hour, so I said I'd take you home with me and she'll collect you from the vicarage.' She saw Charlotte look uncertainly at Caroline and said in a low voice, 'She does understand what I'm saying, doesn't she?'

Charlotte had understood, but she was nervous about being left with no one she recognised. She'd hoped that she and Clare would be in the same place, but Clare had been hurried off by a harassed-looking woman with her hair tied up in a scarf who'd said, 'Hurry up, dear, Mr Prynne will be home for his tea shortly.' Clare had turned to wave, and then disappeared out of the door, encouraged by Mrs Prynne bumping the suitcase against her legs.

She watched the other children being collected and taken away, until she was left standing alone as the Dawson children gathered round the woman who seemed to be in charge. Somewhere in the back of her mind she felt that this was familiar, that she'd done all this before, but try as she might, she had no idea where or when. Then Miss Morrison came over and smiled at her.

'My sister says the lady who you're going to live with, Miss Everard, is very nice. She lives by herself, so I'm sure she'll be more than glad of your company. We're all going over to my sister's house now and Miss Everard will come and fetch you when she gets home from work.'

They left the hall and Avril led them in through the vicarage gate. As they reached the front door it was flung open and David Swanson was there to greet them.

'Welcome, welcome to Wynsdown,' he cried. 'Come along in and we'll soon get you settled.' They trooped indoors and David took them into the kitchen.

'Here we are,' he said. 'Now then, who are you?'

The boy stepped forward and said, 'Please sir, I'm Paul and these is Frances and Valerie.' He pointed to his sisters who were hiding behind Miss Morrison's back. 'But we call them Fran and Val… if that's all right, sir.'

'That's excellent,' replied David. 'Fran and Val they shall be. Now, I'm Mr Swanson, but everyone calls me "vicar", so I think you'd better call me "vicar" too.'

'Please, sir, what do we call her?' asked Paul nervously, pointing to Avril who was standing watching her husband take charge. 'Do we call her Mrs Vicar?'

This was greeted with laughter which made the boy flush red with embarrassment, but the vicar said, 'I think that's the perfect name for her. Mrs Vicar! Good idea, Paul. Well done.' He turned to his wife. 'Now, Mrs Vicar, I think you'd better show them where they're sleeping, don't you?'

Avril swept them off upstairs and Charlotte was left waiting in the kitchen with the vicar and Miss Morrison. She could hear excited voices upstairs as the Dawson children were shown their bedrooms and wished she was going to stay in this warm, welcoming house. The vicar told her to sit down and she perched on one of the chairs by the table. He and Miss Morrison were chatting together, both eager to catch up on what had been happening and Charlotte let her thoughts wander as she so often did these days. She remembered the advice given to her by Sister Miller: 'Just let things float to the front of your mind.'

It's so stupid, she thought for the umpteenth time. I can remember her advice, I can remember what she looked like, I can remember *her* name. Why can't I remember my own?

It was as the Dawsons and Mrs Vicar came back downstairs that the doorbell rang. Mrs Vicar opened the door and there standing on the step was a tall thin woman, her hair scraped back into a bun, her expression strangely lifeless. When she forced a smile to her lips it didn't reach her dark, deep-set eyes.

'Oh, Miss Everard,' cried Avril. 'You're here. That's good. Charlotte is here in the kitchen waiting for you.'

Charlotte turned to see the woman she was going to live with

and her heart sank. She wanted to cry, 'No! Please not with her!'
Her thoughts must have shown on her face because Miss Morrison
said briskly, 'Say hallo to Miss Everard, Charlotte.'

Chapter Seventeen

It was cold and dark as Charlotte followed the bobbing light of Miss Everard's torch through the village. She set a good pace and Charlotte almost had to run to keep up with her, scurrying along, changing her suitcase from hand to hand as she went. At the edge of the village they turned up a narrow lane and came to a small house, set back from the road behind high hedges. Miss Everard paused at the gate, waiting for her new charge to catch up, and then led her up the path to the house.

'Come in,' she said as she opened the front door, 'and wait here while I see to the blackout.'

Charlotte stood, waiting in the darkness, as Miss Everard put down her bag and disappeared. Suddenly the house was flooded with light and Miss Everard reappeared in the hall. 'What did you say your name was?'

'I don't know my name,' Charlotte said, a trace of misery in her voice, 'but I'm called Charlotte.'

'Well, don't just stand there, Charlotte,' Miss Everard said testily. 'Take your coat off and come into the warm.'

Charlotte did as she was told and followed her hostess into the kitchen, where a solid-fuel stove just managed to take the chill from the air. This, Miss Everard attacked with a poker, riddling it violently before grabbing a hod of coke and pouring it in through the top.

'Hadn't gone out,' she said, 'so it'll soon warm up in here.' She turned and seemed to look at Charlotte properly for the first time.

'Charlotte,' she said, 'the vicar's wife tells me you've lost your memory. We'll have to see if we can get it back for you. Come along upstairs now and I'll show you your room.' Miss Everard had an abrupt way of speaking, so that she always sounded irritable when she spoke.

Is she always cross? wondered Charlotte as she followed her out of the kitchen.

Miss Everard led the way up the stairs to a square landing, off which there were four doors.

'This room's yours,' she said, opening one of them. 'Used to be mine when I was a child.' The room was chilly, with its blackout curtains already drawn across the windows, but it was neatly and comfortably furnished with a bed, a chair and table and a chest of drawers. A wardrobe with a long mirror on its door stood in one corner and under the blacked-out window was a broad window seat.

'Bathroom's next door,' Miss Everard said, with a wave of her hand. 'Now, why don't you get yourself unpacked and then come down for supper. Turn off the light when you come.'

Charlotte opened her small suitcase and took out the clothes she'd been given by Matron. They were few enough, but adequate, and she laid them carefully in the chest of drawers. She caught sight of herself in the mirror and paused in front of it for a moment or two, staring at her reflection. Staring back at her was a pale-faced girl with straggly dark hair and brown eyes, thin, almost skinny. Thin wrists stuck out from the sleeves of her red jersey and her skirt seemed to hang off her. The reflection startled her; there'd been no mirrors at St Michael's, she hadn't seen herself since before she was injured and she hardly recognised herself.

Who am I? she wondered for the millionth time. Where do I come from?

This had become her most recent question. She knew that she could speak both English and German, so perhaps she was German. Sometimes she caught herself thinking in German, but she tried not to. After all, Germany was bombing London, killing thousands, and she didn't *want* to be German. But suppose she was. Why had she been in London?

Miss Morrison had tried to come up with an answer for her. 'It could be that you're a refugee,' she suggested. 'Perhaps you're Jewish. You could have been sent here to escape from the Nazis; lots of children were, you know.'

But why had she been out on the street during an air raid?

'Probably just bad luck,' Miss Morrison said. 'You don't like going into the air raid shelter, do you? So perhaps you were caught in the street but wouldn't go into a shelter. What do you think?'

Charlotte didn't know what to think. All she knew for sure was that she couldn't remember, she'd been concussed and had broken her arm. The plaster had been removed just before she'd left London, but her arm still ached when she was cold and she cradled it against her now. Then she shrugged and turning off the light went down to the warmth of the kitchen.

Downstairs she paused at the kitchen door. Miss Everard was busy at the stove, stirring something in a large saucepan.

'Soup to warm us up,' she said, glancing over her shoulder. On the table was the heel of a loaf and a wedge of cheese. Two places had been laid with plates, knives and spoons. 'Glasses in the cupboard,' she said, pointing towards a cupboard in the corner.

Charlotte fetched the glasses and put them on the table. There was a water jug in the cupboard as well, so she took it to the sink and filled it. Miss Everard gave a nod of approval and then, lifting the pan from the stove, poured the soup into two bowls.

'Right,' she said, 'let's eat before it gets cold.'

The soup was thick with vegetables, hot and delicious. Miss Everard cut two generous slices of bread and passing one to Charlotte, dipped her own into the soup. Charlotte followed suit, and for a moment or two they ate in silence.

'Tomorrow is Saturday,' Miss Everard said. 'You and all the new children are going to a meeting in the church hall when everything will be explained to you, about school and the village and such. I'll come with you so that we can plan how we'll do things. All right?'

'Yes, Miss Everard,' Charlotte replied.

'I don't think you can call me that now you're living here,' Miss Everard said with a tight smile. 'Miss Edie will do.'

'Yes, Miss Edie.'

Silence fell again as they finished the soup and ate their bread and cheese, then Charlotte, plucking up courage said, 'The soup is very good, thank you, and the cheese tastes good, too.' She had hardly spoken since she arrived and it was only now that Edie Everard noticed her accent. Certainly not the gentle West Country burr of the local area, but not the loud and to her ear, slovenly, accents of the earlier evacuees either; something harsher, more guttural. European, but not quick and light like the French.

'You speak good English,' she remarked. 'Do you speak German as well?' The question was sharp and Charlotte hesitated.

That hesitation said it all as far as Edith Everard was concerned. She had been given a German child to foster, to have living here with her in her home.

'You do, don't you?' she said, a sudden expression of hatred flickering across her face. 'You're German, aren't you?'

'I don't know,' came the simple reply. 'I don't know who I am.'

Edith set about clearing the table, banging the plates together, clattering the cutlery. That vicar's wife had foisted a German child on her, without so much as a warning. A sudden rage flooded through her as she filled the sink with water and began to wash up. How dare they do this to her? She, who had lost everything to the Germans in 1918. She could hardly breathe and her furious silence enveloped the kitchen, a thick fog of anger smothering everything, leaving Charlotte bewildered and afraid. Not knowing what else to do, she took a tea towel from the rail beside the stove and started to dry up the dishes as Miss Edie slammed them down on the draining board.

'I think you should go to bed, now,' Miss Edie said when at last she had regained control of her emotions. 'I will see you in the morning.'

Charlotte said nothing. She simply turned and went upstairs. As she lay in bed later she found she was shaking. She saw again the flash of hatred on Miss Edie's face. People here in England hated Germans and she, Charlotte, almost certainly was one. As this thought came to her she realised that once again her thoughts had been in German. Tired as she was after the long journey from London, it took Charlotte a very long time to fall asleep, lying awake long after she heard Miss Edie come up the stairs, use the bathroom and close her bedroom door.

Miss Edie didn't sleep easily either. The rage which had almost consumed her downstairs when she realised that the child was a German, had eased somewhat now. But the familiar ache, the one she had embraced and clung to ever since she'd received the telegram in August 1918, was still there, a part of her. She thought about Herbert as she did every night before she went to sleep. His picture, a faded sepia, stood on her bedside table, the last thing she saw at night, the first thing she looked at in the morning. Forever young, he smiled out at her, erect and proud of the sergeant's stripes on his arm, his young face, with its neat moustache, as handsome as the day she had kissed him goodbye at the end of his leave. The day she had worn, for the first time, her engagement ring. Turning on the light again, she opened the drawer of her bedside table and pulled out the telegram still folded into its buff envelope, dog-eared and faded. She unfolded it and read again the fateful words...

Regret to inform you that Sergeant Herbert Clapham of the Cheshire Regiment was Missing in Action, presumed killed 10th August 1918. Secretary of War extends his sympathy.

How many times had she read it? It would be impossible to count. Herbert was never coming home to marry her. She would mourn him for the rest of her life.

His body was never recovered. His name was recorded on the Menin Gate with thirty-eight thousand others, named but with no known resting place. Edith's life had ended the day the telegram arrived.

Oh, she still lived with her parents in Blackdown House, where she'd been born. She'd nursed her father when he'd caught Spanish flu in 1919 and died. She'd nursed her mother, who'd recovered, and she continued to care for her until the day she died in 1930, but Edith had never recovered from the loss of the man she loved.

Something inside her had shrivelled up when she'd opened that telegram, and it had never blossomed again. She hated everything
German. No longer able to enjoy the music of German composers,
Beethoven, Brahms, Mendelssohn, she refused to listen and thus
denied herself a pleasure that she'd enjoyed since her youth. She had
lived alone at Blackdown House ever since, cutting herself off from
friends to live with her memories. Once a member of the church
choir, she had ceased to believe in God; a god who could allow her
Herbert to die and leave her alone in the wasteland of the rest of her
life was no comfort to her.

Her offer of a home for an evacuated child had been her first real
act of unselfishness for years and now that had backfired. Who had
she been landed with? A German child.

Not the child's fault, she had to admit, but whether the people
who had brought her here chose to admit it or not, she, Edith
Everard, knew that the child was German. She could tell.

The next morning dawned bright and cold. Charlotte, wrapped in
a blanket in her unheated room, pulled back the curtains and,
perching on the window seat, looked out. Below her was a carefully
tended vegetable garden, with neat rows of sprouts and cabbages,
and she guessed where all the vegetables in last night's soup had
come from. She didn't know what any of them were, but it was clear
that Miss Edie was obeying the instruction to dig for victory. Dig for
Victory. Charlotte had seen that written up somewhere, not just on
a poster – they were everywhere – but in huge letters. Where?

She stared out across the country beyond the garden, undulating
fields marked with hedges or stone walls and the occasional stand
of trees stark against the winter sky. Tussocks of grass and patches
of winter bramble caught the sunlight, while dips and hollows
remained shadowed, a patchwork of winter colour. Sheep were
grazing in several of the fields, some cattle stood together under the
trees in another and away in the distance, she could just make out
some farm buildings, grey stone with slate roofs as if they'd grown
up from the limestone beneath them. Further off was a line of hills,
hardly more than a smudge on the skyline. Charlotte had never been

in such remote countryside before. It seemed to stretch endlessly in every direction. When they had driven up through the lanes from Cheddar the previous afternoon, the road had been between high hedges and she'd seen nothing to prepare her for the wide expanses she could see from here. There was something a little scary about so much space.

As she sat on the window seat Charlotte wondered what was going to happen to her next. She knew Miss Edie had been angry when she realised that she, Charlotte, was German, but what was she going to do about it? If she'd had somewhere else to go, Charlotte would have packed up her suitcase again and left. But she had nowhere except out into the endless fields that surrounded the village.

Miss Edie called her to come down for breakfast and dishing up a bowl of porridge set it down before her. It was clear that she had already eaten hers as the empty bowl lay on the draining board.

'The meeting in the church hall is at half past ten. I am going to work in the garden until then. You are to wash the dishes and clean the kitchen. I have made my own bed, you are to make yours. Do you understand?' She had spoken in a strangely slow and deliberate manner as if afraid that her German charge wouldn't be able to understand her.

'Yes, I understand you very well,' Charlotte replied. 'You do not have to come with me to the meeting. I will pack my case and go to Mrs Vicar. Her sister goes to London today. I will go with her. You do not want me here and me, I do not wish to stay.'

'Don't be ridiculous, child,' snapped Edith. 'You'll do no such thing.' She was taken aback at and not a little impressed at Charlotte's confrontation. 'I'm merely asking you to help with some of the chores, while I get on in the garden. Be ready to go at quarter past ten.'

Charlotte washed up the few breakfast pots and then went back upstairs. She was just going into her room when she noticed the door of Miss Edie's room was ajar and curiosity overcame her; pushing it wider she crept into the room and looked about her. It was much bigger than her own and had probably been that of Miss

Edie's parents when she was a child. It was furnished comfortably enough, but the furniture was old and shabby and it was clear that nothing had been done to smarten the room up for many years. The walls were papered with a floral wallpaper, but the colours were dim and in places the paper was torn. A threadbare rug covered much of the floor and the blackout curtains hanging on either side of the window had seen better days. Charlotte tiptoed over to the window and peeped through a gap in the curtain. In the garden below she saw Miss Edie, busy hoeing. Safe from interruption, Charlotte turned her attention back to the room. There on the table by the bed lay a book, a pair of spectacles and an old photograph in a silver frame. A uniformed soldier with curly hair stared out at her with smiling eyes.

Who was he? she wondered as she picked him up for a closer look. A husband? A brother? A boyfriend? The photo looked quite old.

There was nothing much else to see. The bed had been neatly made and Miss Edie's dressing gown hung on a peg on the back of the door. Charlotte left the room, making sure that the door was left a little ajar as she'd found it. There was one more door on the landing and, wondering what was in that room, she gently turned the handle. The door was jammed or locked. Either way, it wouldn't open. Charlotte went back into her own room and made her bed as she'd been told. She was still sorely tempted to pack her case and take it with her to the meeting in the church hall. She hadn't lied. If Miss Edie didn't want her here, she didn't want to stay. She would ask Miss Morrison if she could go back to London with her, then she'd return and fetch her things.

She went back downstairs and looked into the two other rooms. The one next to the kitchen was a dining room, rather dark, its heavy furniture covered with an overlay of dust. Clearly it hadn't been used, or cleaned, for some time. The other door opened into a sitting room. It was furnished with shabby but comfortable-looking armchairs and could have made a cosy place to sit and read or listen to the wireless had the fire been lit. A piano stood against one wall and a bookcase full of books against another, but this room, too, felt cold and unused. These two rooms had no blackout curtains or screens and Charlotte guessed they didn't need them, so seldom were they used. She was just investigating the cupboard under the stairs when she heard the back door open and, not wanting to be found prying, she beat a hasty retreat upstairs; by the time Miss Edie reached the landing, Charlotte was sitting on her window seat staring out across the Mendip Hills.

Together they walked back into the village and arrived at the church hall just as it began to fill up with the evacuees and their hosts and hostesses. Mrs Vicar was at the door greeting everyone and as soon as Charlotte saw Clare she broke away and went over to say hallo.

Clare was sitting next to a large woman wearing a cross-over apron and a scarf tied round the back of her head. Charlotte flopped down on her other side.

'What's your place like?' she muttered.

With a quick sideways glance to make sure Mrs Prynne wasn't listening, Clare said, 'Not too bad. Had some sort of stew last night. Weren't too bad. Have to share a room with Sandra, Mrs Prynne's daughter. Don't like that, she snores something rotten. What about you?'

'Got a room to myself,' Charlotte admitted, 'and the supper was good. She don't like the Germans though.'

'Nor does anyone!' exclaimed Clare.

'But she thinks I am one.'

'But that's stupid!' cried Clare. 'You ain't!'

'Think I might be,' Charlotte said. 'That's the trouble.'

'Well, even if you was, you ain't one of *those* Germans, are you? Stands to reason. If you was one of them you'd be in Germany, wouldn't you?'

'Anyway, I think she's going to say she won't have me, an' if she does I'm going to ask Miss Morrison to take me back to London. I don't like the country. There's no houses, just fields and sheep an' that.'

At that moment Avril Swanson moved to the front of the hall and clapping her hands, asked everyone to sit down so she could start the meeting.

'First of all I'd like to ask my sister, Caroline Morrison, to say a few words about the children she's brought down here and her reason for doing so. After that I'll explain how we plan to make these children welcome in our village and to integrate them into village life.

'What's "integrate"?' Charlotte murmured to Clare, who shrugged and said, 'Have to wait and see.'

Caroline Morrison got to her feet and, looking at the expectant faces before her, treated them to her most charming smile.

'First of all I'd like to thank you all, all the people of Wynsdown, for making the children from St Michael's home in Streatham so welcome. St Michael's is a home for children who, due to the war, have been left with no other home and often with no family to care for them. We at St Michael's take these children in and look after them until we can find them somewhere, better, safer to live. Sometimes they are able to return to their families when they have been rehoused, others may move on to another home, perhaps more suitable to their age, and yet others may be evacuated to villages like yours, which are, we hope, too small to interest the bombers. The trouble with St Michael's is that it is close to Croydon airport and thus in a target area for the bombers. Many of the houses round our home have been completely destroyed or at the least made uninhab-itable. There have been casualties, sadly some fatalities, and so I have been allowed to bring these children here, to you, knowing that it may be this that saves their lives. You, taking in these children, are doing more than offering them a home. You're offering them a future, a future they might otherwise not have. So we all thank you and will do our best to make sure that you never regret your gener-osity.' Miss Morrison treated them all to another smile and, to a round of applause, sat down beside her sister.

Avril, applauding too, stood up again. 'Now, this afternoon we're going to have a party here in the church hall so that we can all get to know one another. All the children in the village are invited, as are those of you who are looking after them. The sooner we get to know everyone the better it will be. However, in the meantime, we need to sort out schools. Now, children, if I call your name please stand up so we can see who you are and I'll tell you what you'll be doing after the weekend. Fred Moore, please stand.' Flushing a furious red, Fred stood up, followed by Malcom Flint, Molly Hart, Charlotte Smith and Clare Pitt, as their names were called.

'Now, all of you will be going down to Cheddar on the school bus with the other children who attend Cheddar Secondary School. You must be on the village green, outside the Magpie, by a quarter past eight. The bus won't wait for you if you're late, so please do be there in plenty of time. Right, children, you can sit down again now.' Clare and Charlotte subsided on to the seats, pleased that at least they'd be going to school together. 'That's if I stay,' muttered Charlotte. She had seen Miss Edie speaking to Mrs Vicar before the meeting began and she was wondering what had been said about her.

'Course you'll be staying,' replied Clare softly. 'Not going to send you back to all them bombs now, are they?'

As they had been whispering together, the rest of the children had been called to stand and be recognised. When they'd all answered their names they were told to sit down again and Mr Hampton stepped forward to introduce both himself and Miss Mason, who would be teaching this group.

'No need to be frightened,' he assured them with a grin. 'Miss Mason and I are both very nice and we don't bite. Just come to school a little bit early on Monday morning and we'll get you settled in before the other children arrive.'

The meeting broke up, but before it did Avril reminded everyone they were asked to the party that afternoon. 'And there'll be roast chestnuts for us all. Dr Masters has collected loads from the tree in his garden and he'll be roasting them here this afternoon.'

As soon as she could, Charlotte edged her way through the crowd to where Miss Morrison stood.

'I don't like it here,' she said without preamble. 'I want to come back to London with you.'

'Charlotte, my dear,' Miss Morrison replied, 'I'm afraid that's impossible. We've managed to get you all safely away from the bombing and I'm afraid you won't be able to come back until the war's over.'

'But that may not be for years,' wailed Charlotte.

'I know, but it's for your own safety. Charlotte, dear, we don't even know, yet, where you belong. When we do we want to be able to hand you back to your family, safe and sound.'

'What happens if I remember?' Charlotte demanded. 'If I remember who I am? What happens then?'

'If you remember, write to me at St Michael's and tell me. Then I'll see what I can do. In the meantime, you have to stay here.'

'That Miss Edie, the one what I'm staying with, don't want me,' she said.

'Actually you're wrong there, Charlotte. I was talking to her earlier and she told me and my sister that she did want you. She wants you to stay.'

'She doesn't like me because I'm German,' said Charlotte flatly.

'That's not quite true, but I will tell you something if you promise not to mention it to Miss Everard.'

'What?'

'She is still very sad because the man she was going to marry was killed at the end of the last war. He was in the trenches and was killed. You have to understand it's very difficult to get over something like that,' Caroline said, thinking as she said it that Edith Everard ought to make an effort and not wallow in self-pity for twenty years.

Charlotte remembered the photo she'd seen in Miss Edie's bedroom that morning of a soldier in uniform. A young man, much younger than Miss Edie, she had thought, but of course not much younger than Miss Edie would have been in 1918.

'Give it a few days, Charlotte, and see how you get on. If things are too difficult, tell my sister and I promise you she'll move you.'

At the end of the morning the two of them walked home to Blackdown House. Miss Edie heated some more of her special soup, saying as she did so, 'I managed to get some mince at the butcher in Cheddar yesterday, so I thought I'd make a cottage pie for this evening. Do you like cottage pie?'

'I don't know,' Charlotte said cautiously.

Miss Edie gave her a smile and said, 'Well, we'll find out tonight, won't we?'

Chapter Eighteen

The party in the church hall was only a qualified success. The village children all turned up, seduced by the promise of roast chestnuts and jammy buns. Marjorie Bellinger produced the buns and Avril raided her stock of home-made blackberry jam to go inside. The evacuees were brought along by their host families and the two groups stood on either side of the hall eyeing each other up.

'It's like when we were youngsters going to the village dance,' Janet Tewson said to Sally Prynne. 'Remember how we used to be one side of the hall, watching the lads on the other?'

Sally laughed. 'I remember you trying to catch the eye of your Frank,' she said.

Janet laughed too. 'Well,' she said, 'caught more than his eye, didn't I?' She beckoned her twins over. 'Dick, Chris, you look after our Polly, she's your little sister now, remember.'

Dick pulled a face, but Chris went across to Polly who was hiding among the other children from St Michael's. He grabbed her by the hand and said, 'Mum says you're to come with us.' Polly started to cry and he said angrily, 'What you making that din for? I was going to get you a hot chestnut and a bun.'

'Don't like hot chestnuts,' wailed Polly, who had never had one.

'Bet you like jammy buns though,' persisted Chris. 'Come on, Polly-dolly. Mum says come over and have a bun.'

Gradually, the two groups began to mix. Dr Masters was doing a roaring trade with his hot chestnuts and once the London children had tasted them they were back for more.

'I thought you had hot-chestnut men in the streets of London,' Nancy said to Caroline.

'Used to and probably will again,' answered Caroline, 'but just now the streets of London are not what they used to be. The older kids might remember, but some of these are only five or six.'

Caroline was watching Charlotte quite carefully. She had decided to stay another night before returning to London and not simply because her old friend, Henry Masters, had asked her round for supper, but because she was genuinely worried about Charlotte and her placement. Avril had been accosted before the morning meeting by Edith Everard, demanding to know why she hadn't been told that her charge was a German.

Avril, a little thrown by the vehemence of her question, said, 'We're not sure she is. But does it really matter?' She was about to say, 'She's a child that needs a loving home, isn't that what you were offering?' when Miss Everard interrupted.

'It matters to me,' she said. 'We're at *war* with the Germans... for the *second time* in twenty years!'

'I'm well aware of that, Miss Everard, but we aren't at war with Charlotte Smith.'

At that moment Caroline looked across the room and seeing the expression on Miss Everard's face realised that Avril was having problems, so she walked over to join the two women.

'Everything all right, Avril?' she asked cheerfully.

'I'm afraid we shall have to move Charlotte. Miss Everard doesn't want her and—'

'I didn't say I didn't want her,' snapped Miss Everard. 'I simply said it would have been a courtesy to tell me in advance that the child was German. I'm perfectly happy to give her a home, but I think you should have warned me.'

'I apologise if you think I misled you, Miss Everard,' said Avril, keeping a tight rein on her temper, 'it was entirely unintentional; but now we have to be sure that she's in a home where she's welcome.'

'Well, she is,' insisted Miss Everard, 'and I want her to stay.' Perversely, she found it was indeed so. She had come to complain about the situation, but as soon as the vicar's wife said she was removing Charlotte from her care, Miss Edie discovered she wanted her to stay. 'I'm happy to have the girl,' she said, now furiously back-pedalling, 'it's the lack of courtesy, the lack of communication, that I was complaining about.'

'Very well, if you're sure,' Avril agreed, biting her tongue to remain civil, 'but if you change your mind at any time, or if things ever become difficult, please tell me at once and I shall move her in with us at the vicarage.'

'I'm sure that won't be necessary,' Miss Everard said stiffly, adding, 'Is there anything else I ought to know about her?'

'She doesn't like small spaces, doesn't like being shut in. She will go into a shelter if she has to, provided she feels she can get out in a hurry, so we usually sit her near the door.'

Miss Everard nodded. 'I'll remember,' she said, and turning, stalked away.

'I hope we've made the right decision,' Avril said to her sister. 'It's not going to be easy for the child.'

'She's tougher than you think,' Caroline assured her. 'Don't know what her past is, but it's clear it hasn't been easy and she's come through it all.'

'What was all that about?' Nancy Bright had seen the confrontation and had wandered over to discover what was going on.

'It's just that we think Charlotte Smith is probably half German, or possibly a German refugee, and Miss Everard is up in arms because we didn't tell her so.'

'You've fostered a German girl with Edith Everard?' Nancy stared at Avril in disbelief.

'Well, why not?' Avril was disconcerted by Nancy's incredulity.

'She lost her fiancé at the very end of the Great War and it turned her peculiar. She's never forgiven the Germans for killing him. She's lived alone since her parents died and quite frankly I think she's a bit potty.'

'Good gracious,' cried Avril, 'why on earth didn't you tell me?'

'Well, I'm not one to gossip,' Nancy replied, perfectly straight-faced, 'but I'd have assumed you knew. Anyway, I didn't know that

Edie had offered to take in a vaccie and I didn't know the child was German.'

'We don't know she is,' cried Avril in frustration. 'We don't know who she is and nor does she, poor kid. God, I wish we'd just made room for her at the vicarage.'

'Leave her for now,' Caro advised. 'She's been moved from pillar to post enough; but keep a strict eye on her.'

After the meeting Edith and Charlotte had left together and later, both had come back for the party. As soon as she got there, Charlotte sought out Clare who had already devoured one bun and was licking every last speck of jam from her fingers.

'Hey, Charlotte, you should have one of these. They're ever so good.'

Charlotte and Clare discussed the homes where they had been billeted. Clare, now living with Mr and Mrs Prynne and their daughter, Sandra, was fairly philosophical.

'Could be worse,' she said. 'We listened to the wireless last night. Sandra's not coming to school with us yet. She's not eleven till the spring.'

'At least you got a proper family to live with. I only got Miss Edie,' Charlotte said.

'Is that what you call her?' asked Clare, intrigued. 'Miss Edie? Bit of a mouthful, ain't it?'

'What do you call yours?' Charlotte asked.

'She said to call her Ma, like Sandra and Mr Prynne both do. Easy that.'

'What d'you think this school will be like?' wondered Charlotte. 'We got to go on the bus and have our dinner there.'

'Be all right,' Clare said. 'I like school.'

Suddenly there was the sound of a bell and Mr Hampton moved into the middle of the room.

'Right, you lot,' he said. 'We're going to play some games now. Miss Mason's going to play the piano and you can all play musical bumps.'

Miss Mason settled herself at the piano and began to play. The older children looked on with disdain as the younger ones rushed into the middle to join in. Charlotte and Clare watched. They wouldn't have minded joining in, especially when the winner was given a twist of liquorice, but by then it was too late.

It was cold outside, but it didn't stop them going out to run races across the village green. Mr Hampton, Dr Masters and the vicar put them all into teams, being careful not only to mix up the St Michael's children with the Wynsdown ones, but to mix girls with boys. They had laid out a track, marked with bean bags, and for half an hour the noise on the green was raucous as the children screamed their team-mates home in relay races, three-legged races and lastly, a sack race.

Charlotte found herself in a team with Teddy Baker and little Valerie Dawson from St Michael's. Another older boy from the village was chosen as the team leader. His name was Billy Shepherd. He was tall and muscular with fair, curly hair and deep-set blue eyes. He looked round his team and, seeing little Val standing to one side, went across and bending down to her said, 'Hallo. Who are you?' Val cowered away from him and Charlotte said, 'That's Val. She's only five. She doesn't know who you are.'

'I'm Billy Shepherd and I live at Charing Farm on the hill. Who are you?'

For the first time since she had left the hospital Charlotte did not say she didn't know. Looking up into Billy's wide friendly face she answered, 'Charlotte Smith. I come from St Michael's.'

'I know that,' he said. 'I been watching you.'

Charlotte looked startled. 'Have you? Why do you watch me?'

'Don't know,' Billy replied, scratching his head. 'Liked the look of you, I suppose.'

Somehow an unacknowledged link had been forged. Billy organised his team carefully, making sure everyone was included. When little Valerie Dawson was running in the relay race, he encouraged her with raucous cheers, and when Charlotte was tied to a local girl, Emmy Gripton, to run three-legged, he led the applause when they won.

However, when the races were over and the last of the liquorice awarded, the children quickly returned to their two groups, locals on one side of the hall and evacuees on the other; each group eyeing the other with suspicion.

'They'll soon sort themselves out,' Michael Hampton assured Caroline Morrison when she commented on this. 'Children are very tribal, you know, but they'll soon shake down together. See that child over there?' He pointed to a small red-haired boy standing with the village children. 'That's Sidney Morgan. He and his twin, Stephen, came with the first batch of evacuees, but, as you can see, he regards himself as a local now.'

As the evening drew in and the chill of the November day slipped towards freezing, the villagers gathered up their families and new charges and hurried home to the warmth of their own firesides.

Miss Edie set the usual brisk pace as she and Charlotte left the village green and it wasn't long before they were back at Blackdown House with Miss Edie again attacking the recalcitrant stove.

'I'll put the pie in the oven,' Miss Edie said. 'I pulled some leeks earlier, why don't you clean and chop those?'

'Please, Miss Edie, what's leeks?'

Miss Edie seemed about to snap out an answer, when she thought better of it and said, 'Here, I'll show you.' She reached into a bucket at the back door and pulled out a bundle of leeks, mud clinging to their roots. She banged them against the side of the bucket to get the worst off and then put them on the draining board.

'Here,' she said, 'watch.' With the sweep of a sharp knife she cut one lengthways and showed Charlotte how to clean out any mud from inside, rinsing the leek clean in the sink before chopping it into rings. She passed the knife over and returned her attention to the cottage pie. Charlotte picked up a leek and was soon chopping and cleaning as if she'd done it all her life. When she'd finished Miss Edie handed her some carrots. Charlotte didn't need lessons in peeling carrots, she simply picked up the knife and began to pare away the skin.

'Well,' said Miss Edie, 'you've obviously done that before. Perhaps you used to help your mother in the kitchen.'

Charlotte was about to say 'I don't know,' but Miss Edie interrupted her. 'I know you don't think you know, but it's snippets like these that will help you remember. You've made your bed, you've washed the dishes, you've helped lay the table. Clearly you've done this at home.'

'Yes,' Charlotte agreed slowly, 'yes, you must be right.'

Supper was a much easier meal than the night before. Now she had got over her shock about Charlotte's probable nationality, Miss Edie found that she was intrigued by the girl. Clearly she didn't remember anything about her family, but she did certain things as a matter of course. Certainly she was intelligent; she spoke two languages. And she was courageous, too, confronting her, Miss Edie, this morning, taking the initiative and threatening to leave when she realised that she was unwanted. It was probably this show of courage and determination that had changed Miss Edie's mind; she had indeed been going to demand that Avril Swanson take the girl back, but on the point of losing her, she suddenly realised that she wanted her to stay.

Monday morning saw the older children waiting on the village green for the school bus. Charlotte stood with Clare and the four other St Michael's children, a separate group from the locals. Charlotte recognised some of the children who had been in her team at the party, but none of them seemed to notice her. When the bus rumbled round the corner it already carried a few children. The Wynsdown children clambered aboard, the locals loudly confident, St Michael's almost silent and apprehensive.

The journey was noisy, with children from another village added to the load and when they arrived at school the children poured out of the bus and into the school yard, leaving the newcomers standing outside.

'Come on,' said Malcolm Flint, taking charge, 'we'd better go in.'

It wasn't easy, but once they'd been allocated to classes and the actual school day started, they began to find their feet. Charlotte, Clare and Molly were in the same class, so at least they had each other, staying together when they went out at break times and at dinner time. Their class teacher, Miss Davis, spoke to each one, taking down her name and address to pass on to the school secretary. When she came to Charlotte, Charlotte simply said, 'Charlotte Smith, Blackdown House, Wynsdown.'

The trouble began the next morning, waiting outside the Magpie. As the bus drew to a halt, one of the village boys, Tommy Gurney, shoved Fred Moore aside as he tried to get on to the bus and said, 'Vaccies go last.' Fred, in the same class as Tommy, had been taunted with 'Vaccie' all the previous day and now he'd had enough. He smashed his fist into Tommy's face and Tommy found himself on the ground, blood streaming from his nose. Immediately, Tommy's mates turned on Fred and there was a free-for-all. Sam, the bus driver, clambered out of his cab and came round to try and sort it out, but by this time fists were flying in all directions, the village boys being cheered on by their sisters. Jack Barrett, landlord of the Magpie, saw what was happening and he and his wife, Mabel, stormed out of the pub and into the fray. Mabel, a large woman whose strong arms were used to hefting barrels, grabbed hold of the girls who were standing, watching in horror, and pushed them on to the bus.

'You kids get on the bus and stay there,' she ordered before turning back to grasp two of the younger boys.

Once Jack had managed to pull Fred off Tommy and hold them apart and Sam had collared Malcolm, who'd immediately gone to Fred's aid, the fight fizzled out.

'On the bus, sharpish!' roared Sam, still holding Malcolm in a vice-like grip. The other boys, encouraged by cuffs from Mabel, scrambled on to the bus and only then did the two men release the three boys. Tommy's nose was still bleeding and Mabel stuffed her handkerchief into his hand.

'Here,' she said gruffly, 'mop yourself up.'

'You,' Sam said to Malcom, 'you sit on the seat behind me.' He turned to Tommy. 'You go to the back, and you, troublemaker,' he pointed an accusing finger at Fred, 'get in there, next to her,' and he pushed Fred into the spare seat next to Molly. Then he got back into the driving seat. 'I don't want to hear a sound from you lot,' he bellowed down the bus, 'or swelpme God, I'll put you out in the road.'

'It was the vaccie what started it,' said a girl's voice from somewhere near the back of the bus.

Sam glared in her direction and said, 'One more word...' before he let in the clutch and the bus moved off.

News of the Wynsdown fight spread like wildfire round the school. All those concerned were called into the headmaster's office and all returned, chastened, to their classrooms. Notes were sent home to the parents of the three main protagonists, and they were dealt with there as well.

Peter Bellinger listened to Fred and Malcolm's side of the story before he gave them both a severe warning about the beating they would get if they started any more fights. He and Marjorie had a sneaking sympathy for the boys, whom, they realised, had been ganged up on, but they were determined to nip such behaviour in the bud before it got out of hand. Fred and Malcolm accepted their warning without a word. They both knew that they had a very good billet at the manor and neither of them wanted to risk losing it.

Tommy Gurney's dad, Bert, a labourer at Charing Farm, said, 'Well, you got a bloody nose for it and serve you right. Make sure you win next time, boy. Don't want them vaccies to get too big for their boots, do we?'

For the next few days there was a stand-off outside the pub as they waited for the bus to arrive, but there were no further scuffles. As the weeks went by, Malcolm was discovered to be a first-class footballer and the Wynsdown children were very proud of him when he made the school team. Fred, who was no mean footballer either, lived in his reflected glory. A sort of wary truce existed between the vaccies and the local children. They met about the village at weekends and the boys joined the scouts. Sid Slater, a bachelor farmer who lived with his mother on a smallholding just outside the village fence, was the scout master, and every Thursday evening they met in the church hall. Once the evacuee boys had been integrated into the troop and worked together on various projects round the village, the antagonism between the groups almost disappeared. The odd shout of 'Vaccie!' was sometimes heard across the village green, but all the children gradually shook down together. If there was any rivalry with the kids from another village, there was no doubt that the Wynsdown children were united in the defence of their own.

Charlotte got used to living with Miss Edie. There was little warmth between them, but neither was there any further animosity. On the days when Miss Edie was working down in Cheddar, Charlotte often went home after school with Clare, to the Prynnes. She liked going there and playing in the kitchen with Sandra and Clare. Ma Prynne was very easygoing and though housework wasn't high on her list of priorities she kept a warm and comfortable home. Compared with the chilly, immaculately tidy Blackdown House, it had a welcoming warmth. When Miss Edie came home on the evening bus, she knocked on the Prynnes' door and Charlotte joined her for the dark walk home.

In the evenings they sat together in the kitchen, Charlotte doing her homework at the kitchen table, Miss Edie reading gardening books, doing the mending or altering clothes.

'We should make some for you,' she said, one Saturday after-noon when Charlotte had finished her homework and was sewing a button back on to her winter coat. 'I think there's a box of my mother's in the attic. There might be things in that which we could adapt for you. Let's go and see.'

They both put down their sewing and trooped upstairs to the third bedroom. Miss Edie unlocked the door and together they went in.

Charlotte looked round her with interest. She'd never been in here and had always wondered why it had to be kept locked. As far as she could see there was nothing of value in the room, simply a bed, and a few other sticks of furniture, nothing worth locking the door for. In one corner she noticed a small triangular door tucked into the slope of the eaves. Miss Edie crossed the room and bent to open it. The door was stiff and it took several sharp jerks to pull it open. She knelt down and shone her torch inside.

'This is the attic,' she said, over her shoulder. 'All my parents' things are in here.' She crawled through the door and disappeared. Charlotte, approaching the door, put her head through. Beyond was the roof space, about five foot high on one side, sloping sharply to the eaves on the other. Stacked against a central wall were suitcases and boxes. Some of these had labels stuck to their sides and by the light of Miss Edie's torch, Charlotte could see a box labelled, *Mother's Shoes* and another marked *Winter Clothes* and yet another *Father's Suit.*

Miss Edie grasped the handle of the one labelled *Winter Clothes* and said, 'This one looks hopeful. Come and help me pull it out and we can take it downstairs into the warm.'

For a moment Charlotte hesitated, then taking a deep breath as she'd learned to do going into St Michael's air raid shelter, she crawled through the little door and into the attic space beyond. There was no room to stand up and she stayed on her hands and knees, breathing deeply.

'Here we are,' called Miss Edie from behind a pile of boxes. 'Just come over here and get hold of this handle with me. It seems to have got caught on something.' Together they manoeuvred boxes to release the suitcase, but it wasn't the case that came free, it was the boxes, crashing down around Charlotte, knocking her sideways and trapping her under the eaves. Miss Edie's torch was knocked from her hand and clattering to the floor, went out.

Miss Edie swore under her breath but Charlotte began to sob.

'Are you all right, Charlotte?' she asked. 'What's the matter?'

'Let me out! Let me out!' Charlotte cried, her voice rising in panic. 'I can't get out. Let me out!' Miss Edie struggled to extricate herself from the pile of boxes and then began to pull them away, pushing them out through the attic door into the bedroom. The faded light of the winter's afternoon coming through the bedroom window was enough to see by and she managed to clamber out herself, pulling more boxes and the suitcase out behind her. She crawled back in, now able to get to the boxes that were trapping Charlotte into the space under the eaves and pull them away. Needing more light, Miss Edie felt round for the fallen torch, but when she did find it, it refused to light and she shook it in frustration.

She could hear the girl sobbing and she called out to her, 'It's all right, Charlotte, it's all right, I'm coming. Don't panic, I'm coming to get you out. You're all right.'

Was the child hurt in some way? she wondered as she wrestled her way through the accumulated junk to reach her. The attic space was larger than she remembered, running the length of the house. Where had all this stuff come from? When her parents had died, she had simply boxed everything up and shoved it in, stacking it against the chimney breast. Where had the rest come from?

At last she managed to clear a space and could see through to where Charlotte was stuck. With only the light through the open door to aid her, she could see little more than the girl's face, but she continued to move things out of the way and at last managed to clear a pathway. She lay down on her stomach and reached her hand through.

'You're all right, you're all right,' she soothed. 'I'm here now and you can get out. Take my hand.' At first Charlotte seemed not to hear, then suddenly Miss Edie found her hand gripped so tightly that her fingers were crushed.

'Well done, good girl, see if you can turn round a bit and slide out backwards. Easy does it. Good girl, nearly there.' As she continued to encourage the child, she felt her shifting under the sloping roof, her head almost touching the rafters. The further she squirmed back the higher the roof was over her head, the more room she had to move.

'Come towards the light, Charlotte,' Miss Edie said, trying to keep her voice calm. 'That's the way, good girl, I've got you.' She backed out through the door into the bedroom, almost dragging Charlotte behind her. Once they were both safely back in the bedroom she flopped on to the floor, gathering the girl into her arms and hugging her close. For a moment Charlotte remained rigid and then she seemed to relax, her body soft against Miss Edie's rather angular one, and for a long moment they rested on the bedroom floor in silence. Then Charlotte pulled away, rubbing her tear-streaked face with her hand.

'Sorry,' she muttered, ashamed of her panic.

'It doesn't matter. Go in the bathroom and wash your face,' suggested Miss Edie, gently, 'and then we'll go back downstairs and have some tea.'

When Charlotte got to her feet and went into the bathroom, Miss Edie continued to sit on the floor. She longed for Charlotte to be back beside her, to feel the warmth of her body against her own. She couldn't remember the last time she'd hugged anyone at all, certainly not her parents, they weren't the hugging sort. Herbert, then. She hadn't held anyone in her arms since Herbert had held her in his and kissed her goodbye. They had stood on the platform at Temple Meads station in a world of their own as they waited for the train. Others were also saying goodbye, but Edie, with the engagement ring newly on her finger, was entirely unaware of them. Herbert was returning to France and every moment spent with him was precious. People might have frowned at them, kissing in public, but they didn't care, and they held each other tight until the train steamed into the station. Dearest Herbert, it was all so long ago.

She heard the lavatory flush and got stiffly to her feet. All round her were the boxes and cases she'd dragged from the attic in her efforts to release Charlotte. The whole room was a mess and for the first time, Miss Edie, who had a place for everything and everything in its place, didn't care. She picked up the case marked *Winter Clothes* and closed the door.

Chapter Nineteen

Christmas approached and the village bazaar became the talking point. Marjorie Bellinger and Avril Swanson took on the organisation. There were to be stalls of Christmas items, decorations made by the children in the village school, pieces of handicraft brought home from the secondary school. The scouts were running a bran tub and had been round the village collecting unwanted or outgrown toys to wrap in newspaper and hide in the barrel they'd begged from Jack and Mabel at the Magpie. The Morgan twins had decided to have their own stall. Nobody knew what they were going to sell, but Marjorie agreed to give them a small table in the corner. Miss Mason at the school had taught the girls two country dances and there was to be a display in the afternoon when the selling part of the bazaar was over.

All the money raised was to go to the Red Cross, who were doing such wonderful work with the wounded, both civilians and servicemen. When they had finally opened the suitcase rescued from the attic, Miss Edie and Charlotte found several jerseys and some warm winter dresses, blouses and skirts. Miss Edie held each one up, marvelling that she could remember her mother wearing this or that.

'We'll unravel this old woolly,' she said, holding up a blue cardigan which was misshapen and had certainly seen better days. 'I'll make you a new cardigan.'

At the bottom of the case were some old napkins, a checked table cloth, three torn pillowcases and some sheets.

'I don't remember any of these,' Miss Edie said, holding them up. 'I don't think there's much we can do with them.'

'Can I take them to school?' asked Charlotte. 'Miss Gardener who does handicraft has asked if we can bring in any unwanted pieces of material. We're making things for the bazaar.'

'Of course you can,' agreed Miss Edie. 'I expect I can find you some more.'

Charlotte took the pile of fabric into school. She was delighted. She had decided to make a patchwork cushion cover for Miss Edie for Christmas. Several of the other girls were doing the same and they pooled all the scraps of material they'd brought so that there were lots of colours and patterns to choose from. Charlotte enjoyed handicraft lessons. She enjoyed sewing and planned her cushion cover with care, joining her chosen patchwork pieces with tiny stitches. When she had finished the patchwork front of the cushion, Miss Gardener found a piece of smooth blue fabric in the handicraft cupboard to make the back.

Clare looked at the finished cushion cover and sighed. 'You sew ever so well,' she said. 'Look at my handkerchief. It's all creased and all my stitches show. It's taken me for ever and Miss Gardener says I've got to make two of them, or it isn't enough for a Christmas present.'

'It'll be fine when you've washed and ironed it,' Charlotte told her, though secretly she had her doubts. But it had been such hard labour, surely Mrs Prynne, for whom it was intended, would like it, however it looked.

Once they had finished their own Christmas presents, the girls were expected to make things for the bazaar. Charlotte happily hemmed squares of coloured cotton to make hankies, and Molly, who preferred to knit, had learned to turn a heel and was making socks.

The day of the bazaar arrived two Saturdays before Christmas. There was great bustle as stalls were set out in the church hall. Just before it was declared open by Major Bellinger, the Morgan twins arrived to set out their wares. They arrived at the hall with two wheelbarrows full of bundles of sticks. They had been out 'sticking' every weekend since they'd heard about the bazaar and the wood they'd collected had been tied up in bundles to use for kindling. They were charging sixpence a bundle, delivered.

Mrs Prynne looked at the bundles and said, 'That's a bit cheeky! Sixpence for wood we could go and collect ourselves for free.'

The vicar, overhearing, smiled and remarked, 'Ah but you didn't, you see, and this is for such a good cause!' He beamed at the red-faced Mrs Prynne and moved on round the room, leaving her to buy a bundle out of shame and to get himself a raffle ticket for a chance to win the Christmas cake made by the Mothers' Union.

'We pooled all our butter and sugar ration,' Janet Tewson told him proudly. 'They say it won't be long before they ration eggs as well.' She grinned at him. 'Not that you'll be short, what with those hens scratching about your garden, vicar.'

'I'm sure we can always swap some eggs for a jar or two of your delicious honey, Mrs Tewson,' the vicar said.

'Do you think my mother would like these?'

Charlotte turned round to find Billy Shepherd standing beside her at the fancywork stall. He was holding up two of the hankies that Charlotte had hemmed herself.

'I expect she would,' said Charlotte, adding with a smile, 'Hankies are always useful and I made those.'

'You did?' Billy peered at them. 'I thought they were shop ones! The thing is, I saw some with initials in the corner, you know, done in coloured thread, but it looks as if they've all gone.'

'I can put initials on the corner if you like?' Charlotte offered. She had seen Billy around the village from time to time and they'd exchanged smiles, but he hadn't spoken to her since the day of the welcome party. He wasn't at school any more, he'd left to help his father on the farm, but she'd not forgotten how much trouble he'd taken to make little Val enjoy the races that day and she wanted to do something for him in return.

'Really?' Billy sounded impressed. 'Could you?'

'If you buy them now, I'll take them home and embroider them so they're really special. What's her name?'

'Margaret,' he replied, 'Margaret Shepherd. Can you do the M and the S?'

'Yes, if you like,' answered Charlotte.

'Hmm, but I can't afford much extra... for the M and S, you know?'

Charlotte burst out laughing. 'I'm not asking you to pay me,' she cried. 'I'll do it for you because... it's Christmas.'

'You're on!' Billy handed over the money for the hankies and then gave them to Charlotte, who put them in her pocket. 'I'll do them tonight, or tomorrow,' she promised. 'What colour would you like?'

Billy thought for a moment. 'Think her favourite colour is green,' he said. 'Have you got green?'

'I expect so, I'll do my best.'

Good as her word, Charlotte found some pale green cotton in Miss Edie's workbox and carefully worked the initials M and S, intertwined, in the corner of each hankie. Miss Edie watched with interest as, working without a pattern, Charlotte embroidered the initials.

'You sew very well, Charlotte,' she said. 'You must have been well taught.'

'I like sewing,' Charlotte said. 'I always have.'

As each of them realised what she had said, they smiled. Another tiny piece of the jigsaw of her life was turned face up.

Billy was delighted with the embroidered hankies. He called at Blackdown House next time he was in the village to collect them. Charlotte had washed and ironed them again, so that there were no marks or creases from her sewing.

'That's lovely,' Billy said. 'My mum'll be dead pleased.' He stood awkwardly in the kitchen for a moment and then said in a rush, 'Would you like to come out to the farm one day and see the animals? Our dog, Maisie, had pups a couple of weeks ago. You'd like to see those, wouldn't you?'

'Can I?' Charlotte turned pleading eyes on Miss Edie. 'Can I go?'

Miss Edie smiled. 'I expect so, in the Christmas holidays.' She turned to Billy and said, firmly, 'You'll have to come and fetch her and bring her home. I'm not having her wandering about the hill on her own.'

School ended the Friday before Christmas and on Saturday Billy arrived at Blackdown House to fetch Charlotte.

'Mother says to ask if Charlotte can stay for dinner,' he said, and to Charlotte's delight Miss Edie agreed. It suited her very well to have Charlotte out of the house for a few hours, she had plans of her own.

Charlotte put on her coat and together she and Billy walked the mile and a half to Charing Farm where Billy's mother greeted her kindly. Margaret Shepherd was large, both in height and girth, her greying hair caught up behind her ears with two large combs; a comfortable, motherly woman who guessed how difficult it must be for any child being away from home.

'You'll stay and have your dinner,' she said, a statement, not a question, and Charlotte, standing in the warm, welcoming kitchen, said, 'Thank you, I'd love to.'

'I'm going to show Charlotte round the farm,' Billy said.

'Well, she can't go in those shoes,' his mother said firmly, looking down at Charlotte's black school shoes. 'Look in the back porch and see if you can find her some boots, there'll probably be a pair of Jane's that might not be too bad.'

Billy led Charlotte into the back porch, where there was a row of wellington boots. 'These look about right,' he said, picking up a pair at the far end. 'Belong to my sister. She keeps them here for when she comes home.'

'Where is she now?' asked Charlotte.

'Jane? She's training as a nurse in Bristol. Here, try them on.'

Charlotte pushed her feet into the proffered wellies. They were on the large side, but she could manage to walk without too much difficulty.

'Right,' said Billy, his own feet in work boots, 'let's go.' He led the way out of the back porch into the farmyard. It was almost square, paved with cobblestones, among which some hens were scratching, pecking peacefully.

'Have to shut them up at night,' Billy said. 'Foxes. But we have a steady supply of eggs, and Mum says we'll have chicken for dinner on Christmas Day.' He walked across to a stable opposite. 'My dad keeps his horse in here,' he explained as he opened the door and went inside. 'He's out today, gone over to look at the sheep in the far field. Some of them'll be lambing before long. Come on in,' he went on. 'I want to show you these.'

Charlotte followed him into the stable, waited in the gloom while he lit an oil lamp and set it on a high shelf. To her delight she found herself looking over the half door into a loosebox full of puppies. The mother dog was lying comfortably in the hay while her pups explored their restricted world. There were five of them, black and white collie dogs, snuffling in the hay. One came at once to the door and Billy reached in and picked him up.

'Three boys, two girls,' he said. 'This one's a boy. He's always the brave one. Dad says I can keep him to train up as my own dog.' He rubbed the puppy behind the ears and it wriggled ecstatically. 'Here, you hold him,' Billy said, passing the black and white bundle over to her. Charlotte reached out for the puppy and cuddled his warm furry body against her neck.

'He's so sweet,' she cried, 'and you're so lucky to have a dog of your own. What's his name?'

'Jet,' replied Billy, and the dog immediately turned his head towards Billy. 'See, he knows my voice already and his name too.' He reached out to take the pup from Charlotte. Reluctantly she handed him back. 'You're so lucky,' she said again. 'I'd love to have a dog of my own.'

'Got to find homes for all of these,' Billy said. 'P'raps you could have one.'

'Really?' For a moment Charlotte's face lit with joy at the prospect, but then her face fell. 'Don't think Miss Edie'd let me. She doesn't like mess about the house.'

'Dogs aren't messy,' Billy assured her, 'not if you train them properly.' He put the puppy back into the pen. 'Anyhow, these won't be ready to leave their mother till after Christmas, so you got time to ask her.'

They went on round the farmyard and Charlotte looked at the huge pig in her sty. 'She should farrow in about three weeks from now,' Billy said.

'Farrow? What's farrow?'

'Have her babies,' replied Billy, adding, 'You don't know much about animals, do you?'

'I've never lived on a farm,' Charlotte protested, and even as she said it she thought, I know I haven't, and stored away this piece of information to add to the others.

They were out in the field looking at the cows, grazing the meagre grass in the winter sunshine, when the loud clanging of a bell summoned them back to the farmhouse for dinner. Billy led the way into the kitchen where the long wooden table had been laid with eight places. The day was overcast and Mrs Shepherd had lighted three oil lamps, which suffused the room with a warm glow and Charlotte realised, with a jolt of surprise, that the farmhouse had no electricity.

'Billy, show Charlotte where she can wash her hands,' instructed Mrs Shepherd, 'the men'll be in in a minute.'

Billy showed Charlotte a large downstairs cloakroom, where, besides the lavatory and wash basin, coats hung on pegs and buckets and brooms stood against the wall. When she emerged into the kitchen, Charlotte found five men coming in from the outside.

'You sit here, Charlotte, my lover,' Mrs Shepherd said, pointing to a chair next to her own, 'and Billy'll sit next to you.' The men all took their places at the table and Mrs Shepherd said, 'This is Charlotte, a friend of Billy's. She's having dinner with us today.'

'You're very welcome, Charlotte,' Mr Shepherd said from his place at the opposite end of the table.

Mrs Shepherd began to ladle stew on to plates from a big pot on the range and as these were passed along the table, one of the men said, 'You're a vaccie, aren't yer?'

Before Charlotte could even open her mouth Mrs Shepherd said, 'We don't use that word here, Bert Gurney.'

'It's what she is,' muttered Bert.

'What she is, is a guest in our house and someone who's come to live in our village, that's what she is,' Mrs Shepherd retorted and a silence fell round the table.

To change the subject Billy said, 'I told Charlotte that she might be able to have one of the puppies, Dad.'

'Did you now?' His father raised his eyebrows. 'And what did she say?'

'She said—' began Billy cautiously, but Charlotte interrupted him.

'I said I'd love one, but Miss Edie'll probably say no.'

'We haven't sold them all, have we, Dad?' demanded Billy. 'You said I could have Jet, but there's four more.'

'We'll talk about it later,' his father said, ending the discussion. 'Don't forget I'll need you to help with milking this afternoon, Billy.'

'But I promised Miss Everard that I'd bring Charlotte home,' Billy protested.

'Then you'll have to go sharpish after dinner, because I need you back here. You've had the morning off.'

'She can walk home with me,' suggested Bert Gurney. 'I'm going her way.' But Billy immediately said, 'No, it's all right, I'll take her, I promised. I'll be back for milking.' Charlotte felt relief flooding through her. She didn't want to walk back to the village with Tommy Gurney's dad, who thought she was only a 'vaccie'.

The dinner was delicious and filling. 'Have to give the men plenty to eat midday,' Mrs Shepherd said when they'd gone back out. 'Heavy work on a farm.'

Back at Blackdown House, Edie hadn't been wasting her day. She'd been out to the copse at the end of the lane and cut some branches of holly and twists of ivy. These she'd brought home, thinking that together she and Charlotte could decorate the house and perhaps make a wreath for the front door. It was so long since Edie had paid any attention to Christmas she suddenly found she was enjoying the preparations. She had finished the blue cardigan for Charlotte's Christmas present and had bought her an atlas and a dictionary from the bookstall at the bazaar. She was also planning a special lunch for Christmas Day. Not a Christmas dinner as such, but she'd saved up her meat ration to make a meat pie which she knew was one of Charlotte's favourites.

When she got back from collecting the greenery, Edie went up into the attic again. Somewhere, she was sure, was a box with some old Christmas decorations in it. She opened the triangular door and crawled through, her torch lighting her way. The boxes were all tumbled as they'd been left when Charlotte had been trapped. Which might hold the decorations, she wondered. She hadn't seen them since... She thrust the thought of Herbert away and began reading the labels, many of them in her mother's neat hand. She must have put them up here. Sure enough, on a small cardboard box near the back, was the word *Xmas*. Edie hauled it out and carried it downstairs. She decided not to open it until Charlotte got home.

Her morning had been interrupted by a ring on the doorbell and she had been amazed when she opened the door to find the vicar's wife on her step.

'Miss Everard,' said Avril Swanson, 'may I come in?'

Miss Edie nodded and stepped back to allow her into the house. 'Have to be the kitchen, I'm afraid,' she said, leading the way. 'It's the only warm room.' She waved her guest to a chair and sat down opposite her.

'Would you like some tea?' she asked, rather belatedly.

Avril shook her head. 'No, thank you. I won't stay long. Is Charlotte here?'

'No, she's gone to spend the day with the Shepherds at Charing Farm.'

Avril was surprised, but she smiled and said, 'That sounds nice. I'm glad she's making friends among the village children. Look, I'll come straight to the point...'

'Yes, please do.'

'Yes, well, what we wondered, David and I, was, well, whether you and Charlotte would like to come to us for Christmas dinner on Wednesday. David will be having a service in the church in the morning, but we'll all be back to have lunch at about one and we hoped you and Charlotte would join us.' She hesitated and then added, 'We've got the three Dawson children, of course, and we thought Charlotte... I mean, well, it might be fun for her to have some other youngsters around.'

'Well, I don't know...' Miss Edie was completely taken aback by the invitation.

'Perhaps you'd like time to think it over,' Avril said hastily, not wanting to bounce Miss Everard into saying no. 'You don't have to say now, just let me know by Christmas Eve so I know how many potatoes to peel. We've killed a chicken and it's quite big enough for all of us. So think it over, perhaps see what Charlotte thinks.'

'No, I make the decisions here,' said Miss Edie. 'I thank you very much for thinking of us and for thinking of Charlotte, being on her own here with only me for company,' she raised her hand as Avril seemed about to protest at her bald statement of the facts, 'and we'd be delighted to accept. Thank you.'

Avril was surprised but pleased. She had come in the expectation of being roundly refused, but David had agreed it was worth the effort to go and ask and he'd been right.

'Lovely,' she said. 'We'll expect you any time after half past twelve.'

When Charlotte got back to Blackdown House, Miss Edie was waiting for her in the kitchen. 'Did you have a nice time?' she asked.

'Yes, it was lovely,' Charlotte said. 'They've got cows and sheep and the pig's about to... farrow?'

'Is she now? You'll be able to see the piglets next time you go over, won't you?'

Charlotte was pleased that Miss Edie thought she could go again. 'They had puppies, too,' she said. 'They were ever so sweet!'

'Guess who came here today?' Miss Edie said, adding before Charlotte had a chance to answer, 'Mrs Swanson.'

'Mrs Vicar?'

'Yes, Mrs Vicar, and she's asked us to go to the vicarage for Christmas dinner. Would you like to go?'

Charlotte bit her lip. She did want to go, but she wasn't sure if that would be the right answer. Miss Edie came to her rescue saying, 'I said we'd love to,' and was rewarded with a wide smile. 'Now then,' she went on, 'I got some holly and some ivy today. I thought you could make a wreath for the front door and perhaps we could put some up in the house for decoration.'

They sat together at the kitchen table and managed to fashion a wreath from the greenery. Miss Edie found a piece of red ribbon in her workbox and when they'd added that to their creation, they went to the front door and hung it on the knocker.

'Now we must look in here,' Miss Edie said and pulled a box out from under the table. She undid the string and said, 'Open it and let's see what's inside.'

Charlotte pulled the lid off and peered inside. 'Paper flowers,' she said and lifted out a long chain of paper roses. Edie took it from her and laid it aside. She remembered her father hanging that paper chain, looping it across the sitting room, and she was glad that she'd made her preparations in there too. The roses should take their usual place.

Charlotte reached into the box again and pulled out four angels with gold paper wings, each attached to a piece of string. Mother used to hang those on the Christmas tree, thought Edie, and realised with a pang of regret that she could have got a tree if she'd thought of it in time. Never mind, they'd make the most of what they'd got.

They spent the rest of the evening putting the remaining greenery behind pictures and hanging the old decorations. Miss Edie had planned to use the sitting room on Christmas Day and when she opened the door Charlotte saw that the room had been spring-cleaned. She hadn't been into the room since her first day at the house. Now she saw that it had been dusted and the window, which had been thick with grime, had been cleaned. The fireplace had been brushed and there was a fire laid ready for lighting. She glanced across at the piano and saw that it, too, had been polished and that there were two new candles in the holders.

'I thought we'd use this room over Christmas,' Miss Edie said. 'My father always put the roses up in here.' She fetched the steps and Charlotte held one end of the chain while she attached the other to the wall.

'Now we're ready for Christmas,' Miss Edie said when they'd finished. 'It all looks very cheerful, doesn't it? We'll light the fire in here tomorrow.'

Christmas Day dawned dry and cold. Miss Edie and Charlotte exchanged presents at breakfast. Edie was charmed and delighted with her cushion cover. She'd had no idea that Charlotte was making it, but she could see the immense care and effort that had gone into it. Charlotte had known about the blue cardigan, but she was pleased to wear it with her new navy winter dress that they had adapted from one found in the attic suitcase, adding her blue beads as a finishing touch. The atlas and dictionary were a complete surprise and she was thrilled with them.

'Thank you, Miss Edie, I love them,' she cried and to the surprise of both of them, she gave her foster mother a hug. 'We should put the dictionary on the kitchen mantelpiece,' she said. 'That's where it's always kept.'

Edie noticed another jigsaw piece of Charlotte's memory, though this time Charlotte, in her delight with her Christmas presents, hadn't noticed what she'd said.

At Miss Edie's suggestion she had hemmed two more hankies cut from an old sheet, and embroidered the initials AS and DS in the corner to give the vicar and Mrs Vicar as Christmas gifts. Sitting by the fire in the newly cleaned sitting room on the Sunday evening, she had worked Avril's in pink and David's in blue and as before, Edie was impressed with her skill. These were now wrapped in paper, decorated by Charlotte and tied with coloured thread, ready for when they went to the vicarage for lunch.

Just before eleven Miss Edie asked, 'Would you like to go to the service in church, Charlotte?'

Charlotte looked doubtful. 'I don't know,' she said. 'I shan't know what to do.'

'It'll be lovely,' Miss Edie assured her. 'Candles and singing. We can just sit at the back and you'll see what happens.'

'All right,' Charlotte agreed and they walked down into the village. There were no bells ringing, there had been no bells since the outbreak of war – but as they approached, it seemed that the entire village was heading towards the church. Charlotte saw Clare walking with the Prynnes and ran to catch up with her.

'Happy Christmas!' Clare cried when she saw her. 'You coming to church, too? Sandra's singing a carol with the other school kids. What did you get for Christmas?'

'An atlas and a dictionary,' Charlotte told her proudly, quite forgetting the painstakingly knitted blue cardigan she was wearing. 'What about you?'

'They've done up Ma's old bike for me!' Clare beamed. 'Means I can bike anywhere I want to now.'

'Ooh, lucky you!' Charlotte said enviously.

They arrived at the church door and there was the vicar welcoming them inside. Clare and the Prynnes went in together, but Charlotte hung back, wanting to go in last and sit at the back where no one could see her. She and Miss Edie waited until the vicar had gone in himself and then slipped into the back pew.

Miss Edie had surprised herself when she'd suggested that they go to the service. She hadn't been to church for years, but having got back into the spirit of Christmas, she felt that the village service on Christmas morning was part of it all. When the service started with 'O Come, All Ye Faithful' she lifted her head and sang as she used to. Charlotte didn't know the words, but they were supplied in the hymn book that Miss Edie had handed her as they'd gone in and she, too, sang.

When the service was over the vicar stood at the door and shook hands with everyone as they came out. As their turn came, he showed no surprise at seeing Charlotte and Miss Edie among his congregation, simply saying, 'Lovely to see you both. Merry Christmas.'

It was a cold day, but everyone stood about outside again, talking, laughing and exchanging Christmas greetings. Charlotte was surprised at how many people smiled at her and wished her 'Merry Christmas!' For the first time she felt that she was really part of Wynsdown and she returned their smiles. Even Tommy Gurney saying, 'Happy Christmas, vaccie,' didn't dampen her day.

When they arrived at the vicarage for lunch, David and Avril made them very welcome, David saying again how lovely it had been to see them at church. Miss Edie had brought a bottle of her home-made elderflower wine and Charlotte had her parcel of hankies.

'We're having presents after lunch,' said Avril, shooing the children away from the kitchen and into the drawing room, warm for the first time since Christmas the year before. There was a tree in the corner and underneath it were Christmas gifts, wrapped, waiting to be opened. Charlotte placed her parcels there and Miss Edie added her bottle of wine.

Christmas lunch was delicious; the chicken and roast potatoes disappeared like magic and the Christmas pudding, though short on dried fruit, yielded, to the delight of the four children, a three-penny bit for each of them. After the meal they all gathered in the drawing room and listened to the king speaking on the radio. He said it was, above all, a children's day and he was sure that everyone was doing their best to make it a happy one wherever those children were.

'He knows we ain't at home,' Paul said, marvelling at the king's prescience. 'How does he know that?'

When the speech was over they gave and received their presents. There was a toy for each of the Dawson children, a book about animals for Charlotte, a tiny bar of perfumed soap for Miss Edie, and an extra twist of coloured paper full of sweets for the children.

Charlotte presented her presents to the vicar and his wife and they were both delighted with their embroidered handkerchiefs.

'They're beautifully done, Charlotte,' said Avril as she admired the needlework. 'They must have taken you ages.'

'Not as long as Miss Edie took to make my cardigan,' Charlotte said, holding out her arms to show it off. 'She took an old one apart and made me this.'

'It's lovely,' said Avril, adding, as she noticed Charlotte's necklace, 'and your necklace matches it perfectly.'

'Harry gave it to me,' Charlotte said.

'Harry? Who's Harry?' asked Avril gently.

Charlotte looked at her for a moment and then said, 'He comes from my town. He comes from Hanau.'

Chapter Twenty

$\mathbf{H}$arry spent his Christmas in an internment camp on the Isle of Man. When he'd been arrested at the hostel he was taken to the local police station and put into a cell. He was searched and the money that he'd stashed in his pocket was removed and put in an envelope.

'Hey!' he cried, trying to grab it back. 'That's mine. That's my money. Give it back! Give it back!'

'It's all right, son,' the policeman said to him placatingly. 'It's still your money, look, it's in an envelope with your name on it, see?'

They'd taken his ID card, which was in the name of Heinrich Schwarz, and put it with all the documents Mr Pate had given them into a folder labelled *Heinrich Schwarz*, and his money was put into it as well.

'I need the toilet,' he said as they took him to the cells, hoping that he'd be taken to a lavatory and might be able to make a dash for it before he was locked up. The constable kept a firm grip on his arm. 'Sorry, mate,' he said and pushed Harry into the cell. It was furnished with a narrow wooden shelf for a bed, with blanket and pillow. A bucket stood in a corner. The constable pointed to the bucket and said, 'You need a piss? You can piss in that.'

When the door clanged shut behind him, Harry looked round him, wondering if there was any way of escape. High above him was a window crossed with vertical iron bars. No way out through that. He reached for the bars and managed to haul himself up, scrabbling for purchase with his toes, until he could see out through the grubby panes. The window faced into a yard, surrounded by a high wall. A double gate stood open at one end and there were two police cars parked below.

Before it got dark he was given a plate of fish with some soggy chips, and then warning him that everything had to be blacked out, they switched off the lights. It was only early evening and as Harry sat in the darkened cell, he could hear the world going on outside without him. As the moon rose and he could make out shapes within the cell, the sirens began their nightly wail. Almost immediately he could hear the aircraft overhead and the pounding of the anti-air-craft guns in a nearby street. Suddenly he heard the sound of a key in the door and a voice said, 'All right, Schwarz! We're coming in to take you down to the shelter. Any nonsense from you and you'll be back in handcuffs.' The door opened and two burly policemen came in, one with a torch. Harry allowed himself to be led from the cell and down into the basement of the station, which had been fitted out as an air raid shelter. There was a table and a couple of chairs, but nowhere to lie down. He was told to sit and he flopped down on to a chair in a corner. He appeared to be the only prisoner and he sat there, accompanied by one of the police officers, to wait the raid out. For a brief moment, as they had gone along the passage to the base-ment steps, Harry had considered trying to make a break for it, but common sense prevailed; he would never have made it to the front door of the police station, and even if he had, he'd have been on the streets in what sounded like the father and mother of a raid. They could hear the continual clamour of the Blitz outside, the drone of planes, the boom of the ack-ack, the howl and whistle of the bombs before the ground shuddered under their impact and explosion. Fire engines, their bells clanging, hurtled through the streets to douse fires before they spread beyond control. It was mayhem.

'Sounds like a bad 'un,' said the constable. 'We're better off down here, mate.'

Though he had hoped to be back with Dan, firefighting, Harry had to agree with him. Casualties in a raid like this would be enor-mous; he was better off where he was. However, as the constable seemed ready to talk, Harry thought he'd try and discover what was going to happen to him.

'Why am I here?' he asked. 'I ain't no enemy alien. I escape from Nazis in Germany. On the train.'

'Yeah, well, you're still German though, ain't you?'

'Not all Germans Nazis,' Harry said.

'Trouble is, we don't know which of you is an' which ain't.'

'My family Jewish,' Harry told him. 'Nazis kill my father and mother. I hate Nazis.'

'I'm sure you do, mate. Still, you're a German, see, an' your papers say you're sixteen, so...' He raised his hands dismissively.

'So, what going to happen to me?'

'Dunno.' The constable clearly didn't care. 'You'll probably go up north or somewheres first, then, well who knows? Some of you lot've been sent to Canada or Australia where you can't do no harm. 'Spect you'll be looked after, put somewhere safe and at the end of the war you'll be let go.'

Harry stared at him. 'Till the end of the war? Suppose the Nazis win?' he said. 'What happen to *me* then?'

The policeman gave him a hostile stare. 'Who gives a fuck? They ain't gonna win,' he snarled. 'Now, shut your face.'

It was another hour and a half before the all-clear sounded and Harry was led back to his cell. The constable had said not another word to him. They'd sat in stony silence waiting for the all-clear.

Back in the cell with the blackout still in force, Harry could see very little. He hauled himself up on the bars of his window again and peered out. The whole sky was lit with a lurid orange glow, smoke wafting lazily in the wind. The Luftwaffe had done its job and swathes of London were ablaze once more. He could hear the continual ringing of fire engine bells as the firefighters raced from one blaze to another. Men shouted and there was the occasional rumble of falling masonry, the occasional boom of a delayed-action bomb. Day dawned outside and a few fingers of sunlight forced their way through the dirty panes of his window, but still no one came near him and he had to make use of his bucket. He was very thirsty, but no one brought water and no food was offered. The watch he'd bought from one of Mikey's stalls had been taken with his other personal possessions and he had no idea of the time, but eventually he heard heavy footsteps approaching his door and the constable who had escorted him to the cell the day before appeared.

'Let's 'ave you,' he said by way of greeting.

'Water, want water,' Harry said, his voice croaky in his dry throat.

'You'll get some soon enough,' replied the constable and led him along the passage to an interview room where another officer was already waiting.

'Here he is, Dawes,' said the constable. 'The inspector'll be along directly.' He turned to Harry, still standing just inside the room, and pointed to a chair. 'You, sit down there and wait.'

Harry sat as he was told and waited. Dawes, the officer left with him, took no notice of him, simply stood with his back to the door apparently staring into space. After about half an hour Harry got to his feet and stretched. Dawes still ignored him, so Harry went across to the window and looked out. The day outside was sunny and bright. He could see little beyond the high wall he'd seen from his cell, a tall building opposite, the tops of a few trees, their leaves burnished orange, red and gold in the autumn sun-light, and in the distance a church steeple, its crowning cross leaning at a drunken angle.

Harry went back to his chair and flopped down to wait. 'I want water,' he said to the man on the door. 'Please, I want water.'

Dawes continued to ignore him. He'd been talking to Constable Brown from the night shift who had guarded this man during the air raid and Brown had told him that this prisoner was a Nazi who wanted Germany to win the war. Thirsty, was he? Well, he could die of thirst for all Dawes cared.

At last the door opened and another man came in. He was not wearing uniform, but he was clearly Dawes's superior officer as the man came to attention. Harry remained seated and the plain-clothes officer took the chair opposite him.

'Now then, young man,' he began, 'I'm Inspector Gordon. Can you understand what I'm saying to you?'

'Course I can,' replied Harry. 'I want water.'

'You had water with your breakfast,' snapped Gordon.

'No breakfast,' said Harry.

'What d'you mean?' demanded the inspector. He glanced at Dawes, still standing stony-faced at the door. 'Has this man had breakfast?'

'Dunno, sir.'

'Well, get out there and find out,' snapped Gordon, 'and bring some water.' He turned his attention back to Harry. 'We'll wait.'

Moments later Dawes was back with a glass of water which he put down with a thump in front of Harry. Harry snatched it up, draining it in one go. It was the first liquid he'd had since he'd been arrested. A few minutes later the first constable came in with a bread and marge sandwich on a plate which he, too, dumped unceremoniously in front of Harry. Harry grabbed the sandwich and crammed it into his mouth. He wasn't going to risk them taking it away again.

'Well, Heinrich, let's start again,' said Inspector Gordon.

'Harry,' Harry said through a mouthful of bread. 'My name Harry Black.'

'Not what it says on your identity card.'

'Stopped being Heinrich when I come here.'

'Well, Harry then, you haven't made yourself very popular here, have you? First you make a run for it, then you kick one of my officers in the eye, then you resist arrest and last night you told Constable Brown that you want the Germans to win the war. Not the way to make friends, is it?'

'I didn't say,' protested Harry hotly. 'My father was murdered by Nazis! Why I want them to win the war? So they can murder me too?'

'The thing is, Harry, that you've made a nuisance of yourself, and we haven't time to deal with nuisances like you. It's better that you're shut away where you can't cause any more trouble.'

'But I not cause trouble,' Harry almost shouted. 'I living in hostel, I have job, I help firefighters.'

'Yes, so I heard. Still, the government want to be sure. So, today you'll be transferred to Brixton prison for a few days while they decide where to send you.'

'I want my money,' Harry said harshly. 'Policeman steal it.'

'There you go again, Harry, saying stupid things that will annoy people. No one has stolen your money. It is with your papers and will travel with you. You'll get it back if and when you're released, OK?'

Harry opened his mouth to protest but Inspector Gordon cut him off. 'Enough, Harry. You'll be returned to your cell to await your transfer. Take him down, Dawes, and make sure he slops out before he leaves.'

Dawes moved up behind Harry and yanked him to his feet. 'Come on, you,' he said and, keeping a firm grip on Harry's arm, he led him back to his cell.

Harry wasn't transferred that day, nor the next, so he had to endure two more nights in the basement of the police station in the company of Constable Brown. On the first night when the sirens went, he told Brown he'd rather stay and take his chances in the cell.

'What, so's you can signal to those bastards up there?'

'How? By whistling to them?' Harry felt the frustrated fury boiling up inside him.

'Cut the crap, smartarse,' snarled Brown, 'and get a move on.'

The third night Brown was even more contemptuous, addressing Harry as a Nazi Jew-boy. They were once again in the basement shelter, but now Harry was in handcuffs. They had seen the resentment in his eyes and they didn't trust him any more. Any residual sympathy there might have been for the plight of a sixteen-year-old boy alone in a foreign country was long gone.

'They shot down four of your gallant Nazis last night,' Brown told him. 'Not sure why we're so keen on keeping you safe down here. If I didn't have to guard you, I could be out there helping the poor sods being blown to bits by your lot. What have you got to say to that, Jew-boy?'

Suddenly Harry had had enough. Brown was the Hitler Youth, the Gestapo, the fascist Brownshirts all rolled into one. The street fighter in him burst out and with one swift movement he was across the room. Pushing Brown to the floor he forced his cuffed arms round the policeman's neck, pulling the metal handcuffs hard against his throat. If a second officer hadn't come in at that moment Harry might well have committed murder, but the policeman grabbed him, smashing his fist into Harry's face, and it was all over. He was marched back to his cell, the door slammed behind him, the cop's voice echoing along the passage. 'And you can stay in there and be damned to you.'

Harry was lucky that no further action was taken about his second assault on a police officer. The inspector had no wish for the provocation to be brought out into the open. Public opinion about the internment of German and Italian nationals had begun to swing against the idea. So many had been refugees from the Fascists that many were already being released to do valuable war work. No, Inspector Gordon was just pleased to get shot of the troublemaker Heinrich Schwarz, or Harry Black or whoever he was. He'd happily off-load him and make him someone else's responsibility.

Harry was taken to Brixton the following morning and a memo on his papers warned that he'd attacked a police officer and should be regarded as dangerous.

Harry's confinement in His Majesty's Prison Brixton lasted seven weeks and they were the seven most miserable weeks in his life. The prison was overcrowded. Harry was now regarded as a prisoner rather than an internee and the regime was harsh. However, Brixton was only being used as a transit prison and from there he was moved first to Huyton Internment camp outside Liverpool and then at length by boat to the Isle of Man.

At Huyton he had been housed in a half-built housing estate. Cramped and cold, hundreds of internees had been living on a building site, housed in half-finished council houses, surrounded by barbed wire. Autumn had turned to winter and the facilities were basic to say the least and the food minimal. Always hungry, the inmates had a strict regime among themselves, adding everything edible they could find to spin out their meagre rations. Morale was very low and more than one internee considered suicide as a convenient way out. Most, however, were determined not to be cowed by the harsh conditions. Some of them had already suffered the torment of a Nazi concentration camp and though the conditions were bad they were nothing like those they'd already experienced. Harry and several of the other, younger internees were constantly looking for a way of escape, but they were strictly guarded and no opportunity presented itself.

Then one day, just a week before Christmas, Harry and twenty others were told they were moving again.

'Where to now?' Harry demanded.

'Never you mind,' came the reply. 'You'll see. Get your stuff.'

There was very little 'stuff' to get. Harry still had his case with him; it had been returned when he left Brixton. He had his clothes but there was no sign of his money or his watch. He had long ago given up hope of ever seeing those again. The police were the same everywhere, they were thieves, he'd always said so. They'd nicked his valuables and there was nothing he could do about it.

The next day they were taken to Fleetwood where they were put aboard a ship, *The Lady of Man*, and they realised they were going to the Isle of Man. Everyone had heard about the camps over there and their spirits rose. Several internees had already been released from there, so perhaps the end was in sight. If only they could find some way to prove that they were no threat to the security of England, that they truly hated the Nazis as much as the English did. Harry decided he would be the model prisoner.

When they reached Douglas and disembarked, they were formed up into groups and marched along the sea front. The sea they had just crossed looked grey and brooding. As Harry looked out across the endless expanse of water, he knew that there'd be no escape from here; his mood was grey and brooding, too.

Knew I should've made a break for it before we was put on that ship, he thought bleakly. I'm stuck here now till the Nazis invade and come looking for me and all the other Jews holed up here on this bloody island. Like rats in a trap we'll be.

They were marched through a gate and along the promenade to what looked like a hotel and a row of large houses, looking out over the sea. All this was surrounded by barbed wire, cutting off the whole promenade, and with it those who were constrained to live beyond the gates. The new internees were logged in and assigned to a house along the front. They were all together and for once their accommodation, though cramped with several to a room, was dry and comparatively warm. They were also assigned weekly rations to cook and share. They chose a house leader, Alfred Muller, who had actually been born in England of German Jewish parents. Alfred, who had been the headmaster of a large school in Birmingham, had a talent for organisation and soon sorted out rotas for the cooking and the household duties. It was a step up from jumping to obey the shouted order of some loud-mouthed NCO who had been invalided out of the army. They were to organise themselves. They were responsible for themselves and it returned them some measure of dignity. For the first time in months they were not actively hungry. The food was plain, but at least it was there.

The whole camp had a life of its own with a set routine. Reveille was sounded at seven o'clock, after which the roll was called, followed by some sort of physical exercise before breakfast. Then there was the rest of the day, stretching out before them. Boredom was acknowledged as the main enemy within the camp and it was to counteract this that several of the inmates organised talks, classes, lectures. So many of them were professional men, doctors, lawyers, lecturers, musicians and actors – top men in their fields – and a sort of open university opened up, with tutors of the highest calibre.

On Christmas Eve there were services led by various clergy and the singing of carols raised everyone's spirits. Harry had never celebrated Christmas before. His parents did not because of their faith; their celebration had been Hanukkah. Since the death of his parents Harry had had no faith and didn't miss it. He was Harry and he was master of his own destiny. Even so, he was glad there was extra to eat on this day that was so special to others.

Harry's Christmas dinner was rabbit stew with potatoes and carrots, and it was the best meal he'd eaten in years.

Chapter Twenty-One

By Christmas Eve London had been subjected to nearly a hundred days of almost continuous bombing. Not only London, but other major cities considered by Hitler as targets. Coventry, Southampton, Plymouth, Liverpool, Manchester and Bristol had all received visits from the Luftwaffe with heavy bombing and firestorms, but despite this attack on the fabric of Britain and on the morale of her citizens, though aghast at the damage inflicted, people refused to be cowed. Christmas was upon them and, war or no war, everyone was determined to celebrate the season of goodwill.

'Season of goodwill, that's a joke,' Arthur said gloomily as he and Dan were fire-watching once again on the paint warehouse roof. 'Hitler'll probably send us an extra-special present for Christmas.'

'Well, I shan't be here to receive it, mate, I'm off to Feneton tomorrow to see my Naomi.'

'How's she keeping?' Arthur asked. 'Babby's due soon, isn't it?'

'Middle of January, so they say.' Dan couldn't keep the pride out of his voice and Arthur, the father of three daughters, smiled. He could well remember the excitement of an imminent birth.

'So a few weeks to go yet,' he said equably. 'Hope it all goes well.'

'No reason why it shouldn't, the doc says,' replied Dan. 'Still, I'm looking forward to being there over Christmas.'

Dan had managed to get to Feneton only once since Naomi and Shirley had moved there. He had taken the train from Liverpool Street three weeks after they had left and Naomi had met him at the station. She flung herself into his arms, oblivious of the half-envious, half-disapproving looks from the other travellers.

'Danny, oh Danny, I've missed you so,' she cried. 'Thank God you're safe. That dreadful bombing!' She hugged him to her and he returned her hug as tightly as he dared.

'Got to be careful of the baby,' he said as he held her away from him and looked into her eyes. He could feel tears springing to his own as he saw the joy and love he felt reflected there. 'God,' he muttered, 'I've missed you, an' all.'

'Baby's all right,' Naomi assured him and, taking his hand, said, 'Come on, let's get away from here.' She led him out of the station and across the street to a little tea room opposite. As she opened the door a bell jingled and Shirley appeared through a curtain at the back.

'Look who's here, Shirley,' Naomi cried. 'Two teas please.'

They sat in the window and held hands across the table. Suddenly shy, Naomi said, 'I hope you don't mind, Dan, but I've booked us a room at the Feneton Arms. It's the local pub.'

'Mind?' exclaimed Dan. 'Why should I mind? I want you to myself while I'm here. I've missed you, girl.'

Naomi flushed with pleasure. 'Thought it'd be just as well. I share a room with Shirley and of course she said she'd move out, sleep downstairs, but I wanted us to be more private... you know.'

Dan did know and was wondering why they had stopped in the teashop for tea when their time together was so precious, but he only squeezed her hand and said, 'Yeah, I want us to be private, too.'

Shirley came out to the table with a pot of tea and two rather tired-looking pieces of sponge cake.

'Saved you a piece of your own,' she said, putting the tray on the table. 'Glad to see you, Dan,' she added.

'What did she mean, "a piece of your own"?' asked Dan as he took one of the pieces of cake and dunked it in his tea.

'It's a little job I've got,' Naomi explained. 'Now, don't look like that, Dan. I got to do something, even if it's try to bake cakes without butter or eggs! I bake stuff for the teashop and Mrs Grant, what owns the shop, pays me. Gives me the rent money for Maud. Means I can save for when I can't work cos of the baby. We been trying out some of them recipes the government gives out. We made Woolton Pie last week. Didn't taste too bad and we wasn't hungry after.' She looked up at her husband suddenly and said, 'You been getting enough to eat, Dan? With me not there to cook for you?'

'Course I do,' he assured her. 'Don't you worry about me, I do all right.' He finished his soggy cake and then gulped down the rest of his tea. 'Shall we go, then?'

Naomi finished her tea, saying, 'Just wanted you to see where Shirley and I work, that's all. I got today off and Sunday.' She went to the curtain at the back of the shop and lifting a corner called through, 'Off now, Shirley. Thanks for saving us a bit of cake.'

They wandered out into the late-autumn sunshine and, hand in hand, sauntered along the village street until they came to an old coaching inn fronting the main road with an arched entry to the stable yard at the back. Above the door swung a creaking wooden sign board, but its name had been painted out in dark red paint. 'It's cos it's called the Feneton Arms,' Naomi explained when Dan looked up in surprise. 'All the village names have been painted out cos of German parachutists. The pub would give away the name of the village, see?'

'Let's hope that any don't arrive today,' said Dan as he pushed open the door. 'We don't want no interruptions from Hitler or anyone else today!'

They had a wonderful two days away from the bombing in London. The peace of the evening was broken by the distant sound of planes and anti-aircraft fire, but they were able to sleep in each other's arms without the night sky raining down death and destruction on them.

Now, for the second time, Dan took the train and arrived at Feneton. Again Naomi was there to greet him and in the bitter cold and gathering dusk they hurried straight to the Feneton Arms. Naomi was looking tired, her face pale and drawn. Once upstairs in their room he took her in his arms and kissed her. She returned his kiss and then pulled away.

'Sorry, love,' she said, 'got to sit down. Got a bit of back ache.'

Dan was immediately all solicitude. 'Here,' he said, leading her to the dressing-table chair, the only chair in the room. 'Or do you want a proper lie-down?'

Naomi smiled. 'No,' she insisted, 'I'll be fine in a minute, it's probably just that your train was a bit late and I was standing out in the cold for a while. I'll be fine once I get warmed up again.'

When she felt a little better she suggested that they go downstairs to the bar and get a drink. 'After all,' she said, 'it's Christmas Eve. We deserve a drink to start our Christmas.'

They went down to the bar, which was decorated with paper chains made by the landlord's daughter. They looped across the ceiling, hoops of newspaper painted bright colours. Branches of holly were tucked behind the pictures on the walls and ivy twisted up the narrow pillars supporting the canopy over the bar counter. There was a fire burning in a wide, old-fashioned fireplace, the logs glowing red under the dancing flames. The blackout curtains were already closely drawn and in the yellow lamplight the bar looked warm and welcoming.

Dan bought a beer for himself and a warm port and lemon for Naomi and they took their drinks to a small sofa beside the fire.

'You all right, Naomi?' Dan asked. 'You look a bit peaky.'

'Just tired,' Naomi assured him. 'I always seem to be tired now. Don't worry,' she smiled across at him, 'it's only cos of the baby. The doctor says it's to be expected.'

'Well, just as long as you're sure.'

The landlady provided them with a supper of liver and onions and they each had another drink by the fire before Naomi said, 'Sorry, Dan, but I got to go to bed.'

They went upstairs and got undressed. Naomi sighed and flopped down on the bed. Dan looked at her anxiously. 'You sure you're all right, girlie?'

'Still got a bit of back ache,' Naomi admitted, 'but I expect it'll be gone in the morning. Come on, get in beside me and warm me up.'

They snuggled down together under the blankets, Naomi nestled in Dan's arms, reassured by the warmth of his body next to hers.

Dan, feeling her heart beat against him, knew an overwhelming burst of love and murmured softly into her hair, 'You're everything to me.'

It was only a couple of hours later that Naomi awoke with a start. A sharp pain knifed through her and she sat up with a gasp. Dan was immediately awake.

'What? What is it?'

'A bit of a pain,' Naomi said when she could say anything at all.

'What sort of pain?'

'It's all right, it's gone now,' she said. 'Go back to sleep.'

Dan lay down again but could feel Naomi lying, tense now, beside him.

It can't be yet, she was thinking. It isn't due for another fortnight. Must be a false alarm.

It wasn't. The next pain, coming about twenty minutes later, just as she had drifted off to sleep again, made her gasp. As the contraction wore off she lay still, trying to calm her thoughts. If the baby was indeed about to put in an appearance, how was she going to get to Ipswich to the hospital? The doctor had assured her everything should go well.

'But,' he'd said when she'd last seen him two weeks ago, 'I think it would be a good idea, Mrs Federman, if you had your baby in hospital since you're a slightly older mother and this is your first. Means we're all on hand, just in case.'

'Just in case what?' demanded Naomi. 'I thought you said it was all going to be OK.'

'I did, and I'm sure it will be, but just in case we're needed.' He had put her name down for the maternity unit for a couple of weeks in mid-January. 'Can't be sure when the baby will put in an appearance,' he went on, 'but this way at least we'll be expecting you.'

Well, thought Naomi now, they certainly aren't expecting me on Christmas Eve. It must be a false alarm, and she forced herself to try and relax. It wasn't any use and once she'd struggled through the next contraction she shook Dan awake.

'Dan,' she whispered. 'Danny, I think the baby's coming.'

Dan sat up with a start. 'What did you say?'

'The baby. I think it's coming. I'm having contractions.'

'But it isn't due for another two or three weeks yet,' he cried in dismay.

Naomi gave a weak laugh and said, 'Don't think it's going to wait that long.'

Dan leaped out of bed and pulled on his trousers over his pyjamas. 'What are we going to do? What shall I do?'

'I'm supposed to go to the hospital, but I think we'd better ring the doctor first. The number's in my bag. You could ring from downstairs.'

Dan passed Naomi her bag and she pulled out a scrap of paper with a phone number scrawled on it. 'Here,' she said, but as he reached to take it from her she doubled up with yet another contraction. 'Tell him,' she gasped, 'tell him they're coming every fifteen minutes or so and ask him if we should try and get to the hospital.'

Dan snatched the paper and ran to the door. 'Won't be long,' he promised. 'Back in a minute.' He ran downstairs to where he'd seen a phone behind the bar, but when he reached it he found a metal grille had been pulled down over the bar and locked so that the phone was inaccessible.

'Shit!' He ran back upstairs and along the landing to a door marked *Private* at the far end. He banged on it hard with both his fists. At first there was no sound in answer to his knock and he beat on the door again, shouting, 'Open up. Please open up.'

After a moment the door creaked open and the landlord peered out on to the landing. 'What's up?' he demanded grumpily. 'It's after midnight, for Christ's sake!'

'My wife,' cried Dan, 'the baby's coming. I got to ring the doctor.'

The landlord turned back and shouted up the stairs, 'Jenny, need you down here, sharpish!'

Moments later the landlady, wearing an old dressing gown and with her hair in an untidy plait, appeared beside her husband.

'What's the matter?' she asked.

'Got to phone the doctor,' insisted Dan. 'My wife's gone into labour.'

'Right.' Jenny immediately took charge. 'Jim, go down and show him the phone. Got the number?' and when Dan nodded she said, 'Right, go and ring then, I'll go to your wife.'

When Dan came back from the phone he found Naomi sitting up in bed, gripping Jenny's hands as she dealt with another contraction.

'What did he say?' she asked as the pain subsided.

'He's on his way,' Dan replied. 'Says you're to stay put.' He turned to Jenny and said, 'Dr Phelps'll be here in a minute. He said please can you find some clean towels and put some water on to boil.'

'Of course.' Jenny got to her feet and Dan took her place at the bedside. Jenny despatched Jim to put the kettle on and wait downstairs to let the doctor in while she went to a cupboard on the landing and pulled out some towels and an extra couple of pillows.

The contractions were coming regularly now and as each grabbed her, Naomi gripped Dan's hands, trying not to cry out.

'It'll be all right,' he soothed, 'the doc's on his way, it'll be all right.' But as another contraction took hold he was beginning to wonder where on earth the doctor could be.

Moments later Dr Phelps appeared at the door, bag in hand, and came straight across to the bed. Jenny had helped Naomi to move on to a folded towel and had propped her up with extra pillows. He looked at the anxious father and said, 'You'll be best off downstairs, just ask Mrs Dow to come up, will you?'

Dan bent forward and kissed Naomi on the cheek. 'I'll be just downstairs, girlie,' he said. 'You'll be OK now the doc's here.'

He left the room with relief. He had felt so helpless in the face of Naomi's pain. There was nothing he could do to alleviate it except hold her hand.

Better, he thought, to be out of the way now the doc was here to do his stuff.

Jenny Dow bustled upstairs and as she went into the bedroom, she gave Dan a smile and shut the door firmly behind her. Dan stood on the landing for a moment or two, but when he heard Naomi cry out, he couldn't bear it and ran downstairs.

He and Jim sat at the bar and Jim poured them each a glass of brandy. 'Need a good stiff drink at a time like this,' Jim insisted. 'We've got a kid, Gwen, she's called. I remember when she were born, eight she is, but I remember that night like yesterday.'

It seemed for ever to Dan before Jenny came down again and said that things were fine but would be a little time yet, and wasn't it exciting, oh, and Happy Christmas!

Jim went back to bed and Dan sat by the dying embers of the fire, dozing fitfully. He woke with a start when Jenny reappeared in the bar and threw back the blackout curtains; it was daylight outside.

'Congratulations, Mr Federman,' she said with a tired smile. 'You have a son.'

'A son,' echoed Dan. 'And Naomi? How's Naomi?'

'Tired, as you'd expect,' came the reply, 'but she's fine. The doctor'll be down in a minute, then you'll be able to go up and see them. I'm putting the kettle on for some tea, would you like some?'

'A son! We've got a son!' breathed Dan, hardly daring to believe it.

It was about ten minutes later that Dr Phelps came downstairs. He walked wearily into the bar and shook Dan's hand. 'Congratulations,' he said. 'Your son decided to put in rather an early appearance, so he's a bit on the small side, but he'll be fine.'

'Is she all right?' Dan asked. 'Is Naomi all right?'

'Yes, she is, but she needs a rest. I suggest you take her up a cup of tea, admire your son and then let them both get some sleep.'

'Thank you, doctor,' Dan said. 'Thank you for all you did, coming out in the night, an' that. Don't know what we'd have done without you.'

Jenny appeared at the door with a tray of teacups. She poured two for Dan and he hurried upstairs with them. He pushed the door open and edged his way in. Naomi was sitting up in bed, pale, but radiant. Her hair had been brushed and tied back off her face and she greeted him with a dazzling smile. Lying beside her in a drawer from the chest in the corner was a small bundle of... something.

'Look, Danny,' she whispered. 'Look at our son. Isn't he beautiful?'

Dan put down the tea and peered into the drawer. The bundle was tiny, swathed in a white cloth of some sort, with only his head poking out and a tiny fist thrust into his mouth. He had a dark quiff of hair standing on the top of his head and Dan, staring down at him, began to smile, truly believing now that he was indeed a father and this scrap of humanity was his son, his responsibility.

He bent down and very gently placed a kiss on the baby's head before going round the bed to gather his beloved wife into his arms.

'Careful,' she admonished. 'I'm a bit sore.'

'Sorry,' he said and pulling up the chair, sat down beside the bed.

Together they sat and drank their tea, looking at the miracle that was their son.

'We haven't even got a name for him,' Dan said at last. 'We should've had a name ready. What do you think?'

'I think I'd like to call him Nicholas,' Naomi said.

'Nicholas,' repeated Dan. 'OK, but why Nicholas?'

'It's Dr Phelps's name. I asked him, because if he hadn't come so quickly we might not have a baby.'

'Nicholas. Nicholas Federman. It's a good name,' said Dan. He went back round to the drawer and looking down said, 'Hallo, Nick, mate.'

Chapter Twenty-Two

'Hanau's in Germany. My name is Lisa Becker and I come from Hanau. I came on a train.'

For a moment the three adults stood in silence, stunned as they realised the import of what Charlotte had actually said. She had remembered who she was and where she came from; but was that all, some fragments of her earlier life, or had she remembered everything?

Charlotte's recollection of Harry was a double-edged sword. She stood for a moment in the vicarage drawing room as her mind processed what she'd just said. Hanau. Mutti, Papa and Martin. They all came flooding back to her, her beloved family trapped in Germany and disappeared. The letter marked GONE AWAY. Her face crumpled and without a word she turned and ran out of the room. Avril made to follow her, but the vicar put a restraining hand on her arm and she stood aside, allowing Miss Edie to go.

Unaware of what was going on round them the Dawson children were playing with the toys they'd received. Paul had a football, which he couldn't use in the house, but the girls had been given a glove puppet each, a dog and a cat, and at David's suggestion they were going to make up a puppet show. All three disappeared behind the settee and there was great giggling.

Avril looked anxiously at David. 'What do you think she's remembered? Everything?'

David shook his head. 'Who knows? She's remembered someone called Harry, but goodness alone knows if that's a good or bad thing.'

'It sounds as if they came over on one of those refugee trains, you know, the ones we heard about bringing Jewish children out of Germany?'

David nodded. 'Yes, does indeed.'

'In which case, do you think Miss Everard is the right person to deal with... well, whatever it is?' Avril was thinking about Miss Everard's reaction when she'd discovered that Charlotte was probably German. Now it appeared that Charlotte's memory had come back, at least in part, and that she was indeed German, how would Miss Everard react?

'I don't know,' David said, 'but I think we have to let her try. They've been living together for nearly six weeks now and they seem to have come to an understanding. I think having Charlotte to think about instead of just herself has probably been a turning point for Miss Everard.'

'Yes, it has.'

They both spun round to find Miss Everard coming back into the room. Clearly she had heard some of their conversation, but all she said was, 'If you'll excuse us, vicar, Mrs Swanson, I think Charlotte and I'll be going home now. Thank you for inviting us today, it's been a lovely Christmas.'

'Shall I walk home with you?' offered the vicar. 'I could do with a breath of fresh air.'

Miss Everard shook her head. 'No, thank you. You've the other children here. We'll be fine.' She gave a brief smile and said to Avril, 'You don't have to worry about Charlotte, Mrs Swanson, I'll look after her.'

'I'm sure you will,' replied Avril, 'but if there's anything I can do—'

'I won't hesitate to ask,' interrupted Miss Everard, 'I promise you.'

Avril saw them to the door and stood watching them walking together through the winter afternoon, Charlotte clutching her coat around her and Miss Edie tempering her steps to match those of her charge. It was dusk and the evening closed round them as they followed the beam of Miss Edie's torch.

Avril closed the door and returned to the drawing room, where David was helping with the puppet show, and Christmas Day went on. The king had said that everyone should do all they could to make it a happy day for children wherever they were and the Swansons were doing all they could to make it so for their evacuees.

When the three children were at last tucked up in bed, the girls cuddling their glove puppets and Paul with his arms round his football, Avril came back downstairs and flopped into her armchair.

'What a day!' she said. 'It seems an age since we woke up this morning and opened the children's stockings with them.'

David opened Miss Edie's bottle of elderflower wine and poured a glass for each of them. He handed Avril hers and raising his own said, 'Cheers, darling. You made it a very special Christmas.' They both took a sip of the wine and then, spluttering, David said, 'Goodness, what has she put in this?'

'Don't know, but,' Avril took another mouthful and smiled, 'I think it might grow on me!' She put down her glass and went on, 'I've been thinking, David, perhaps I ought to ring Caro and tell her that Charlotte has remembered her name and where she comes from. What do you think?'

'I think I'd leave it for a couple of days until we know a little more,' David replied, risking another sip of the wine.

'But now she's remembered her name, perhaps her family can be traced.'

'It sounds to me as if her family is still in Germany.'

'Yes, but she must have been living with someone in London. They must be worried sick about her. They may even think she's dead.'

'I still think we should wait and see what else she can remember,' David said. 'She may not have total recall yet. And she may find it difficult to reassimilate what she does remember, specially if it's painful.'

'So what do you think we should do? We can't leave it all to Miss Everard. Charlotte may need specialist help; at the very least I think she should see Dr Masters.'

'You can keep a watching brief, my love,' said David, 'but I don't think you can interfere.'

'Is it interfering to want what's best for the child?' asked Avril hotly.

'Calm down, darling. All I'm saying is that we give it a couple more days to see how she is and then we'll contact Caroline and see if having Charlotte's real name can help us find out more about her. What she was doing in London. Who this Mr Peter Smith was; you know, the man they found her with? And why she was out in the street in the middle of an air raid. All that.'

'But the sooner we get on to Caro the sooner we can start to discover the answers,' Avril protested.

'Darling, it's Christmas Day, tomorrow is Boxing Day. With the best will in the world Caro wouldn't be able to discover anything until after the weekend. So, let's wait and see what Charlotte can remember.'

'I suppose you're right,' Avril sighed. She didn't want an argument with David now that they finally had a couple of hours to themselves. Instead, she held out her glass for a refill and they drank another glass of the wine before they went upstairs to bed. When they reached the children's rooms, Avril looked in on them as she always did. The girls were both fast asleep, heads under the blankets, and Paul was lying on his back, his new football still clutched in his arms. Avril stood at the door for a moment, smiling, but her smile faded as she turned away, wondering if Charlotte was asleep or if she lay awake, memories flooding her mind.

Charlotte was still up, sitting by the fire in the living room and trying to come to terms with what she had remembered.

When Miss Edie had followed her out of the vicarage drawing room, she'd found Charlotte sitting on the stairs, her whole body heaving with sobs, tears pouring down her cheeks. Miss Edie sat on the stair beside her and held her close, knowing there was nothing else she could do while Charlotte's grief at what she'd remembered consumed her. Gradually the sobs subsided and Charlotte, turning her tear-blotched face to her said, 'Can we go home now?'

Miss Edie handed her a hankie. 'Of course we can. Blow your nose and then we'll say goodbye and go.' She got to her feet and went back into the drawing room, leaving Charlotte to dry her eyes.

They had walked home in silence, each wrapped in her own thoughts. When they got in, Miss Edie put a match to fire she'd laid ready in the sitting room and then went into the kitchen to put the kettle on. Charlotte went straight up to her room.

'I'm making some tea,' Miss Edie called up to her. 'Come down when you're ready.'

Upstairs, Charlotte lay on her bed and stared bleakly at the ceiling. She knew who she was now, she knew her name, she recognised the people in the photograph that stood by her bed. Miss Morrison had put it into a frame for her, so that she could have it at her bedside, perhaps to jog her memory. She picked it up now and looked at it. There they all were, Mutti, Papa and Martin, smiling for the camera. How could she have not recognised them? She'd looked at that picture a thousand times without recognition and yet now she knew them at once. She'd had this picture, but surely, there should have been letters, too. She remembered that she'd had a letter from Mutti saying they were well and that Papa had come home again. She'd written back but her letter had been returned to her marked GONE AWAY. Her letters, where were they? She opened the drawer in her bedside table and tipped everything out, but there were no letters. A feeling of panic overcame her and she crossed to the chest in the corner, pulling out its drawers and upending them on to the floor, clothes, underclothes, socks, hankies, school books, pencils, pen, a bottle of ink, a ruler, everything she owned all heaped together as she searched frantically for her letters. They were not there. Desolate, she sat down on her bed holding the picture of her family in her hand. GONE AWAY, she remembered that clearly now, stamped across the envelope. But where had they gone? Harry had shrugged and said they weren't coming back. 'You got to make your own life now,' he'd said. 'I learned that the hard way, too.'

Harry. Harry kept coming into her mind. He came from Hanau. She remembered coming on the train. Harry said he'd been on the same train, but she hadn't seen him. It had been he who had recognised her. But where? School. But where was school?

Charlotte heard Miss Edie call from downstairs, but she didn't go down. She wasn't ready to talk about her family. Miss Edie wouldn't understand what it was like, not to know what had happened to them. So Charlotte simply sat on her bed, holding her photograph. She didn't cry, she felt dried up inside, a husk with no tears left.

At last there was a tap on the door and Miss Edie came in, carrying a cup of tea. She looked at everything, heaped on the floor, but she made no comment.

'Charlotte,' she said softly. 'I've brought you a cup of tea. You need something to warm you up. It's cold up here.' She put the tea down on the bedside table and then sat down next to Charlotte on the bed and took her hand. Charlotte didn't pull away, but her hand was icy in Miss Edie's and Miss Edie chafed it in her own before saying, 'Come on, Charlotte, drink a little tea.' She reached for the tea, holding the saucer while Charlotte sipped from the cup.

'I've lit the fire downstairs,' Miss Edie said, 'so the sitting room is lovely and warm now. Why don't you come down? We can make some toast by the fire and I've got some crab apple jelly I bought at the bazaar.'

Charlotte didn't answer, but when Miss Edie pulled her gently to her feet she didn't resist. Still clutching the photograph, she allowed herself to be led back down into the warmth of the sitting room and settled into one of the armchairs beside the fire. Miss Edie had already brought the bread and jelly in from the kitchen and now she reached for the toasting fork. Spiking a piece of bread on its prongs, she held it towards the fire.

As the bread began to toast she said, 'Oh, I've left my tea in the kitchen. You do this while I fetch it, will you?' She handed Charlotte the toasting fork and left the room.

Normality, she had decided. Normality was the thing. She had to get Charlotte thinking about everyday things, doing everyday things, so that her memories could gradually become absorbed into her life that was now. She was about to drink her tea when she smelled burning and dashed back into the sitting room.

Charlotte had been staring into the flames, the heat from the fire warming her cheeks, so that they flushed red. Where are they now? she wondered. How's Martin coping in another new place without being able to see? She paid no attention when the toast caught fire and Miss Edie rushed back into the room in time to snatch the toasting fork out of her hand and shake the blackened toast into the fire.

'Don't want to burn the house down,' she said mildly. She made more toast and spread it with the crab apple jelly, then she passed a piece to Charlotte and began to eat a piece herself.

'I didn't think I'd have room for any more food today, after that lovely lunch,' she said as she munched her toast. There was no response from Charlotte and she let the silence lapse round them before she said, 'Is that your brother in the photo?'

Charlotte looked down at the picture lying in her lap. 'Martin,' she said. 'He's my brother and he's blind.' Silence wrapped them again and then Charlotte said, 'I can't find my letters.'

'Your letters?'

'I had a letter from my mother when I got here and I wrote back but she didn't get it. It came back to me marked "Gone Away". I don't know where they are and now I can't find the letters.'

'Are they what you were looking for upstairs?'

'They aren't in my room.'

'I don't think you had them with you when you came here,' Miss Edie said. 'No one mentioned to me that you had any letters. Just the photo which had been in your pocket. It was the only thing you had when you were found, the only thing that might identify you.'

'I must have dropped them in the raid,' Charlotte said miserably.

'Where were you when your mother wrote to you? When you first got here? Can you remember? You said you came on the train. Who met you in London?'

'Aunt Naomi and Uncle Dan.'

'And where did they live, your aunt and uncle?'

'They weren't my aunt and uncle. I've no one left and I don't know what's happened to them. The Gestapo took Papa and we had to move out of our home. We lived with my aunt Trudi for a short while, but then Mutti found somewhere...' Her voice trailed off.

After a while Miss Edie said, 'And then you came on the train.'

'Yes, but I don't know what happened to them.' Charlotte's voice rose to a wail. 'My letter came back with "Gone Away" on it. I don't know where they are.' She looked at Miss Edie almost accusingly. 'You wouldn't understand. You don't know what it's like to lose your family and not know what's happened to them.'

Miss Edie looked at her for a moment. She knew all right. She knew what it was to lose someone and not know what had happened to them. Herbert had simply disappeared in a battle, probably blown to bits. That vision had haunted her for years, an explosion and Herbert... gone. She had never spoken of her grief at his loss, of her misery at the emptiness it left; the sliver of hope that perhaps, just perhaps, he'd survived and would come home. She'd been young at the time, but not as young as Charlotte. She couldn't leave this child to bear her sorrow alone, thinking that no one could understand. Now, for the first time, she must tell her own story; make it clear that she did understand.

Taking a deep breath, Miss Edie reached for Charlotte's hand. 'Not to lose my family, no, I don't. But I do know what it's like to lose someone I loved and not know whether he's dead or alive. To wonder every day if there'll be news of him.' She pressed Charlotte's hand to her cheek for a moment. 'In the war, the last war I mean, I knew a soldier. His name was Herbert and we were going to be married. He came home on leave and on the day he went back to France, he asked me to marry him.' She was still holding Charlotte's hand and as she spoke she felt a quickening interest in what she was saying. She went on quietly. 'Herbert wasn't someone my parents knew. We met in Bristol when I went there to help pack Red Cross parcels. He came from Yorkshire, but he'd been wounded at Passchendaele and been in hospital for several months. My parents wouldn't have approved of him, he wasn't an officer, just a corporal in the infantry.' She lapsed into silence as she thought of their brief courtship.

'What happened to him?' Charlotte asked.

'When he was signed off fit for duty, he was posted back up north for a few months. We wrote to each other almost every day. And then they sent him back to France. He was given a week's leave and he came back down to Somerset. I introduced him to my parents. They were very polite to him, but we both knew they thought he was... unsuitable.' Miss Edie said the word in the condescending tone her father would have used. 'When he caught the train from Bristol I went to see him off, and that's when he proposed to me, in the waiting room at Temple Meads station.' She smiled sadly at the recollection. 'He'd bought a ring and put it on my finger. And he went, back to the front.'

'And he didn't come back?' asked Charlotte softly, forgetting her own sadness as she was drawn into Miss Edie's.

'No. He was killed, in August 1918. So near the end of the war. There was a battle near Amiens. A great offensive, they said. All the Australians and Canadians alongside the British and French, pushing the Germans back.'

'And he died?'

'He was killed in the advance. He was posted missing in action. He had no family and he'd put me as next of kin on his pay book, so the telegram came to me.' She dashed a tear from her eye. 'His body was never found.'

'How do you know he's dead,' asked Charlotte, 'if they never found him?'

'They never found thousands of them,' Miss Edie said. 'Of course I kept on hoping that he'd turn up somewhere, alive and well. For years I thought he might suddenly come knocking on my door, but of course he never did. I'll never know what happened to him that day. I learned to live with it. I had my parents to look after. That was hard, because I knew they were relieved he'd been killed. I had to do my duty by them, but I hated them because they were glad he'd died, my Herbert.'

'I told Harry they'd gone,' Charlotte said. 'He said I'd got to make my own life now.'

'He was right,' said Miss Edie. 'You must. I should have, instead of living in a past full of regrets. All I have left of Herbert is a photo he sent me when he was promoted sergeant.'

'And your ring.'

'I took it off.'

'Took it off?'

'The day I got the telegram.'

'Why?' asked Charlotte. 'Why did you take it off?'

'Herbert wasn't well off. He'd bought me the ring he could afford, but my parents, well they... I took it off. I didn't want his ring despised.' Silence enfolded them again and they both stared into the embers of the fire.

'I wish I had my letters,' Charlotte said.

'You mustn't give up hope, Charlotte,' Miss Edie said. '"Gone Away" doesn't mean they're dead. It may simply mean they've moved again and whoever is living at that address now, doesn't know where.' Silence lapsed round them for a moment or two as they both stared into the fire as if they could see the faces of their loved ones in the flames.

'Tell me about Aunt Naomi and Uncle Dan,' suggested Miss Edie.

'I went to them when I got to London,' Charlotte said. 'Sixty-five Kemble Street. They were very kind to me.'

'Have they got a telephone?' asked Miss Edie.

Charlotte shook her head.

'Then, in the morning, I think you should write to them and tell them where you are and explain what's happened. They must be so worried about you. But now,' Miss Edie got to her feet and put a guard over the dying embers of the fire, 'now, I think we should both go to bed and try and get some sleep.' She smiled at the child who had altered her life and added, 'I know some of your memories are sad, Charlotte, but at least you know who you are now. On the whole, a good Christmas present, I think.' Another thought struck her and she asked, 'Would you like us to call you Lisa, now?'

Charlotte considered for a moment and then shook her head. 'No,' she replied. 'In Wynsdown I'm Charlotte.'

Chapter Twenty-Three

Dan had planned to stay only two nights in Feneton, but with the unexpected arrival of his son, he stayed an extra two. Shirley came to visit them at the pub and admire the baby.

'Looks a bit on the small side,' she said as she peered down at him sleeping peacefully in his drawer.

'That's cos he was early,' Naomi said. 'Dr Phelps says he'll catch up in no time. He's ever so nice, Dr Phelps.'

Shirley said, 'Well, that's good then,' but she wasn't really thinking about the baby, she was wondering if Naomi thought she could move back into Cousin Maud's house. Shirley had been willing enough to share her room with Naomi, but she had no intention of sharing it with a squalling baby. She'd been planning to tell Naomi that she'd have to find somewhere else to live when the baby came, but now it had happened and she'd left it too late. Still, she'd say it anyway, she decided. Dan was here, he could find them somewhere else; after all, they were his responsibility.

'Maud says she doesn't think you can come back with the baby,' Shirley said, pushing the blame for her decision on to the cousin who'd given her refuge. 'Says she's sorry, but there isn't really room for two of you.'

'No matter,' Naomi said. She wasn't surprised; she'd been half expecting it. It had been all right sharing with Shirley, though on occasion her untidiness had nearly driven Naomi mad, but she knew it would be hopeless if there were three of them crammed into the small bedroom. 'We'll find somewhere else. Dan might take us back with him tomorrow.'

'What? Back to the Blitz?' Shirley was startled. She hadn't meant them to go back to London, just find somewhere else.

When Dan came in, Naomi told him that she no longer had anywhere to stay. 'I'm quite glad really,' she said. 'We was beginning to get on each other's nerves, sharing that room. Think we'd better come back to London, with you.'

Dan looked at Nicholas, now at his mother's breast, and shook his head. 'No,' he said firmly. 'We ain't going to risk either of you back there. We'll find somewhere else round here. There must be families who've got a spare room and would like the extra bit of cash. I'll ask Jenny, she's sure to know of someone.' He gave Naomi a reassuring grin. 'Don't you fret, girlie, we'll find you somewhere to stay, you and young Nick.' He left her feeding Nicholas and went downstairs to find Jenny. When he'd explained the situation Jenny smiled.

'I did wonder how they was all going to fit in,' she said, 'and I talked it over with Jim. We don't have many visitors staying just now, so we thought Naomi and Nicholas might like to stay here, with us. She can have a couple of rooms, and when she's on her feet again she can help in the bar. I know she was cooking for the café down the road, so if she wants to help in the kitchen here too, so much the better.'

'How much rent would you want?' Dan asked. It seemed a perfect solution, but he thought they'd want more than Maud had been asking.

'You're not listening, Dan,' laughed Jenny. 'I'm offering board and lodging to Naomi and the baby in return for her help in running the pub. We're busy in the evenings with the RAF base only five miles away. I could do with another pair of hands. Naomi can work down here in the bar and know that Nicholas is perfectly safe asleep upstairs. And when she has to feed him, she only has to pop upstairs.' She cocked her head at him. 'So, what d'you think?'

'I think it's a brilliant idea,' Dan said, 'and I'm sure Naomi will too.'

'Good,' said Jenny. 'Go up and see what she says.'

It was all agreed. Naomi should keep her room and for the first two weeks, while she was still recovering from the birth, Dan would pay Jenny what they'd been paying Maud. After that Naomi would be earning her keep and the money they'd been paying Maud would be Naomi's to use for Nicholas.

'You've fallen on your feet all right,' Shirley said when they told her of their arrangement. 'Does that mean you won't be working for Mrs Grant no more?'

'It'll depend on when Jenny wants me,' Naomi replied. 'If I have spare time I'll happily bake for the café, but I shan't know till I see how it all works. I'll come and see Mrs Grant when I'm back on my feet. Dr Phelps says I got to rest for another week yet.'

With everything settled Dan set off back to London on Sunday morning.

'Can't afford not to work any longer,' he said. 'Need to be out in the cab.' He bent over and kissed her long and hard on the mouth. 'Look after yourself and the boy,' he said gruffly. 'I can phone you here, Jenny's given me the number.' And with that, he hurried out of the room before the sight of his wife and his sleeping son could unman him.

When he'd gone Naomi gathered Nicholas into her arms and held him as he slept. She knew they'd taken the right decision. It would have been madness for her to take a young baby away from the relative security of a Suffolk village, back into the horror of bomb-blasted London, but she was already missing Dan and he was on his way back into the battleground London had become.

'Try not to worry about him,' Jenny said when she came up and sat with Naomi for an hour that afternoon. 'There hasn't been a raid since before Christmas. It may be easing off now. P'raps the worst is over, eh?'

She was wrong. The worst wasn't over. Dan got back to a cold house in Kemble Street late in the afternoon and, having made himself a sandwich to take with him, went straight out again to join his fire-watching team at the paint warehouse. As darkness fell and he walked through the chilly streets, he thought of Naomi and Nicholas back in their warm room at the Feneton Arms and smiled. They were safe.

He reported in to John Anderson and then joined Arthur.

'Peaceful here over Christmas,' Arthur remarked as they climbed the iron fire escape to the warehouse roof. 'Your missus all right, is she? Only we was expecting you back two days ago.'

'She certainly is,' Dan said. 'We've got a son! Born on Christmas morning, he was.'

'But she weren't due yet,' Arthur said.

'No,' Dan agreed with a grin. 'But young Nicholas made his own mind up!'

'Nicholas. That's a nice name. Congratulations, Dan, boy, you must be a very proud dad. Staying up there, are they?'

'Yes.' Dan was about to explain how everything had been settled when the sirens began to wail. They hurried the last two flights and emerging out on to the roof saw the starburst of anti-aircraft shells further south and east and heard the steady drone of incoming aircraft, a swarm of loud and angry wasps invading the sky. Bombs began to fall, pounding the city with high explosive, but even more devastating, incendiaries in their hundreds began pouring downward out of the night. In the darkness of the streets below them, Dan and Arthur could see fires erupting in every direction, flickering flames taking hold faster than the firefighters could smother them.

A second wave of bombers came over, the air filled with the roar of their engines. As they passed overhead one of the incendiary bombs swirled down and landed with a brilliant flash on the warehouse roof. For a moment, both Arthur and Dan ducked away from it, but then training took hold and they rushed forward to where the bomb fizzed, dazzling white, beginning its lethal work. The two men grabbed sandbags from the stack kept ready on the roof and rushed forward with them. Arthur, slashing the bags with his knife, tipped their contents on to the infant fire. Dan grabbed a spade and began to shovel the loose sand, heaping it on to the simmering flames. Arthur went back for more bags and as the fire, now starved of the oxygen it needed, began to subside, they piled yet more sand on top until they were quite sure that it had been put out and rendered harmless. Even as they finished dealing with this first incendiary, another dropped on the other side of the roof and a third almost on top of the first.

'Christ,' yelled Arthur, 'you take that one, Dan, I'll do this.'

Dan dashed to the further bomb, dragging a sandbag with him. The bomb was already fizzing, the heat intense, burning the leaded roof of the warehouse. Dan heaped the sand on to the fire and went back for more. It wasn't enough. He couldn't smother it fast enough and it was now burning furiously. Rushing back for more sand, he caught a glimpse of Arthur, spade in hand, furiously shovelling sand on to his bomb. Dan grabbed another bag and turned back to the third, but despite his efforts he knew there was no way he could extinguish the fire.

'Arthur,' he bellowed, desperately trying to make himself heard over the continuous throb of aero engines, 'Arthur, help!'

Arthur had managed to subdue his fire, the heaped sand doing its work, but even the two of them couldn't put out the third fire, and even as they made one more valiant attempt, another bomb dropped down, past them and into the street below.

'Time to go down,' Arthur cried. 'Come on, can't do more here.' He grabbed Dan by the arm and pulled him towards the fire escape. Dan held back for a moment, staring at the raging fire on the far side of the roof. They'd failed. The roof was aflame and probably the whole warehouse would go up.

'Dan! Come on!' shrieked Arthur as he ran for the iron ladder and disappeared over the parapet. With one final backward glance at the inferno now burning out of control, Dan followed, his cheeks scarlet from the increasing heat, his lungs bursting with the hot smoke.

They scrambled down the escape, and reached the ground to find the whole unit battling fires and more bursting out in every direction.

'Fire on the warehouse roof,' they reported to John Anderson. 'Three bombs at once.'

'Too big for us,' John shouted, reaching for the phone. 'I'll call the brigade, see if we can save it. You get out into the street. There's fires everywhere.'

Dan and Arthur left the post and headed back out into the night. The sky was no longer dark, it blazed red and orange. The bombers still came, wave after wave of them, flying up the river to target docks and city alike. It was Sunday night and the buildings in the commercial area were mostly empty, few had their regular fire-watchers in position. The two men joined with another team and tackled fire after fire, sometimes dealing with a bomb that had yet to explode into flame, at others pumping water on those which had already taken hold, heaving sandbags, shovelling sand. Fireboats on the Thames pumped the river over to the city in a desperate attempt to provide more water to quench the flames, but the tide was low and lack of water reaching the shore hampered the continuing and increasingly desperate attempts to save the city from this blistering firestorm.

When at last the all-clear went the whole of London seemed to be ablaze. There was no respite for the firefighters, as they fought to save homes, wharfs, warehouses, factories and some of London's beautiful historic buildings. Hundreds of firefighters risked their lives in their efforts to bring the inferno under control and, working with them, Dan felt exhausted beyond exhaustion. By the time John Anderson sent them home, he and Arthur were gritty-eyed, their lungs full of the smoke which still billowed across the sky, their legs hardly able to carry them.

'Sleep,' John ordered. 'Come back when you've had some shut-eye. We'll still be at it. We ain't done yet; the bastards ain't going to win.'

Dan dragged himself home. Everywhere showed the devastation of the raid. Ruined buildings, some collapsed, some standing, black-ened shells, silhouetted against the burning sky, testified to its ferocity. Offices, factories, churches, homes all targeted to instil fear and misery, to destroy the morale of the Londoners who suf-fered the attack.

When Dan turned into Kemble Street he stopped in his tracks. The whole of one side of the street, his side of the street, had virtu-ally been destroyed. The houses, though not flattened, had been taken by the fire. Blackened walls, jagged roof trees, the spike of a chimney breast, crumbling masonry, all that was left of the five houses in the terrace; fire had swept through them all. Few people were about; most, surely, would have spent the night in the Hope Street shelter. When they emerged they'd find their homes gone.

With leaden feet Dan walked down the road until he came to the remains of his own house. Thank God, he thought as he surveyed the blackened shell, thank God he'd refused to let Naomi come home. He stared at the remains of the house he'd been born in. The fire must have swept through it at great speed. The roof had gone, the window frames stood, empty of glass, on blackened walls. The inside was gutted and even as he watched smoke drifted up into the early-morning sky, smoke to join the smoke of the second Great Fire of London. Everything Dan owned had been in that house; he had the clothes he stood up in, the money actually in his pocket and his taxi, still garaged under the railway arches. Unless, he thought miserably, they've collapsed on top of it, or taken a direct hit. What's left? Firefighters had done their job and moved on. The fire was out, but they had saved little.

Dan was so tired that he could hardly take in what he was looking at; all he could think was that Naomi and Nicholas were safe. He had no home left, but he did have a family. The thought gave him a sudden spurt of energy and he did something that he would have castigated anyone else for and broke all the rules. With a quick glance to see if anyone was looking at him, he walked up to what had, until last night, been his front door. There was no door now, just a gaping hole into the ruin of his home. Carefully he stepped across the threshold – inside, the smell was damp and acrid. He edged his way down the hall to the kitchen at the back. Wet ash covered the floor, black and clinging as his feet disturbed it. In the kitchen, now little more than a shell, were the remnants of the few pieces of furniture it had contained. In the far corner was the cellar door. It, too, was burned black, but the firemen must have got to the blaze before that, too, was consumed by the flames. Dan put his hand on the handle and pulled. The door fell towards him, knocking him sideways and clattering to the floor, exploding a cloud of ash around him. Coughing, but determined, Dan stood at the top of the cellar steps and peered down into the dark. By the little light which filtered down from the kitchen he could see that the fire hadn't reached the shelter he'd made to protect his family. Edging down the steps, he peered into the gloom. He could just make out the mattress, still on the floor, the old armchair tucked into the corner. Dan had nowhere else to go, at least for now and so, almost dead on his feet, he went down the last few steps and lay down on the mattress. He was asleep within seconds and it was only when the sound of voices shouting in the street above woke him, that he crawled out of his subterranean lair to face the day.

He staggered out into the street to find a crowd of men working their way along the street, looking into every house and marking what had to be done.

'Hey, mate,' called one who had a clipboard and seemed to be in charge. 'What the hell were you doing in there?'

'It's my home,' replied Dan.

'But what're you doing in it now? Don't you know how dangerous that is? For Christ's sake it's people like you who put people like us in danger. You go into an unsafe building and we have to crawl in and pull you out.' He shook his head in fury. 'Where were you last night anyways?'

'Out fighting bloody fires,' snapped Dan. 'Pity some bugger didn't put this one out!'

'Well, you can't stay here. Better get along to the rescue centre and see if they can find you somewhere to doss down,' said the man. 'Reckon they'll be along to flatten this lot soon. Too dangerous to leave.' Unaware of the look of horror on Dan's face, he studied his clipboard and made a note. Looking up again he said, 'Don't go back inside, right? Too dangerous.' And with this warning he and his men continued along the road. Dan watched them until they were round the corner and out of sight and then turned back into the house. Burned-out shell it might be, but it was still his home. He didn't risk trying to get upstairs; the stairs were gone and the odd protruding struts were burned and brittle. He looked into what had been the front room. Nothing to retrieve from there, either. In the kitchen he found the savings tin that had been kept in a hollowed hidey-hole under the cooker and pulled it out. He looked inside and found a small roll of notes, carefully saved and hidden by Naomi;

neither of them trusted banks. Now at least he had a little money to tide him over. He returned to the shelter of the cellar, which had escaped almost unscathed, and looked about him. He wouldn't go to the rescue centre, not yet. There was no reason that Dan could see why he shouldn't sleep here until he found somewhere better. There was no way of securing it, but even if someone did get in there was nothing worth stealing.

Stuffing the cash into his pocket, Dan set out to find a telephone box that worked. Much as he dreaded the call, he had to tell Naomi what had happened to their home.

Chapter Twenty-Four

When Charlotte woke up on Boxing Day her bedroom was suffused with an eerie light. Going to the window she drew back the blackout to find that it was snowing. Huge white flakes drifted down, swirling gently to lay a smooth white carpet over the fields. The hedge at the bottom of the garden was already losing its angularity, becoming just another snow-covered shape, and away in the distance the woods were no more than a heavier whiteness against the leaden sky.

Charlotte shivered and, leaving the curtains open, climbed back into bed. As she lay watching the snow falling steadily, she thought about the previous day, cut into two distinct halves: before memory returned and after. Before, she had been enjoying a happy and peaceful Christmas, with presents and church and lunch. The warmth of her welcome at the vicarage had given her a glow of pleasure. She didn't remember any other Christmases and so this one had taken on a magic of its own. After, as the gates of her recollection opened and her memories came flooding through, the misery she felt as she remembered her family threatened to overwhelm her. However, a gradual calmness had followed as she sat by the fire with Miss Edie and began, once again, to come to terms with what had happened. She had known about her parents and Martin before she'd lost her memory, she reasoned, and must have learned then to accept the possibility of their loss, so now she should be able to do so again.

She remembered Aunt Naomi and Uncle Dan and 65 Kemble Street, a house that had given her refuge and become a home. She recalled the patience Aunt Naomi and Uncle Dan had shown as she tried to settle down in England, the affection they had given her and how, over the year, she had grown to love them in return. Where were they now? In Kemble Street? And where did they think she was?

And then there was Harry. What had happened to him? The last thing she remembered was going to meet him in the park. They were going up west and he'd promised to buy her dinner in a real café. She could remember going into the park and finding Harry sitting waiting for her in the September sunshine. She must have been wearing the necklace he'd given her, as she still had it. Had he noticed? But try as she might, she could remember nothing more until she woke up in the hospital.

Did we go to London? she wondered. Did Harry buy me dinner in a café? Where else did we go and why weren't we together when the raid struck? Why wasn't Harry found with me?

Remembering the nurse's advice to stop trying to remember, Charlotte turned her thoughts to the previous evening. Miss Edie had told her about Herbert, how he had been lost; how she'd never known exactly what had happened to him. It was a very sad story, but at some level Charlotte knew that she was being warned. Don't let the loss of your loved ones destroy the rest of your life. Mourn them, grieve for them, remember them with love and then gradually, gently, ease them into a secret compartment of your mind and move on. Easily said, Charlotte thought, but it was too soon for her. The ache of her grief would be with her for a long time yet.

Snow was building up on the outside sill and the strange white light pervading the room made it feel cold. Charlotte slid out of bed and got dressed as quickly as she could. Everything she had tipped from the drawers last night was still heaped on the floor.

I wish I could find my letters, she thought sadly as she stared at the mess she'd made. With a sigh, she began to pick up her clothes and checking them once again just in case she had missed something, she folded them into the drawers. She shook each of her school books in turn just to be sure that nothing had been tucked into the pages, but by the time she'd restored some sort of order to her things, she had to accept that the letters weren't there.

She could hear Miss Edie moving about downstairs and so closing her door on her bedroom, she went down.

'Hallo, love,' said Miss Edie as she came into the kitchen. 'Did you manage to sleep?' Miss Edie had never addressed Charlotte by any term of endearment and it surprised both of them when she did so now. The confidences of the previous night had changed her, changed them both.

Charlotte smiled. 'Yes, thank you,' she replied.

'That's good. What would you like for breakfast? Poached egg on toast?'

Charlotte watched as Miss Edie slid two eggs into the waiting pan.

'Keep an eye on the toast, will you?' Miss Edie said as she put two slices under the grill.

Together they made their breakfast and together they sat down and ate it.

'I've been thinking,' Miss Edie said as she poured them each a cup of tea, 'it might be a good idea if you wrote down what you do remember, so that we know as much about you as possible. What do you think?'

Charlotte agreed. Perhaps if she did that, the hours that were still missing might come back to her. After breakfast she sat down at the kitchen table and on a clean sheet of paper she began to write.

Lieselotte Becker. Born in Hanau 11th June 1926.

My parents: Franz and Marta Becker.

Papa is a doctor. Mutti is a housewife and looks after me and my brother Martin.

Martin is two years older than me and he is blind.

We used to live in Waldstrasse 9 Hanau where Papa had his surgery. He was arrested and we were turned out into the street.

We went first to Aunt Trudi's and then Mutti found us a room in an apartment house.

I came to England on the train in July 1939.

I was taken in by Aunt Naomi and Uncle Dan, the Federmans, and we live at 65 Kemble Street. They are very kind to me. Uncle Dan drives a taxi. Aunt Naomi works making uniforms for soldiers.

I go to school at Francis Drake. My friends are Harry Black and Hilda Lang.

Harry comes from Hanau too and lives in a hostel. He has left school and works for a man at the market.

Hilda's mum is German and Hilda speaks German and English. They helped me learn English. They live in Grove Avenue.

She paused and looked up, chewing the end of her pencil. What else could she write? She thought about the letter she'd had from Mutti. She'd said Papa had come home but wasn't well. She said to write to them through Cousin Nikolaus in Zurich.

My parents were trying to go to Switzerland to Papa's cousin, Nikolaus. Mutti wrote his address on a piece of paper, but I haven't got that now and I don't know where it is.

'That's excellent,' Miss Edie said, coming to read what she'd written over her shoulder. 'Can you write about that last day, when you got caught in the raid? Do you know why you were where you were?'

'A bit,' Charlotte said. 'Harry and I were going up west. I met him in the park. It was warm and sunny.'

'Did you go?'

Charlotte shrugged. 'Must've.'

'By Tube,' suggested Miss Edie.

'No,' answered Charlotte vehemently. 'I never go underground!'

Miss Edie thought of Charlotte's panic when she'd been trapped in a dark corner of the attic and remembered she'd been told

Charlotte had to be coaxed into St Michael's air raid shelter. It was probably why she was in the street during that first dreadful Blitz raid. However, she simply nodded and said, 'By bus then.'

Charlotte shrugged again. 'I suppose.'

'What did you do when you got there?' It was one question too many and Charlotte snapped, 'I don't know, do I?'

At that moment there came a knock at the back door and when Miss Edie opened it, she found Billy Shepherd standing in the porch, his coat thick with clinging snow and his hat a flat white pancake on his head.

'Billy!' she exclaimed in surprise. 'What are you doing here?' adding before he could reply, 'You'd better come in.'

'I'm a bit snowy, Miss Everard.'

'Never mind that, come in before you freeze to death and all our heat gets out!'

Billy stamped his feet on the mat and took off his boots, hung his coat and hat on a spare peg and followed Miss Everard indoors. Looking up from what she was writing, Charlotte saw who it was and her face broke into a smile and she jumped to her feet. 'Billy!' she cried.

'How you doing, Char? Happy Christmas.'

Charlotte looked from Billy to Miss Everard before saying, 'Happy Christmas, Billy... but Christmas is over.'

Billy laughed. 'Christmas Day is, silly, but today's Boxing Day. That's a holiday too. We wondered if you'd like to come over to the farm for your dinner.' He looked at Miss Everard a little uncertainly. 'Both of you, of course. Ma said to say you was both more than welcome. I know it's a bit snowy,' he hurried on, 'but it has stopped snowing now and I'll walk you there and back.'

Charlotte turned hopeful eyes on Miss Edie, who said, 'What a kind invitation, Billy. I'm sure Charlotte would love to come, but I'm afraid I won't accept. Please thank your mother, but I have things I need to do here before I go back to work tomorrow.' She turned and smiled at Charlotte's eager face. 'You go with Billy,' she said, 'but make sure you're back here before dark. I don't want you two wandering about in the dark and the snow. Go on upstairs and put some warmer clothes on, and I'll find you some boots.'

When Charlotte and Billy had gone, Miss Edie sat down and squeezed another cup of tea from the pot. Going to Charing Farm for the day was just the distraction Charlotte needed, she thought. She wouldn't have time to brood on the memories that had returned to her.

Miss Edie reread what Charlotte had written that morning and then folded the piece of paper, putting it into her pocket. She put on her coat and, finding her scarf, gloves and hat and donning her own boots, she set off to the vicarage. The snow had indeed stopped and a weak sun was filtering through the blanket of cloud, striking diamonds in the fallen snow. There were already footprints along the lane and as she reached the village green, she saw a group of children, red-nosed from the cold, building a snowman. Among them were the Dawson children and the two lads who now lived with the Bellingers. There was a great deal of laughter and shouting, and even as she watched the two older boys began to pelt each other with snowballs. As she turned in the vicarage gate, a snowball flew past her ear and she turned back to glower at the boys, but to their surprise and her own, she suddenly bent down, grabbed a handful of snow and returned fire. The boys darted out of range with shrieks of laughter and Miss Edie headed for the house.

Avril had seen her from the window and was already at the front door when Miss Edie dodged into the relative shelter of the front porch.

'Miss Everard!' she cried. 'Those naughty boys! Are you wet? Come in, do!'

'They missed me,' Miss Edie said, laughing, but she was glad not to have got snow down the back of her neck.

Avril took her coat and then led her into the kitchen. 'We only heat the drawing room on high days and holidays,' she said. 'This is the warmest place in the whole house. Sit down, do.' She waved at a chair by the fire and Miss Edie sat down. Before Avril took the one opposite she said, 'Can I get you anything to drink? Tea?'

'No, thank you,' Miss Edie said. Avril looked at her expectantly and she went on, 'Charlotte has gone over to the Shepherds' for lunch and so I thought I'd take the opportunity to bring you up to date.' She took the paper out of her pocket and passed it over. Avril took it and read it through. She looked up.

'And this is what she remembers?'

'I did try asking a few more questions, but so far, I think, she's remembered all she can. It'll probably all return to her before long. Her mind must have blocked it out till now, but maybe from now on the rest will gradually come back. The thing is, I thought perhaps you could get in touch with your sister and see if she can contact the foster parents, the Federmans, and let them know where she is and that she's all right.'

'Yes, indeed,' Avril agreed. 'I'm sure Caroline could find them for us now we have an address. I don't know where this Kemble Street is, but even if Caro doesn't either she'll be able to find out.'

'I've suggested Charlotte write to them straight away,' Miss Edie told her, 'to set their minds at rest, but she hasn't begun that letter yet. I thought she ought to do it in her own time so I haven't pressed that. After all, we don't know how well they all got on.' Miss Edie had remembered the suggestion that she'd made the night before about writing to the Federmans, but she hadn't reminded Charlotte. Suppose the foster parents wanted her to come back to them? She didn't want to lose Charlotte just as she was getting used to sharing her life with someone who needed her.

'You don't think they'll want Charlotte to go back to London, do you?' Miss Edie voiced her fear now.

'I wouldn't think so,' Avril replied, trying to sound reassuring. 'She'd be in far more danger living in London than she'll be in down here.'

'Yes, that's what I thought,' said Miss Everard, the relief clear in her voice.

At that moment the vicar came in, shaking snow off his coat. 'Direct hit,' he said ruefully. 'That Malcolm Flint's a dead-eye shot!' He smiled at Miss Edie and said, 'Hallo, Miss Everard, how nice to see you. How's Charlotte this morning?'

'She's doing well,' answered Miss Edie. 'Young Billy Shepherd came over and took her back to the farm for lunch. Just what she needed, a change of scene and something else to think about.' She gestured to the paper Avril still held in her hand. 'I've just been showing your wife what Charlotte wrote this morning.'

'Let's have a look.' David held out his hand for the paper. 'Quite a lot of information there,' he said. 'Only a few gaps.'

'I thought I'd ring Caro with the information about the foster parents and see if she can find them,' Avril said.

'Good idea,' David said, 'provided Miss Everard agrees that's the way forward. She's Charlotte's foster mother now.'

All the way home Miss Edie nursed those words in her heart: 'her foster mother'. She was standing in for Charlotte's lost mother. She was a mother. Something she never thought she'd be. A mother.

When she'd gone Avril said, 'Well, that's good news, isn't it? We should be able to find her London foster parents and set their minds at rest as to where Charlotte is. Caro will be delighted.'

By the time Billy and Charlotte arrived at the farm the sun had broken through and the whole landscape was shining, the trees and buildings etched against the pale blue sky, the distant hills rising against the last of the clouds. It was bitterly cold and the wind that had blown away the snow clouds cut through their many layers of clothes, making them shiver.

'Better go and tell Ma you've come,' Billy said, 'let her know it's just you and not Miss Everard, too.' They went to the back door and shed their boots and coats before going into the warm and welcoming kitchen.

'Charlotte, you've come, my lover. Welcome. Miss Everard not coming too?'

'No,' answered Charlotte, 'but she said thank you for asking her. She goes back to work tomorrow and had things to do.'

'I understand,' said Mrs Shepherd comfortably. She hadn't expected that weird old stick, Miss Everard, to come all that way through the snow. Indeed, she thought, it was much better that she didn't. It was still a holiday and she didn't want a ghost sitting at her feast.

'Well, lunch won't be ready for another hour at least, so why don't you go and have a look at they puppies?'

They went back outside and across to the stable. It was chilly over there, but Billy assured Charlotte that the hay in the dogs' loosebox made it quite warm enough for the puppies. As soon as they closed the stable door behind them, two of the puppies came prancing over to the loosebox door to see who was there. Billy opened this door and the two of them edged inside before the curious puppies could escape. One of them was Jet, the dog Billy had already chosen for his own, but for a moment Billy ignored him and bent down to pick up the other one. He passed her over to Charlotte, who held her close, her face against the dog's warm fur.

'Oh, you're beautiful,' she cooed and was rewarded by having her face washed with a small pink tongue. Billy sat down in the hay to play with his dog and Charlotte, putting the puppy back on the ground, sat down beside him. The puppy danced forward again, darting away when Charlotte held out her hand.

'You have to move slowly or you spook them,' Billy said. 'Just sit there for a moment and they'll come to you. They're very nosy.'

He was right and within minutes not only the original puppy came back to her, but the others, made braver by their siblings, edged closer, sniffing and snuffling at the two humans who'd invaded their world.

'Doesn't their mother mind them coming to us?' wondered Charlotte, as one of the puppies attempted to clamber over her legs and fell backwards, its little legs paddling helplessly in the air.

Maisie was lying against a straw bale, watching her offspring exploring, apparently indifferent to their excursions.

Bill laughed. 'No, she knows they're safe enough with us. If another dog appeared, well, that'd be a different matter.'

As they sat in the hay, playing with the pups, Charlotte said, 'I got my memory back now, a bit anyway.'

'Have you?' Billy didn't sound particularly interested. 'What you remembered then?'

'That I'm German...'

'Well, we *knew* that,' Billy said, bending forward to extricate his trouser leg from Jet's needle-sharp teeth.

'But I'm not a Nazi, I'm a refugee. My parents have disappeared, and my brother. I think the Nazis have taken them away some-where, but I don't know where.'

'That's sad,' Billy said, 'but I expect you'll find them again when we've won the war.'

'Will we win?'

'Of course we will,' asserted Billy. 'It may take a while, but we will win, I promise you.' And it was clear to Charlotte that he had no doubt at all about that. It cheered her a little to hear his confidence.

'You don't mind that I'm German?' she asked tentatively, almost dreading the answer.

'Mind? No, why should I? You're you. That's what matters.'

At that moment the bell sounded out across the farm and reluc-tantly they shut the puppies into their loosebox and went back to the kitchen. Today there was only one extra hand at the dinner table, a small, quiet man whom Mrs Shepherd introduced as Ned Barnes.

'Pity Jane's not here,' said John Shepherd as they sat down to the table. He turned to Charlotte. 'She's a nurse, you know, but couldn't get leave for Christmas. Still, we hope she'll be home for a couple of days before too long.'

Mrs Shepherd picked up a huge pan from the range and began to dole out piping hot bubble and squeak. The fried vegetables, well flavoured with home-grown onions, smelt wonderful, and scattered among them were chopped pieces of chicken from the previous day's roast. Each plate was piled high and topped off with a fried egg.

As they all tucked in, Billy said, 'Remember what you said, Dad?'

'Said about what?'

Billy pulled a face. 'You *know* what about.'

'Oh, that!' his father replied airily. 'No, I haven't forgotten.'

'Well?' Billy's voice took on a note of frustration.

'Well, let your dad eat his dinner,' said his mother, but she was smiling.

'The thing is, Charlotte,' said Mr Shepherd as if he and Charlotte were already in the middle of a conversation. 'I was wondering if you could help me out.'

Charlotte look across at him in surprise. 'Please. How can I help you?'

'I need a good home for one of my puppies and I wondered if you'd be kind enough to give her one.'

'A puppy? For me?' Charlotte's face lit up with pure joy, causing everyone to laugh with her. 'You're giving me a puppy?'

'If you would like one and,' John Shepherd added seriously, 'if Miss Everard will let you have one.'

Charlotte's smile faded and she said, 'This I don't know.'

'I will write a note to her, explaining,' Mr Shepherd said. 'The pup's not quite ready to leave her mother yet, and when she is we'll keep her for a few more weeks and get her house-trained, so that there is no problem for Miss Everard. Before you go home today come and get the letter from me.'

Charlotte was so excited that she couldn't stop beaming. When they had finished their dinner, she and Billy went back to the stable.

'You can have whichever of the bitches you want,' Billy said as he opened the loosebox door.

'Bitches? What is "bitches"?'

'Girl dogs.'

As before, Jet pranced forward as soon as he heard Billy's voice, and the other brave one was soon behind him. Charlotte picked her up.

'Is this a girl dog?' she asked.

Billy laughed. 'Yes, she is.'

'Then I choose her,' said Charlotte, gathering the little dog up into her arms.

'I think she's already chosen you,' Billy replied.

When they reached Blackdown House, just before it got dark, Charlotte had the note from John Shepherd safely in her pocket.

'Don't say anything to Miss Edie about the puppy,' she said to Billy. 'I will ask her later.'

Billy shrugged. 'All right,' he said.

'Did you enjoy yourself?' Miss Edie asked when the curtains were drawn against the night and they were settled by the fire.

'Yes, it was a lovely dinner. Bubbles.'

'Bubbles?'

'All potatoes and vegetables.'

'Bubble and squeak,' laughed Miss Edie.

'Yes, with an egg.'

'Sounds delicious, I'm sorry I missed it. I don't know the Shepherds, only by sight. They sound very kind.'

Now, Charlotte decided, was the moment to produce the note that was burning a hole in her pocket. Miss Edie seemed relaxed and was thinking well of Billy's family.

'Mr Shepherd gave me this,' she said, extracting the letter from her pocket and handing it over.

Miss Edie saw her name on the envelope and opened it. Charlotte watched her read the short note it contained. When she looked up Miss Edie saw such hope mixed with entreaty in Charlotte's eyes that the reservations that had come to her mind were dashed away. Charlotte needed something to love, something that would return her love unconditionally. They'd overcome the problems of having a dog as they occurred. She smiled at her charge and said, 'What a kind offer. A dog of your own. You lucky girl!'

Charlotte stared at Miss Edie for moment and then flung her arms round her, enveloping her in a huge hug, and Miss Edie knew that whatever problems having a young dog in the house meant, they were worth it.

And so a month later, Bessie, named for Princess Elizabeth, joined the household at Blackdown House.

Chapter Twenty-Five

When Dan had finally got through to Naomi and told them that their home had gone, she broke down and begged him to come up to Feneton and stay with her.

'You ain't got nowhere to live now,' she said, her voice quavering with shock. 'Just get out of London, now, while you still can.'

'Not as easy as that,' Dan said gently. 'I still have to earn us a living. Can't just jack it all in.'

'Come up here and get a job,' Naomi begged. 'Just get out of London before you're killed. Nicholas and I need you, Danny. Please?'

As Dan was about to answer, the pips went and the call was over. He'd heard the tears, the desperation in her voice, and he was tempted to ring straight back and say he was on his way, but a moment's thought made him wait. He didn't know what to do and until he'd thought through all the possibilities, he didn't want to commit himself. He went back to the house and down into the cellar. He didn't relish sleeping there, but at least he was on hand if decisions were to be taken about what was going to happen to the house.

The London sky was still filled with smoke, swirling in the wind among the gently swaying barrage balloons, and it was clear that many fires were still burning. Perhaps he should go to the fire post to see what he could do to help. He would go later, he decided, but first he'd go to the railway arches to pick up his cab. It was already nearly midday, but he might as well ply for hire during the afternoon. In the evening he'd go back to the post as usual and join his fire-watching team. On his way to the arches he went into the Dog

and Duck and used the men's toilet. It was cold and dank and supplied only cold water, but at least he could wash his hands and
remove the soot and grime from his face before he tried to pick up
passengers. There was a cracked mirror over the single basin and
Dan stared at himself. Unshaven, with red-rimmed eyes and hair
standing up on end, he didn't look a good prospect for any work
today, but until he could sort out some more clothes there was little
more he could do. He damped his hair and tried to smooth it down
with his hands. There was no towel, and so he came out of the toilet
flapping his hands before wiping them on his trousers.

Feeling marginally better, he had a pint and a sandwich and then
set out for the railway arches. The taxi was still there, undamaged
by the raid, and Dan gave a sigh of relief. He still had a way of supporting them all. He was about to get into the cab and drive out into
the street, when a man in the uniform of a fire service officer
appeared at the entrance.

'This your cab?' he demanded without preamble.

'Yes,' Dan said cautiously.

'Requisitioning it,' said the man. 'Need it for the fire service.'

Dan stared at him. He knew they'd been requisitioning cabs on
and off for some time now, but his had not been taken. 'My cab? Am
I to drive it?' he asked.

'No,' replied the man. 'It'll be converted to carry water tanks
and hoses. A regular fireman'll drive it. You're to take it to this
depot.' He handed Dan an official-looking form with an address on
it. 'Take it there now and you'll be given the requisition paperwork.
Weren't enough vehicles last night,' he added, 'and we've lost too
many.' He looked round at the two other taxis which were still
parked under the arches. 'Know who owns these?' he asked.

Dan did, but he wasn't going to say so. 'Not always the same
cabs parked here,' he hedged.

'I see,' replied the man. 'Well, you get along to the depot, the
sooner they get to work converting yours the sooner it'll be out on
the street.'

'Yeah, all right,' said Dan, knowing there was nothing he could
do about the requisition.

The fire officer seemed to relent a little and said, 'Good man. Need all the help we can get. Bad raid last night.'

'I know,' snapped Dan, resenting the man's patronising attitude. 'I was firefighting till dawn.'

'Weren't we all,' the man retorted. 'Bloody fires are still burning. Still,' he added as he turned away, 'at least we saved St Paul's.'

Dan drove his cab to the depot and there he handed it over to the fire service. He was given a receipt and told that when the war was over he might seek recompense.

Recompense indeed! he thought as he strode away to reach his fire post on foot. Be lucky if I see a single penny.

John Anderson was already back at the post when Dan got there, but the scene round it had entirely changed. The warehouse where Dan and Arthur had been watching had lost its roof and top floors. A thin column of smoke still drifted up from this blackened section. The fire brigade had sent a fire engine as soon as the fire had been phoned in. Paint, so combustible, would burn out of control and they'd done all they could to contain the blaze. They'd had some measure of success; it was the upper floors, where the offices were, that had been burned out, the lower levels had survived the attack and the feared inferno had not burst forth. All round the area were damaged buildings, skeletal trees and blackened patches on road and pavement where incendiaries had been doused before they could take hold.

'Christ, Dan, you look rough!' John Anderson exclaimed by way of greeting. Dan pulled a face.

'Lost my house last night,' he snapped. 'No other clothes and nowhere to clean up!'

John looked lost for words and simply clapped Dan on the shoulder and said, 'So sorry, chum. Glad you came back. We'll need every pair of hands tonight if they come again.'

'Where're you going to stay if your house has gone?' demanded Arthur when he heard what had happened to Kemble Street.

'Cellar's still all right,' Dan told him. 'It's got a mattress, I can doss down there.'

'Don't be silly, mate,' cried Arthur. 'Come round ours. Matty'll be pleased to see you.'

271

Dan smiled wearily. 'Thanks, pal,' he said, 'but I'll go back home when we've done here. Need to keep an eye on the place. Not much to steal, you know, but don't want anyone else moving in just cos I'm not there. Assessor bloke was round this morning. Thinks they may bulldoze the lot. Need to be there, you know?'

The night was another busy one; so many fires from the raid the previous night were still burning, a beacon to the incoming planes, but at last John Anderson sent them home.

'You sure you won't come to us?' Arthur offered again. 'Be no problem, for a few days at least. You know, just till you get sorted?'

'No, thanks again, mate, but I think I'll head on home for now. Maybe take you up on it later, if they flatten.'

Dan had told none of the firefighters that his taxi had been requisitioned. He'd keep that to himself until he'd decided what to do next. He had no income now and no way of earning any. As he walked back to his burned-out home, he thought about Naomi and Nicholas in Feneton. He had no reason not to go up and join them now – well, the fire-watching – but he was a volunteer, not part of the auxiliary fire service. He had nothing to bind him to London and perhaps Naomi was right, he could get some sort of work up in Suffolk. Suddenly he wanted to be back at the Feneton Arms, his own arms round his wife. His longing for her was intense, a physical ache.

It was almost dawn when he reached home and he crept into the ruined house and down into the cellar. It was bitterly cold, but at least he could lie down and catch a few hours' sleep before finally making up his mind. He gathered the blankets they'd kept down there and, lying down on the lumpy mattress, piled them on top of himself in an attempt to keep warm. At last, despite the cold and his continuously churning thoughts, he finally drifted off to sleep. He awoke in the late morning, his mind made up as he slept. He'd go to Suffolk and look after his wife and son. He'd done his bit in London, he'd fought fires and he'd given up his cab. Now, he decided, he'd do his proper job in life and provide, somehow, for his wife and child.

He crawled out from under the blankets and went back up into the burnt-out kitchen. He tried turning on the tap, but no water came out. He had no other clothes and nothing to eat. Nothing left but a ruined house and a few quid in his pocket. He looked round to see if there was anything else he could salvage, but could see nothing. He returned to the cellar and there he picked up the blankets and bundled them into their box. He couldn't take them with him and he could do nothing with the mattress, so he left them where they were. Suddenly he caught sight of the biscuit tin Naomi had put on the shelf and he grabbed it and, pulling the lid off, he found there were half a dozen biscuits inside. He took out two and crammed them into his mouth while he searched along the shelf for anything else that might be edible. There was a pot of jam, half full, and he stuck his fingers into it, scooping the jam out in dollops into his mouth. He hadn't eaten, he realised, since midday yesterday.

He was about to leave the cellar, his pockets full of biscuits and the now almost-empty jam jar, when he caught sight of the small suitcase Naomi had insisted on storing in safety. Lisa's suitcase. It was all they had left of her and so, catching it up, he carried it upstairs to take with him. He stood in the kitchen and looked round. Everything was black and the smell of smoke still almost overpowering. He looked at the cellar door still lying in the ash on the kitchen floor. Perhaps he could secure it, so that anyone wanting to break in would have to make an effort to do so, not just walk in off the street. He knew there were squatters everywhere as people looked for somewhere to sleep when their homes had gone.

He heaved the door up and pushed it against the door frame, wedging it so that at a casual glance it appeared closed. It didn't really matter, he supposed, but somehow it made him feel better that a small part of their home was still their own.

When Dan finally emerged into the street it was deserted. A chilly wind was blowing and the sky was dark, threatening rain, or possibly snow. He had made his plans. He would go first to the rescue centre where they could perhaps give him another set of clothes and maybe even a square meal, then he would go the station and catch his train. He would be out of London before dark, away before the next raid. He felt a stab of guilt at leaving John Anderson, and particularly Arthur, in the lurch, but he pushed it aside. His place was now with Naomi and Nicholas. Surely there'd be war work he could do in Suffolk.

The WVS woman at the rescue centre was as helpful as she could be.

'I suppose you're looking for somewhere to stay,' she said wearily.

'No,' Dan replied. 'I got somewhere to stay, just wondered if you'd got any clothes, you know, what have been given for people what have been bombed out.' He held his arms out and looked down ruefully at his grimy, soot-covered clothes. His shirt was black and the knees of his trousers were ragged where he'd struggled moving rubble and heaving water tanks.

She was so relieved that he wasn't looking for shelter that she gave him a huge smile. Looking at his filthy clothes, she waved her hand to the door of the next room. 'You do look a bit the worse for wear,' she agreed. 'Have a look in there. I expect you can find something.'

Half an hour later, Dan, clad in clean clothes and carrying the old ones in a bundle tied with string and Lisa's suitcase, made his way to the station. He was leaving London like so many others already had and, as the train drew out of Liverpool Street, he looked back at the pall of smoke that still hung over the city and felt himself well out of it.

Naomi was in the pub kitchen when he arrived, unannounced, in the bar. Jenny sent him through and Naomi greeted him with a shriek of joy, dropping the rolling pin she'd been using to roll a pie crust and flinging herself into his arms.

'Danny, oh Danny,' she cried, over and over as they kissed and kissed again. 'Thank God you've come. I was so afraid for you in London. How long can you stay?'

Jenny sent them upstairs for a short while together and Dan was able to admire his son, just a week old, but already putting on an ounce or two. It was still a miracle to him that he had a son at all, but seeing him, such a beautiful baby with tiny fingers curled in sleep, gave him an unexpected jolt of joy.

'They're calling it the Second Great Fire of London,' Naomi told him. 'There was a picture of St Paul's Cathedral in the paper Jim had today. The fire and smoke all round the dome. It must have been the worst raid yet!'

Dan told her a little of what he'd seen. He didn't mention the incendiaries on the warehouse roof – she was quite alarmed enough already – but then went on to explain about his cab being requisitioned. 'So, you see, girlie, I can't work as a cabby no more, so I thought I might as well come up here with you and try and get something here.'

'You mean you've come... to stay?' Naomi's face was suffused with joy. 'Oh, Dan, really? You ain't going back?'

'Nothing to go back for,' Dan replied. 'The house is in ruins, though perhaps it can be repaired one day. I've no work down there and we need to be together as a family.' He hugged her to him again. 'I'll have to find something up here, of course. But I did bring the savings pot from under the stove, so we've a little cash in hand.'

'And Lisa's suitcase,' murmured Naomi. 'I'm so pleased you thought to bring that, Dan. When this dreadful war is over I want to be able to give her things back to her family.'

'Yeah, I know,' answered Dan and neither of them mentioned that Lisa's family had disappeared and wouldn't come looking for her. They needed something to cling to.

Chapter Twenty-Six

The snow lay heavily on the hills for several days after Christmas. Wynsdown was snowed in, the road down to Cheddar blocked with drifts and impassable. Miss Edie wasn't able to go to work and people were turned in on their own resources. Charlotte went out and joined the other village children as they played in the deep white snow. Billy came into the village several times, trudging in pulling a sledge to carry home his family's rations from the village store, but he never stayed, he was needed by his father on the farm. There were sheep to be brought in from fields before they were buried in drifts, or fell into snow-filled ditches and couldn't get out. Some were almost ready to lamb and they were kept close to the barn.

Sometimes Charlotte went back to the farm with him, longing to play with Bessie. Bessie was already learning her voice and every time she went into the stable the little dog capered towards her in delight. And then there were the piglets to see. The pig had farrowed and Charlotte was enchanted by the ten pink piglets that now squirmed about their mother in the sty.

However busy she seemed, Mrs Shepherd always made Charlotte welcome, often inviting her to join in the communal midday meal, but they followed Miss Edie's rules and she was always home again before it got dark.

On one of those evenings she had just reached Blackdown House when the air raid siren in Cheddar began its swooping warning. Miss Edie went immediately to check on the blackout. Charlotte listened to the siren and shivered. At least here there was no cellar.

They had nowhere to shelter but the cupboard under the stairs or under the heavy kitchen table.

'No need to worry unless we hear them overhead,' Miss Edie assured her, hoping that she was indeed right. 'They don't waste bombs on the hills. They'll be heading for Bristol again.'

They heard the planes in the distance, but they were still high and far away. They sat at the table and ate their supper as if there were no raid going on. It seemed strange to Charlotte to be ignoring the Luftwaffe, but she was only too pleased that they didn't have to take shelter. They went to bed in the usual way, sleeping in their own rooms. The sound of planes continued on and off for the rest of the night and it wasn't till early morning they heard the all-clear.

'It must have been a dreadful raid,' Miss Edie said as they ate their breakfast. 'Nearly twelve hours.'

After breakfast Charlotte went out into the village to see if Clare was about. As she passed the vicarage Mrs Swanson came out and called to her.

'Charlotte, are you going over to Charing Farm today?'

'I don't know,' answered Charlotte.

'I have a message for the Shepherds,' explained the vicar's wife. 'There was a big raid on Bristol last night and their daughter, Jane, has just rung to say that she's all right. You know she's nursing there?'

'Yes, this I know. Billy said she was coming home very soon.'

'Yes, well that's the other part of the message. She says the hospital's been inundated with people who've been injured in the raid, so she won't be coming home for a while yet.'

'In-inun...?'

'The hospital's very busy,' said Avril, 'so she can't come. Can you take them the message? They haven't a phone and they must be so worried.'

'Yes. I'll go now.'

'Thank you, dear.' The vicar's wife looked relieved that it was one less thing for her husband to worry about and hurried back into the vicarage.

Charlotte set off at once, taking the now familiar path across the fields to Charing Farm. Margaret Shepherd, who was feeding the hens when she walked into the farmyard, looked up in surprise.

'Hallo, my lover,' she said. 'Didn't know you was coming over today.'

'Mrs Vicar asked me to come,' Charlotte said. 'She sends you a message from Jane.'

'From Jane?' Mrs Shepherd's face creased into a smile. 'She's heard from her?'

'Yes. She phoned this morning to say that the raid was very bad in Bristol, but she is all right. She can't come home because the hospital is in-inun... very busy. Many people are hurt after the bombing. She has to stay.'

'That doesn't matter,' cried Mrs Shepherd and Charlotte could see tears of relief on her cheeks. 'She's safe. That's all that matters.' She dashed the tears away with the back of her hand and said, 'We must tell John and Billy straight away. We've been so worried. Just let me put on my boots and we'll go and find them.'

Together they tramped out across the fields to where Billy and his father were mending a fence that had collapsed under the weight of the snow. They both looked up as they saw Charlotte and Mrs Shepherd hurrying towards them. Charlotte could see from the expression on John's face that he was expecting the worst. His wife saw it too and called out to him, 'It's all right! Jane's all right. She's rung the vicarage and Charlotte's brought us the message.'

'Thank God,' John cried and he hugged his wife to him in relief. 'What did she say?' he demanded of Charlotte as he let his wife go again.

'She said the raid was bad and many people were hurt. She is all right but can't come because the hospital is... very busy.'

They all stood together in the field for a while discussing the news, the Shepherds apparently unaware of the cold, but when Charlotte shivered Mrs Shepherd said, 'We must get back to the house or there won't be any dinner. I'll ring the bell when we're ready.'

She and Charlotte walked back to the farm. 'You go and say hallo to Bessie for a moment,' she said to Charlotte, 'and then you can collect the eggs for me. I hadn't done that when you arrived.'

Charlotte needed no second bidding and scurried across to the stable where the puppies were still living with their mother. As always, as soon as Bessie heard the door open she came to the door of the loosebox. Charlotte spent ten minutes playing with her and then, a little reluctantly, she collected the egg basket from the back porch and went to the hen house. The hens were scratching about in the run outside where Mrs Shepherd had tossed the corn earlier. Billy had cleared away the snow, but the ground looked extremely hard. Charlotte went along the back of the hen house, feeling in the nesting boxes among the hay for any new-laid eggs. She collected eight, still warm, and placing them in the basket, she took them into the kitchen.

'Thank you, Charlotte. You'll stay for your dinner?'

'Yes, please.'

'And when you go you must take some eggs with you, a little thank-you for bringing us the message from Jane.'

Later that afternoon, when Billy walked with her back to the village, she carried half a dozen eggs in a borrowed basket. Miss Edie would be delighted with them, she knew.

When she reached Blackdown House she found Miss Edie standing at the door, peering out into the dusk.

'Charlotte!' she cried. 'Where on earth have you been? You haven't been home since breakfast and I didn't know where you were.'

Charlotte saw the worry on Miss Edie's face and felt guilty. She hadn't even thought of telling her where she was going.

'I'm sorry, Miss Edie,' she said. 'Mrs Vicar sent me with a message for Charing Farm and I stayed for dinner. Mrs Shepherd sent you these.' She held out the basket of eggs as a peace offering.

'What was so important that you couldn't come home here first to tell me where you were going? I've been all round the village looking for you.'

'Mrs Vicar said—' began Charlotte, but Billy interrupted.

'She came to tell us that my sister, Jane, was safe after the raid on Bristol last night. She'd rung the vicarage because we haven't got a phone and Mrs Swanson asked Charlotte to bring us the message.'

'I see.' Miss Edie was still angry, but the explanation rather took the wind out of her sails. She had asked Clare and all the other children she'd seen in the village, but hadn't thought to go and ask at the vicarage. 'Well, you're back now. Come inside and get warm.' It was clear to Billy that this invitation didn't apply to him and he turned away, saying, 'Bye Char. See you soon.'

Suddenly remembering the basket still being held out to her, Miss Edie called after him. 'Please thank your mother for the eggs, Billy. It's very generous of her.' Billy raised a hand in acknowledgement and disappeared down the lane.

That evening Charlotte was sitting at the kitchen table when Miss Edie said, 'I really think you should write to the Federmans, you know.'

Miss Edie knew that such a letter was well overdue, but she hadn't pressed the matter. Inside she was still afraid these London foster parents would ask for Charlotte to come back. She had spent the day worrying as to Charlotte's whereabouts and it had made her realise what the Federmans must be going through, not knowing what had happened to the child, and now she provided Charlotte with notepaper and an envelope.

Charlotte looked at the paper and wondered what she should write. What should she tell them? She hadn't retrieved all her memories yet. She thought hard for some time and then, at last, pulled the paper towards her and wrote.

Dear Aunt Naomi and Uncle Dan,
I hope you are well.
I was caught out in a big air raid on my way to Hilda's and broke my arm. I got taken to a hospital and when I woke up I can't remember who I am. I can't remember where I live or remember anything. I have a new name and I am called Charlotte Smith. I was put in St Michael's and when more

raids came we all came to Somerset. That is where I am now.
Miss Edie is looking after me and I am getting a puppy. She is
called Bessie.

I go to school in Cheddar. It is lots of snow here.

Please tell Hilda where I am. She will wonder why I didn't
come for tea.

When the bombs stop I will come to London again. There
were bombs near here last night but not here. They were in
Bristol.

Please be careful in London. I hear on the wireless that
London is burning down.

I hope you will write to me. I have put my house at the top
of this letter.

Love from Lisa

When she had finished writing, she passed the letter over to Miss Edie and said, 'I have told them about me and my lost memory.'

'So I see,' Miss Edie said when she'd scanned the letter. 'Well, you'd better address the envelope and then you can post it tomorrow. They say the road up from Cheddar is open again today. Mr Shepherd took his tractor down this morning and managed to clear a way through.'

Charlotte did as she was told and the letter, addressed to Mr and Federman, 65 Kemble Street, London, was put by the front door ready for posting.

Miss Edie was right and the next day the school bus made it to the village. Warned by a phone message to the vicarage, which was quickly passed round the village, all the senior school children were outside the Magpie when it arrived. Charlotte slipped the letter into the post box before joining the crowd of children who stood waiting, stamping their feet against the cold.

Avril had phoned Caroline on Boxing Day to tell her what Charlotte had remembered.

'She says she lived in a place called Kemble Street, do you know it?'

'Never heard of it,' Caroline replied. 'But that's not surprising, there must be thousands of streets in London that I've never heard of.'

'I realise that,' Avril said with a laugh, 'but I wondered if you could find out.'

'I expect so,' Caroline said. 'What do you want me to do when I have?'

'Well, we just thought you might be able to go and see her foster parents. They're called Federman. They must assume she's dead, I think, but if not they must be worrying themselves sick about her.'

'Couldn't she just write to them?' suggested Caroline wearily. 'I haven't got much time for junketing around London, looking for people. St Michael's is already full again, and there's been no let-up in the bombing except for yesterday and today. I have my hands full trying to find suitable homes for these children. You can't take any more, I suppose?' she added, a hopeful note creeping into her voice.

'Oh Caro, we can't...' began Avril.

'Don't be silly, I *know* you can't, but I'm just trying to explain to you that I'm up to my eyes. I'll try and find out where this Kemble Street is and then if it isn't too far away, I'll do my best to visit the Federmans, but I doubt if it'll be in the next few days.'

'Don't worry about it,' Avril said, hearing the note of exhaustion in her sister's voice. 'Miss Everard said she'd get her to write, I just thought... well, never mind. By the way, Dr Masters was asking whether you'd be visiting us again soon. D'you know, I think he's taken quite a shine to you, Caro.'

Caroline recognised her sister's teasing, but what she said brought a smile to Caro's lips. She liked Henry Masters and from what she could tell from a very reserved and private man, he seemed to like her, too. However, all she said was, 'Doubt if I'll be down for some time, not unless Hitler decides to lay off us for a while.' As if the talk of Dr Masters triggered an idea she went on, 'Has he seen Charlotte? Dr Masters, I mean. Perhaps he should give her the once-over now that her amnesia has gone.'

'Not entirely gone,' Avril reminded her. 'She still doesn't remember the raid or the hours leading up to it.'

'All the more reason to let Dr Masters have a look at her. She may have some physical damage to her brain.'

'Yes,' agreed Avril. 'Well, I'll mention it to Miss Everard and see what she thinks. As David is constantly reminding me, it's Miss Everard who is her foster mother, not me.'

'How's that going?' asked Caro with interest. 'The Miss Everard thing?'

'Amazingly well, as far as I can tell. They came over for Christmas dinner as I told you and there seemed to be a comfortable understanding between them. Charlotte's not afraid of her, if that's what you're worried about.'

It had been what Caroline was worried about, but now all she said was, 'That's all right then, good.'

When Avril had rung off, Caroline got out a map of London and tried to find Kemble Street. She had no idea where to look and stared at the myriad of streets in frustration. Some of them were so small that the name wasn't even written on the actual street. How was she going to find this Kemble Street, let alone go there? St Michael's was again full to capacity with children who'd lost their homes and, some of them, their families. They were as close to Croydon as they'd ever been and the bombing had been significant right up until Christmas Eve. As no raids materialised on Christmas Day, nor the two days thereafter, she began to feel a glimmer of hope that the worst was over. It wasn't, of course, and on the evening of Sunday 29 December the firestorm launched by the Luftwaffe engulfed not only the city and docks area, but outlying parts of the capital as well. When the siren began its warning, she took the children into the shelter in the garden and there they stayed from six p.m. to early the next morning. They'd heard bombs falling with booming explosions that shook the ground, they'd heard the bombers droning across the sky over their heads, a steady roar, they'd heard the clanging of fire engine bells as the fire engines hurtled from place to place to try and contain the conflagration that London had become. When the all-clear sounded and they finally crept out of the shelter, Caroline Morrison first, they found themselves looking at the remains of what had been St Michael's. The roof gone, the walls collapsed inward, leaving only a few brave fingers of stone pointing defiantly to the sky.

For a moment Caroline stared at the ruins and then with a tremendous effort gathered her wits about her. The children in her care had to be housed somewhere else and quickly. She led them out of the cramped, cold shelter into what had been the garden.

'Now then,' she said, 'we need everyone to be very sensible. We're all going to walk down the road to the rescue centre. You may see people being helped by the fire brigade and we mustn't stop and stare, or get in their way. Get into twos and hold hands. You older children look after the younger ones.' With Matron leading them at the front and Mrs Downs bringing up the rear, Caroline Morrison kept walking along beside the crocodile of children, making sure no one dropped out and that no by-stander said anything that would halt their progress.

When they reached the rescue centre they found it completely overwhelmed with people who had been bombed or burned out. Miss Morrison, turning up with an extra twenty-five children, found the person in charge, a Mrs Small, at her wits' end.

'I don't know what to do with them all,' she cried.

Caroline was very sympathetic, but adamant that space had to be found for them somewhere. She stayed at the centre all day, demanding that some of the children should be syphoned off and sent to other homes across London.

'How many orphanages and homes are there?' she demanded of poor Mrs Small. 'They don't all have to go to the same one!'

'I'm doing the best I can,' snapped Mrs Small, and indeed she was. By the end of the day every child had been found a place to sleep, for that night at least. It took another four days to find each of them a satisfactory longer-term solution to their homelessness. Caroline refused to be fobbed off with promises.

'This is the second time these children have been bombed out,' she said. 'We need to find them somewhere, quickly, where they can feel safe.' At last it was achieved and Caroline, Matron and Mrs Downs were suddenly at a loose end. None of them had a place to go, but they didn't mind that; provided the St Michael's children had new homes, they were satisfied. The three of them had moved into a local pub, miraculously still standing, which had guest rooms upstairs. They had to share a room, but at least they had a roof over their heads.

'What'll we do now?' wondered Mrs Downs.

'Well, we're not needed here for a while,' Caroline said. 'There's no home left for us to run. I expect they'll find us something very soon, but I suggest we each go somewhere and have a few days' rest, or rather, I should say, a few nights' rest. None of us have had any leave for more than a year, so it's time for a break to recharge our batteries before they find us another place for our children's home.'

'Where should we go?' wondered Mrs Downs. 'I haven't got anywhere except perhaps to my cousin in Yorkshire.'

'Then I suggest you go there,' Caroline said. 'We all need to sleep, undisturbed, for a few nights. I shall go down and stay with my sister. I suggest you leave your contact details with the local authority. That's what I'm going to do, then they can contact you when they have a new job lined up.'

The day Caroline was going to take the train down to Somerset she remembered her promise to try and find Kemble Street and the Federmans. She still had no idea where the street might be, but decided that the quickest way to find it was to take a taxi. All taxi drivers had to know where every street in London was and the quickest way to reach it. It would cost, she knew, but she decided that it was worth the money simply to find Charlotte's foster parents and tell them that she was all right. She'd tell them how much safer Wynsdown would be and try and convince them to let Charlotte stay there for the duration of, if not the war, then at least the Blitz.

She had no luggage to speak of. All her possessions had been destroyed in the bombing, but she did have a bank account and she withdrew enough money to buy herself another set of clothes. This she accomplished very quickly and then began to look for a taxi. She found one at Oxford Circus and persuaded him to take her to Kemble Street, which he assured her was in Shoreditch. As they travelled through the town she stared out of the window, horrified at the havoc caused by Sunday's bombing raid. She had seen in a newspaper a picture of St Paul's, standing tall, its famous dome silhouetted against the battle-torn sky, but it hadn't conveyed the devastation she could see round her now.

The cab turned into Kemble Street and as she looked along it, Caroline's heart sank.

'What number, lady?' asked the cabby, leaning back to speak through the glass partition.

'Sixty-five,' murmured Caroline.

The driver pulled in to the side of the road and she got out. 'Will you wait a minute?' she asked. 'I shan't be long.' And she knew she wouldn't. A row of odd-numbered houses had been burned out, standing stark and black against the afternoon sky, and sixty-five was in the middle of them. She walked slowly towards it, her eyes taking in the damage. No one could be living in these houses now, blackened and roofless. As she stood and looked at them a man appeared from the far end of the street. He walked up the road, his eyes fixed in front of him as if to avoid looking at the ruined houses.

'Excuse me.' Caroline put out a hand to halt him. He stopped and looked at her blankly, as if seeing her for the first time. 'Excuse me,' she said again. 'Can you tell me what happened to the people who lived here? I mean, are they all right? Were they safely in a shelter?'

The man glanced at the houses and said, 'Who knows?'

'I just thought you might know what had happened to them. I'm looking for a couple called Federman. I think they lived at number sixty-five. Did you know them?'

The man still didn't seem quite with it, as if he didn't really understand the question. 'They've gone,' he said.

'Gone? Gone where?'

The man gave a strangled laugh. 'How should I know? Gone, that's all. Burned to bits in Hitler's Blitz.' He grinned and, seeming to like the rhyme, he repeated it in a sing-song voice. 'Burned to bits in Hitler's Blitz. Burned to bits in Hitler's Blitz.' He looked round him and added, 'Just like my Mary. I'm looking for her. She's gone, too. I'm looking for Mary. Have you seen her?'

At that moment a younger woman came hurrying along the street and reached out an anxious hand to take the man's sleeve.

'Come along, Tom, it's time to go home.'

'I'm just looking for Mary,' he said plaintively.

'I know you are,' the woman said gently, 'but she ain't here no more. Come on, Tom, time to go home.'

She gave Caroline an apologetic smile and led the man away, holding tightly to his hand as she would that of a young child.

Caroline wanted to ask her if she knew the Federmans, but it seemed pointless. The poor woman had other things to think about, and it was clear that even if the Federmans had survived the raid, they were no longer here. She returned to the still-waiting cab and climbed back in.

'Paddington station,' she said. It would be almost as quick and much cheaper to take the Tube as she normally would have done, but she felt worn out, both mentally and physically. She sat back in the taxi and allowed herself to be driven across London. She still had a long journey ahead of her and knowing how the trains were behaving these days it could take anything from three hours to twenty-three. But Caroline didn't mind. She was going to see Avril, to stay a few days and be cosseted. She would have to tell poor Charlotte that her home in Kemble Street was no more and she wasn't looking forward to that. How much more, she wondered, could the poor child take?

The journey was long and cold. When she finally arrived at the station in Cheddar, Caroline was exhausted. The train was unheated and she'd had to change twice, waiting on freezing platforms as night fell. She managed to put a call through to the vicarage to say she was coming and she'd stay the night in Cheddar and come up on the morning bus. However, to her amazement and delight, Henry Masters was waiting for her at the station.

'The vicar told me you were on your way, so I thought I'd come and get you. Don't want to have to find a place to stay at this time of night.' Henry picked up her small bag and led the way to his car.

'Oh, that's wonderful,' cried Caroline. 'How long have you been waiting? I had no idea when I'd get here.'

'Oh, not too long,' Henry said airily as he opened the passenger door for her. 'Come on, get in and let's get you home.'

Henry drove slowly up the lanes to Wynsdown. The snow still lay on the fields and was heaped at the side of the road, but with the occasional spin of its wheels, his little car made it up to the village.

When Avril opened the front door and saw Caroline standing, pale-faced, on the step, she gathered her into her arms.

'Caro!' she cried. 'You're here!'

There was no reply to Charlotte's letter to the Federmans. She waited for the post every day, but in vain. Miss Morrison had been to see her soon after she'd arrived in Wynsdown and gently broke the news that 65 Kemble Street was a burned-out ruin.

'All the houses on that side of the road were destroyed by fire,' Miss Morrison told her. 'No one could live there now, but it doesn't mean that your foster parents were killed. I expect they were in a shelter somewhere and are quite safe.'

Charlotte didn't agree. She knew that they wouldn't have gone to Hope Street, the nearest shelter. If they'd been in the house they'd have been sheltering in the cellar. For a moment she could picture the underground room with its mattress and two old armchairs, the candles and the blankets in their box. Uncle Dan had always said it wasn't deep enough to protect them from a direct hit, but was it deep enough, Charlotte wondered now, to protect them from a fire-storm sweeping through the building above them?

'Did you see anybody in the street?' she asked. 'Was there anyone there you could ask about them?'

'No,' replied Caroline, 'well, only a man who was looking for his wife, Mary. But I think he was a little crazy... from the bombing, you know. It takes some people that way.' She nearly went on to say, 'I think she must have been killed,' but just caught herself in time. No point in robbing the child of the tiny scrap of hope she was holding on to, if indeed the strange man had been looking for someone who lived in one of the houses. And indeed there was no real reason to think that the Federmans had been in the house during the raid; surely they'd have been sheltering somewhere.

'Did you look in the cellar?' asked Charlotte.

'The cellar?'

'Yes. It's where we went to shelter. Uncle Dan fitted it out for air raids.'

'No,' said Caroline, 'no, I didn't look in the cellar, I'm afraid. I didn't know there was one. But I'm sure the houses must have been searched by the rescue services.'

'So they didn't get my letter,' Charlotte said. 'If there is no house the postman won't leave any letters, will he? What do they do with all the letters sent to bombed houses?'

'I don't know, my dear,' Caroline said gently.

Charlotte nodded. 'So, I have lost them, also.'

Caroline longed to hug her, but the girl held herself aloof, though tears brimmed in her eyes. Caroline knew that she had to deal with the news in her own way and it was clear that she was determined not to break down. Caroline admired her courage, but felt it would be better for Charlotte in the long run to cry her unshed tears.

Chapter Twenty-Seven

It was freezing. A cold fog rolled in off the sea and invaded every quarter of the camp, its damp greyness matching the mood of all the inmates. The weather had been cold and miserable for the past three weeks and everyone was getting on everyone else's nerves. Rows broke out over the smallest things, the slightest of issues boiling over into violence. Boredom was the great enemy. There was little for the internees to do apart from the day-to-day running of each house, and that took up little time. They played cards and wrote letters, anxious to keep in touch with families still living at home. But Harry Black knew better than to set himself against the card sharks, and he had no one to write to.

Harry hated being cooped up indoors and went out, walking round the camp even in the most foul weather, simply to get away from the others in the house. His worn clothes offered little protection against the icy wind and smothering fog and when he returned his teeth were chattering with the cold.

'Better to stay in during this weather,' Alfred Muller said to him one evening. 'I know you're bored, but there're things you could do to counter the boredom, you know.'

'What things?' snapped Harry. 'There's nothing I want to do here in this shithouse.'

'Getting angry with me won't help,' said Alfred calmly. 'You're an intelligent man,' he went on, consciously using the word 'man'. Many of the other inmates treated Harry as a boy to be ordered about, a boy with no say in how things should be done, and Alfred knew Harry resented it. 'You could set your mind to learning something new; something that'll stand you in good stead for when you get out of here.'

'Oh yeah,' Harry drawled, 'like what?'

'Perhaps you could improve your English,' suggested Alfred. Since all the internees in the house were German, that was the language they spoke and Harry had reverted to his native tongue. 'Are you planning to stay in England after the war?'

'No,' said Harry firmly, 'I've had enough of England. I came as refugee from the Nazis and the English locked me up. If this bloody war ever ends I'm off to Australia.'

'They speak English in Australia,' pointed out Alfred. He was used to dealing with recalcitrant teenage boys and Harry was no different from many he'd worked with during his career as a teacher.

'Yeah, well so do I,' Harry snarled and, turning on his heel, slammed out of the kitchen, leaving Alfred staring at the door with a rueful smile. Not ready to learn yet, he thought, but even so, he's a bright boy and with a little help he could go far.

Harry went upstairs and flung himself on his bed. He hadn't been to school for years and he sure as hell wasn't going back now. He didn't need to learn anything new, he knew how the world wagged. It was everyone for himself and Harry worked hard at getting what he wanted. Or at least he had until he'd been dumped in here. He looked round the room which he shared with three others. The beds were crammed in a row, with scarcely room to walk between them. A narrow locker beside each provided the only storage space for each man's personal belongings. Harry had very few. The suitcase he'd had with him when he was arrested had been returned to him when he left Brixton, but it contained very little, just his few clothes. He had no books or pictures, nothing to remind him of his parents or his home in Hanau. His money, he'd been assured, would be returned to him when he left the camp. When he left the camp! The very words filled him with fury. He was expected to stay here and rot until either the British won, which seemed increasingly unlikely, or the Nazis invaded and took over the country. Then, no doubt, he'd be recognised as a Jew and find himself in yet another camp and he'd heard enough about those to be chilled by that prospect.

The door opened and one of his room-mates came in, Rolf Heffer. He looked at Harry suspiciously.

'What you doing in here?' he growled. 'You been touching my things?'

'No.' Harry's tone was sullen. A few weeks ago he'd been caught by another of his room-mates, Bernd Bauer, going through Bernd's locker and a fight had ensued. Bernd was much older and broader than Harry, but Harry had given a good account of himself. They'd been dragged apart before any real damage had been done and they'd both ended up in the camp cooler for a week. When they came out Bernd, though still in the same house, had been moved into a different room, his place taken by Rolf Heffer.

Rolf had been picked up from a drifting German fishing boat in the North Sea and brought ashore, but despite his rescue he hated the English and resented being locked up. He'd a vicious temper that flared in a moment and he was fast with his fists. Harry knew, like everyone else in the house, that you didn't mess with Rolf Heffer. Once, only, he had dared peek into Rolf's locker and there he'd seen it, a kitchen knife, pointed, its blade honed to razor sharpness. Harry had swiftly closed the locker door, his heart thumping. Never again would he touch anything that belonged to Rolf Heffer.

'Alfred says to tell you you're on kitchen duty and to get back downstairs,' Rolf said now.

Harry was about to protest, but thought better of it. He got to his feet and slouched out of the room.

I can't stay in this hellhole till the end of the war, he thought as he stumped back downstairs. There must be *some* way I can get out of here.

As Harry helped prepare some vegetables for the midday broth, he turned various possibilities over in his mind. The obvious problem was that they were incarcerated on an island. Even if he managed to escape from the camp, where was he to go? There were boats enough in the harbour, but he knew nothing about boats, nothing about navigation. It meant, he had to accept, that he couldn't go it alone. He'd have to have a co-conspirator, someone who did know these things. It made it twice as dangerous; two people in a secret were, Harry knew, one too many.

'You're deep in thought,' remarked Hans Bruch, who had taken charge of the kitchen and was making the soup. 'Planning your escape?'

Harry looked up sharply and Hans saw, for a second, the truth in Harry's expression. His eyes widened and he laughed. 'You were, weren't you?' He cuffed Harry gently on the shoulder. 'Don't be silly, lad,' he said. 'There's no way out of this camp and there's no way off this island. If you want to get away from here, your best bet is to volunteer for the army.'

'The army?' Harry looked stunned.

'That way,' Hans explained, 'you get the two things you want most just now. You get off the island and you get to take a swipe at Hitler.'

'And you?' demanded Harry. 'Are you going to volunteer for the army?'

Hans shook his head. 'No,' he sighed. 'I'm no Nazi, I hate all they stand for, but I'm a German, born and brought up in Heidelberg. I was in London training as a chef when war was declared, but I won't willingly fight against my own country. No, I'll have to stay here until it's over. But you? When you left Germany it was to escape persecution and Germany ceased to be your home.'

'And that's different?' asked Harry, interested.

'It is in my eyes,' Hans replied. Then, changing the subject, he waved at the table. 'Come on, Harry,' he cried, 'put the things on the table. The rest'll be in in a minute.'

Harry did as he was told, but he thought about what Hans had said. He hadn't discarded his escape ideas completely, but volunteering for the army might indeed be another way out.

After the meal of broth and bread and cheese, Alfred called Harry over and taking a book out of his pocket, handed it to him.

'Thought this might interest you,' he said.

Harry looked at it. It was a book about Australia. He knew it was a book about Australia because there was a map of Australia on the front cover. He wouldn't have known otherwise because he couldn't read. He wasn't going to admit that, though, and so he said, 'About Australia! That'll be interesting.'

Alfred watched him glance through the pages, pausing at the set of photographs in the middle. The text was in German, but Harry didn't register that. All printing looked alike to him. Alfred saw at once that Harry couldn't read and was not surprised. A boy who'd been running from the Nazis all his childhood had not spent time learning his letters. He waited until the other inmates had left the room and then he said quietly, 'I could teach you to read, Harry. You'd get on far better in Australia if you could read and write.'

'I can read and write,' Harry said hotly.

'Of course you can,' Alfred agreed mildly, 'but I was thinking of teaching you to read and write in English. Far more use to you after the war, especially if you do decide to go to Australia.'

Harry handed him the book back. 'No, thanks,' he said.

'Fine,' Alfred said. 'I just thought you might like to improve your spoken English as well. It's my first language.'

'But you speak German.'

'Yes, I do. My mother was German, but I was born in England.'

'If you was born here, what you doing in the camp?' demanded Harry. 'You ever been to Germany?'

Alfred shook his head. 'No, never. But because my mother was German I still have relatives over there, so, I'm suspect.'

'Can't you volunteer to join the army and fight?' Harry asked. 'That'd prove which side you was on.'

'Too old,' Alfred sighed. 'The army wouldn't want an old school-master like me.' He smiled across at Harry. 'Whereas you might be very useful to them, especially if you spoke good English.' He switched to English and said, 'Why don't you and I talk in English? You speak it well enough to be understood, but we can improve on that.'

Harry looked at him suspiciously but answered in English. 'Why?' he said. 'Why you want help me?'

'Why not? It'd give us both something to do. To keep us occupied.'

'I don't want to be "occupied",' replied Harry, lapsing back into German. 'I just want to get out of here.'

'Don't we all?' agreed Alfred, still speaking English, 'but until we can, we need to pass the time and we might as well do it usefully, not simply wandering about in the rain and getting wet.'

Harry put the book on Australia down on the table. 'I don't want to read that,' he said and stalked out of the room.

Later that evening Alfred called all the inmates of the house together. 'I was a headmaster of a big school before I was interned,' he began. 'And I've decided that I'll start teaching again here. Is there anyone who'd like to learn something new or different? Is there anyone else who can teach us all something new or different?'

There was a general murmur among the inmates and then Bernd Bauer said, 'I'm not very good at maths. I never got the hang of it at school, but maybe you could make me understand.'

'I'll certainly try,' promised Alfred. 'Anyone else?'

'I'm an artist,' said another man, Richard Scholz. 'I can teach drawing if anyone's interested.'

'I thought English conversation might be helpful,' Alfred said. 'I know some of you are refugees and you may want to stay in England after the war or go to the States or Australia.' He directed his gaze at Harry. 'What about you, Heinrich?'

'My name is Harry,' Harry snarled.

'Precisely,' smiled Alfred, completely unfazed by his rudeness. 'You came to live in England and changed your name to an English one, so I'd have thought you'd want to speak good idiomatic English.' He regarded Harry through quizzical eyes. Harry looked away.

There was a general discussion about what lessons might be offered, but though several people thought the whole idea stupid, others saw that they could benefit from learning something new.

Several days later Rolf cornered Harry in the corridor. He pushed him against the wall, stretching out his arms and trapping Harry with his body.

'You're a lad with some guts,' he said, his voice surprisingly soft. 'I'm getting out of here. You coming with me?'

Harry stared at the big man, looming over him. 'Getting out?' he croaked.

'Getting out of this camp and off this island.' Rolf looked at him with fierce eyes. 'You do *want* to get out of this fucking place, don't you?'

Harry nodded.

'Right, well, that's what we're going to do. You and me.'

Harry couldn't believe he was hearing this. 'How?' he whispered.

'Never mind how,' snapped Rolf. 'I'll tell you when you need to know. Got a plan, but it needs the two of us.'

'Why me?' faltered Harry.

'You're a survivor because you got the guts to look after yourself. I need a survivor and I need someone who speaks English. You.'

'I speak some English,' Harry said cautiously.

'Yeah, well you'd better go an' have a few lessons with old Alfred, hadn't you? Make sure you know how to get us about.'

'About where?' Harry still didn't believe what he was hearing.

Rolf grasped him by the arm and led him to their room. None of the others was there and he closed the door behind them.

'If we get away from here,' he said, 'we shall land either in England or Ireland. In either case one of us needs to speak English. I don't know a word, but you do.' He grabbed Harry by the shoulders and shook him. 'I got things to do before we can go,' he said. 'Your job is to practise your English, right? And remember,' he went on speaking softly, 'if anyone else hears of our idea, if you so much as hint at what we're planning to anyone, I'll kill you.' He lowered his face to Harry's, so close that Harry could feel his foul breath on his cheeks. 'You believe me, boy?'

Harry believed him. He nodded, unable to speak.

'Good,' said Rolf, letting him go so suddenly that Harry fell on to his bed. 'Just remember, it's just you and me. Don't come near me. I'll come to you when we need to talk. You, you just learn your English.' With that Rolf stalked out of the room leaving Harry sitting on his bed, excited by the idea but very afraid.

Thinking about escaping was one thing, actually going through with it quite another. Harry didn't know how Rolf intended to get them out of the camp, but if they were going to England or Ireland, they must be going to steal a boat. At least Rolf was a seaman. He'd know how to sail the boat and he'd know how to navigate, but though part of him still liked the idea of escape, the more Harry went over the idea in his mind, the more frightened it made him. They'd never get out of the camp, they'd never make it to the harbour and if they did, how could just the two of them steal a boat big enough to take them across the sea? Harry remembered the dreadful crossing they'd had coming from Liverpool and that was in a much bigger boat than the two of them would be able to manage. Suppose he told Alfred about the plan? But if he did, Rolf would know and would kill him. He shuddered as he thought of the sharpened blade in the big man's locker. What if he simply said he wouldn't go? Would Rolf kill him anyway, to ensure his silence?

The various classes started and every morning Alfred gathered his five students together in the common room and the English con-versation lessons began. Richard Scholz taught drawing in the latter part of the morning and then Alfred taught maths in the afternoon.

Alfred made no comment when Harry turned up to his next class. The five who had been coming simply accepted that Harry had changed his mind, but Alfred was aware that Harry himself had changed. He had lost some of his cockiness. He stopped giving smart answers and answering back. Alfred's long experience with boys of his age knew at once that something was the matter. After the class a few days later, he called Harry back.

'Are you all right, Harry?' he asked. 'Is something troubling you?'

Harry looked up and answered sharply, 'No! Why should there be?'

Alfred shrugged. 'You look a bit down, that's all.'

'Well, who wouldn't be, stuck in this hellhole?' demanded Harry.

'Fair enough.' Alfred knew when to back off. 'Just thought there might be something I could help you with, that's all.'

'Who d'you think you are? My father?'

'I'm old enough to be,' admitted Alfred with a rueful smile. 'But if you're all right, then that's fine.'

Alfred thought about the change in Harry. He noticed that the boy had been giving Rolf Heffer a wide berth, moving away from him if they met in the communal rooms. Rolf seemed to be keeping clear of Harry, too. Was something going on there? Alfred wondered. Was there something between them? Rolf was a big man and there was no doubt that he could have his way with a skinny urchin like Harry. Despite his bravado, Harry was only a lad and no match physically for a man like Rolf. Was Rolf abusing the boy? Things like that happened, especially when men were confined together with no female company. Alfred decided to watch the two more carefully. If it was what he feared, he would definitely intervene and get Rolf moved to a different part of the camp.

Harry thought about what Alfred had said. He wished he could tell him about Rolf and his plans. They were getting more scary every day. But the thought of the sharpened kitchen knife in Rolf's locker kept him silent. He didn't doubt for one moment that Rolf would use it if he thought Harry was going to betray him.

The previous day Rolf had followed him on his walk round the camp. As they walked along the path that followed the promenade behind the wire, Rolf outlined his plan. He had got hold of some wire-cutters from one of the camp workshops. Volunteering to go on a work party outside the camp he had managed to secrete the wire-cutters down the leg of his trousers. The guard who marched them back from the fence-mending they'd been doing for a local farmer had not counted the tools in and out properly.

'So, next morning there's a fog, boy, we go out into the camp and along by the beach, away from the gate. We simply cut our way through the wire and we're out. I saw a place we can hide if need be until it's dark and then we get along to the harbour and take a boat.'

'What about evening roll-call?' asked Harry.

'What about it? We'll be long gone by then. The fog's the thing, you see.'

'What if someone sees us? One of the guards?'

'If anyone gets in our way, I'll deal with them, never fear.' His eyes gleamed as he leaned in close to Harry's ear. 'I got a knife!' he hissed. 'No one's going to stop us, boy, you'll see.'

Harry looked into Rolf's glittering eyes and was almost overcome with fear. The man was mad. Did he really think they'd simply cut through the wire and walk away? And if they did meet a guard in the fog, was he really going to stab him with the kitchen knife?

Rolf clearly saw his fear because he said, 'Don't you get any funny ideas now, boy. You're in this, same as me.' He grasped Harry by the hair and said, 'If I think I can't trust you, you know what'll happen to you.' He let him go again and added more calmly, 'It's all right, boy, I ain't going to hurt you, am I? Need you to speak English when we get to the other side, don't I.'

And when you don't? thought Harry, panic-stricken. What'll happen to me then?

Harry was dreading the next foggy day. Each morning he woke up to see clear skies he breathed a sigh of relief and headed to his English class. To his surprise he was enjoying these and, with his earlier knowledge as a basis, he was making good progress. Alfred was a patient, encouraging teacher. He hoped to teach Harry to read in due course, but had decided to wait for a while. Spoken English was the more important.

It was nearly two weeks later that the fog rolled in once more. Not first thing as was so often the way, but creeping over the island in the late afternoon. Harry crept out of the house to find somewhere to hide from Rolf. As he slipped into the mist, Rolf materialised beside him.

'Right,' he hissed. 'We go now.'

'We haven't got anything with us,' muttered Harry. 'We need food and water for the journey.'

'We do without,' Rolf growled. 'Now's our chance. Come on.' He grabbed Harry by the arm and dragged him along the path by the sea. The fog swallowed them up and though Alfred had seen them leave the house, he hadn't seen which way they were going. He was filled with a dreadful foreboding. Where were they going, out there in the fog? He hurried outside and peered into the shifting mist, but the two had disappeared. He had to make a decision and quickly. If Rolf and Harry were up to no good, surely they would be going away from the main gate. He turned left and followed the path inside the wire. Once he thought he heard voices, but it was difficult to know from which direction they came. He walked on, moving as quietly as he could. Rolf and Harry seemed to have disappeared, but Alfred knew there was only so far they could go in any direction within the camp. Then he heard it, a clump and a muttered oath. He'd almost stumbled on them in the fog.

'Harry?' he called.

There was no reply, but Alfred could feel that someone was there. He called again. 'Harry? Are you there?'

Suddenly a shrill voice cried out, 'He's got a knife!'

Alfred froze. Was the knife threatening Harry or himself? 'Harry, where are you?'

'Stay where you are!' Rolf's voice was a low growl. 'This ain't nothing to do with you.'

'Are you all right, Harry?' Alfred spoke in English, knowing that Rolf couldn't understand him. 'Answer me in English.'

'He's got a knife,' Harry said. 'He'll use it on me if you come too close.'

'Speak German!' bellowed Rolf. 'Speak German, damn you!'

'I've come to fetch Harry back to the house,' Alfred said mildly, edging softly forward through the fog.

'Well, he ain't going!' snapped Rolf. 'He's coming with me.'

'Coming with you where?' asked Alfred, easing himself nearer. 'Where are you going?'

'He cut the wire,' Harry shouted in English. His shout was followed by a scream and Alfred lurched forward, bursting from the fog to see Rolf with his knife at Harry's throat. A trickle of blood was running down the boy's neck and he was arching himself away in a desperate attempt to avoid being cut again.

'Told you to stay where you are,' shouted Rolf, his eyes blazing.

'I'm not coming near you,' Alfred said gently. 'Just let him go. He's only a boy. Let me take him back, you can go on through the wire if you want to, I shan't report you.'

'No!' Rolf took a step towards Alfred and his grip on Harry loosened a fraction. It was all Harry needed. With a sharp twist he broke free and as Rolf turned to grab him again Harry kicked him as hard as he could between the legs. Harry, the street fighter, knew exactly where to kick and with a roar of pain, Rolf doubled over, dropping the knife as he clutched at himself.

Harry caught up the knife and would have returned to the attack had Alfred not shouted, 'No, Harry!' He grabbed him, pulling him away and put himself between Harry and the agonised Rolf. Still facing Rolf he said, 'I'm taking Harry back to the house now, Rolf. What you do is up to you. But if I see you here in the camp again, I shall report you to the commander and see that you're locked up for attempted murder.' Though his heart was pounding, Alfred knew he had to face Rolf down.

At that moment a drift of air parted the fog and he could see where the wire had been cut. Another few moments and they'd have made their doomed escape. Harry saw the gap as well and was almost overwhelmed with relief. Alfred had saved him. He didn't have to try and reach the harbour, he didn't have to put out to sea in a stolen boat. He was close to tears.

Holding firmly on to Harry, Alfred backed away from Rolf. A breath of wind and Rolf disappeared again, wreathed in the shifting mist. It was their chance.

'Hurry!' Alfred hissed and turned back along the path, pushing Harry in front of him. It was a mistake. Roaring his fury, Rolf erupted out of the shrouding mist, cannoning into Alfred and knocking him flying. Harry was thrown aside as he fell and the knife clattered out of his hand, disappearing into the fog. Rolf made a grab for Harry, shouting at him as he tried to force him back towards the cut wire, but again Harry twisted free, scrabbling along the ground in his efforts to escape.

'Get away from me!' he screamed, his voice shrill with fear. 'Get away from me!'

Alfred lay winded on the ground, but he knew that he had to do something. Rolf seemed completely manic and might do anything to the boy. He lurched upward and caught hold of Rolf's leg, bellowing as he did so, 'Run, Harry! Run.'

He had little strength and it was a feeble attempt, but he held on just long enough for Harry to vanish into the gloom before Rolf pulled himself free. Out of his mind with rage, he drove his heavy boots into Alfred's body, kicking his side, his back and his head.

Harry had run, but as he did so he continued screaming, this time for help. Within moments three camp guards appeared at the double, bursting through the fog, guns in their hands.

'What's going on?'

'What's up?'

'What's happening here?' they shouted as they made a grab for Harry.

'Over there!' shrieked Harry, pointing into the fog. 'Over there! He's killing Alfred!'

As the mist parted again, they saw Alfred on the ground, curled into a ball in a vain attempt to protect himself from Rolf's boots.

'Stop! Stop or I'll fire,' bellowed the first guard.

Beyond reason now, Rolf didn't seem to have heard. Unsure of his target in the fog, the guard didn't shoot, but all three guards launched themselves at the rampaging figure. It took their combined strength to overcome him and force him to the ground. Even then he struggled fiercely and it was only when one of the guards hit him a blow to the head with his pistol butt that he finally slumped, unconscious.

After that things moved very quickly. Reinforcements were summoned and Rolf was removed, restrained with handcuffs, to the cooler. Alfred was put on a stretcher and carried straight to the hospital that overlooked the camp. Harry was taken to the commander for questioning. As the fog drifted away on the evening breeze the guards searched the path and surrounding area. They soon found the knife and further on the wire-cutters, lying beside the cut wire. Harry's account of how Rolf had forced him to go with him, backed up by Alfred when he too was questioned, was believed.

It was clear to everyone that a man the size of Rolf would have very little difficulty in intimidating a young lad like Harry. It was also clear that Rolf had become unhinged during his incarceration. He was shipped off the island, back to the mainland and Liverpool gaol, where he could do no further damage.

It took several weeks before Alfred returned to the house. Harry had been allowed to go and see him in the hospital. Alfred had put his own life on the line to save Harry and he was truly grateful.

'Why on earth didn't you tell me what was going on?' Alfred demanded as soon as he saw him. 'I could have dealt with it.'

'He had a knife,' Harry replied. 'He said if I spoke to anyone about his plan he'd kill me and I believed him.'

Chapter Twenty-Eight

It was a cold, hard winter and on several occasions the people of Wynsdown found themselves snowed in, cut off from the outside world by the drifting snow that made the lanes all but impassable. Its inhabitants were stoical about such winter conditions and with a few exceptions life in the village continued much as usual. When the older children were unable to get down to Cheddar because of the snow, Michael Hampton commandeered the church hall and set up trestle tables so they could continue with at least some of their lessons. Farmers struggled to look after their stock and once lambing started in earnest they were out in the fields at all hours of the day and night. The occasional thaw reduced the tracks and footpaths to deep squelching mud which, with the return of the frost, became hard rutted furrows laced with iced puddles.

The children, particularly the younger ones, revelled in the wintry days, longing to be out in the snow sledging, building snowmen or making ice slides on the frozen pathways. The older inhabitants were less delighted by a fresh fall of snow, struggling to the village shop or edging fearfully along the slippery roads. Dr Masters had to set more than one broken wrist when a trip to the hospital was impossible.

Miss Edie had managed to find Charlotte some sturdy walking boots and a heavy overcoat. With the socks and gloves they knitted from another unravelled jumper, Charlotte was able to brave the outdoors.

On weekday evenings she stayed at home. There was plenty to keep her busy with school work, making and mending clothes, and an added pleasure: she was learning to play the piano. Miss Edie had caught her one afternoon trying to pick out a tune on the piano in the sitting room. They seldom used the room as it was cold and what little fuel there was for the fire came from their 'sticking' excursions, when she and Miss Edie ventured out together to the small spinney at the end of the lane with an old wheelbarrow, to gather any fallen twigs and dead wood they could find. They had just returned from one of these and Charlotte was stacking their haul beside the fireplace. As she had so often before, she looked across at the piano that stood in the corner of the room, but this time she opened the polished lid and touched the keys.

'I can teach you to play properly,' came a voice from the door, and Charlotte spun round guiltily to find Miss Edie watching her. 'Would you like to learn?'

Charlotte's face creased into a smile. 'I'd love to,' she said and her lessons had begun.

At the weekends she spent much of her time at Charing Farm. There were always jobs that needed doing there and she loved to help Mrs Shepherd with the hens and in the kitchen. Often, when Billy had finished his work, they took the two young dogs out over the hills, roaming the fields and woods, completely happy in each other's company. Billy knew the hills like the back of his hand. He led Charlotte down tracks and woodland rides where the dogs went mad among the trees in search of rabbits. He took her up steep paths to a hilltop from where she could see out across the countryside to the Bristol Channel, the sea a shining polished steel in the winter sunshine. On one occasion they emerged at the top of Cheddar Gorge and peered down into the deep ravine, carved out by an age-old river.

One Saturday afternoon they had wandered further than usual. It was a bright winter's day and as they'd set out, a pale blue sky arched over the greys, browns and scrubby greens of the winter hills. For a while shafts of sunlight warmed their faces as they wandered over the fields, climbing stiles and following muddy tracks and paths across the hillside. Charlotte, aware of a new lightness of heart as she watched the dogs chasing each other through a stand of trees, thought she'd never been so happy. She had a home with Miss Edie, she had a dog called Bessie and she had a friend in Billy. She could walk out across hills that stretched into the distance and come home to a warm fire and a warm welcome. The war seemed a world away.

She looked across at Billy, striding along beside her, and knew a sudden burst of affection for him. His thick, curly, fair hair sticking out from under his cap, his strong hands grasping the thumb-stick he always carried, his shoulders broad under his waterproof jacket, now all so familiar to her. As if feeling her eyes on him, Billy stopped and turned to her.

'What?' he demanded, his blue eyes searching her face.

'What, nothing.' Charlotte felt the colour rising in her cheeks and, looking away, added, 'I'm getting cold.'

'Come on then,' Billy said as they emerged from a copse out on to the upland once again, 'we should get back.'

The weather was changing. A sharp wind knifed across the hillside and dark clouds looming from the west obscured the sun, presaging rain.

Turning back to the spinney, Billy whistled for Jet, who had been snuffling about in the undergrowth further down the hill. Charlotte shivered and began to call Bessie. Neither dog came back and Billy gave an angry shout.

'Jet! Come here, dog! Where are you?' Jet did not reappear. Nor did Bessie.

'Damn dogs!' Billy strode back to the copse and went in among the trees, calling and whistling. Charlotte went further out on to the hill, screwing her eyes against the wind as she called, trying to catch sight of either dog. She couldn't see them and she wandered further across the open hill, her feet sinking into the deep mud of the track, calling and calling, but no dogs came back.

Billy came back up the hill to join her. 'Any luck?' he called.

'No, can't see either of them.'

'Trouble is, one leads the other on.'

Billy set off along a rough path that skirted the edge of the trees.

'They could have come out of the wood on the other side,' he called back. 'You wait here in case they come back this way.'

Charlotte waited, stamping her feet to keep warm. The sky continued to darken and she could feel rain on the wind. She didn't like being here alone on the hill by herself. It was a bleak place with no houses in sight, and though she knew she was only a mile or two from Wynsdown, she wasn't sure in which direction. She wished Billy would come back. She tried calling Bessie again, but heard nothing but the wind through the dark branches of the trees. Then, suddenly, in the distance she heard a faint bark. It came from the opposite side of the copse, in the direction Billy had taken.

He must have found them! she thought, and I've got Bessie's lead.

Glad to be moving again, she set off along the path that Billy had taken. On the far side of the trees it wound away up the hill and in the distance she could see Billy, standing, silhouetted against the sky. There was someone with him, but Charlotte couldn't see either of the dogs. She began to run, her breath misting out in front of her as she struggled up the hill.

'Billy!' she called. 'Billy! I heard them barking. They're down the other way!' Billy didn't turn and as she neared him she realised that the other person was a man in uniform and that he was armed with a gun, pointed at Billy.

'Now then,' said the soldier, looking at her over Billy's shoulder, 'who've we got here then?'

'That's my friend Charlotte. I told you, we've lost our dogs.'

'Yes, I know. You said. But you shouldn't be up here at all.'

'Why ever not?'

'This is MOD land, now.' The soldier had lowered the gun and he waved a hand, encompassing the hill behind him. 'Military. You kids better get out of here, sharpish. Where d'you say you come from?'

'Wynsdown,' said Billy, pointing back across the hill. 'About three miles that way.'

'Long walk then,' said the soldier, squinting at the sky. 'You're going to get wet!'

At that moment they heard more barking and saw the two dogs burst from a thicket further down the hill, happily chasing each other.

'Better get your dogs then,' the soldier said and stood and watched as Billy and Charlotte hurried down the path to grab their joyful dogs and snap on their leads. The rain was falling in earnest now as they set off along the track that led across the hill and over the ridge towards the village. When they reached the top of the rise, Billy paused and looked back. The soldier was still where they had left him, standing in the rain, watching them.

By the time they reached Charing Farm they were soaked to the skin and freezing cold. Her boots, caked in mud, made Charlotte's feet leaden and she'd plodded the last half-mile, wondering if she'd ever get home. The dogs, wet and covered in mud, were banished straight to the stable, where Billy and Charlotte rubbed them down and fed them before going into the welcome warmth of the Shepherds' kitchen.

'I can't imagine what you were doing staying out there in this dreadful weather, Billy,' scolded Margaret. 'Didn't you see it closing in? Poor Charlotte's turned blue!'

'We did, Mum, but the dogs took it into their heads to go rabbiting and we lost them.'

Margaret Shepherd sighed. 'Well, you'd best get yourselves dry. Give me your coat, Charlotte, and I'll put it to dry by the range. Did you tell Miss Everard you were coming to us?'

'I said I was going to take the dogs out with Billy.'

'Well then, let's hope she'll guess you're safely here with us.'

'Mum, where's Dad?'

On their way home Billy had said, 'I think we should tell someone about that bloke, Char. It's a bit strange, suddenly finding him up on the hill.'

'What was he doing, do you think?' Charlotte asked.

Billy shrugged. 'Don't know, but he was in RAF uniform. I think I'll talk to Dad about it. You know he's second to Major Bellinger in the Home Guard. Better not to say anything to anyone till I've told him.'

Charlotte had agreed. All she wanted to do was get warm and dry. She didn't care what some airman was doing on the hill.

'Dad's in the village doing Home Guard drill,' his mother replied now. 'He'll be back later.'

It had become a familiar sight in the village, the Home Guard drilling and training several nights a week. After the fall of France, the secretary of state for war, Anthony Eden, had made a wireless broadcast calling for men, aged between seventeen and sixty-five, to volunteer for a local defence force. The response was enormous. Thousands of men who were not in the services due to their age or being in a reserved occupation, flocked to volunteer and the Local Defence Volunteers, soon renamed the Home Guard, was born.

In Wynsdown, as elsewhere, there had been no lack of volunteers. Being a farming community there were plenty of men who had not been called up. They were too important, working on the land in an effort to feed the nation, but the idea of being part of a defence force ready to defeat the invaders when they came, appealed to those who were needed at home.

The squire, Major Peter Bellinger, was the natural choice of leader. He had come through the first war with distinction and he longed to be of military help in this one. His son, Felix, was a pilot in the RAF, and his brother, James, was something hush-hush in the War Office, but Major Bellinger had felt sidelined in the country and longed for more active involvement.

Once his volunteers had been recruited the major did his best to train them into some sort of fighting force. At first the whole village used to turn out to see them drilling on the green, but they lacked uniforms and equipment so it wasn't long before the novelty wore off and they were left to their own devices.

'Don't know what good Bert Gurney with a broomstick's going to be,' muttered Ma Prynne to Mabel over a port and lemon at the Magpie one evening. 'Germans're going to be terrified of him, I *don't* think!'

It was how many of the village saw the local Home Guard, but Peter Bellinger remained undeterred and gradually licked his army into shape. John Shepherd was his second in command and Billy had been keen to join, too, but he was only sixteen and the major had refused to take him on.

'No, lad,' he said. 'You're doing good work with your father, there on the farm. Maybe next summer, eh?'

Despite the hard winter, the Home Guard kept up their training, sometimes in joint exercises with other branches, putting into use what they'd learned. Local signs had been removed to confuse an invader, but the local lads didn't need them, they knew their way around their own hills and exercises across the countryside improved their field-craft and more importantly, their morale.

Margaret and the two youngsters were at the kitchen table eating their tea when John Shepherd came in.

'Ah, Billy, Charlotte. Glad you're both here. Need to have a word before you go home, Charlotte. I saw Miss Everard, by the way. Said I'd run you home in the car, after tea.'

The two children looked at each other and Billy said, 'Yes, all right, Dad, we need to tell you something, too.'

'All sounds very mysterious,' Margaret said as she took a pot of stew out of the oven and dished up a portion for her husband.

'No, not really,' answered John between mouthfuls. 'Just need to ask them a couple of things, that's all.'

When they had finished eating he looked round the table and asked, 'Where did you two go this afternoon?'

'Up over the top, Beacon way.'

'Yes, I thought it must've been you.'

'Been us, what?' asked Billy.

'Been you up towards the trig. With the dogs.'

'Yes. We lost them for a while and we were looking for them when this bloke appeared and asked what I was doing. He was in uniform, RAF I think, and he had a gun.'

'Yes,' put in Charlotte, 'and he was pointing it at Billy.'

'He wasn't one of your Home Guard blokes, was he, Dad?'

'No, he wasn't. Now, Billy, Charlotte,' John spoke seriously, 'today you seem to have wandered rather close to a new military installation.'

'What's an installation?' asked Billy, intrigued.

'The military have taken over an area of land and no one is allowed to go there. We don't know what they're doing there, but that doesn't matter. They're doing something for the war effort and people have got to stay away. The man you met today was a sentry.'

'But that bloke wasn't guarding anything!'

'You didn't see what was there because he stopped you from going too close,' pointed out his father. 'It's a military zone now and there are wide boundaries. Whoever is in command up there heard how close you'd been and rang Home Guard HQ. Did you say you came from Wynsdown?'

'Yes,' answered Billy. 'The man asked and I told him.'

'Well, the message came through to Major Bellinger and we guessed it was you two because they mentioned the dogs. I said I'd speak to you.'

'And tell us what they're doing?' asked Bill excitedly.

'No, quite the opposite. I don't know what they're doing and we're not going to discuss it. But, and this is important, you are not to tell anyone about what happened today, understand?'

They both nodded and John smiled as he added, 'It's top secret and it has to stay top secret.'

It didn't, of course. Billy and Charlotte weren't the only ones to be warned off and before long everyone was talking about it. Several people went to look and all sorts of rumours began to fly.

'What d'you think they're doing?'

'Enemy alien camp?'

'POWs?'

'I heard it was an explosives factory.'

'Secret weapon plant. Had it from the brother of a bloke who's working there.'

'They're training spies. You'll see. Keep our eyes open for them.'

'How will we know?'

'We won't, not if they're any good.'

'I reckon it's another anti-aircraft battery, to help protect Bristol and Weston.'

'Bet the Home Guard know.'

'No, they wouldn't tell them.'

There was certainly activity, men coming and going, lorries

arriving and departing, but usually at night. No one knew what it was all about but speculation was rife.

'You reckon they're building a POW camp, Dad?' Billy asked his father one dinner time.

'I don't know what they're doing,' John Shepherd maintained. 'Maybe.'

'But you're number two in the Home Guard. Can't you ask Major Bellinger? He must know.'

'He may do, but if he does, I doubt if he'd tell me or anyone else.'

'There's loads of men working on it, whatever it is,' Billy said. 'The Morgan twins went to look and saw them. Got shouted at by a guard with a huge Alsatian, so they ran for it. Must be very secret, mustn't it, Dad, if they're guarding it with dogs?'

His father shrugged. 'Which is probably why we don't know nothing about it.'

Billy remained intrigued, but though he had the feeling that his father knew more than he was saying, he was unable to prise any more out of him. Rumours continued to flourish, but no one knew for sure what was happening in the military zone. Except Major Bellinger.

Peter Bellinger had been informed about what was going on because there could come a day when it affected all the nearby villages. He had been called in to the local Home Guard HQ and had the situation explained to him.

'Last raids on Bristol were pretty bad,' the CO said. 'Once the pathfinders have come over and dropped their flares, the bombers just home in on the fires to drop their load.'

Peter Bellinger nodded.

'So we're going to fool them.'

'Fool them?' Bellinger exclaimed.

'Yes. We're laying out a mock town up on the hill. They've modelled it on Bristol; designed a decoy city with fake streets and factories and even railway yards. If they're heading for Bristol again we'll put it into action, allowing a little light, the occasional flame to escape as the pathfinders come over. With a little luck they'll drop their flares on the decoy and the following bombers will do the same with their bombs. Should save Bristol a pasting!'

Peter Bellinger stared at him in amazement. 'Do you think it'll work?' he asked.

'Better bloody work,' came the reply. 'It's taken enough time, effort and money. The thing is, if it does, it may put some of the nearby villages at greater risk. You and your men must patrol your village at night and enforce the blackout rigorously. If there's the slightest sliver of light in the wrong place it could defeat the object of the exercise and also destroy your village.'

'But from the air, does it really mimic Bristol?' Peter Bellinger couldn't quite believe what he was hearing.

'So I'm told,' replied the CO. 'Haven't been up to see myself. The thing is, your job is two-fold. You have to enforce the blackout and you have to ensure that no one from your area wanders over there to have a look. The perimeter is well guarded, but we must ensure that no civilians get wind of what's going on.'

'They'll know straight away if the decoy works,' pointed out the major. 'Mendips'll suddenly be bombed to bits.'

'With careful information management that can be passed off as a German miscalculation... which of course it will be. There's no need for the general public to know about the decoy.'

Major Bellinger was sworn to secrecy and so he returned home unable to share any of this amazing information even with his wife. He simply had to tell his men that no one was to be allowed to approach the new military zone.

'If you see anyone hanging round over there,' he said, 'then you arrest them and bring them to me.'

'But what *is* going on over there, sir?' asked Bert Gurney.

'I have no idea, Gurney. Our orders are simply to ensure no one goes near the place. It's all part of an exercise we've been ordered to join.' It was the only explanation he would give.

His men accepted this and patrols were set up to monitor the blackout and to keep any inquisitive folk away from the military zone.

It was the early hours of a Sunday morning some weeks later that the air raid sirens began to wail. Though there was no moon, the sky was clear and it wasn't long before the roar of approaching air-craft and the blast of ack-ack could be heard. The Home Guard were out in force, checking all the houses in the village and the out-lying farms to be sure no lights were showing. Billy and his mother, asleep at Charing Farm, woke with a start and Billy hurriedly pulled on some trousers and a thick jersey over his pyjamas.

'I'm going out to the barn, Mother,' Billy said. 'Dad's out on patrol and someone should be in there with the last of the ewes. This noise'll terrify them.'

Reluctantly his mother agreed and Billy hurried out across the yard. The thunder of the planes filled the sky now and as he reached the barn he looked up. Coming in from the south, the planes flew in formation, dark sinister shapes against the night sky.

Heading for Bristol again, he thought as he watched them. Hope Jane'll be all right. The first flight were almost out of sight when they seemed to release a trail of lights. Bright flares spiralled down-wards, erupting into brilliant yellow and white fires, targets for the bombers following in their wake.

'They're dropping short!' Billy cried as he watched the incen-diaries burst into flame somewhere beyond the ridge on the distant hillside. Anti-aircraft guns, dug in somewhere up on the hill, pounded away at the incoming planes, blasting the sky with shells in an effort to bring down the enemy, or at least to drive them away.

The first aircraft peeled away, their job as pathfinders done, but the roar of engines didn't fade as another flight passed overhead and, homing in on the incendiary-lit target, off-loaded their bombs. Explosions cracked the air as the waves of bombers emptied their bomb bays before swinging south again towards France.

Billy wasn't the only one watching, fascinated, as the Luftwaffe mistook its target and bombed the open hillside. The bombing sounded so close that people from most of the villages that nestled among the hills were at their windows, staring incredulously as the last of the raiders flew away. How had the Germans made such an incredible mistake? Surely they must have been aiming for Bristol. No one could speak of anything else.

In Wynsdown they gathered outside the church for morning service, exchanging ideas as to what could have happened.

'How did they come to miss Bristol like that?' Billy asked his father as they went out to the sheep. 'You were out on patrol, you must've seen the whole raid from out there.'

'I don't know,' replied John. 'It's the pathfinders must've got it wrong. They drop their lights and the bombers drop their bombs. If the pathfinders get it wrong, like last night, then the bombers do, too. Just thank God they did. Saved Bristol from a rough night.'

'Thank God indeed,' echoed his wife, her thoughts flying to Jane working in Bristol.

Billy thought about the bombs. There must be huge damage after such a heavy bombardment. He knew roughly where they had landed and was even more intrigued.

'You know what, Dad? I reckon they were targeting that military zone. P'raps it wasn't a mistake. P'raps they knew there was something top secret there and bombed it specially.' He shook his head. 'The poor buggers underneath it all. Whatever it was, it must be destroyed now.'

It was a plausible explanation and one which many local people came up with. Somehow the Germans had learned that there was a top-secret project and had set out to destroy it, but, surprisingly, the army land was still occupied and so they must have failed.

All built safely underground was the perceived wisdom, so the project, whatever it might be, was safe.

'Must have been told by a spy,' said Bert Gurney. 'Stands to reason, don't it? There's spies about, fifth column.'

Chapter Twenty-Nine

'My dad says there's a German spy round here,' Tommy Gurney announced to the school bus two days later. 'He says there must be, cos how else did they know where to bomb?'

'But they missed Bristol,' pointed out Fred Moore.

'Yeah, but maybe they didn't.'

'Didn't what?'

'Didn't miss Bristol. Maybe they hit their target. My dad says that they must've knowed that there was a top-secret place up there and that's what they was aiming for.'

'Well, it's certainly top secret,' put in Stephen Morgan. 'Me and Sid went over that way the other day and we was chased off by a man with a big dog.'

'Yeah,' Sid agreed. 'Couldn't get close enough to nothing, so must be top, top secret. Them Germans'd want to bomb that, wouldn't they.'

'Yeah, that's what I'm saying,' Tommy averred. 'My dad says someone must've tipped 'em off. Someone what knew it was there. Someone who's German!' He stood up and looked round the bus. 'And who do we know who's German?'

'Sit down, Tommy Gurney,' Sam roared from the front of the bus. 'No standing up while we're moving.'

Tommy flopped back down on to his seat, but he could see he'd made his point and he grinned wolfishly at Charlotte, sitting pink-faced beside Clare halfway down the bus.

Clare turned to face him. 'You talking about Charlotte?' she demanded.

'Anyone else we know German?'

'That's just stupid, Tommy Gurney,' Clare shouted at him. 'How would Charlotte get a message to Hitler?'

'That's what we'd all like to know,' shouted Sidney Morgan. 'Spies have ways.'

'Yeah, they send messages in code!' cried his brother.

'Charlotte's not a spy!' cried Clare.

'How do you know? You don't know. She might be.'

'Nobody knows where she came from, do they? Just turned up with you vaccies.'

'She could be fifth column,' called out Ernie Clegg. 'She's probably been telling them all about us ever since she got here.'

'She's fourteen,' Clare said dismissively. 'What Nazi is going to use a fourteen-year-old as a spy?'

'She's German,' stated Tommy, undeterred. 'She's German and we hate Germans, don't we?'

There was a murmur of assent all around the bus.

'So,' continued Tommy, triumphant, 'we don't want nothing to do with her.'

'You're just stupid,' declared Clare. 'A stupid, stupid boy!'

'And we don't want nothing to do with you, neither, stupid vaccie!'

By the time they got off the bus, Charlotte and Clare were on their own. All the other children preferred to side with Tommy Gurney, seeing safety in numbers. Whether Charlotte was a spy or not they neither knew nor cared, but she was German and therefore the enemy and fair game.

For Charlotte it was a return to the early days in London. She remembered only too well the days back at Francis Drake Secondary, Roger Davis and his gang with their taunting and bullying; until, that was, Harry had hurtled to her rescue, fists flying. Tears pricked her eyes at the thought of Harry. She could do with him now. This time, however, Charlotte knew that she had to stand up for herself; there was no Harry to come to her rescue.

She got through the day with pale-faced determination, ignoring the collective spite of the other children. Clare stayed with her in the playground in the morning, but like Hilda, she fell victim by association. On the bus home she sat with Charlotte, but it was an uncomfortable journey for them both as the jeering continued.

That evening Charlotte's spirits were low, her face pale, and a haunted look in her eyes. She'd become used to being part of Wynsdown. That she was German had ceased to be important; she was just Charlotte Smith, who lived with Miss Everard and was popular with the girls at school.

'What's the matter, Charlotte?' Miss Edie asked over their supper. 'You seem a bit down. Aren't you feeling well?'

'I'm all right.'

Miss Edie's lips tightened. 'No, you're not. Come on, tell me what's the matter.' She waited, watching Charlotte struggling with her decision. Clearly something was wrong but unless Charlotte confided in her, Miss Edie knew she could do nothing but wait.

Her silence was rewarded when, with a deep sigh, Charlotte said, 'They say at school that a German spy told the bombers about that army place.'

'So?' prompted Miss Edie.

'They say it was me.'

'You!' Miss Edie gave an incredulous laugh. 'Don't be ridiculous, my dear.'

'It is not ridiculous if you are me and no one speaks to you.'

'Is that what's happening?' Miss Edie's laughter died as she saw the misery on Charlotte's face.

'It was Tommy Gurney's idea, I think,' said Charlotte and she explained what was being said about her.

'I'll come down there tomorrow and speak to the headmaster.'

'For me... better not,' Charlotte said. 'It'll stop soon.'

Yes it will! thought Edie. If she doesn't want me to go to the head, I won't, but I will get it stopped.

That evening, while Charlotte was doing her homework, Edie went out.

'I shan't be long,' she said, 'I just have to see the vicar about something. Don't forget your piano practice if I'm held up.'

Charlotte, struggling with an algebra problem, just nodded and Edie went to the vicarage.

'Is the vicar in?' she asked as soon as Avril opened the door.

'He's in his office, but he's got Peter Bellinger and John Shepherd with him. I don't suppose he'll be long. Would you like to wait?'

'Yes, please,' Edie replied. 'Actually, I wanted to talk to the major as well, so perhaps I can kill two birds with one stone.'

They waited in the kitchen and Avril, always someone unhappy with an uneasy silence, said, 'Nancy Bright was telling me that you used to sing in the church choir.'

Edie gave a knowing laugh. 'Well, Nancy Bright would, wouldn't she?'

Avril smiled ruefully. 'I'm afraid we were talking about the choir and your name came up. It's a pity you don't still come and sing. We're a bit thin on the ground these days and Nancy says you've got a lovely voice.'

'Does she now?' Miss Edie's face was hard for a moment and then she said, 'So's she, for that matter!'

'Would you like to rejoin?' Avril asked tentatively.

'I'll think about it.'

Before either of them could say more, the door opened and the vicar came in with John Shepherd and Peter Bellinger.

'Miss Everard! What a lovely surprise,' the vicar cried. 'We were just going to have a drink before Peter and John went. Can I tempt you to one too?'

Miss Edie shook her head. 'No, thank you, vicar, but don't let me stop you. I just wanted a word with both you and Major Bellinger.'

'Sounds serious,' said the major, watching as the vicar poured each of them a measure of whisky.

'Well, I think it is,' Miss Edie replied.

'Now,' said David settling himself at the kitchen table with the others. 'What's the problem?'

As quickly as she could Miss Edie repeated what Charlotte had told her. 'I have no idea what's going on in that military place over the hill,' she said, 'and I'm not asking. But somehow I want it scotched that there was a German spy. My poor Charlotte has been taking flak at school today because she's German and the stupid children, led by Tommy Gurney, of course, and egged on by the Morgan twins and that Clegg boy, are saying she told the Luftwaffe where the military zone was so they could bomb it.'

Peter Bellinger gave a guffaw. 'But that's ridiculous!'

'I have to admit, I laughed, too, when she first told me,' Miss Edie said, 'until I saw her face. As far as I understand it, she's been sent to Coventry. The children are calling her a spy. It's a bit of excitement. Charlotte's German and it's an excuse for bullying.'

'This is ridiculous,' insisted Avril. 'You must speak to the headmaster. He'll have to deal with it once and for all.'

'I can't, she's asked me not to. I think this sort of thing happened to her in London when she first arrived and she weathered that storm, but now it's happening again. Children can be very cruel, particularly in a gang, and they're ganging up on Charlotte now.' She turned to Peter Bellinger. 'I was wondering if you could have a word with Tommy's father. He's in your Home Guard, isn't he?'

The major grimaced. 'Yes he is, and I imagine that's where the stupid idea came from in the first place. He'll have said something like it and Tommy's just parroting his father. I'll see what I can do, of course, but Bert Gurney isn't an intelligent man and once he's got an idea in his head it'll be difficult to shift it.'

'Billy and Charlotte were found up by the zone that day,' John Shepherd reminded them. 'That was before the raid. They've said nothing, but anyone could have seen them. The rumour could have come from there.'

'But the whole thing is utterly preposterous,' said the vicar. 'As if a fourteen-year-old girl had the means to contact the Germans.'

'I believe they're suggesting she's in touch with the fifth column,' Miss Edie said.

'Leave it with me, Miss Edie,' Peter Bellinger said. 'I'll do what I can to put a stop to it.'

But it wasn't Major Bellinger who put a stop to it, it was Billy Shepherd. When his father got home and told him what was going on, Billy felt rigid with rage. How dare they bully his Charlotte? His Charlotte. She was the first and only girl he'd ever been interested in and that was how he'd come to think of her. He listened to what his dad was saying and then spent the night awake, planning what he was going to do about it. Next morning he went to Blackdown House.

'I've come to walk Charlotte to the bus,' he told Miss Edie when she opened the door.

A smile flashed across her face. 'Billy, how very nice. Come in. I'll tell her you're here.'

Charlotte was amazed that Billy had turned up so unexpectedly on her doorstep.

'Hallo, Billy,' she said. 'You're early into the village.'

'Yes,' Billy answered casually. 'Had something to do, so I thought I'd walk you to the bus.'

Miss Edie watched them set off down the lane with relief. Billy's father must have told Billy about Tommy Gurney's rubbish and he was going to deal with it.

Charlotte had no idea Billy knew about the events of the previous day, but she wasn't looking forward to school.

'You're very quiet,' Billy remarked. 'You all right?'

'Yes, I'm fine,' Charlotte replied, and they walked on in silence.

As they came towards the green they could see the children, gathered outside the Magpie, waiting for the bus. Charlotte hung back a little, but Billy, not appearing to notice her reluctance, walked on to the waiting group.

'She won't dare show her face today,' Tommy Gurney was boasting to the Morgan twins. 'Not now we've found her out. My dad's going to tell Major Bellinger an' I 'spect she'll be arrested soon.' He didn't see Billy coming, but all of a sudden found himself being spun round and held in a vice-like grip.

'What were you saying?' Billy enquired softly, his face menacingly close to Tommy's.

Tommy's eyes widened. Billy was two years older, six inches taller and had broadened from hard physical work on the farm. Tommy saw the cold anger in Billy's eyes, felt warm breath on his face. 'N-n-nothing,' he stammered.

'Oh, I think you were.' Billy remained icy cold and was all the more terrifying for it. 'Say it again, so I can hear what lies you're spreading about my girl.'

'Your girl?' echoed Tommy faintly.

'Yes, my girl.'

'Your girl's a German spy!' called a voice from the safety of the group.

'My girl is German. A German who's lost her parents, her brother and her home. A refugee from the very people you pretend she's spying for. Charlotte... is... not... a... spy.' He spaced the words out for emphasis. 'And if I hear any more of such utter nonsense from anyone... they'll regret it.' His grip tightened on Tommy and the boy squeaked with fear.

'Now,' Billy went on conversationally, 'I've heard that you've all been treating my girl very badly.' His eyes turned to the Morgan twins who were standing amid the others. 'I know who the bullies are.' His eyes flicked to Ernie Clegg, who squirmed away behind Fred Moore. 'And this I promise you: one more word from any of you about spies, fifth columns and hating German girls and I'll come and get you, each and every one, and you'll wish I hadn't.' He jerked Tommy's arm sharply up behind him, making the boy cry out in pain. 'Understand, Gurney?' He waited for a response and when there was none he jerked again and repeated, 'Understand, do you?'

'Yes,' gasped Tommy.

'Good,' said Billy and released him. Billy turned his attention to the other boys. 'You lot better believe me, an' all,' he said. 'Another word from any of you and I'll find you, wherever you are, and you'll truly wish I hadn't.'

'Bully!' muttered Stephen Morgan.

'Takes one to know one,' remarked Billy calmly, and turned his back on them all.

Charlotte, still standing a little way off, had watched the whole encounter in amazement. Now when Billy came towards her, she could feel colour flooding her cheeks. Billy had called her his girl.

'Who told you?' she asked as he reached her side. 'Miss Edie?'

'Nope,' replied Billy. 'Heard it on the grapevine. But you just let me know if you have any more trouble from any of these little shits and I'll sort them out.'

They all heard the sound of the bus coming up the hill into the village, and the children scuffled together, ready to get on. Billy linked his arm through Charlotte's and led her to the bus. He allowed everyone to get on first and then, very deliberately, kissed her gently on the cheek before she, too, got on the bus. As it pulled away he could see her inside, taking her seat next to Clare. He had claimed her, his girl, and he set off back to Charing Farm with a light heart to begin his day's work.

The mood in the school bus was subdued to begin with, but gradually the noise rose to its normal level. Clare squeezed Charlotte's hand.

'It'll be all right, now,' she said. 'They're all afraid of Billy.'

Charlotte smiled. She was in a world of her own. How could anyone be afraid of Billy? He was kind and gentle, but not so, she now knew, if anyone threatened his girl. His girl. Charlotte's heart raced at his words and she touched her cheek where he'd kissed her. He had claimed her publicly and she was his.

Chapter Thirty

There had been no repercussions for Harry after the unsuccessful escape. Everyone assumed that he had been the unwilling victim of an insane prisoner. Harry readily accepted this version of events. He knew that both he and Alfred had been in real danger from Rolf and that it was Alfred's courage that had saved them. That made Alfred his hero. Only Hans Bruch looked at him askance when he returned to the house after his adventure and Harry knew Hans thought he had been a willing participant in Rolf's plan. However, Hans said nothing and Harry, banishing any thoughts of escape, soon came to believe the accepted story himself.

When Alfred returned to the house, he was still weak and needed rest, but it wasn't in his nature to sit about and before long he started up his classes again and this time Harry joined in with enthusiasm. During Harry's visits to Alfred in the hospital, a closeness had developed between them. It surprised Alfred. He had been right when he'd said that he was old enough to be Harry's father, but he hadn't expected his affection for the prickly boy to be so strong. He had saved him from Rolf, but more importantly he'd also saved him from himself. Alfred knew that, despite Harry's protestations that he'd been too afraid of Rolf to betray him, the hope of escape had long been in Harry's mind too. Alfred could only hope that after the fright Rolf had given him, Harry would put all such thoughts aside and set about acquiring the skills he would need after the war.

'You really do need to improve your English,' he insisted, 'and from now on you and I will only speak English to each other.'

Harry gave him a rueful shrug. 'All right, Alfred. You win. English it is.'

Alfred was an excellent teacher and an exacting taskmaster, continually correcting grammar, vocabulary and accent, and over the weeks, Harry's spoken English improved out of all recognition.

Alfred had been right, Harry was intelligent, and now he was self-motivated it took him little time to learn to read and write. Once he could read, Harry discovered a whole new world open to him and he devoured the books from the camp library that Alfred suggested.

'Now it's time to try and get you out of here,' Alfred said to him one evening. 'You know they're gradually releasing people, don't you?'

Harry shrugged. 'Yes, but it's not going to be me, is it?'

'Why not?'

'Why would it be?'

'Well, you clearly aren't a threat to national security, are you? And they could use you in the war effort.'

'I don't think anyone knows I'm here. Who's going to let me out?'

'You have to make contact with the right people, Harry. Don't forget, as a refugee you can volunteer for the army. The Pioneer Corps is taking men from the occupied countries and using them to support the front-line troops. You should ask to see the camp commander and it's time you wrote some letters.'

'But who do I write to?'

'Anyone and everyone,' answered Alfred, 'from the chiefs of staff to the secretary of state for war!'

Thus the letter-writing began.

All through the spring and early summer Harry had been going out of camp on work parties and had earned himself some pay. It was credited to his camp account and with it he could buy the stamps he needed for his letters. He was not the only one writing such letters, of course, and some of the letter-writers had managed to reach the right people. At five o'clock each day the names of those who were to be released the next day were announced. Those who had applied for release waited with baited breath to hear if they had been successful. If so, they were called in to see the camp commander. The wheels of bureaucracy moved incredibly slowly and most of those waiting hopefully to hear their names were disappointed, but the lucky few were jubilant.

One evening in June, Harry was listening to the list of names, when a name leaped out at him. 'Alfred Muller'. Harry was dumbstruck. Alfred had been summoned to the commander's office, which meant, almost certainly, he was going to be released… tomorrow. He'd be taken to the dock and put on a ship for Liverpool. Alfred was going home to his family. Alfred was leaving and Harry hadn't even realised he'd been applying for release.

'That's stupid!' he told himself. 'Of course he was applying, everyone is!' But even so, somehow he felt betrayed. Alfred was leaving and he, Harry, was still stuck here in this shithole. He looked round but couldn't see Alfred anywhere. That made him angry too. The man had applied to be released and he wasn't even here to hear his summons.

Harry turned away and stumped back to the house. Alfred was in the kitchen with Hans, overseeing preparation of the evening meal.

Harry barged in and said, 'Better pack your bag, Alfred. You're leaving tomorrow!'

Alfred laughed. 'What a great idea, Harry. You know I think I will, just in case!' Then he turned back to Hans and the supper.

'Listen!' Harry was almost shouting now. 'Listen, you stupid bastard, you've been called to see the commander. You must be on the list for release. I didn't know you'd even applied!'

'Of course I've applied,' answered Alfred mildly. 'I've been applying ever since I got here.'

'So why the hell didn't you go and find out?' demanded Harry, a little more quietly.

'Because, Harry,' Alfred answered with a sigh, 'I got tired of being disappointed. So, let's forget it and get this meal on the table.'

'But Alfred,' Harry said, 'it's true. Your name was called this evening. You're going home tomorrow.'

Alfred turned slowly back to look at him. 'You're not joking, Harry? It's a pretty poor joke if you are!'

Harry, now containing his own disappointment, managed a smile and replied, 'No, Alfred. I wouldn't joke about anything so important.'

Alfred stared at him for a moment and then he gathered him into a bear hug and began to weep.

Harry watched Alfred leave the following morning and felt utterly bereft. Alfred had become his mainstay and now he'd gone, Harry was alone.

'Keep writing those letters,' Alfred said as he gave Harry a final hug. 'They're sure to let you out soon, they'll need people who speak both English and German. I'll keep writing on your behalf, too. One way or another we'll get you out.'

Harry wasn't so sure. He'd been to see the camp commander some weeks earlier, but he hadn't seemed very helpful, simply saying he'd look into his case.

'You're under age,' he'd said. 'Can't join up until you're eighteen.'

'I can join then though?'

'Maybe. It's not up to me.'

'You mean I'm stuck in this... camp,' Harry changed the word he'd been going to use just in time, 'until I'm eighteen? That's another eighteen months.'

The commander shrugged. 'Probably,' he conceded, 'unless someone finds a use for you before that. Then you might get out.'

Harry had left the office extremely depressed, but Alfred had encouraged him to go on writing to people in London.

'You never know, someone might pick you up.'

Now Alfred had gone Harry's spirits plummeted. He knew he was on the Isle of Man for the duration.

Harry still went out on work parties; he quite enjoyed the physical work and at least it got him out of the camp for a while. Spending days working in the fields and with enough regular food, he grew stronger, growing another couple of inches and filling out so that he looked more like a healthy young man and less like a scrawny street urchin. He missed Alfred more than he would have thought possible and though he still continued with his reading, his morale was low.

Sometimes the internees were escorted out of the camp and taken to the beach, where they could exercise and swim in the sea. Occasionally Harry went too, but he found such excursions made it increasingly difficult to return to the confines of the camp. Many of those around him seemed content to live life a day at time like this, but Harry became increasingly bored and low-spirited.

It was early August before he came up for release and like Alfred, he'd almost given up.

'Heinrich Schwarz. To the commander's office.'

At first Harry didn't react. No one called him Heinrich now, but of course it was how he was registered within the camp. Like Alfred the news almost brought him to tears. Tomorrow! Tomorrow he'd be out of this place and on his way.

Harry left the camp next morning. First thing, he had reported to the guard room, where he was given his papers and the belongings that had been taken from him on his arrival. It was the beginning of the long release process. He was still listed as an alien and so there were still restrictions, but he was no longer a prisoner. The ship took him to Fleetwood and once his documents had been checked, yet again, by the police there, he was free to continue his journey. Harry was on his way back to London. He'd been given a travel warrant and asked to supply an address where he could be contacted and reminded he must report to the police on his arrival. To begin with he was at a loss for an address. There was no way he was going back to the hostel where he'd been arrested nearly nine months ago, but he was terrified that they might not let him leave unless he wrote something. He was about to wing it and make up an address when he remembered Dan Federman. He'd stayed the night in his house, been fire-watching with him; surely he wouldn't mind Harry giving his address, 65 Kemble Street. The house where Lisa had lived. His only link with her.

Harry had given occasional thought to Lisa while he'd been incarcerated, but she hadn't been at the forefront of his mind. Harry had long ago learned not to dwell on the past and those who peopled it. He'd been fond of Lisa, but she was dead. He had moved on from her as he'd moved on from his parents. Kemble Street, however, was another matter altogether. Perhaps Dan would let him sleep in the cellar again, just until he found somewhere.

Harry was not sure why he'd suddenly been given his freedom. He still wasn't eighteen but he'd said in all of his letters that if he were allowed to go free he would do anything to help the war effort. He reminded everyone that he was fluent in both German and English, this last not quite true but near enough to get him by. Whatever it had been that had convinced the powers that be that he was no longer a security risk, Harry didn't care. He was out! Once through the formalities at Fleetwood, he was allowed to board the London train. With a jubilant heart, he climbed into the carriage. The compartment was crowded but Harry didn't care, he was free.

The journey took hours, as the train was often shunted into a siding to let a more important train steam by, but when at last he arrived at Euston it was the early hours of the following morning.

Harry not only had his suitcase, but the money he'd had on him at the time of his arrest. He'd been amazed by that. He'd expected that to have disappeared into someone else's pocket along the way. Added to this was the small amount he'd earned while working from the camp. Despite his tiredness, Harry walked along the blacked-out platform with a spring in his step. He was a man of means, he could read and write and he was determined, he was about to go up in the world.

As the sun began to climb above the roofs of London, still tired and gritty-eyed, Harry made his way to Kemble Street. He hoped the Federmans might let him live with them as a boarder, at least for a short while, then he could report his address, as required, to the police station. The sight that met him when he turned off the main road into Kemble Street made him pull up short and stare. One side of the street still provided homes, though many of the houses had minor damage with doors and windows boarded up, and one or two houses wore tarpaulin caps. The other side of the street was a line of derelict houses. Clearly fire had swept through them some time ago and they'd been left standing empty throughout the winter. The ravages of the freezing weather and the northerly winds were obvious as the houses sagged together as if relying on each other for strength to stay upright.

Harry walked slowly along the pavement until he came to number sixty-five. It looked as bad as the others, its roof burned out, its window frames twisted by the heat and holding only a few shards of broken, smoke-streaked glass; weeds flourished beside what had been the front door.

Harry wondered what had happened to the Federmans. Had they been killed in the fire? Harry thought about Dan. He, surely, must have been out fire-watching when this had happened. Had his wife survived? She'd been left in the cellar shelter the night Harry had gone to the fire post with Dan.

Has the cellar survived? Harry wondered suddenly. Can I still get into the house and down into the cellar?

He still needed somewhere to sleep himself and he remembered the cellar had a mattress. Perhaps he could still use it as his place until the Federmans came back.

He cast his eyes up and down the road, but there was no one about, so he walked up to the gaping front door and edged his way inside.

The whole of the house was burned out, all the furniture destroyed, blackened walls and ceilings bearing witness to the strength of the fire. He walked down the narrow passage that led to the kitchen. As he'd remembered, the door to the cellar was in the far corner. It was charred, but made of good solid wood, it seemed to have withstood the ravages of the fire better than the rest of the house. The closed door stood behind a festoon of cobwebs, clearly unopened for a long time. Harry tried to turn the handle but it was stiff and unmoving. Grasping it in both hands he tried again. This time it gave a little and he realised that the door wasn't on its hinges, it was simply pushed into its frame and wedged into place with a sliver of wood at the bottom. A good hard pull was all it needed to pull it free. Harry pulled and the door, suddenly released, fell towards him, nearly knocking him to the ground. He propped it against the wall and peered down the steps that lay beyond. The only light came through the broken kitchen window, but dusty fingers of sunlight probed the stairs and Harry made his way carefully down them. He wished he had a torch, but remembered that there had been some candle and matches on a shelf, and as his eyes grew accustomed to the gloom, he felt his way round the walls until he found what he was looking for. He struck a match and lit a stub of candle, still pushed into the top of a beer bottle. By its flickering light he saw the cellar still had chairs and a mattress.

This'll do, he thought, delighted. It's dry and a place to sleep. They aren't here, so there's no reason why I shouldn't move in.

Harry had never been a great respecter of other people's property and dumping his case on the floor, he blew out the candle and went back up the steps. He heaved the door back into place and wedged it carefully as it had been before.

His visit to the police station went without a hitch. He registered himself at 65 Kemble Street with a busy desk sergeant and then set off to buy himself a few necessities. He'd been given back his ration book along with his identity papers and so he bought a few provisions, and to make the cellar a little more habitable he managed to get hold of a Tilley lamp. Carrying his purchases back to Kemble Street he once more slipped in through the front door of number sixty-five. He'd have to make sure no light leaked out from his underground haven at night, but otherwise he'd be snug and dry, with a place to lay his head. He managed to pull the cellar door closed behind him and, having unloaded his shopping, he ate some bread and cheese. Then, pulling a couple of blankets from a box, he flung himself down on the mattress and slept the clock round.

The next evening he went to the fire post Dan had taken him to. He hoped that someone there might have news of the Federmans and he'd be able to find them. Perhaps, he thought, as he hurried through the streets, they'll be living somewhere nearby and I can shack up with them after all. He was all too aware that if the police came round and checked on the address he'd given them, they'd realise he was a squatter and he might be turned out.

He was greeted by John Anderson at the fire post.

'Eh, lad, I've seen you here before.'

'Yes, I came once with Dan Federman.'

'And never again.'

Harry glared at Anderson and said, 'The day after I was here, I was arrested as an enemy alien. I've only just been released.'

'So you aren't an enemy any more?' asked Anderson with a grin.

'I never was,' snapped Harry. 'I'm a Jewish refugee from Germany. I hate the Nazis and want to fight.'

'Well, if you want to fight fires, lad,' Anderson replied, 'you're more than welcome here.'

'But where is Dan Federman?' Harry asked. 'It's him I'm looking for.'

'Don't know, lad. His house was burnt and we think he must have moved out of London to be with his wife in Suffolk. We haven't seen him for months. We haven't had any raids since the end of May, just a few alarms that came to nothing, so the volunteers have dropped away, Dan Federman with them.'

'Oh, well,' shrugged Harry, anxious to change the subject, 'never mind.' He raised a hand and slipped away. He didn't want to be called as a volunteer again now that he'd heard the Federmans had moved away. Now he had their house to himself. 'I'm a friend of Dan Federman's,' he would say if anyone challenged him. 'He said I could sleep in his cellar till I found somewhere permanent.'

John Anderson made no move to stop him and once he was out of sight Harry hurried back to Kemble Street. Once inside number sixty-five, he went back down to the cellar and took stock. He had very little money and needed to find a way to make some. Could he go back and work for Mikey again? Perhaps as a last resort.

The next day, as he emerged from the house, a man was passing. He looked at Harry and said, 'Who're you then? What you doing in there?'

'Who's asking?' Harry countered.

'Albert Johnson, citizen patrol,' came the reply. 'Keeping an eye...'

'I'm a friend of Dan Federman's...' Harry trotted out the prepared line.

'Cellar-rat, are you?' said the man. 'Well, I suppose you need somewhere to sleep and if Dan said you could stay... I'm just keeping an eye... you know, to see there ain't no looting.' Albert Johnson nodded and passed on along the road, his head swivelling from side to side as if searching out hidden looters among the ruins. Harry's ruse had worked and it gave him confidence. Perhaps the police would accept it, too, if they should bother to come round checking on him.

'Looting', the man had said. Surely, Harry thought, there was nothing left to loot, if there ever had been. The houses stood bare and stark against the September sky. There was surely nothing left of value in any of them. But it had given him an idea. There might be other places, other bomb sites in richer areas might be worth a look. And if he did find something worth having, well he could always go and see Mikey Sharp again.

Harry needed money while he waited for his call-up, so in the meantime he got himself a job in the docks. It was heavy work, but Harry didn't mind. He was happy to be working in the fresh air and being paid enough to live on. His work also gave him the opportunity to expand his own private and lucrative business.

It had begun in a very small way. He had been walking through a cleared bomb site near the docks – a patch of wilderness, scrub and weeds covering the rubble and debris left behind – and there it was, winking at him as a shaft of sunshine struck through a tuft of willowherb, something bright. Looking round to be sure he was unobserved, Harry bent down as if to tie his shoe and reaching in among the weeds his fingers closed on his prize. A ring. Without looking at it, he slipped it into his pocket and continued to walk slowly across the open ground where once a row of houses had stood. As he walked his eyes scoured the derelict ground about him, but there was nothing else to see.

Safely back in the cellar in Kemble Street away from prying eyes, he pulled the ring from his pocket and looked at it. A gold band, if it was gold, with a diamond set in a cluster of tiny red stones. Could that diamond be real? Harry wondered. It was quite big. And the little red stones, rubies? He considered what to do with it. He could go back to the market and sell it to Mikey Sharp, but before he did, he needed to find out if it was real, not just a piece of glass. He needed to know what it might be worth. He didn't intend to let Mikey cheat him. Harry had learned a lot during his incarceration on the Isle of Man, but reading and writing weren't everything. He'd always been streetwise and he knew finding this ring was his big chance.

Next day, when his shift was finished, he found a small jeweller's shop in Hackney. The name ING was painted in faded gold letters above the window and hanging above the door were the three gold balls indicating that Mr Ing was also a pawnbroker. Harry peered in through the window at the items of jewellery offered for sale. He needed a shop where few questions would be asked and this seemed the right sort of place. He had prepared his story and so with one last glance at the watches and brooches displayed in the window, he pushed open the door and went in. A bell jangled as he entered and a small man emerged from behind a curtain. He stood behind the counter and regarded Harry through wire-rimmed spectacles, before saying in a soft voice, 'Good afternoon. Can I be of help?'

'Are you Mr Ing?' Harry asked.

The man nodded. 'I am indeed,' he said.

'Good,' said Harry. 'Well, my mum wants her ring valued, see.' He placed the ring on the counter.

'Does she now?' The man looked sceptical.

Innocently, Harry met his eye, apparently completely unaware of the jeweller's scepticism. 'Yeah, she was bombed out. My dad was killed in the raid and she's lost everything. She don't want to sell it, she just wants to know what it might fetch, just in case, know what I mean?'

Mr Ing thought he did. 'Yes, I see,' he said. 'Well, let me have a look at it.' He removed his spectacles and fixed an eyeglass into his eye. Holding the ring up to the light, he peered at it. 'A pretty thing,' he said. 'But you say she doesn't want to sell it?'

'No,' Harry replied firmly. 'It's not for sale.'

Mr Ing nodded. 'Would she care to borrow against it?'

'Well,' Harry sounded hesitant, 'what would you lend... if she did?'

'I would have to consider,' Mr Ing said thoughtfully. 'If I was lending, maybe ten pounds.'

'Pull the other one,' Harry jeered. 'I know what my dad give for it.'

'I'm sure you do,' agreed Mr Ing in a tone that belied his words. 'But things are different now...' He didn't say 'there's a war on' but the words hung in the air.

Harry picked up the ring and put it back in his pocket. 'No,' he said, 'she wouldn't want to hock it for that. Sentimental value, you know? Thanks anyway.'

As he turned to the door Mr Ing said, 'I might be able to raise my offer a little, seeing as your mother's circumstances are so sad. Say twelve pounds ten?'

'I'll tell her,' said Harry and left the shop. He'd learned what he wanted to know. Mr Ing might even have gone a little higher than twelve pounds ten shillings, but he'd sell the ring on for more, so Harry felt certain that it must be worth at least twenty pounds. He set off to find Mikey Sharp.

Since then, Harry had gradually increased his business. Unloading ships at the docks meant there were occasions when small items came his way and were easily concealed in the pockets of his work clothes, but his main source was the bomb sites. The east end of the city still revealed the determination of the Luftwaffe to bring it into submission. Skeletal buildings still stood, their precarious walls displaying ragged wallpaper and hanging fireplaces. Such buildings were cordoned off, but for a street-rat like Harry, the barriers presented no problems and under cover of dusk, he crept through ruins, climbed up broken walls into the remains of upper rooms, searching for treasure. And he found it. Not huge amounts, but occasional pieces abandoned or lost in an air raid, things that could be quickly turned into cash through Mikey and others, like Mr Ing, not too choosy where such items came from.

Harry wasn't making a fortune, but his savings, stashed safely in the cellar at 65 Kemble Street, were building up. He kept the money in a cocoa tin which he hid in a small cavity he'd hollowed out under the cellar steps. He was still determined to go to

Australia after the war and he was equally determined not to go empty-handed.

When his call-up papers came through he found that he was to be deferred as he was now a docker and thus in a reserved occupation. He continued to live in the cellar of sixty-five and people in the area got used to seeing him coming and going. If questioned he always said he was a friend of the Federmans who, as they must know, had moved out of London when Mrs Federman's baby was due.

So many of the houses in the street had been damaged, many of the people who'd known the Federmans no longer lived there, and those few who did, accepted his story. With the destruction of so many homes during the months of the Blitz, people were living wherever they could find a roof. The man had called him a 'cellar-rat', well, Harry knew he was not the only one.

Chapter Thirty-One

June 1942

It was Saturday evening. The day had been hot and the air was still warm as the midsummer evening sun still lingered over the village. Many of the people of Wynsdown had been hard at work in their gardens, tending the vegetables that added so importantly to the meagre rations they could buy in the shops. Miss Edie had been weeding the vegetable plot and Charlotte had been picking and podding broad beans. These would be salted to preserve them for use later in the year.

'Save us two portions for supper this evening,' Miss Edie called over her shoulder.

'Billy's coming to fetch me at half past seven,' Charlotte reminded her.

'I know, I hadn't forgotten, but you can't go to the dance with no food inside you.'

Charlotte was very excited. It was the Wynsdown midsummer dance at the village hall and she was going with Billy. He had come specially to ask Miss Edie if he might take her.

'Everyone will be going,' he said, 'so if I could fetch Charlotte and we could go together, that would be great.'

'Can I go, Miss Edie? Please say I can go.'

Miss Edie had smiled. Charlotte was sixteen now and there was no reason why she shouldn't go to the village dance. All her school friends would be there and Miss Edie knew that Billy would take good care of her. Since Billy had claimed Charlotte as his girl, there had been no further bullying from Tommy and his mates, and over the subsequent months few people gave thought to the fact that Charlotte was a German refugee. Her friendship with Billy was accepted, he was recognised as her protector, but in fact very little had changed between them. Billy continued to treat her as he might a younger sister and Charlotte, after the first flush of pleasure that he had claimed her as his girl, came to realise that it had been his way of dealing with the bullies. She was just his friend and that was enough.

'I can't see why not,' Miss Edie said in answer to Billy's request, 'provided you bring her home again before eleven.'

'Oh, Miss Edie, the dance doesn't end till half past,' cried Charlotte. 'Can't I stay to the end?'

'In the door by midnight!' replied Miss Edie and was rewarded with a huge smile that illuminated Charlotte's face.

'What are you going to wear?' Clare asked on their way to school one morning.

'Miss Edie found a skirt that belonged to her mother,' Charlotte said, 'and she's altered it for me. It's dark green with white daisies on it and I've got a white blouse to go on top.'

'Lucky you,' sighed Clare. 'Ma hasn't got anything to alter for me. She's cut up a bedspread to make a skirt for Sandra and though there's enough material to make me one too, she says we can't wear the same thing.'

It meant that Clare was going to have to wear her old summer dress and as she pointed out to Charlotte in despair, 'It was too tight last time I wore it, so goodness only knows how I'll get into it now! I haven't even got a decent skirt and blouse, only my school uniform and I'm not wearing that! No, I'll have to squeeze into my old dress, but no one'll want to dance with me in a scruffy dress which I'm bursting out of!'

'Malcolm will!' Charlotte assured her. 'You know he likes you. He won't care if you're wearing your old dress.'

'He may not,' Clare said bitterly, 'but I will.'

'But you like him, don't you?'

'Yes,' muttered Clare, 'you know I do... that's the point!'

'Can I give Clare my yellow check skirt?' Charlotte asked Miss Edie later, when she got home. 'It's too small for me really, isn't it? But it'd fit Clare all right and she hasn't got anything pretty to wear for the dance.'

'You could offer to lend it to her,' suggested Miss Edie. She had found the length of yellow gingham in the market in Wells last summer and had bought it to make Charlotte a summer skirt. She had indeed grown out of it now, but Miss Edie had it earmarked for further alteration.

Charlotte shook her head. 'No,' she said, 'that's not the same. I have to give it to her so that it's hers.'

Miss Edie could see the point and reluctantly she agreed, so that evening Charlotte took the skirt round to Mrs Prynne's and gave it to Clare.

'Everyone'll know it's yours,' objected Clare.

'Course they won't!' Charlotte assured her. 'I haven't been wearing it cos it's too small for me. They won't remember. And what if they do? Since rationing, everyone's swapping clothes.'

Billy had called for Charlotte at exactly half past seven. He was waiting in the hallway of Blackdown House when she came down the stairs, pausing at the turn to smile down at him. Billy had claimed her as his girl over a year ago, but as she walked down the stairs, dressed for her first dance, it was as if scales had fallen from his eyes and he were seeing her for the first time. No longer was she the scruffy Charlotte in dungarees and wellington boots who helped him muck out the pig and feed the hens, the Charlotte who, with her dog at her heels, strode out over the hills with him, the Charlotte who wobbled along behind him on his sister's bike. Now, she was transformed into a new and exotic Charlotte whom he hardly recognised.

Her hair had grown longer over the last months and this evening Miss Edie had helped her put it up for the first time. Swept back smoothly from her face, it was held in place by two tortoiseshell combs, its length coiled at the nape of her neck. The confused and frightened school girl who had arrived from London all those months ago with no memory of who she was, had emerged as a tall and confident young woman with glossy brown hair, warm brown eyes and a generous mouth that curved into a wide smile as she looked down at him. A wave of love surged through Billy, leaving him hot and breathless, and with it he recognised, for the first time, the depth of his feelings for her. Charlotte. His girl. He'd been fond of her, enjoyed being with her, felt the need to protect her, but now, suddenly, he felt awkward and shy. Could this beautiful girl really be his? Could she possibly feel the same about him as he did about her? For the first time Billy felt diffident, hesitant, unsure of what had been so certain before. Charlotte smiled across at him, apparently unaware of the effect she was having on him, and his heart turned a somersault before he pulled himself together and stepping forward said, 'Charlotte, you look fantastic.' And there was no disguising the admiration in his eyes.

'Doesn't she just?' agreed Miss Edie, beaming.

'So do you,' replied Charlotte, for it was the first time she'd ever seen Billy in a suit, a shirt with a collar and tie, his curly, fair hair smoothed down within an inch of its life. His deep-set blue eyes shone bright from his summer-tanned face and she thought she'd never seen him look more handsome.

'Midnight,' Miss Edie reminded them, 'and not a minute later.' She watched them walk out into the evening sun and knew a moment of melancholy, remembering how she and Herbert had walked together so many years ago. But her memories were no longer bitter. Herbert had loved her and she him, but he was long gone, and since this strange child had been catapulted into her life and she'd learned to love her, Miss Edie had, at last, been able to revisit her memories without pain and move on.

The hall was hot despite the windows being open and the doors propped wide to allow the thick summer air to circulate. It was almost dusk and when darkness fell they knew they would have to shut the doors and fix the blackout screens, but for just a little longer they were able to continue dancing by the light of the evening sun.

A four-piece band was playing, Paul Rollett thumping away on the village hall piano, Bob Fountain playing his accordion, Andy

Hallman blowing mournfully into his saxophone and Dennis Bird beating his drums to keep them in time. Everyone was at the mid-summer dance; it was the high spot of the summer and eagerly awaited. Almost every household in Wynsdown had contributed something to the feast and Jack at the Magpie was providing the beer and lemonade.

Some of the senior school children had spent the afternoon decorating the hall with bunting, draping the flags across the ceiling and filling the windowsills with vases of wild flowers gathered from the hedgerows that morning.

It was a wonderful evening. Everyone had managed to find something festive to wear, even if it was only some flowers for a girl's hair or a jacket from the back of a cupboard, ironed and pressed into uncomfortable service for the evening. Everyone was chattering, sharing plates of food and, of course, dancing. Charlotte grinned across at Clare when she saw her with Malcolm Flint, his arm around her shoulders, and Clare dressed in the yellow skirt and a white lacy blouse that might have once been a net curtain, beaming with pleasure as they walked out on to the tiny space that served as the dance floor.

The vicar and Mrs Vicar were there, as were many of those who had offered homes to the evacuees. Caroline Morrison had come down for the weekend and was being squired by Dr Masters. It was an evening the village was to remember for a long time to come; an evening of good food, good cheer and warmth. Once it grew dark outside, the doors were closed and the blackout shutters put in place. It made the hall unutterably hot and more than one couple slipped out into the warm darkness beyond its walls.

Billy, still a little disorientated by the sudden revelation of his feelings, stood watching the dancing for some time. He didn't know how to talk to this new, confident Charlotte. For the first time in his life he felt out of his depth.

'Come on, Billy,' called Clare from the dance floor. 'Why aren't you dancing?'

Charlotte looked up at Billy with a mischievous grin. 'Why aren't we dancing, Billy?' she demanded.

'I'm not very good at dancing,' he replied awkwardly, still hesitating.

'Don't be silly,' cried Charlotte, turning to him with a smile that raised his heart-rate. 'We've come to a dance. Let's dance!' She held out her hand to him and together they joined the dancers on the floor.

Charlotte was thistledown in his arms, but Billy felt as if he had two left feet.

'Told you I wasn't very good,' he mumbled as he trod on her toe, but Charlotte simply laughed and, holding tight to his arm, refused to let him leave the dance floor.

The band stopped for a well-earned break and with some relief Billy went to the bar to fetch them a drink. Charlotte stood watching the people gathered in the hall, people she'd come to know over the months she'd been in Wynsdown.

'Hallo, Charlotte.'

Charlotte turned to find Miss Morrison standing beside her, smiling. 'You look as if you're enjoying yourself. I saw you dancing!'

'Oh, I am, Miss Morrison,' Charlotte cried. 'We've been having dancing lessons at school and I love it.'

'It's lovely to see you so happy,' Miss Morrison said. 'How's Miss Everard?'

'Miss Edie? Oh, she's fine. I tried to get her to come here tonight, but she said she had a bit of a headache and anyway she's too old for gallivanting.' Charlotte looked up at Caroline Morrison and said softly, 'You don't have to worry about me, Miss Morrison. I'm very happy with Miss Edie.'

'Good,' said Miss Morrison, 'that's all I wanted to know. Enjoy the rest of your evening.'

'What did she want?' asked Billy when he came back with their drinks.

'She just wanted to know if I was all right. She's always been very kind to me, Billy.'

Billy nodded and handed her a glass of lemonade before taking a long pull at his pint of scrumpy.

'It's hot in here,' Charlotte said as she sipped her drink. 'Shall we go outside and see if it's a bit cooler?'

Billy would never have dared suggest this to her on this evening, when suddenly their relationship seemed to have changed, but when the suggestion came from her he turned towards the door and holding aside the blackout curtain, led her outside.

'That's better,' Charlotte said as they sat down on one of the benches set around the green. A three-quarter moon sailed out from behind a cloud, bathing the village in silver, the church tower across the green standing in stark relief against the night sky. It was certainly cooler outside and the change in temperature made Charlotte shiver.

'You're cold,' Billy said.

She looked up at him, her face lifted to his. 'No,' she whispered, 'not really.'

Awkwardly, Billy slipped his arm around her shoulders and felt the warmth of her body against his. His kiss was gentle, little more than a brush of his lips against hers, but when she sighed with pleasure, he kissed her again and this time she responded, slipping her arms round his neck to hold him close. After a long moment they broke apart, breathless.

'Oh, Charlotte,' was all he could say, but it seemed to be enough as she sighed and snuggled against him.

Other couples had drifted out into the darkness, but as they heard the band strike up again they were returning to the party inside the hall. Suddenly shy, Charlotte got to her feet and said, 'We should go in.'

It was a magical evening and, floating on a cloud of happiness, Charlotte didn't want it to end. With Billy's arms around her she felt she could dance for ever. When the band finally struck up the last waltz, everyone crowded on to the dance floor and there was hardly room to move. Charlotte danced with her head on Billy's shoulder, enfolded in his arms, so that she felt the steady beat of his heart, beating in rhythm with her own.

As promised, Billy left Charlotte at the door of Blackdown House at a minute to midnight. They had walked slowly home along the lane, arms entwined, complete in their new-found happiness. Outside the gate they paused for one last kiss, before Charlotte slipped from his arms and ran lightly up to the front door. With one hand on the latch she turned for a final blown kiss and then she opened the door and was gone.

Billy turned back down the lane and as he walked home his whole being was filled with Charlotte. His girl. His love. But as he walked across the fields, silvered in the moonlight, he found himself thinking of what he'd recently been asked to do and, for the first time, he wished he'd refused.

Charlotte, safely home at Blackdown House, sat on her bed and relived the evening. Her evening with Billy. The feel of his arms round her as they danced, his cheek against her hair, his breath on her cheek, the pressure of his hand in the small of her back and above all the way he'd kissed her. The evening had been wonderful. The exuberance of the dance in the hall, the laughter and the gaiety, despite the wartime austerity, had lifted the spirits of the whole village. They had raised a collective two fingers to Hitler and his crew and the jollity of the evening had left everyone with a sense of wellbeing as they walked home through the warm darkness of a midsummer's night.

Chapter Thirty-Two

The peace of that summer night was shattered just over an hour later by the howl of the air raid sirens. Most of the people of Wynsdown had fallen into bed, exhausted after the night's festivities in the village hall, and were rudely roused again by the unexpected warning.

Charlotte jerked awake, pulled from the depths of sleep by the insistent wail that echoed across the hills. Miss Edie, startled from a deep sleep, got out of bed and crossed to her window. Careful to show no light, she pulled aside the blackout and looked out into the night. There was nothing to see, but it was not long before the sound of sirens was overlaid by the throb of aircraft.

A moment later Charlotte was beside her at the window. The drone of the aircraft was quite distinct now and in the distance star-bursts of anti-aircraft fire lit the sky.

'Do you think they're headed for Bristol?' Charlotte said as she craned her neck looking for the approaching planes.

'Maybe,' agreed Miss Edie, 'but I can't see any planes, can you?'

'No. Perhaps they're not as close as they sound.'

Major Bellinger and his Home Guards turned out at once to patrol the village and surrounding area, checking for leaking light and manning the prepared observation posts, but there was little more they could do.

Billy had not been asleep when the siren began and he was soon dressed in his Home Guard uniform and following his father out into the night. The moon was still in the sky, gleaming intermittently between rags of cloud, and they quickly made their way to the small stone shelter perched on a rise above the farm that served as an observation post. Once their eyes were accustomed to the midsummer darkness, they found their way across the familiar fields quite easily and were soon ensconced on the top of the hillock with their binoculars, scanning the sky towards Weston-Super-Mare, Wales and the sea. The post was connected by field telephone to Major Bellinger's HQ at the manor, but though they stayed in the shelter until the all-clear sounded, there was nothing to report.

Other members of the platoon continued their patrols, dark shapes that could be seen prowling the village, keeping their vigil. They could hear distant explosions and vivid flashes of brilliance lit the western sky, too far away to pinpoint the targets, but close enough to fill the night air with the clamour of the raid.

Throughout the village people stood at their windows watching the sky. Few took shelter these days; the raids had fallen off in recent months and few people felt in danger when the sirens went off.

'Looks as if Weston's the target tonight,' David Swanson said to his wife as they and the three children, who had crept from their beds, watched from a bedroom window. Little Val slipped her hand into his.

'I don't like it,' she whispered.

'No,' David agreed softly, 'nor do I. But the bombs are too far away to hurt us here.'

'But why?' asked Avril. 'Why Weston, I mean.'

'The Oldmixon factory, I expect, or maybe Banwell,' replied David. 'Obvious targets, really, aircraft factories.'

'But how do they know about those?' wondered Avril.

David shrugged. 'Reconnaissance flights, I suppose.'

'And the airfield,' put in Paul. 'They'd want to bomb that.'

'And the airfield,' David agreed and not wanting to frighten the girls any further said, 'Come on, all of you, back to bed. You'll catch cold out here.' He picked Val up in his arms and, followed by the other two, carried her back to her bed, sitting beside her until she drifted off to sleep again.

When the all-clear finally sounded most of the inhabitants of Wynsdown had gone back to bed and later awoke to a peaceful

Sunday morning. News of the attack on Weston reached the village early on. Martha Mason, the village schoolteacher, had a cousin who lived in Weston and she had spoken to her briefly on the phone.

'There's an awful lot of damage,' she reported to those around her as she stood outside the church waiting for morning service. 'My cousin Angela lives just off Moorland Road and she says there's lots of damage there. It's quite dreadful. The civil defence people are out searching for survivors in the ruined houses.'

There was an immediate buzz among the parishioners still gathered at the church gate and Martha became the centre of attention until the vicar came out to encourage his flock inside for the service. He, too, had news of the raid on Weston, where his elderly aunt now lived. She had rung the vicarage to let them know that she was safe and her home undamaged.

'Some of the roads are badly affected,' she'd told him. 'But don't worry about me. I'm fine and I don't need to go out.'

David had been relieved and during the service he offered prayers for those who had been killed, injured or had lost their homes.

Charlotte and Miss Edie, who some months before had been prevailed upon to rejoin the choir, had been invited to the vicarage for lunch, and it was with a certain air of gloom that they all gathered in the vicarage garden in the summer sunshine for an alfresco meal. Caroline Morrison was there with Dr Masters.

'I'm going back up to London tomorrow,' Caroline told them. 'I'm taking over a new children's refuge in North London. It's a home that was damaged in the Blitz, but it's been repaired and is up and running again. It'll be quite a challenge, but I'm looking forward to it.'

'Has the bombing stopped in London now?' asked Miss Edie.

'Well, there isn't the blanket bombing like during the Blitz,' Caroline replied, 'but there are occasional raids still.'

'They said on the wireless that Hitler's turned his attention elsewhere, now. Just bombing towns and cities at random.'

'You mean like Weston?' said Avril bleakly.

'Caro'd come down to get away from bombs for a bit,' said Dr Masters, 'and now they've started bombing here!'

'Well,' said David, 'let's hope this was a one-off and we've seen the last of them.'

It wasn't and they hadn't. That night, soon after midnight, the sirens warned of another raid and once more a flight of enemy aircraft appeared over the horizon, sinister dark shapes in the night sky occasionally fixed for a moment in the beam of a pursuing searchlight. Anti-aircraft guns along the coast pounded away, sending shell after shell to explode among the marauding planes and below, the boom of explosions made clear the toll being exacted on the town.

Once more, the Home Guard were out on patrol. Most of them had had little or no sleep the previous night and several of them were slow to appear on duty that evening. Billy and his father returned to their observation post. From their perch on the hillside they could see across the fields down to the village in one direction and out towards the coast in the other.

'Determined to finish what they started,' John said as he scanned the sky with his binoculars. 'Sent the buggers over from France, I expect. They're too bloody close for comfort these days. Trying to soften us up. Reckon the invasion's still on the cards.'

Sitting together in the darkness, watching the sky, Billy was tempted to tell his father the real reason for his recent special training weekend. He had been allowed to join the Home Guard when he'd turned seventeen and he'd turned out with them for training ever since. But a few weeks ago he'd been 'invited' to a special meeting. He had been down in Cheddar collecting supplies for his mother and had stopped at a pub for a quick pint of cider before going home again. As he sat at the bar nursing his pint, he was joined by an older man, wearing a Home Guard uniform.

'Billy Shepherd, isn't it?' said the man as he hoisted himself up on to an adjacent bar stool.

Billy turned to find himself looking at Mr Tavistock, who had taught him history at school. Billy hadn't seen him since he'd left school, though he'd heard that 'Old Tavy', as he'd been known, had retired soon after. Billy hadn't been surprised; after all, Old Tavy *was* old, at least fifty. He'd been in the last war.

'Mr Tavistock?'

'Surprised to see me in uniform, lad? They're calling on all of us old men these days. You in the Home Guard?'

Billy said that he was.

'Thought so,' said Mr Tavistock. 'Thought I heard you were in the Wynsdown lot. Still farming up there with your dad, are you?'

'Yes,' replied Billy cautiously, wondering how the old man knew, or remembered, so much about him.

'Important work that,' remarked Mr Tavistock, signalling to the barmaid for a pint for himself and another for Billy.

'Not much to do, if you ask me,' Billy said. 'A lot of parading and drill and that, and some exercises on the hills, but nothing exciting.'

'Getting fed up with it, are you?'

'I think we all are,' answered Billy. 'I mean, defending our country is vital, I know, and we have to stay in training, but at the moment most of us are bored with the whole thing.'

'Well, there are ways of making it more interesting,' Mr Tavistock said as he took a pull at his pint and smiled, savouring the first mouthful. 'Special duties.'

Billy's curiosity was piqued and he said, 'What sort of special duties?'

Mr Tavistock tapped the side of his nose. 'Can't tell you that, lad. But if you think you might be interested, come to the Cliff Hotel on Saturday night and maybe you'll find out.' Then, inexplicably leaving the rest of his cider almost untouched on the bar, Old Tavy had slipped down from his stool and said, 'Must be off. Think about Saturday. Come on your own. I'll be there.'

Billy had thought about Saturday all week, and when Saturday evening came he'd ridden his bike down to Cheddar and made his way to the Cliff Hotel. Mr Tavistock was in the hallway and when he saw Billy he greeted him with a smile and led him upstairs into a room where three other men were waiting, sitting in awkward silence on the chairs which had obviously been set out for them. One of them, Kenny Blaker, had been at school with Billy and greeted him with a nod, but said nothing. As he took one of the seats, Billy wondered if Old Tavy had sent Kenny along, too. Didn't he work for a builder? A few minutes later an officer came into the room and they all stood up.

'Sit down, gentlemen,' the officer said and, moving to the front of the room, looked round at them all. He didn't introduce himself, simply said, 'Thank you for coming.' He continued to stand although a chair had been placed for him.

'What I am about to say to you is extremely hush-hush,' he began. 'You will not repeat any of it to anyone. You've been asked here because we think that you are the men we need for one of our local auxiliary units. It means extra training and some secret and almost certainly dangerous work, in defence of your homes and your country, but each of you has been recommended by someone who knows you, which is why you're here. If you are interested in hearing more about what we want you to sign up to, then stay and listen; if not, you should leave now and no one will think the worse of you. But I have to emphasise, we're only asking for volunteers.' He waited a moment, watching them. Billy looked back at him. This officer was asking him to do something secret and special in defence. He didn't know what, but if he volunteered, he thought, he'd be doing something real for the war effort.

He remained seated, as did Kenny Blaker and the other two men.

The officer looked pleased. 'Good,' he said. 'I'll give you a brief outline and then over the next few weeks you'll be called for additional training to join a new signalling corps. At least, that's how you'll explain the additional training you'll be receiving beyond the usual Home Guard exercises.

'The possibility of a German invasion is still with us,' the officer went on. 'And we must be prepared. We're training a secret resistance force, men who will continue to resist in the case of German occupation. They will be the men who disappear underground when the Germans arrive. They will be the men who continue to fight; who harry the invading troops, attacking, and running. Sabotage will be the order of the day, destruction of anything and everything that might aid the Germans in their occupation. They

will be putting their lives on the line in every operation they under-
take. Many of them will not survive, but we will not allow the
Nazis simply to walk in and take our country from us.' He paused
and looked again at the young men seated in front of him. 'You will
be among these men. In the case of invasion, you will simply disappear. You men have been chosen because you know your own area
inside out. Preparations are already being made locally, with hidden
dumps of weaponry, ammunition, explosives and, of course, food
and water, for your survival. You have been recruited into this
resistance force, but you must never, ever, reveal to anyone else that
such a force even exists. You are the Home Guard, but you are
more, much more. You are our secret underground army and your
very survival may depend on no one knowing that such an army
exists. What people don't know they cannot betray – even under
pressure.'

'You mean under torture.' The words were said softly, but the
officer pounced on them.

'That's exactly what I mean,' he said. 'When you return home
after this training, you will say nothing of where you've been or
what you've been doing. You will maintain absolute silence on the
matter even with your closest friends and family... your wives and
children, your parents and siblings, your girlfriend, your lover...
none must have an inkling of what you're being trained for. This is
what you're signing up to, this is what must be maintained, for your
own safety, for the safety of us all.

'If the worst comes to the worst, many people will be against
what you're doing. There will be German reprisals, as there have
been in France, and people may well turn against such a resistance
force. That is why you will never be able to tell anyone what you've
been trained to do. As far as your friends and family are concerned,
your wives, particularly your wives, you're in the ordinary Home
Guard. This is for your security, but also for their own.'

Later, as he'd ridden back up the hill to Wynsdown, Billy knew
a strange mixture of pride and fear that had been with him ever
since. He had been chosen to fight to the last. If the Germans landed
he would be among the last defenders of his country.

A week later he'd been called for extra training, duly explained as a signalling course. It was training totally different from anything he had done previously, and before he returned to Wynsdown he was accepted into a secret force, unknown to the outside world, unknown to anyone not directly involved, and had signed secrecy papers.

Despite the insistence on total secrecy, as he and his father sat in the observation post, watching the bombers unloading death on those beneath them, Billy was sorely tempted to tell his dad what he'd signed up to. Surely *he* would never tell anyone? Except perhaps his mother. And she wouldn't tell...

At that moment they heard the sound of a plane approaching very close and very fast. Its engine shrieked as it came diving towards them.

'Christ almighty, it's on fire!' bellowed John, and even as they watched they saw a dark figure fall from the cockpit and hurtle towards the ground until, with a jerk, its descent was slowed as a parachute opened up above him. The plane continued its screaming descent and crashed beyond the ridge in a ball of fire.

John snatched up the field telephone and reported back to base.

'Enemy plane down above Charing Farm!' he shouted. 'On fire. Crew unlikely to have survived. One bailed out. Parachute opened. Headed for Charing Coppice.'

He listened for a moment and then said, 'Right, sir. We're on our way.'

As his father reported in, Billy watched the parachute continue to drift down, the man hanging from it, a limp form like a broken doll. As it neared the ground the wind carried it away from the observation post and into the patch of woodland known as Charing Coppice on the far side to the next field. The parachute became entangled in the top branches and the airman was left dangling twenty feet above the ground.

'Come on, Dad,' Billy cried, jumping down from the shelter. 'We can catch this one.'

'On our way,' John shouted. 'Major Bellinger's going to the plane. He's sending reinforcements up to us as well.'

They grabbed their rifles and scrambled down the hill and across to the trees, where the parachute caught in the branches showed white in the moonlight. Below its canopy hung the figure of a man, twirling gently in the wind.

They approached the scene with care, creeping in through the shelter of the trees, unsure if the man was armed, injured or possibly dead.

'Keep him covered, Billy,' murmured John, 'while I see what's happening.'

Billy edged forward through the undergrowth until he had a clear line of fire, while his father circled round to the other side of the tree, his own rifle aimed at the gently twirling body. For a moment he didn't know what to do; there was no sign of life, so he called out.

'Are you alive? We've got you covered.'

For a moment there was no response and then far above them came a faint groan. John pulled his torch from his pocket and shone it upward. He could see the man's face, twisted with pain, but his eyes were open and he was staring, terrified, down at the man with the rifle below.

'No shoot,' he called. '*Beine kaputt.*'

'No,' John called back. 'No shoot.' Keeping his eyes firmly on the man above him, John said, 'Come out, Billy. We have to get this bloke down. He's been hit in the leg, I think.' He was looking at the man's ragged trousers and could see blood trickling on to his flying boots. The man's face was a mask of pain and he groaned again.

'What are we going to do?' asked Billy as he set his rifle aside and looked up at the airman.

'Have to cut him down,' replied John. 'But it'll be a difficult operation in the dark. We may have to wait till daylight.'

'I could climb up and cut his harness away,' Billy said, 'but then he'd simply crash down to the ground.'

'Needs two of us up in the tree, so we can lower him down. But we need someone on the ground, too.'

'I'll climb up and have a look,' Billy said, and watched by the German he began to scramble up the tree. When he got level with the dangling man he called, 'Shine your torch this way, Dad.' John directed the torch beam at the parachute harness and Billy studied it carefully.

'We can cut him loose from the parachute and then ease him down to the ground.' He looked across at the man and gave him a nod. 'You'll be OK, mate,' he said.

The airman latched on to the word 'OK' and rasped, 'No OK. *Beine kaputt.*'

'Sorry,' Billy said gruffly, 'don't speak German.' He turned his attention back to the parachute lines and then called down to his father. 'Not too difficult, Dad. Once we've got manpower on the ground, two of us can manage this end.'

While they waited for their reinforcements to arrive, Billy went back out into the field where there were some sheep hurdles stacked against a wall. He heaved one of them free and carried it back to the edge of the wood.

'Need something to carry the poor bugger on,' he said as he laid it on the ground.

'Good thinking,' said his father. 'Shouldn't be too long before help gets here.'

It was only fifteen minutes later when three more members of Wynsdown Home Guard arrived at Charing Coppice. Led by a puffing Charlie Marston, with Bert Gurney and Frank Tewson bringing up the rear, they pushed their way through the bushes into the wood. Daylight was beginning to creep into the eastern sky, and in the half-light of dawn they all surveyed the airman, suspended in the tree.

'Shoot the bugger and be done with it, I say.' Bert was his usual bullish self.

'Don't be ridiculous, Bert,' snapped John. 'He's a prisoner of war.'

'Whatever he is, he's up a gum tree,' said Frank and then laughed at his own joke.

'He's wounded,' Billy said, 'and he's losing blood. We have to get him down.'

'Diddums!' said Bert. 'Poor little Jerry! Is he hurt then?'

'For Christ's sake, Bert, put a sock in it,' said John. He turned to Charlie who, wearing his corporal's stripes, was the senior man after himself. 'Right, Charlie. We've worked out what to do, all we need is for you three to wait here at the bottom of the tree and we'll lower him down to you. He's wounded in the legs, but we don't know how bad. You have to catch him and ease him on to the ground. Understand?'

'Yes, sir.'

Billy was already back up the tree and John climbed up beside him.

'Take his weight, Billy, while I cut the webbing free.'

Billy took the strain and after some quick work with his knife, John had cut the man free of the parachute and together they held him, still suspended in his harness. The airman moaned, but he seemed only half conscious now and unaware of what was happening to him.

'He's coming down,' called John. 'Ready, men?'

It was hard to hold the dead weight of the airman as they paid out the harness ropes, but with Billy taking the strain as the anchor man, they gradually lowered him from the tree. Despite the fact that the men below were there to catch him, the airman shrieked with pain as his legs bumped the ground and by the time John and Billy had climbed down again, it was clear that the boy had passed out. For now that they could see his face properly, they could see he was indeed not much older than Billy, possibly about twenty, but no more.

'Now then,' ordered John, 'get him on the hurdle while he's still out cold.'

Billy fetched the hurdle and three of them lifted him on to it. His legs were covered in blood and through the tatters of his uniform, John could see bone projecting through the pale flesh. He turned to Billy. 'Run back to the farm and tell your ma to get a bed ready for him. Then on down to the village and bring Doc Masters up to have a look at him. Tell him he'll need pain killers of some sort. The lad's legs are shattered.'

Billy nodded and set off at a run.

'Right, men,' John said. 'One on each corner, and try not to bump him.'

By the time they reached the farm, Margaret had made up a bed on the sofa in the sitting room, lighted the fire to warm the seldom-used room and made tea. Hot water simmered on the stove and all was ready when the doctor arrived with Billy only moments later.

'I saw Major Bellinger, Dad,' Billy told him as they waited for the doctor to examine his patient. 'He said to tell you he's been out to the crash. The plane is burnt out and there are three more crew still inside, well, what's left of them, anyway. Didn't stand a chance, poor sods. He's put a guard on the plane to stop souvenir hunters and rung HQ for them to come and deal with the wreck and to take over our man.'

'Doubt if our man can be moved for a bit,' his father replied. 'Luckily he was out cold all the way back here, but he's in great pain and unless they knock him out again, it'll be difficult to transport him.'

At that moment Dr Masters came into the room, looking grave.

'He's in a bad way,' he said. 'Not a lot I can do for him here, just keep him sedated and try and control the pain. I think it'll be a case of amputation, certainly for one of his legs. They may be able to save the other.'

'The poor boy,' Margaret said.

'He's come round again, but of course there's the language barrier. I can't explain to him what needs to be done, or even what I'm doing to help until we can get him to hospital.'

'You could fetch Charlotte, Billy,' said his mother. 'At least she could talk to him, try and reassure him. What do you think, doctor?'

'It might be helpful,' replied the doctor, but he sounded dubious.

Margaret took this as yes and despatched Billy to Blackdown House to fetch Charlotte. When she saw who was at the door she felt suddenly shy. Would Billy feel the way he seemed to feel on Saturday night, or would it be like last time when everything reverted to normal and he treated her like a little sister again?

'Hallo, Billy,' she said, adding as she took in his Home Guard uniform, 'have you been up all night?'

'Yes, since the siren went, anyway.'

'Come in.'

'I can't. Look, Charlotte, we need your help back at the farm.' He told her quickly what had happened.

Charlotte wasn't at all sure she wanted to speak to a German airman who'd been bombing them one minute and shot down the next. 'Serve him right,' she muttered as Billy explained why he'd come. 'He shouldn't have been there at all.'

'Come on, Char, don't be like that,' coaxed Billy. 'If you saw him you'd be sorry for him. He's going to lose at least one of his legs.'

'I've lost my family thanks to people like him,' snapped Charlotte. 'Not just a leg.' However, not wanting to cause a rift between them, she put on her jacket and followed Billy back to Charing Farm. There she was greeted by Margaret, who gave her a warm hug and said softly, 'You're a good girl to come. It can't be easy for you. He's in here.' She led her through the kitchen and into the sitting room. After a brief hesitation Charlotte went in and Margaret softly closed the door behind her.

Charlotte was shocked when she saw the young man lying on the sofa, his legs hidden under a makeshift cage to keep the covers away from them. His skin was ashen, his eyes huge in the pallor of his face. It was obvious that, despite Dr Masters's best efforts, he was in tremendous pain. He'd opened his eyes to see who had come into the room and as soon as he saw it was a young girl, he'd closed them again.

Charlotte walked over to the bed and looked down at him. 'Hallo,' she said in German, 'I'm Lieselotte, who are you?'

Hearing her speak to him in German his eyes flew open and he stared up at her, trying to focus on her face.

'Where am I?' he croaked, his voice hardly audible. 'Who are you?'

'You're… in England.' Charlotte hesitated, unwilling to give him an exact place. 'You were shot down. You were bombing us.'

'Bombing you?' he sounded confused. 'But you're German!'

'Not any more,' Charlotte said firmly, and then remembered she had given him her German name; it had slipped out, she realised,

357

because she was speaking to him in German. 'I've changed my name and I live here now.' She was going to say, 'Germany didn't want me,' but that sounded too dramatic, so she settled for, 'What's your name?'

'Dieter, Dieter Karhausen.'

'Where do you come from, Dieter?'

'Cologne.' He looked up at her with clearer eyes now and asked, 'Am I going to die?'

Despite herself, Charlotte felt moved. She shook her head. 'No, not if our doctor, Dr Masters, has anything to do with it. You're a prisoner of war, but he's arranging for you to be taken to hospital in Bristol.'

'Bristol?'

'That's if the hospital there is still standing,' she couldn't resist saying, 'after your raid. He says you may lose your leg; it was badly damaged when your plane was shot down, but he thinks you'll recover.'

'And my friends? The rest of the crew?'

Charlotte shook her head again. 'I'm sorry,' she said. 'They were killed in the crash.' No need to tell him of the grisly end of the rest of the crew, incinerated in the crashed plane. Even so, the news seemed to suck all the energy from him. Dieter closed his eyes again, turning his head away, but not before Charlotte had seen the tears squeezing out from under his lashes. With sudden, unexpected compassion she said, 'Tell me your address, Dieter, and we'll try and send word to your parents through the Red Cross. I am sure Major Bellinger will do that for you.' She was sure of no such thing, but she felt a desperate need to reassure this frightened young man who yet might die of his wounds. 'I promise we'll try.'

Dieter, drifting away again now, muttered an address before his head dropped into a sedated sleep. Charlotte repeated it to herself and then very quietly left the room.

Back in the kitchen she passed on what she had learned, including the name and address.

Later, soldiers came to take Dieter Karhausen away. Dr Masters was determined that he must be taken to hospital or he would lose both his legs and might die of subsequent infection.

'Our orders is to arrest him and take him to a camp,' insisted the sergeant in charge of those sent to collect him.

'Then he will die,' stated Dr Masters. 'On your conscience be it.'

There was a great deal of talk among those present and finally the sergeant made contact with his commanding officer and put Dr Masters on to explain the situation.

'This young man is going nowhere if he doesn't get his legs seen to immediately,' Dr Masters told him.

Eventually he prevailed and the soldiers who had come to arrest him took him, under armed guard, to hospital in Exeter.

Before she went back to Blackdown House, Charlotte faced Major Bellinger with the promise she'd made to the young airman.

'I'll do my best,' he said, 'but I can't guarantee anything.'

Chapter Thirty-Three

Charlotte and Clare got off the school bus and walked across the green. Outside the churchyard gate Clare flopped down on a bench and Charlotte, dropping her satchel to the ground, sat down beside her. There was only another week of term to go and both girls were looking forward to the summer holidays. Clare was leaving school and was hoping to get herself a job, working in a shop in Cheddar. Charlotte didn't know what she was going to do. Miss Edie was keen for her to continue at school so that she could go to college and train as a teacher, but Charlotte was not so sure.

'It means I have to do at least another year at school,' she said to Clare. 'You'll be out earning your living and I'll be stuck in doing homework!'

'Well, I'm glad I'm leaving school,' Clare admitted, 'but I'll still be here in Wynsdown. I want to join the Wrens, but I'm not old enough yet and in the meantime I got to pay my way at the Prynnes.' She grinned as she added, 'Malcolm'll be staying, too. He's going to work on your Billy's farm. At least they'll both be around.'

'Not sure about Billy,' Charlotte said. 'He's been funny lately. Always off somewhere doing something and he won't tell me what it is.'

'I thought you said he was doing a signalling course.'

'Yes, well, that's what he said, but he's always doing Home Guard stuff now.'

'Well, Home Guard is important,' Clare pointed out.

'I know,' sighed Charlotte, 'but he's so secretive. He doesn't seem to trust me. I've hardly seen him lately. He doesn't seem to have time for me any more.'

It was true, she thought, as she walked home to Blackdown House. Since the night of the raid when the German plane had been shot down, she had seen less and less of Billy. The happiness of the midsummer dance had been destroyed by the German bombers.

Perhaps, she'd thought over the following days, because she'd spoken to the young airman, Dieter Karhausen, and written to his parents as she'd promised, Billy had come to wonder exactly where her loyalties lay. Whatever she'd meant to him up till now, she was still German, still an 'enemy alien'. Since that morning she had hardly seen him and she missed him and their easy companionship more than she'd have believed possible. On several occasions she had walked over to Charing Farm, but though Margaret had been pleased to see her and she'd helped as she had so often before, feeding the hens and the pigs, Billy had been out and about on the farm, only coming in for the midday meal with the other men.

'It's a busy time,' Margaret said. 'I hardly see John, what with the farm and the Home Guard.'

Charlotte knew this was true, but on the few occasions she and Billy did go out together with the dogs as they had so often, Charlotte knew that everything was different and she didn't understand why. It was as if he didn't want to be alone with her. Was Billy regretting their evening together at the summer dance? Regretting they'd kissed and held each other in the way they had? The thought was very painful – she'd thought he'd been as happy as she was – but if he had regrets, well she, too, would distance herself from that evening. This weekend, she decided, she wouldn't go over to Charing Farm. She'd stay at home and help Miss Edie in the garden; she'd practise the piano for her coming music exam and she'd put Billy out of her mind.

As she walked up the path to the house, Bessie barked a welcome from the run Billy had made for her in the garden.

'Quiet, Bess,' she called as she pushed open the door and went into the kitchen. 'It's only me. I'll let you out in a minute.'

The house seemed strangely silent. Charlotte called out, 'I'm home,' but there was no answering call from Miss Edie. Charlotte glanced out of the window, but Miss Edie wasn't in the garden tending her vegetable patch.

'Miss Edie,' Charlotte called again. Still no reply. Was it one of Miss Edie's days for helping down in Cheddar? Charlotte wondered. She didn't think so.

Perhaps she's gone to the village for something and we missed each other, Charlotte thought. The door was on the latch, so she hasn't gone far.

She dumped her school bag on to a chair and went out into the hall. Bessie had stopped barking and the house settled back into silence. She went into the sitting room and, opening the piano, sat down and ran her hands over the keys. Her exam pieces were on the music stand and she played each of them through before spending another quarter of an hour on her scales. Since Miss Edie had been giving her lessons, Charlotte had discovered an unsuspected love for the piano and a talent for playing that had surprised and delighted them both.

Finishing her practice, Charlotte went upstairs to the bathroom, but as she reached the landing she came to an abrupt halt, giving a cry of horror. Miss Edie was lying on the floor half in, half out of her bedroom. She lay face down, her arms thrown out in front of her as if she'd tried to save herself. For a moment time stopped, then Charlotte took a step nearer, staring down at the woman who had taken her into her home. Her eyes were open, but her body was still, no sign of breath or life. Tentatively, Charlotte reached out and touched one of Miss Edie's outflung hands. It was cold.

Slowly she backed away, down the stairs, the chill of disbelief taking hold of her. Miss Edie had been lying, dead, upstairs, while she, Charlotte had been playing the piano. She stood for a moment in the hall, the silence in the house complete, before she turned and ran out of the house. Perhaps I'm wrong, she thought as she raced down the lane to the village, perhaps she's just unconscious and the doctor can bring her round.

Minutes later she was pounding on Dr Masters's door. He was about to start evening surgery and opened the door himself.

'Come quickly,' Charlotte cried. 'Come quickly.'

'Charlotte, my dear girl, whatever has happened?' he asked as he grabbed his bag from the hall stand.

'Miss Edie. It's Miss Edie,' Charlotte cried. 'Come quickly.' She pulled at his hand and together they hurried through the village and up the lane to Blackdown House. From her window Avril Swanson saw them go, saw the wide-eyed panic on Charlotte's face and immediately went to find her husband.

Entering the house, Charlotte led the way into the hall and pointed to the stairs. 'Up there,' she said, the words coming out on a sob. 'She's up there.'

Leaving Charlotte in the hall, Dr Masters strode upstairs. One look was enough to assure him that there was nothing he could do for Miss Edie. She lay on the floor, the chill of death all about her. He reached down and felt for a non-existent pulse, then gently closed the staring eyes. She had been dead for several hours.

Probably a massive stroke, he thought, she'd have known nothing about it. He wasn't surprised. Miss Everard had been to him several times recently, complaining of headaches, and her blood pressure had been too high. He couldn't actually have predicted the stroke, but it didn't surprise him. She was dead and beyond his help, so with a heavy heart he went back downstairs to Charlotte. She was the living and it was she who needed him now. He led her into the kitchen and, pulling out a chair, made her sit down.

'I'm so very sorry, my dear,' he said gently. 'She's gone. There's nothing I can do for her.'

Charlotte, sitting in Miss Edie's chair, stared up at him, silent tears beginning to run down her pale cheeks.

'She won't have known anything about it,' he said.

'I didn't know she was up there,' whispered Charlotte. 'I was playing the piano and I didn't know she was there.'

'You couldn't have done anything for her,' Dr Masters promised. 'It happened some hours ago, before you got home from school.'

'But I didn't come straight home,' Charlotte cried. 'I sat talking to Clare.'

'It would've made no difference if you had,' Dr Masters said. 'Don't blame yourself for not finding her sooner, Charlotte. You couldn't have done anything for her.'

At that moment there was a tap on the back door and on opening it, Dr Masters found the vicar standing in the porch, a questioning look on his face.

'Oh, David,' said Dr Masters, relief in his voice. 'It's you.'

'Has something happened?' the vicar asked. 'Is there anything I can do?'

'I'm afraid Miss Everard has had a stroke.'

'How is she?' the vicar asked, then seeing the look on the doctor's face, realised the answer.

'I'd say it was instantaneous,' said Dr Masters. 'Poor Charlotte has just found her. Will you take her back to the vicarage? She can't stay here, she's in shock.'

'Of course,' replied the vicar.

They both went into the kitchen where Charlotte sat, pale and bleak-eyed. Her tears had stopped, but her cheeks were streaked and wet.

'The vicar's here,' Dr Masters said. 'He's going to take you home with him now, Charlotte.'

'I don't want to go,' Charlotte said flatly.

'You must, my dear. You can't stay here by yourself.'

'I can't leave Miss Edie.'

'I'll look after Miss Edie,' the doctor replied softly. 'You need to go with Mr Swanson. I'll see to everything here, and then I'll come and see how you are. All right?'

Charlotte didn't reply and the vicar said, 'Come along, Charlotte, come back with me and we can all decide what needs to be done.' He held out his hand and though Charlotte didn't take it, obediently she got to her feet.

Dr Masters smiled at her. 'Good. You go with the vicar and I'll be over to see you in a little while,' he said.

Charlotte followed David Swanson out of the door. In the lane she turned back and looked at the house. A vision of Miss Edie lying spreadeagled on the landing filled her mind and she gave a strangled sob. David put an arm round her, but after a moment she pulled away and, turning her back on the house, began to walk down the lane.

Avril saw them coming and was at the door to meet them. She raised an interrogative eyebrow and her husband said, 'I'm afraid Miss Edie's had a stroke.'

'Is she...?' Avril's words hung in the air.

'She's dead!' cried Charlotte in despair. 'And I was playing the piano.' Avril reached out and took the girl in her arms and held her close as she began to sob.

From then on everything was taken out of Charlotte's hands. Avril collected her clothes from Blackdown House and Charlotte stayed at the vicarage. She didn't return to school for the last week of term and though the vicar and his wife had no idea of her decision, Charlotte was determined she was not going back to school in the autumn.

Dr Masters had no hesitation in signing the death certificate. He told Charlotte how Miss Edie had been visiting him over the past few months about her headaches.

'She didn't tell *me*,' Charlotte said. 'Well, I knew she had headaches sometimes, but I didn't know she'd been to you about them.'

'She probably didn't want to worry you,' he replied, adding gently, 'She loved you very much, you know. You gave her a whole new lease of life.'

'She did the same for me,' Charlotte replied.

Miss Edie rested in a closed coffin in her parlour at Blackdown House until the day of the funeral. David and Avril had taken the responsibility for organising it, though they had tried to include Charlotte in their planning. Charlotte had remained cold and detached. She withdrew into herself and only spoke when spoken to. Billy came to see her, but she didn't want him. The burst of love she'd felt for him only a few weeks ago had become a distant memory, fading like a dream in the cold light of reality. She pushed him away. Everyone she loved disappeared and she was determined she would give no more hostages to fate. She was going to leave

Wynsdown. She was sixteen and must take her life in her own hands, take responsibility for herself from now on. She told no one of her decision, not Billy, not Clare, not the vicar or his wife. Her decision was her own, influenced by nobody.

The day before the funeral Caroline Morrison arrived at the vicarage. Avril had rung her and asked if she could possibly come down.

'Difficult,' Caroline had said, but when she heard what Avril was suggesting, she agreed to come for two nights.

The day of the funeral dawned bright and clear. Waking to find sunlight bathing the vicarage garden, Charlotte felt the familiar stab of desolation. How could the sun go on shining? How could everyone else go on about their daily lives as if nothing had happened?

It seemed to Charlotte that the whole village came to the church. She sat with Avril and Caroline in the front pew, but the service meant little to her. David spoke of Miss Edie's life in the village, of the loss of her fiancé, of how she'd stayed at home and nursed her parents, how she'd offered a home to Charlotte. The choir had sung for her, the people of the village, many of whom had always considered her as a curmudgeonly, eccentric old woman, had come to pay their respects… and to gossip about what had happened and what was going to happen to the German girl Miss Everard had taken in. They followed Miss Everard to the graveside and watched as the coffin was lowered into the ground.

Charlotte stood, dry-eyed now, and listened to the vicar saying prayers for the dead and she thought of all her dead. Mutti, Papa, Martin, as distant as the sepia photo she had of them, all disappeared from Hanau, almost certainly dead; Aunt Naomi and Uncle Dan, come and gone from her short life, burned out of their home and also quite possibly dead; and now Miss Edie, who seemed the most real of them all, certainly dead, being lowered into the cold, brown earth. Charlotte tried to picture her, a living woman, digging her garden or wrestling with the vagaries of the kitchen range, but all she could see was Miss Edie, flat, cold and lifeless on the landing floor. She had been back to Blackdown

House the previous afternoon and picked some flowers from Miss Edie's garden and these had been laid on the coffin. Someone had removed them before the coffin was lowered into the ground; Charlotte chose a single rose and stepping forward, dropped it into the open grave.

People began to drift away, many of them heading back to the Magpie to have a drink and discuss the send-off they'd given that strange Miss Everard.

Charlotte didn't follow them, but stood staring, unseeing, into the open grave.

'What are you going to do now, Charlotte?'

Charlotte turned at the question and found Miss Morrison at her shoulder. She shrugged but said nothing.

'If you wanted a change of scene,' Miss Morrison said, 'I could do with another pair of hands at Livingston Road.'

'Livingston Road?' Charlotte looked blank.

'Livingston Road children's home. You know I've just taken over the running of it since it's been rebuilt. Let me know if you'd like to come and help. You'd have plenty to do.' And with that, she smiled and walked away. She'd sown the seed; if it took root, well and good.

Billy was waiting for Charlotte at the churchyard gate. He reached out and took her hand, but though she didn't pull away, Charlotte's hand lay, unresponsive, in his own. It made his heart ache, but he knew it was his own fault. He had indeed been distancing himself a little from Charlotte. He couldn't tell her about being recruited into the secret resistance force and he had the growing fear that, should the invasion really come, Charlotte would be at great risk, being an escaped German living in England. She might be shot as a traitor. If, added to that, she were connected to him, a resistance fighter, she would be in even greater danger.

If only he could explain. But he knew he couldn't; other men relied on his silence, he'd signed the secrecy papers and he was bound by them.

'Thought you might like to get away for a while,' he said. 'We could take the dogs over towards the gorge.'

They had been unable to cope with Bessie at the vicarage and she had gone back to the farm for Billy to look after. On a couple of occasions Avril had suggested that Charlotte should walk up to Charing Farm to see Billy and to take Bessie out, but Charlotte didn't go. Somehow it seemed too much; she couldn't make the effort. Avril was very concerned about her, but seemed unable to break through the invisible shell into which Charlotte had withdrawn.

'If you like,' Charlotte said now, but without enthusiasm. She looked up at him, his blue eyes searching her face, his fair hair its usual unruly self, cut short to disguise its curls. All so familiar, once so dear, now so distant. How strange that in a few short days everything had changed. She held his gaze and for a moment she returned the warm clasp of his hand, but it was momentary, she was sticking to her resolve, offering no more hostages to fate, and she pulled away.

'Come on, then,' he said and together they turned and walked the well-worn path across the fields to Charing Farm. John and Margaret had been at the church and weren't home yet.

'Expect they're in the Magpie,' Billy said. 'It's where most funerals end up.' Even as he said the words he knew he'd made a mistake. Charlotte tensed, moving away from him. Seeming not to notice her withdrawal, he opened the stable door where the two dogs were already barking a welcome and as they hurtled out into the yard, running in crazy circles in their delight, Charlotte bent down catching Bessie to her and hugged the dog's warm body against her. For the first time in days, she felt a moment's comfort.

They set off across the fields, but the gap that divided them was far wider than the couple of feet between them. The sun beat down, but somehow Charlotte still felt cold. As they finally turned and walked back to the farm Billy said, 'What'll you do now, Char?'

Charlotte shrugged. 'Don't know,' she said. But she did know. The awkwardness between them that afternoon had made her decision for her. She would take Miss Morrison up on her suggestion. She'd go back to London with her and help other displaced children.

She had first-hand experience of what that was like, she would understand what they were feeling and there was nothing left for her here in Wynsdown.

Chapter Thirty-Four

After her walk with Billy, Charlotte had returned to the vicarage, sought out Miss Morrison, who was sitting at the kitchen table with her sister, and said, 'I'd like to come back to London with you tomorrow, please.'

Though it was what the two sisters had planned for her, they were both surprised at the immediacy of her decision.

'I do think it'd be a good idea if you went,' Avril said, 'but perhaps tomorrow is a bit early. We need time to get you ready.'

'No,' Charlotte insisted. 'I'm ready to go now. I want to go with Miss Morrison when she goes in the morning.'

'I'm going on an early train,' Miss Morrison said. 'Perhaps it would be better to do as my sister suggests and get yourself sorted out here first.'

'I am sorted out here,' Charlotte said. 'I'll be ready to leave in the morning, however early it is.'

'Well, I don't know...' Avril hesitated.

'Don't know what?' asked her husband as he came in through the door.

'Caro suggested that Charlotte might like to go up to help her at the home,' Avril explained. 'I think it's a good idea, but she wants to go with Caro tomorrow. I think it would be better if we sorted out her things here and then put her on a train in a week or so.'

'There's nothing to sort,' Charlotte said before the vicar had time to answer. 'All my clothes are here. I've nothing else and I want to go... tomorrow.'

'It is a little sudden, Charlotte—' began the vicar, but she rounded on him.

'Miss Edie is dead. I have no home in Wynsdown. I can't stay with you, you've got the Payne children and there isn't room for me. I'm sixteen. I'm not going back to school, so I need to earn my own living.' She looked round at the three adults. 'What Miss Morrison is suggesting is something I can do. I've been there, remember?'

'You're a ward of court,' began Avril uncertainly.

'Then tell the court that I've gone to work at Livingston Road children's home. It's my contribution to the war effort.'

'But everyone here'll miss you,' said Avril in a last-ditch attempt. 'You're part of the village.'

'No,' replied Charlotte. 'I'm not. I've never been part of the village. That's why Miss Edie and I got on so well. She wasn't part of the village either.' Her words were greeted by silence. There was nothing more they could say.

'Well,' said Miss Morrison, 'Dr Masters is coming to pick me up tomorrow morning at half past five. If you're coming with me, you need to be ready in the hall when he gets here.'

'I will be,' replied Charlotte and she went upstairs to put her few things together into her case before walking out into the summer evening for one last look at the village.

Until now she'd only been back to the garden of Blackdown House to pick the flowers for Miss Edie's coffin, but as the sun shone warm on the lane leading to Miss Edie's home, her home, Charlotte found her steps turning that way. Alone, she walked up the lane and in through the garden gate. Miss Edie's flower garden was running riot, but someone had been in to see to the vegetable plot. The vicar had pointed out that Miss Edie wouldn't have wanted the produce to be wasted and Charlotte had agreed, but she didn't know what he'd done about it. Now she saw the runner beans climbing up their poles, the lettuces growing in their neat rows and the tomatoes ripening on the vine and she was glad that all Miss Edie's efforts had not been for nothing. She looked at Bessie's now-empty cage and felt a pang at leaving her beloved dog behind, but Bessie would be miserable in London and Charlotte knew Billy would look after her.

Billy. She hadn't said a proper goodbye to Billy. She hadn't told him what she was going to do. He'd hear she'd gone and she hoped he'd understand that she had to go, that her time in Wynsdown had been simply a chapter of her life and like all the other chapters so far, Hanau, Kemble Street, St Michael's, it was over now and she was about to turn over a new page.

She sat on the bench under the kitchen window, the sun on her face, and for the first time thought about Miss Edie without the tears springing to her eyes. So many things had changed because of her; she'd become part of Charlotte's life, instrumental in its shaping. Whatever happened from now on, Miss Edie's influence would be there. The sun was hanging low in the sky and Charlotte got to her feet. She went into the back porch and, reaching up to the shelf where the spare key was kept, she let herself into the silent house. Quietly she went from the kitchen into the hall and stood for a moment looking round, then steeling herself, she went upstairs and stood on the landing. There was nothing to see. Miss Edie's bedroom door stood open, her dressing gown lay across a chair, her slippers tidily under the bed as if she might walk in at any time; but Miss Edie had gone. The house wasn't cold, just empty.

The door to the spare room was closed and after a glance round her own bedroom, she went back downstairs and into the sitting room. Her music was still on the piano. As the light outside faded to dusk, Charlotte sat down at the piano and played her two exam pieces. She played them without a mistake and when her hands finally came to rest on the keys, she knew she'd said her goodbyes. Quietly she left the house and restoring the key to its place on the shelf, walked out into the twilight, back to the vicarage. At half past five the next morning she was waiting in the hall with her suitcase.

Avril had got up to see them off. She hugged her sister. 'Come down again as soon as you can, Caro. We miss you and,' she teased, 'Doc Masters does too.'

'You mind your own business.' Caro punched her lightly on the arm.

Avril turned to Charlotte. 'You know you've always got a home with us here at the vicarage, don't you?' she said. 'David and I hope you know that you'll always be welcome here.' She gave her a hug and then Dr Masters was at the door and they climbed into the car, heading for the station.

Charlotte settled in quickly at Livingston Road, helping Miss Morrison with the children who'd been put in her care. She was surprised to find Mrs Downs and Mrs Burton, cook and matron from St Michael's, were also installed at Livingston Road. They greeted her warmly, delighted to know she had her memory back. She was given a tiny bedroom in the attic and she was pleased to have somewhere to retreat to at the end of each busy day.

'The children will call you "Miss Charlotte",' said Miss Morrison. 'You haven't got a specific job, but I can assure you, you're going to be very busy.'

Miss Morrison was right. Charlotte had no time to think of anything but the next job that needed doing. The house was home to twenty-five children; children whose homes had been destroyed, waiting to be rehoused with their families, others who had been orphaned by the Blitz and had nowhere to go, yet others waiting for someone to come forward and claim them. Charlotte well remembered the disorientation she'd felt when she'd first come to St Michael's. She could empathise with these children who now found themselves in a similar plight. She was indeed Miss Morrison's extra pair of hands. She helped Mrs Downs in the kitchen, she helped Matron in the laundry and with the never-ending mending, she played with the younger children and helped the older ones with their homework. It was a hectic and busy life and allowed Charlotte little time for introspection. It was exactly what she needed after the trauma of Miss Edie's sudden death.

Hectic as things were at Livingston Road, Miss Morrison insisted that Charlotte had the occasional afternoon off. At first Charlotte hadn't wanted them, seldom going far from the home, always wanting to come back to its security, but gradually over the weeks she felt a growing urge to revisit Kemble Street. She knew Caroline had been there two years earlier, that many of its houses, including number sixty-five, had been destroyed, but she felt the need to go and see for herself. Perhaps she'd go round to Grove

Avenue, too, and see what Hilda was doing. Hilda would be so surprised to see her after so long. Perhaps she'd know what had happened to the Federmans. So, on her next free afternoon, Charlotte made her way across London to Kemble Street, at last getting off the bus and walking again through the once-familiar streets. She'd heard how the East End of London had been devastated during the long nights of the Blitz, but even so she wasn't prepared for what now met her eyes. Ruined houses stood cheek by jowl with those that had survived, burned-out homes faced those undamaged by the fire, patches of uncleared rubble had been reclaimed by creeping vegetation, willowherb, buddleia, buttercups, couch grass, smothering and softening the harsh outlines of the bomb sites, and all around the jagged outline of damaged buildings stood stark against the summer sky. How had anyone survived such destruction?

Despite what she'd seen on the way and what she'd heard from Caroline Morrison, the sight of Kemble Street brought tears to Charlotte's eyes. She walked slowly down the road, looking at the houses. One or two had been demolished, leaving gaps between houses still occupied. Others had been damaged but makeshift repairs seemed to have made them habitable again. Along one side of the street, her side, were the blackened shells that were all that was left of the terrace where she had lived. It was difficult to know which house was which and she had to count twice before she was sure she was looking at number sixty-five. Had Aunt Naomi and Uncle Dan got out, or had they been trapped by the flames in the cellar, dying of smoke or, worse still, burned to death as they tried to escape? Had they been together, or had Uncle Dan still been out when the sirens went off? She stood looking at the house for a long time. Everything she'd owned had been in that house. While she'd been in hospital and later at St Michael's, unable to remember who she was, they must have been wondering what had happened to her. Had they tried to find her?

She thought back to her last night in Wynsdown when she'd visited Blackdown House to say goodbye to Miss Edie. Now, here she was, where she'd lived for over a year with Aunt Naomi and

Uncle Dan. Suddenly she knew that she must close the Kemble Street chapter of her life, as well. She must go into the house that had been her home and bid it and them, farewell.

Hesitantly she went towards it. There was no front door; the way into the house stood open and unguarded. Wild flowers had seeded themselves around the doorway and some had even begun to grow inside the house, drawing sustenance from the moisture in the damp walls and rotting floor. Cautiously, Charlotte stepped inside. The whole place was smothered in damp dust and soot. The walls were black and the breeze blowing through the gaping windows caused little flurries of dust to rise, spin and settle. She edged her way along the passage leading to the kitchen, her feet leaving a trail of footprints on the dirty floor. At the far side of the kitchen she could see the cellar door. How she'd hated that cellar. She walked over and looked at it. It was closed. She put her hand on the handle and tried to turn it, but it was stiff and didn't move.

Oh, well, she thought, glad that it hadn't opened, I didn't really want to go down there anyway. She gave one more cursory twist to the handle and pulled, but the door remained adamantly closed.

'And just what do you think you're doing?' The voice behind her made her jump and she spun round to find the doorway blocked by the bulk of a man, silhouetted against the sunlight outside.

'I… I was just looking,' she faltered.

'Looking for what?'

Just… wondering if—'

'If there was anything you could steal, I suppose.'

'No!' Charlotte almost shouted. 'Of course not! It's just that, well, I used to live here.'

'No you didn't,' snapped the man. 'I know the people who used to live here and it wasn't you.'

'It was,' cried Charlotte. 'I lived here with some people called Federman.'

'Did you, now? And what's your name then?'

'Charlotte Smith,' answered Charlotte and was about to go on when he interrupted.

'Then you didn't live here. There was no Charlotte Smith here.'

'My name was Lisa Becker then. Now, let me out of the house.' She took a step forward, but the man still barred her way. 'Please move,' she said with more determination in her voice than she actually felt. 'I want to go outside.' Who was this man, standing in her way, quizzing her about herself? He wasn't a tall man, but he was broad and sturdy.

'Lisa?' He stood in the doorway, unmoving. 'Lisa, is it really you? I don't believe you.'

'Who are you?' Charlotte demanded. 'Why d'you want to know who I am?'

She edged a little closer to the door, thinking she might make a break for it. As she did so her face was lit by a shaft of dusty sunlight. The man took a step back and with sudden resolve she pushed her way past him, down the passage and out of the doorway. To her surprise he made no move to stop her, simply followed her out into the street.

'Lisa,' he said again, 'it *is* you. We thought you were dead.'

Charlotte looked at him properly for the first time. She hadn't seen him for two years and he'd changed from a scruffy, scrawny boy with fierce dark eyes into a stocky man, sturdy, with powerful shoulders and short cropped hair, but now that she could see him in the light, there was no mistaking him.

'Harry?' She stared at him, seeing his face crease into the irrepressible smile she'd known so well. 'Harry?' Tentatively, she reached out her hand, touched his arm as if to confirm that he was real. 'Is it really you?'

Harry took her hand and held it tightly and nodded before saying, 'Lisa, I can't believe it's you. We all thought you were dead. Thought you'd been killed in the raid.'

Lisa shook her head as if trying to clear her thoughts. Still holding her hand, Harry said, 'Look, there's still a caff in Hope Street. Let's go there and get a cuppa. Come on,' he urged as she hesitated, 'we've got a lot to catch up on.'

Wordlessly she allowed him to lead her along the street, past the derelict Duke and into the café next to the air raid shelter on the corner of Hope Street. He pushed the door open and they went inside. Charlotte sat down at one of the wooden tables in the window while Harry went for tea from the counter.

How strange, Charlotte thought, that the last time I was with Harry we were in a café. It was something she hadn't remembered before, but being with Harry now brought it back. Her hand went to the necklace she always wore, the blue beads Harry had given her a lifetime ago. Harry came back to the table and said the tea was on its way. He sat down opposite her and for a moment neither of them said anything, then they both spoke at once.

'What happened...?'

'Where have...?'

And they both laughed, but their laughter had broken the ice and Harry said, 'You were on the bus, going home. You must have been caught in that first raid of the Blitz.'

'I was. Someone found me unconscious with a broken arm and I was taken to hospital. When I came round, well, I couldn't remember anything, not my name, where I came from, nothing.'

'So what did they do?'

'There was a man found with me...'

'A man? What man?' Harry looked stricken. 'I knew I should have come with you!'

'Just a man. He was dead. They said he was lying on top of me and that's probably what saved my life. His identity card said he was Peter Smith. I didn't have mine with me and they thought I must be his daughter, so they wrote me down as Smith.'

Harry listened, dismayed, as Charlotte told him of the intervening years.

'We all looked for you everywhere,' Harry said. 'Your aunt Naomi went round all the hospitals, but she couldn't find you. They thought you must have got back to Hilda's and been killed there.'

'What?' Charlotte stared at him in horror. 'What d'you mean, killed at Hilda's? Is she dead?'

Harry nodded. 'Whole family,' he said. 'Direct hit.' He saw the colour flee from Charlotte's cheeks and said, 'Sorry, of course you didn't know. Naomi and Dan were desperate to find you, to believe that you hadn't been in the house, but it all came back to the fact that that was where you were going. The house was totally destroyed and it was impossible to know how many people had been inside.'

The waitress appeared at the table carrying a tray of tea, and for a moment neither of them spoke. Charlotte felt sick. She'd been imagining Hilda getting on with her life in London, back at Francis Drake Secondary. She'd been going to walk round to Grove Avenue this afternoon and surprise them all.

'Is that what the Federmans thought?' she asked when the waitress had gone again. 'That I'd been killed by that bomb?'

Harry reached over and took her hand. 'It's what we all thought,' he said.

'I wrote to them,' Charlotte said. 'As soon as my memory came back I wrote to them, but I heard nothing back. Then Miss Morrison, who I work for now, came to Kemble Street to tell them where I was and that I was OK, but she found the house burnt out. She couldn't find anyone to ask.'

'So they don't know you're alive?'

'No, and I don't know if they are, either.'

'They were last time I heard,' Harry said. 'Mrs had moved out of Kemble Street before the house was burnt, she went somewhere safer to have the baby.'

'Baby!' exclaimed Charlotte. 'What baby?'

'Didn't you know she was having one?'

'No.'

'Well she was, and she went away. Dan stayed on. He still drove his cab. Had to make a living, didn't he?'

'So when was the house destroyed?'

Harry shrugged. 'Don't know, I'd been banged up by then.'

'Banged up?' Charlotte was puzzled. It wasn't an expression she'd come across.

'Yeah, interned, you know.'

She didn't know and Harry proceeded to give her an edited version of his arrest and internment.

'So you don't know where the Federmans are now?'

Harry shook his head. 'Nope. Just out of town.'

Charlotte looked disappointed. Now she knew they were alive

and well, she wanted to find them; to tell them she was all right. She longed to see them and explain what had happened to her. She wanted to see the baby.

'Perhaps someone in Kemble Street has an address,' she said hopefully.

'Maybe,' Harry said, but he didn't sound encouraging. He wasn't keen to find the Federmans, not while he was still using their house. To change the subject, he asked her about the village where she'd been evacuated and thus succeeded in diverting her thoughts. There were several ways they might be able to find the Federmans, but for the moment Harry decided to keep them to himself.

Together they sat at the little table in the window, talking, their tea grown cold in the cups until the waitress appeared at their side and said, 'Sorry, but we're closing now. I have to ask you to leave.' She looked down at the half-drunk cups of tea and said with a sniff, 'Hope you enjoyed your tea, then. That'll be a shilling.'

Harry rummaged in his pocket and paid up and then they went out into the evening air.

'So, where's this place you're working at?' he demanded.

'Livingston Road. It's a children's home.'

'How'd you get here?'

'I came on the bus, Harry.'

'Still no Tube?' he teased.

'No,' she said sharply, 'not if I can avoid it.'

'Well, I'll come back with you,' he said, 'so's I'll know where to find you.' He took her hand and together they walked to the main road to catch the bus.

When they reached Livingston Road he followed her to the gate of a large double-fronted grey stone house. 'Looks a bit grim,' he said, looking up at the three rows of windows. 'I wouldn't want to live here.'

'You might if you had nowhere else,' Charlotte snapped. 'Most of the kids don't want to live here either, but they haven't any choice.'

'All right, all right, keep your hair on.' He raised his hands placatingly. 'Aren't you going to introduce me to Miss What's-her-name?'

Charlotte hadn't thought of it, but as Harry had asked, she might as well. 'All right,' she said, and opening the gate she led him up to the front door.

Caroline Morrison was in her box of an office just off the hall and Charlotte knocked on the open door.

'Oh, Charlotte, good, you're back. Have you had a nice afternoon?'

'Yes, thank you, Miss Morrison.' She paused in the doorway and Caroline looked up from what she was doing and said, 'Did you want something?'

'Just wanted you to meet someone,' Charlotte replied. 'I met an old friend this afternoon.'

Caroline put down her pen and got to her feet. 'Of course,' she said. 'Who is it?' She emerged into the hall and saw a young man standing there. He was in workman's clothes, a blue checked shirt open at his throat, his big boots sticking out from under his well-worn dungarees.

Charlotte turned back to her, her eyes dancing. 'This is Harry, Harry Black. He comes from my town in Germany and I knew him in London when...' she hesitated, searching for the right words, 'before I came to St Michael's.'

'Nice to meet you,' Harry said, treating Miss Morrison to his most dazzling smile and sticking out his hand. 'Lisa's been telling me all about what happened to her in the raid and that.'

Caroline Morrison shook the proffered hand. Lisa. He means Charlotte, she thought, but of course he's never known her by that name. 'And I've heard about you, too,' was what she actually said.

'Harry just wanted to see where I live,' Charlotte explained, 'and he wanted to meet you.' Her face was bright with happiness as she looked at her old friend; someone who had known her 'before'. Miss Morrison was pleased to see the change in her meeting Harry had wrought, but she wasn't at all sure about Harry himself. She couldn't put her finger on it, but there was something about him that made her distrust him. Which isn't fair, she told herself firmly. You don't know the lad from Adam, you're in no position to make judgements, especially as he's so important to Charlotte.

'I've got to work, now,' Charlotte was telling him.

'That's OK,' Harry replied as they went back out into the street. 'I know where you are now.'

'But I don't know where you are,' Charlotte reminded him. 'You don't live at Kemble Street, do you?'

'No,' he said. 'Just keeping an eye on it for Dan.' He leaned forward and kissed her on the cheek. 'I can't believe I've found you, Lisa,' he said. 'It's a miracle.'

Impulsively she flung her arms round him and gave him a huge hug. 'I can't believe it either,' she said. Pulling away, suddenly shy, she added, 'But I still don't know where to find you, Harry.'

'Told you, I'm working at the docks, I got a room down there. Don't worry, Lisa, I shan't lose you again, I promise.' With that he turned and with a jaunty wave, set off back the way they'd come.

Charlotte watched him as he rounded the corner before she turned and slowly went back into the house. It had been a miracle to find Harry and in his company she had forgotten, for a while, the feeling of emptiness that she'd been carrying with her for so long. But as Harry had disappeared from sight, it returned, a slow, smothering cloud descending on her. She was here in London, alone, and despite living in a house full of children, she'd never felt so lonely.

That evening, when Charlotte had gone up to bed, Caroline sat in her office and thought about her. She had seen the happiness in the girl's face when she introduced Harry, and despite her own inexplicable reaction, Caroline was pleased for her. However, when he'd left and Charlotte had come back in to the house, that spark had been extinguished. Caroline had called her into the office for a chat.

'How lovely to meet up with Harry,' she said. 'Where did you find him?'

'I went to Kemble Street,' Charlotte said. 'I told you I was going.'

Caroline nodded. She hadn't been sure that was a good idea either, but realised that though it might be painful for Charlotte to see the remains of her former home, it might help her to put that part of her life behind her and look to the future, rather than the past.

'Well, it looked like you said, probably worse. Nothing has been done to clear the ruins or mend the houses.' She sighed and rubbed her eyes as if trying to wipe away the sight of number sixty-five and its neighbours. 'Anyway, I went to look inside.'

'Oh, Charlotte, that was dangerous!' exclaimed Caroline.

Charlotte shrugged. 'I don't think so,' she said. 'The house wasn't going to fall. Anyway, I went inside. It's a complete ruin, still covered in soot. I went into the kitchen and was looking at the cellar door – we used to hide in the cellar during raids – when he came in through the door.'

'Harry did?' Caroline was amazed. 'What was he doing there?'

'That's what he asked me,' Charlotte smiled. 'I didn't recognise him at first. I couldn't see his face and anyway, he's changed. Grown up, I mean. He was a boy when I last saw him. He's not a boy any more.'

'No,' agreed Caroline, remembering the broad-shouldered young man who'd tried to charm her with a smile.

Charlotte described how they'd sat over a cup of tea, talking and talking. 'It was as if I'd seen him yesterday, not two years ago.'

'I think that often happens when you meet up with good friends after a time apart. You pick up where you left off.' For a moment Caroline's thoughts flew to Henry Masters. It was just like that whenever they met and she felt a secret glow.

'They all thought I was dead,' Charlotte went on and she explained why. Her eyes filled with tears as she told Caroline about Hilda and her family. How kind they'd been to her when she'd arrived as a refugee, how Hilda had befriended her at school and how they'd all helped her with her English. 'I can't believe they're all dead, Hilda, her brother, her parents. All gone.' She pulled out a hankie and blew her nose. 'All this time and I didn't know.'

'What was Harry doing at the house?' Caroline asked, more to change the subject than wanting to know.

'He said he was keeping an eye on it.'

'Keeping an eye on it?'

'Yes, he told me he'd stayed with the Federmans for a while when he had nowhere else to live. When they moved, so that Aunt Naomi

was away from the bombs when she had her baby, he said he'd stay
and keep an eye on it.'

'But it's a ruin.'

'I know,' agreed Charlotte, 'but when he found me with my hand
on the cellar door, he thought I was trying to go down there to see
if there was anything to steal.'

'And is there?'

Charlotte shrugged. 'Don't know. I couldn't open the door and
then Harry came. Still,' she brightened a little, 'I know Aunt Naomi
and Uncle Dan are alive... and that they've had a baby. I didn't
know they were having a baby!'

'How exciting,' Caroline said. 'And where are they now?'

'Harry doesn't know. He just knows they were moving away
from the bombing.'

That's strange, Caroline thought, if he promised to keep an eye
on their house, he must know where they've gone. But for the time
being she kept this thought to herself.

'I see,' she said. 'Well, that's a pity, because I'm sure you want to
find them and tell them you're alive and well.'

This drew a smile. 'Oh yes,' cried Charlotte. 'Oh, I do want to
find them.'

'Well, we'll have to see what we can do,' promised Caroline. 'I
expect if we ask around in that area, someone'll know where they
went. At least then you can write to them, if nothing else.'

'I wrote to them before,' Charlotte said, 'but they didn't
answer.'

'I know you did, but that's almost certainly because they never
got your letter. The posts went completely haywire during the Blitz.
There could be a hundred reasons why they never got your letter.'
Or there could be just one, she thought privately. Harry.

When Charlotte went up to bed, Caroline stayed sitting at her
desk, thinking. In her desk drawer was a letter she'd received from
Avril only a couple of weeks earlier. It brought news for Charlotte
and Caroline had been deputed to tell her about it at an opportune
moment. Up until now she hadn't managed to find the right moment
and with the reappearance of Harry Black, she was glad that she

hadn't. It wasn't news she wanted to share with him. She got the letter out and re-read it.

St Mark's Vicarage
Wynsdown

Dear Caro,
I know you're safely back at Livingston Road now and hope that Charlotte is settling in. It can't be easy for her to come to terms with yet another loss, but I'm sure you're keeping her busy which will help!
    We had some interesting news the other day with regard to Charlotte. A few days after you left, Mr Thompson of Thompson, Harris and Thompson came up from Cheddar. He was Miss Everard's solicitor. Anyway, he came to see David about her will. Apparently she's left a small bequest to the church but everything else is left in trust for Charlotte. Till she's 21. You can imagine we were amazed! What's more, she'd named David as a co-trustee with Mr Thompson. You could have knocked us down with a feather! David had no idea. She certainly hadn't asked him. Mr T says he told her to speak to David about it first and he assumed that she'd done so. David can refuse if he wants to but he's not going to. In the meantime it means that Charlotte is quite well off. Miss Everard had some shares or bonds or something that gave her a reasonable income and all that is Charlotte's now. Mr T said Miss E made the will several months ago. Blackdown House is Charlotte's as well, of course, so she does have somewhere to live if she wants to leave London again.
    All this is most unexpected. Mr Thompson is also the executor, but he agreed to leave it to us to tell Charlotte of her inheritance. David and I have discussed it and decided that it isn't something to put in a letter. It would be better to tell her face to face and be ready to answer the questions she will surely have. So, dear Caro, we'd like to leave it to you to break it to her at a suitable moment. You're in loco parentis now... maybe

not legally but certainly de facto. What about all my Latin tags!! Father would have been impressed, don't you think? Still, I know you'll agree it's better to deal with this face to face. I think Mr T is opening a bank account for her, so that she'll have access to some of her money. Not the capital of course, enough to pay her way and for a few little extras, but not so that anyone with an eye to the main chance can get his hooks into her.

Do come down and see us again soon, Caro. Poor Henry is pining away!

Give my love to Charlotte and lots to you,
Avril xx

Though she doesn't know it, Caroline thought now, Charlotte is a wealthy girl and with the recollection of Harry, standing charming and confident in the front hall, she was glad he didn't know it either. He seemed to be a cross between a spiv and a docker and she didn't trust either of them.

Chapter Thirty-Five

Naomi was catching a few minutes' rest while Nicholas was having his afternoon nap when there was a sharp rap on her door. She heaved herself to her feet and when she opened the door she found Shirley Newman outside.

'Shirley,' she said, standing aside for her to come in, 'what can I do for you?'

'I got some news I thought you'd want to hear,' Shirley said, flopping down into a chair. She and Naomi had remained friends over the months they'd both been living in Feneton, but they were not close. Naomi was busy, living and working at the Feneton Arms and Shirley, tired of being at the beck and call of her cousin, Maud, had found work in a factory outside Ipswich and went in daily on the bus.

'What's happened?' Naomi asked.

'Derek's come home on leave,' Shirley said.

This wasn't news to Naomi. 'Yes,' she said. 'I know, you both come in the bar on Saturday.'

'Yeah, but on Sunday we went down to London. Back to Kemble Street.'

Naomi looked at her in surprise. 'Did you? And how did it look?'

'Well, there ain't nothing been done to our house. Looks just like it did before, 'cept that there's weeds growing in the walls. Thing is, Derek says we ought to be repairing it before it gets worse. The bombing's stopped now, so we could try and get it mended.'

'Mended?'

'Well, some repairs anyway. If we could get the roof fixed and board up the windows – you know, make the place water-tight – well, Derek says we could probably move back there.'

'Move back?' Naomi couldn't believe what she was hearing.

'Not now, not straight away, but after the war.'

'That sounds a long way off,' Naomi said.

'I know, but when it does end everyone's going to be looking for places to live, ain't they? Means we'd have a head start. People are going to live in damaged houses to begin with, ain't they?'

Naomi shrugged. She hadn't ever thought that far ahead. She was happy enough as they were now. She had her job, working for Jenny, and Dan was working at the nearby RAF base.

When Dan had come to live there permanently, Jenny had given them two upstairs rooms as their home and they were comfortably settled. Would they, she wondered now, ever go back to Kemble Street? It had always been Dan's home, but they didn't own it and since the fire had made it uninhabitable, they had ceased to pay rent. All their possessions had been destroyed with it. Naomi was in no hurry to go back to face the wreck of what had once been her home. They'd started a new life, here in Suffolk. Nicholas, now two and a half, had made up for his early appearance in the world and was growing fast. He wasn't threatened with death from the skies, he was fed, warm and cared for. Why should they change that?

'So, who's going to pay for all these repairs?' she wondered.

'Landlord'll have to,' said Shirley. 'But listen, Naomi, this isn't what I came to tell you.'

'So, what is?'

'While we was looking at the house, I saw someone going into yours.'

'What?' Naomi stared at her. 'Who?'

'Dunno who,' replied Shirley, 'just a bloke. He went inside but we didn't see him come out.'

'But what was he doing?' demanded Naomi. 'I mean, the whole place is burnt out, least, that's what Dan says.'

'Dunno what he was doing,' returned Shirley, 'just poking about,

I expect. He may have come out again when we wasn't looking. Before we left, Derek went over and looked in. He didn't go inside, but he couldn't see no one and no one answered when he called. Anyway,' she went on, 'Derek said I should come and tell you, case Dan wants to go and have a look-see.'

'Thanks,' Naomi said. 'I'll tell Dan when he gets in, but I don't suppose we can do much. People must be poking about bomb sites all the time.'

When Dan got home that evening Naomi told him what Shirley had said. 'Who d'you think it was?' she wondered. 'And what was he doing in our house?'

'I don't know,' Dan said with a shrug, 'but I bet there are people like him all over London.'

'There isn't anything of ours he could steal, is there?' she asked. 'I mean, you brought all that wasn't burnt with you.'

'I brought all I could carry,' Dan said. 'There was stuff left in the cellar, of course, but that weren't worth nothing. You know, just that old mattress and them chairs. Not stuff I could bring with me, but not worth stealing, neither.'

'Did you lock the cellar door?'

'Couldn't lock it, it was off its hinges.'

'So anyone could get in there.'

'Well, suppose they could. I mean, well, I pushed the door back into place and wedged it. You could open it, but not easily. And why would you even go into the house, let alone try to go into the cellar?'

They had a quick supper and then Naomi went down to do her stint in the bar. Sometimes Dan went down too, to sit in the snug by the fire, but tonight he stayed upstairs. He thought over what Naomi had told him. It did seem odd that someone would go into the burnt-out house and stay there. Of course Derek and Shirley might have missed whoever it was coming out again, but even so, Dan didn't like the idea of someone poking about his home, even if it was a ruin.

He was in bed by the time Naomi had finished closing up downstairs. He heard her go over and look at Nicholas asleep in his cot before she slipped in beside him.

'I've been thinking,' he said as she snuggled close, 'I think I'll go down on Sunday.'

'Down?' Naomi was tired and she sighed. 'Down where?'

'Down to London. To Kemble Street. Have a look around and see what's what. It's months since I was there. I ought to have a shufti.'

'There won't be anything to see,' Naomi said. 'That bloke'll be long gone.'

'P'raps,' agreed Dan, 'but I think I'll go all the same.'

'Well, I can't come with you,' Naomi said.

'Know you can't, love, but even so, I think I'll go. I can have a look and then we can put it out of our minds.' He smiled in the darkness and added, 'I can have a look at the Newmans', too, see if they really can do enough repairs to save it.'

Sunday afternoon saw Dan walking from the Hope Street bus stop into Kemble Street. He walked slowly along the road in which he'd lived all his life, looking at the houses, those with families still living there, those damaged beyond repair and the one or two, like the Newmans', in between. All so familiar and yet bitterly unfamiliar.

There were people about, but no one paid any attention to him. When he reached number sixty-five he paused for a moment on the pavement, looking through the open doorway then, with sudden determination, he stepped across the threshold into the ruins of his home. A glance into the front room told him no one was there. The remains of the stairs in front of him led nowhere; no one would risk going up those. Softly he walked down the passage to the kitchen at the back. There were definitely footprints in the dirt, but they could have been there for months. The kitchen was just as he'd left it on that dreadful day after the fire... except for the door to the cellar. It was still wedged shut, but from the sweep marks in the dust on the floor it was clear that it had been opened, probably quite recently. He crossed the kitchen and looked hard at the door. He could see now that it had been pushed back into the doorway and a piece of rubble had been forced under it to fix it firmly in place. It's what he'd done himself, except that he had used a piece of wood for the wedge, not a stone. Dan looked at it, considering, then he reached down and with several sharp kicks, he dislodged the stone with his boot and the door moved. He eased it open and peered down the steps. No one was there. He'd brought a torch with him and so, with great care, he made his way down into the cellar. Flashing the torch around he saw that the cellar had indeed been in use. The mattress was there with blankets piled on to it. The chairs were there and the small table, but on the table there was a Tilley lamp. They hadn't had a Tilley lamp. That proved it. Someone was using their cellar. Dan looked round to see what else he could see. There was a bottle of water and a row of tinned food on the shelf. Dan was certain he hadn't left any food there. He couldn't remember if there had even been any. Biscuits perhaps? Certainly not tins. Where had they all come from? Too many to have been bought legally, he thought. He wished he had something he could put them in, so that he could take them with him. He didn't know whose they were, nor where they'd come from, but they were in the cellar of his house and as far as he was concerned, that made them his. He picked up a couple of tins of salmon, the like of which he hadn't seen for years, and slid them into his pocket. A treat for Naomi and the boy; at least he'd have something to show for his trip down to London.

He went back up to the kitchen and manoeuvred the cellar door back into place, kicking the piece of rubble underneath it to hold it firmly in place. With one last look round the kitchen he walked back through the house and out into the street. It was still daylight, though it wouldn't be long before the dusk turned to twilight and darkness. He was walking back down the road to catch the bus to the station when he saw someone coming towards him. The man was walking slowly along the road, looking from left to right. A familiar figure and one he immediately recognised.

'Albert?' Dan called. 'Is that you?'

Albert stopped and peered at him. 'Dan Federman?'

'Yes, it's me. Just been down to look at the house. What're you doing?'

'Citizen patrol,' Albert said. 'Keeping an eye... you know.' He glanced round him anxiously as if someone might be watching. 'Keeping an eye...'

'Good for you,' Dan said. Dan knew Albert of old. Not the sharpest tool in the box, Dan's dad would have said, but no harm in him, no harm at all. 'Seen anything, have you?'

'I see lot of things,' Albert said, tapping the side of his nose with his finger. 'Be 'mazed what I see.'

'I'm sure I would,' Dan said, about to move on. 'Keep up the good work.'

'Not the only one.' Albert laid a hand on Dan's arm as if to stop him going. 'Bloke looking after your place, ain't there?'

Dan turned and looked at him. 'What bloke's that?' he said.

'You know the one,' Albert said. 'The one you said could sleep there. Cellar-rat. That's what he is. Cellar-rat. Lots of those about. He's all right, your bloke, cos you told him to look after your house. I don't have to bother with yours.'

'What's his name, this bloke?'

Albert screwed up his face, thinking. 'Don't know his name. Young feller, dark hair. You know his name, he knows yours. Said Dan Federman asked him to keep an eye... You do know his name.' A note of doubt crept into the man's voice and anxious to reassure him, Dan said, 'Course I do, slipped my mind just for a moment. Thanks for letting me know, Albert.'

'My job,' Albert said importantly. 'Citizen patrol. Keeping an eye... you know.'

Well, thought Dan as he made his way to the bus stop, someone is definitely using the cellar, but who? A young bloke with dark hair. Someone who knows I lived there, who knows me by name.

He couldn't think of anyone. Probably a squatter who'd heard whose house it was and simply pretended to know him. Nothing he could do about it now, though, so he got the bus and headed back to Liverpool Street.

Back at the Feneton Arms, Dan told Naomi all he'd discovered. She listened with interest to what he'd found in the cellar and she was delighted with the two tins of salmon.

'Oh, Dan!' she exclaimed. 'Tinned salmon. I haven't seen that since my mother bought it special, when we was courting and you was coming for tea on a Sunday!'

'Albert says he saw someone coming out of our house,' Dan said. 'Young bloke with dark hair who said he knew me.'

'What about that bloke who turned up looking for Lisa that day? What was his name? The one what went fire-watching with you.'

'Oh, I know who you mean,' Dan said. 'Yes, he had dark hair. Can't remember his name though, can you?'

'He was German, wasn't he? Refugee like poor Lisa.'

'That's right. Said he'd come back next night, but he never did.'

'He stayed the night,' Naomi reminded him. 'Slept in the cellar.'

'You're right,' agreed Dan. 'He did sleep in the cellar... so he'd know it's there.'

'Can't think of his name.'

'Well, it don't matter,' Dan pointed out. 'We don't know what happened to him.'

'Whoever it is,' Naomi said, 'is in the black market. Stands to reason, all them tins you saw.'

'Maybe.'

'Course he is,' Naomi said, 'like every other Tom, Dick and Harry.'

'Harry! Wasn't that his name? Harry? Been at school with Lisa?'

'Yeah, could be. Anyway, if it's Lisa's friend I don't mind so much if he's sleeping in our cellar, even if he is black market.'

'Black market, short of two tins of salmon,' grinned Dan.

'Yes, well I'll give one of those to Jen. She'll enjoy a taste of salmon, too.'

'Anyway,' Dan said with a sigh. 'Short of going there and sitting outside the house until he appears, there's no way we're going to catch him at it.'

Dan didn't know how close he'd been to doing just that. Harry Black had been on his way to Kemble Street that very evening. He had been approaching from the far end of the road when he'd seen someone emerge from one of the houses. Was it number sixty-five? He ducked back behind a wall and watched as the man walked away down the street.

Who was it? Harry wondered, and what had he been doing?

He watched as the man stopped to speak to someone. Harry

knew who that was. Citizen Patrol. Barmy, he was, old Citizen Patrol! Harry had seen him several times since their original encounter and had usually managed to avoid him. He wondered if the first man had indeed come out of the Federmans' house. Could it have been Dan Federman? Were he and his wife hoping to come back to get the house repaired? Just the previous week Harry had seen the woman from opposite with her husband, looking over the house they'd lived in. London hadn't been bombed for some time. Perhaps people were beginning to think about coming home. Harry hoped the Federmans weren't. It was useful to have a place to keep his most private stuff. He'd moved to a room near the docks some time ago, registering his new address with the police, so there should be nothing to connect him with Kemble Street if ever anything did go wrong and his stash was discovered.

Citizen Albert continued his patrol and the man moved on. Harry scurried after him, following him not only to the bus stop, but on to Liverpool Street station, watching as he boarded the stopping train to Ipswich. Only once did he get close enough to see the man's face. It was nearly two years since he'd seen Dan Federman, but Harry was pretty certain that's who it was.

Having seen him on to the train, Harry headed straight back to Kemble Street and as the twilight began to deepen, he slipped into the dark doorway of sixty-five. Anxious not to show a light, he felt his way through to the cellar door. There he struck a match and by its flickering light saw at once that the door had indeed been opened. As the match burned down to his fingers, he dropped it on the floor and struck another. The door was still wedged, but the wedge was in an entirely different place to where he'd jammed it in. Quickly Harry released the door, jerked it open and stepped through. Once inside, he pulled it closed and, standing on the top step, struck a third match to light his way down the stairs. With the Tilley lamp lit, he inspected the cellar carefully. He knew exactly what should be there and saw two tins of salmon were missing. Nothing else told him that someone had invaded his domain. His stash of cash was still in the space he'd hollowed out under the stairs and he took it out and counted it. Perhaps, he thought as he looked at the roll of notes, it would be better to keep it somewhere else. If Dan Federman decided to go to the police with what he'd discovered in the cellar, they might come and search. It'd be bad enough to lose his goods, but he couldn't risk losing his money as well. He'd have to find another hiding place, but for the moment he stowed it in an inside trouser pocket.

He'd seen Dan on to the train, so he knew that the police were not on their way just yet, but he decided to take a few of the more portable things with him in case they came to search. After all, tins of food could been left here by anyone, even the Federmans themselves. He turned the mattress over and slid his hand inside the ticking to retrieve a small box containing two brooches and a ring, all of which he'd liberated from a second-floor bedroom on a bomb site. He hadn't shown them to Mikey yet, indeed, he hadn't decided who to go to, Mikey or Mr Ing. Neither knew about the other; Harry liked to keep his options open. He looked at the jewellery in the box and reckoned they would certainly fetch a bob or two.

He pocketed the box and turning off the light, made his way back up into the kitchen. Pale moonlight filtered through the window and Harry secured the door again, this time placing the wedge where the intruder had, in case he returned and realised Harry had been back. He waited in the darkness of the doorway, watching the street until he was certain that there was no one to see him leave, then he stepped outside and melted into the night. He wouldn't come back here for several weeks, he decided, not until he was positive that no one was taking any further interest in the house.

In the meantime, he thought, next weekend I'll go back to Livingston Road and find Lisa. Maybe take her to the flicks.

As when he'd first met her, back in 1939, he was captivated by her. There was something about her that drew him to her and stayed with him even when she wasn't there. He'd relegated her to the back of his mind when he thought she was dead – the dead were the dead – but now that he'd found her again, she had crept her way back into his head, slipping into his thoughts when he least expected it.

When he'd found her in the kitchen in Kemble Street and realised who she was, Harry had been shocked at his own reaction. He had watched her face as they had talked in the Hope Street café, seen the tension and the sadness there, but had also seen how she had changed. No longer was she a small, defiant school girl, in gymslip and blouse, with her hair scraped back off her face, fighting against the bullies. She had blossomed into an attractive young woman, her glossy hair framing a heart-shaped face, her mouth full-lipped and generous, her eyes bright and intelligent. When she'd walked beside him he'd been aware of the movement of her body, no longer awkward and a little ungainly, but smooth and agile with an unconscious sway of the hips. The boy, Harry, had been captivated by the girl, Lisa; the young man, Harry, was captivated anew by the young woman, Lisa.

Harry wasn't new to the charms of women. Since his release from the Isle of Man he'd tasted a few. One old pro had taken him in hand as a favour to Mikey and taught him the pleasures of her trade. He knew women found him attractive and he liked what they did to him, the way they made him feel. But they were simply there for his pleasure; when he finished with them, he never gave them another thought.

Now Lisa kept invading his thoughts and he wasn't at all sure he liked it. He liked to be in control of himself, his mind and his body, and Lisa was threatening them both. He hadn't returned to Livingston Road for a couple of weeks, simply to prove to himself that he didn't need to. She was just another woman, albeit an attractive one, but grown men, like him, didn't get themselves tied up in knots by a woman.

Despite these good intentions, the following weekend found Harry knocking on the door of the Livingston Road home. It wasn't Charlotte who opened the door, but a woman Harry had never seen before. She greeted him with a polite smile and said, 'Can I help you?'

'Come to see Lisa,' Harry said. 'Is she in?'

'Lisa?' The woman looked confused. 'I'm afraid we haven't got a Lisa here.'

'But she works here,' Harry said. And then he remembered. 'Sorry, I forgot. She's called Charlotte now.'

The woman's expression cleared. 'Charlotte. Yes, of course. If you'd like to wait here, I'll see if she's about.'

Harry stood in the hall, waiting. He could hear children's voices from somewhere deeper in the house, the slam of a door and a shout of laughter. It was Saturday afternoon and the children who lived in the home weren't at school. Perhaps Lisa wouldn't be able to come out after all. Harry was about to turn round and leave when Miss Morrison appeared.

'Hallo,' she said. 'I understand you're looking for Charlotte.' Then she recognised him and went on, 'It's Harry, isn't it? Charlotte's friend, Harry? We met before. I'm Caroline Morrison, superintendent of the home.'

'Yes, miss, I remember,' Harry said. He gave her a broad smile. He'd learned that women of a certain age liked his smile.

'Have you come to see Charlotte? Is she expecting you?'

'No, miss. I mean, yes, I've come to see her, but she isn't expecting me.'

'I think she's in the garden with some of the younger children. Do you want to go on out and find her? I'll show you the way.'

She led the way through the house and out of a side door into the back garden. Harry paused on the doorstep and looked out across the grass to where Lisa was playing ball with some little girls. She was dressed in a simple yellow skirt and white blouse and her hair was tied back with a piece of yellow ribbon. She was laughing as she ran to catch the ball and for a moment Harry simply stared at her, knowing in that moment that he wanted her, wanted her in every way.

Caroline, looking back, caught a glimpse of his face and knew a moment's apprehension. But she brushed it aside, she was just being stupid... overprotective.

'Charlotte,' she called, and Charlotte, turning, saw Harry standing in the doorway. Her breath caught in her throat and then she tossed the ball to the waiting children and ran over to greet him.

'Harry,' she cried. 'I thought you'd forgotten me.'

'Never, Lisa,' he said. Then turning to Caroline Morrison he asked, 'Is Lisa free to meet me later this evening? I can see she's busy now.'

'Of course,' Caroline replied. 'Once the children have had their tea, she can certainly go out for the evening if she'd like to. Shall we say about seven? I can manage without her after that.'

Charlotte stood looking from one to the other. What about asking me? she thought.

As if reading her thoughts, Harry asked, 'Will you come, Lisa?'

'Yes, thank you,' she answered, 'I'd like to.'

'I'll be here at seven, then,' he said. He smiled at Caroline again, thinking, Better keep her sweet, then turning he walked back through the house and out of the front door. Caroline and Charlotte watched him go, but their thoughts as they did so were entirely different.

Charlotte was thinking, He did come back to see me. He kept his promise.

Caroline was thinking, The more you smile at me, Harry, the less I trust you.

Good as his word, Harry was at the door promptly at seven o'clock. When he rang the bell the door opened immediately and Charlotte came out. She had changed into the green daisy skirt and white blouse she had worn to the midsummer dance and carried a little white clutch bag lent to her by Caroline.

'Don't be too late,' Caroline had warned. 'You know it'll be an early start in the morning.' She had given Charlotte a key, but she decided to wait up for her. She wanted to be sure she was safely home.

Harry reached out and took Charlotte's hand. 'Where would you like to go?' he asked.

'I don't mind,' Charlotte replied. 'It's just nice to get out for a change.'

'I thought we could go to the flicks,' Harry said. 'P'raps get a bite to eat first. Maybe go dancing after?'

Charlotte looked at him suspiciously. 'Have you got the money, Harry?' she asked. 'I'm not going to duck on and off buses any more.'

'Course I have.' Harry reached into his pocket and pulled out two pound notes.

'Harry! Where did you get all that?'

'Earned it,' Harry said. 'Told you, I work down the docks now.'

'But so much money!'

'Nothing to spend it on till you came along. Come on, Lisa! Let's have a night on the town.'

'I can't be late,' Charlotte said. 'I promised Miss Morrison.'

'Bit of a dragon, is she?'

'No, not at all.' Charlotte spoke sharply. 'She's been very kind to me, and I promised.'

'All right, all right.' Harry held up his hands in surrender. 'I don't mind where we go.' Still holding hands, they walked along the street and found a café. After a fish and chip supper they went into the Odeon and Harry led her to the back row of the stalls. Charlotte had never been to the cinema before. There had been no money for such extravagance while she was living in Kemble Street and no opportunity since. They settled into their seats and watched a cartoon before the main picture, Bob Hope and Bing Crosby in *The Road to Zanzibar*. As soon as the lights went down for the main film, Harry's arm stole round Charlotte's shoulders. At first she stiffened, but as he simply held her gently she gradually relaxed. This was Harry, after all. As the film continued he took her hand in his, gently kneading her other shoulder. She felt a quiver run through her and Harry felt it too. Without haste he gently slid his hand under her arm, so that his fingers rested on her breast. Charlotte felt a burst of heat flood through her and she turned a little towards him. It was all the encouragement he needed. He let go of her hand and, reaching over, turned her face to his. Gently at first he began to kiss her face, his lips roaming over her skin until it seemed on fire. He could feel her warmth and rising excitement and moved his mouth over hers. His lips were demanding, his tongue pushing between her lips. For a moment Charlotte thought of Billy, dear gentle Billy. She thought she'd been kissed before, but his kisses hadn't aroused the response she felt to Harry's. Billy was a boy, Harry was very much a man. Kissing her long and deep, his hands continued their exploration until his fingers began to caress her thighs through the light cotton of her skirt. Suddenly, she broke free and pushed him away.

'What's the matter, Lisa, doll?' he whispered. 'Doesn't it feel good? Don't you like it?'

Charlotte didn't answer. She turned away from him and stared at the screen where Bing Crosby was singing 'It's Always You' to Dorothy Lamour.

'Come on, doll,' Harry murmured. 'It's only a kiss and a cuddle.' He reached for her hand again and stroked her palm with his thumb. 'Only a kiss, because you're so beautiful and I thought I'd lost you.'

Charlotte left her hand in his, but when he slipped his arm back round her shoulders again, she pulled away with a muttered, 'No, Harry!'

Harry sighed and removed his arm. He knew he was going too fast for her, but somehow he couldn't help himself. He'd felt her reaction to his touch and he was aching to go further.

When at last the film finished and the lights went up again, Charlotte looked along the back row and realised that it was all couples, and they'd been making use of the darkness in the same way. The National Anthem sounded through the cinema and everyone stood up. Charlotte stood straight and still; Harry, though on his feet, slouched against the back of the seat in front.

'Harry,' she hissed. 'It's the National Anthem.'

'Not mine, it isn't,' he hissed back.

They walked out into the night. The darkness was complete and Harry produced a tiny pocket torch to light their way to the bus stop.

'Where shall we go now?' he asked.

'I've got to get back,' Charlotte said. 'I told you I couldn't be late.'

Harry sighed. 'All right, doll. But we'll do it again... next Saturday evening? I know a place we can go dancing. You like dancing?'

'Yes,' Charlotte said. 'Very much.'

'Good. Then I'll come next Saturday. Same time. You tell that Morrison lady you're going out again. She can't stop you, can she?'

'No,' Charlotte agreed, 'not if I'm not needed in the home.'

Before he left her outside the home, he pulled her into his arms, holding her close, so that she felt the strength of his body against the softness of her own. For a moment she clung to him, before he gently put her away from him.

'In you go,' he said. 'See you next Saturday.'

'Did you have a nice evening?' Caroline asked as Charlotte came in through the front door for her. 'What did you do?'

'We had fish and chips and then went to the cinema.'

'Sounds fun. What did you see?'

'*The Road to Zanzibar.*'

'Did you? I haven't seen that one yet, but I enjoyed *The Road to Singapore.*'

Charlotte said goodnight and went up to her room under the eaves. As she lay in bed, she relived her evening with Harry, and it was a long time before she fell asleep.

Chapter Thirty-Six

Harry sauntered into Petticoat Lane next Saturday morning. It was a bright September day and he was feeling at one with the world. He'd finished an early shift at the docks and had the rest of the day ahead of him. In his pocket was a gold bracelet he'd 'found' in a bombed-out house in Kensington, probably lost in the flight of its owner. It was a heavy chain with a coiled snake as a clasp. It came from an affluent area, so he had hopes of it fetching a good price. He had thought of taking it in to Mr Ing, but decided against. It wasn't that Mr Ing didn't recognise the provenance of the pieces Harry brought him – he knew perfectly well they were stolen – but business was tough and he asked no questions. However, last time Harry had approached him, with a locket on a chain, Mr Ing had shaken his head.

'No, young man, can't take that. Too recognisable. Rozzers been watching my window.'

It was warning enough. Harry had taken the locket away and hadn't been back since. He had sold it to Mikey Sharp for, he knew, a fraction of its true worth, but even so it had put a decent amount of cash into his pocket and had given him some more capital for his black market trade. The gold bracelet, too, was distinctive, but he thought he'd get a reasonable price from Mikey. Mikey had the contacts to sell it on quickly and discreetly and still make a tidy profit himself.

As he walked between the stalls he didn't notice a young lad, known as Snout, keeping pace with him. Harry was thinking about Lisa, seeing her again this evening. Though he hated to admit it, even to himself, he was longing to see her. He'd take her to the Palais and they would dance, and afterwards…?

He'd decided he'd buy her a present today. He'd never given her the blue bead bracelet he'd bought before she'd disappeared, but he wasn't intending to give her that, he could afford something much better now, especially if he could sell Mikey the gold bracelet in his pocket.

'The Jew-boy's in the market,' Snout reported to Ginger Allsop, Mikey's number two. Ginger nodded.

'Keep your eye on him, Snout. Mikey wants to know where he goes and what he does.'

The lad scampered off and soon picked up Harry again as he was inspecting some jewellery on a stall. He'd seen a brooch he thought Lisa would like; a silver butterfly with delicate filigree wings. It was expensive, but, Harry decided, he would come back and buy it when he'd done his deal with Mikey.

Ginger Allsop headed for the Black Bull and found Mikey sitting, as usual, in the back bar.

'Jew-boy's in the market,' he said.

Mikey gave a wolfish grin. 'Is he now? And where's Parker?'

'Haven't seen him, Mikey.'

'Well, bloody well go and find him! What's the use of a tame copper if he ain't around when you need him?'

'What'll I tell him?'

'Tell him to keep watch. If the Jew comes here to sell me something I shall turn him down, tell 'im I'm thinking about it. When he goes back out into the street, that's when Brenda does her bit and Parker arrests him, OK?' He thought for a moment and then said, 'Did Snout follow him last time he was here?'

'Yeah, he lives in a room down the docks, but his stuff is stashed in a burnt-out in Shoreditch.'

'OK. Stay away from here now and don't let him see you if he comes here looking for me, right?'

'Right, boss.'

'But you lot be ready. If he makes a break for it, an' he will, let 'im go.'

'Let 'im go?'

Mikey leaned forward and very softly, told Ginger of his plan. Ginger grinned. 'OK, boss, I'm on it.'

Ginger hurried back out into the Lane. It was a warm day and it was very busy. The crowds were out, strolling through the market, looking both for true bargains and for stuff from under the counter, but Snout was looking out for him and it wasn't long before Ginger, too, could see Harry Black wandering among the stalls.

'You know that rozzer what stands by the church at the end of the lane?' Ginger said to Snout. 'PC Parker.'

'Yeah, the bloke with the moustache.'

'That's 'im. Well, tell him to come to my stall, fast as he likes. Say Ginger sent you. OK?'

'What about Jew-boy?'

'I'll take care of 'im. You fetch the cop.'

Harry kept his hand in his pocket all the time he was in the market and there was the bracelet, heavy and comforting in his hand. Too many pickpockets in a place like this, he thought. They wouldn't dare touch anyone working for Mikey Sharp, but Harry wasn't, not any more. Harry was his own man. He threaded his way between the Saturday crowds and went into the Bull. He bought himself a drink and sat at the bar for a while, watching and waiting. When he was quite sure no one was interested in him, he walked through to the back, knocked on the door and, without waiting for an answer, went in. He would never have dared do that in the early days, but now he was a player, a man with a business of his own, Mikey's equal.

'Harry boy!' Mikey greeted him with a grin. 'Good to see you, mate. Drink?'

He poured a large measure of whisky from a bottle on the table and handed it to Harry. 'Good to see you, son. What brings you?'

'Just a bit of business.' Harry looked round the room. A couple of Mikey's men were at a table in the corner, big blokes with lived-in faces, who could make short work of any trouble, or troublemakers.

Mikey glanced across at them and with a curt nod of his head, said, 'Charlie, Jumbo, get lost.'

The two men got to their feet and lumbered out of the room. Mikey waved Harry to a chair.

'Well, now, Harry boy. What you got for me today?'

Harry drew the bracelet out of his pocket and laid it on the table. 'Thought this might interest you, Mikey. Solid gold, this is. Worth a bomb!'

'Liberated by a bomb, was it?' Mikey, laughing at his own joke, picked it up, feeling its weight in his hand. He looked at the chain links and the snake clasp.

'Nice piece, if it's real.'

'Course it's real,' retorted Harry. 'Any fool can see that.'

For a moment Mikey's face darkened – no one dared call him a fool – but then he looked up with a grin. 'Snake's a bit obvious,' he said. 'Difficult to shift something so easily recognised.'

'Shouldn't be a problem for a man with your contacts,' Harry said.

Mikey was thinking the same, but his face showed nothing more than a vague interest. 'Have to think about it, mate, sound a few people out, know what I mean?'

'Not leaving it with you,' Harry said.

'No! Course you ain't. Wouldn't expect it, even though we done good business together before. No, you hang on to it, mate. I'll put a few feelers out, see who's in the market. Come back next week, I'll have an answer and some money for you, too, most like.'

Harry scooped up the bracelet from the table and slid it back into his trouser pocket. 'Next Saturday, then.'

Mikey lifted a hand. 'I'll be here,' he said.

Harry left the room and walked out through the front bar. Mikey went to the side window and watched. If everything went to plan, the Jew-boy, Harry Black, wouldn't be here next Saturday, wouldn't be troubling him again, wouldn't be setting up business on Mikey's territory.

Outside in the street Harry paused, wondering if he should change his mind and get some sort of valuation for the bracelet from Mr Ing. As he stood there a young woman bumped into him, grabbing at him as she stumbled over the kerb. He put out a hand to catch her and she gave a piercing scream.

'Let go of me! Let go of me! Take your hands off me. Police!'

From nowhere, it seemed to Harry, a copper in uniform appeared at his side and grabbed hold of his arm. 'Now then, now then, what's going on here?'

'He's took me bracelet!' cried the woman. 'Bumped into me and pulled it off me arm. He's took me bracelet!'

The policeman's grip tightened on Harry's arm. Harry tried to twist free, but his arm was forced up behind him. 'Now then, young man, let's have a look in your pocket, shall we? See if this lady's telling the truth.'

Harry had recognised the 'lady' concerned. Brenda, one of Mikey's Sharp's tarts. Harry had even used her himself once or twice. He glanced back at the pub and saw Mikey standing at the window, smiling. He'd been set up.

'All right,' he said, 'it's in my pocket.' The cop relaxed his grip and reached out his hand to retrieve the bracelet. It was all Harry needed. With a violent twist he hooked his leg round that of his captor, bringing him crashing to the ground. He swung a punch at the girl, catching her full in the face so that she, too, collapsed on to the pavement, blood spouting from her nose. Ginger, Charlie and Jumbo exploded from the crowd, but Harry shoulder-charged Ginger, who fell against Charlie. Jumbo, roaring as he came in for the attack, grabbed Harry's jacket, almost ripping it from his back. As he had so long ago in Hanau, he pulled his arms free, leaving Jumbo holding the torn jacket, but Harry himself free to streak off down the street. Several people made attempts to stop him, grabbing at him as he ran, but the street-rat, when in flight, was unstoppable. Within moments he was out of sight, weaving his way through the Saturday crowds into the maze of streets behind the market.

Outside the Black Bull, Mikey's tame policeman and his other henchmen got to their feet, red-faced and angry. The crowd that had gathered began to disperse, encouraged by PC Parker's angry warnings that 'The excitement's over! There ain't nothing to see here, so move on, before I arrest you for loitering and causing a public nuisance.'

When the crowd had melted away, they all went into the pub and Mikey explained the second part of his plan.

Once Harry was clear of the market and was sure he had lost his pursuers, he made his way back to Shoreditch. He thought Mikey probably knew where he lived, down at the docks, but thought his hide-out in Kemble Street would be safe enough for the time being. He took no risks, however, taking several buses and two Tubes before he was certain that no one was following him. He reached Kemble Street in the middle of the afternoon. Going down into the cellar, he pulled the door closed behind him, lit the Tilley and considered what to do next. Clearly Mikey was behind his 'arrest'. It was one of his tarts who'd started the whole thing off, his henchmen who'd joined the fray. Harry knew he was lucky to have made his escape.

He took the bracelet out of his trouser pocket and slipped it in with his cash in the hidden, inner pocket. Once again he'd proved the wisdom of never having anything valuable in the pockets of his jacket. That was all he'd lost, his jacket. He'd have to steer clear of Petticoat Lane from now on, but there were other markets in other areas of London which were not the province of Mikey Sharp.

He looked along the rows of tins, the bottles of whisky and the box of silk stockings he'd acquired from a bloke in a pub. He had enough here to keep him going for some time. He fed his contacts a little at a time... keeping the prices high. He had a new source of spirits, not just whisky. He'd been in touch with Dickett again and paid a little over the odds for part of a consignment due to go to Mikey. Not the most sensible thing to do, he now realised, but the offer was too good to turn down and he was establishing his own ring of customers. He needed to keep the supplies coming.

Provided he didn't tread on Mikey's toes again, he reckoned he'd be safe enough. He'd move to another patch. In the meantime, he still had the bracelet, which he would offer elsewhere, even if it meant a cut in the expected price.

He'd go to Livingston Road later as planned. In the meantime he might as well have an hour's kip, then he'd go down the public baths and get himself cleaned up, ready to take Lisa dancing. He flopped down on to the mattress and was almost instantly asleep.

He awoke with a jolt an hour later as someone grabbed him and he was dragged to his feet. Despite a struggle, his arms and legs were securely tied and he was pushed down into one of the old armchairs. The cellar was full of men. Mikey's men. Jumbo, holding a wicked-looking knife, stood guard over him, while Charlie, Ginger and PC Parker inspected the items ranged along the shelf.

'Definitely black market stuff, wouldn't you say, constable?' Ginger was asking with mock formality.

'Definitely,' agreed the policeman.

Some of the tins and some bottles of beer were left on the shelf, and the rest Ginger and Charlie packed into boxes they had brought with them.

'What about 'im?' Charlie jerked his head at Harry.

'We check his clothes,' said Ginger, 'and if we think he's hiding anyfink else, we'll ask 'im, ever so politely, where it is.'

Once they had finished with the black market goods, they turned their attention to Harry. 'Stand 'im up, Jumbo,' Ginger said. Jumbo pulled Harry to his feet and held him firmly while Ginger patted him down.

'Something in his pockets,' Ginger said. 'Get his trousers off.' Charlie reached down and cut the ropes round Harry's legs.

Harry struggled, but with his arms still tied and Jumbo holding him in a bear hug from behind, there was little he could do. His trousers were stripped from his legs and the contents of his pockets tipped out on to the table.

'Well, well, what have we 'ere?' Ginger had discovered the inner pocket and pulled out Harry's roll of notes and the gold bracelet.

'Mikey'll be pleased to see this,' Ginger said. 'Makes all this effort worthwhile.'

He stuffed the money into his own pocket, but replaced the bracelet in Harry's. 'Tie 'is legs again and then turn this place over, see if there's anyfink else.'

Harry could only watch helplessly as they searched the cellar, but he knew there was nothing else for them to find. They'd already got everything of value that he owned.

'Anyfink else, Jew-boy?' Ginger demanded. Harry shook his head.

'Right,' said Ginger, convinced Harry was telling the truth. 'Soon as it's dark we'll get this lot moved to the Bull.' He turned to PC Parker. 'Following a tip-off, you came here and found this man, camping out in the cellar of a burnt-out what don't belong to 'im, right?'

'Right,' agreed PC Parker.

'Naturally, you arrested him. The evidence of his black-marketeering is all these tins on the shelf.'

Harry noticed the whisky and the silk stockings had gone. They only needed enough evidence to arrest him. The rest would go to Mikey.

'Better bring another cop with you,' Ginger advised. 'Mikey'll pay. Make sure you make it legal and you make it stick. Mikey don't want to see him again, he wants him banged up and the key thrown away.'

'Yeah, no problem. I got a mate who'll go along with this. Look good on our records to have caught a black-marketeer.'

They pulled his trousers back on, retied his legs, and Harry spent the rest of the afternoon and early evening sitting in the chair in the cellar with Jumbo sitting opposite him, digging the dirt out from under his nails with the point of his knife. Harry looked at the knife. It reminded him of Rolf's and he shuddered. Jumbo looked across at him and gave him a gap-toothed grin.

'You're going down for a long time,' he remarked. 'Shouldn't play with the big boys till you're a big boy yourself.'

As darkness closed in outside, Ginger and Charlie returned and quietly manoeuvred the boxes of contraband up the steps and out into a waiting van.

'Parker'll be back in a bit,' Ginger told Jumbo. 'He'll take 'im away and then you can go 'ome. Keep your eye on 'im though. He's slippery as an eel. Keep 'im tied up and your knife 'andy.'

It was only another hour or so before Harry heard voices upstairs in the kitchen. He looked across at Jumbo. The man was dozing in the opposite chair, but the knife was by his side. Harry looked at it, so near and yet so far. His wrists were bound so tightly that his hands had gone numb and he couldn't move his arms at all. He wondered about trying to kick out at Jumbo with his bound legs, but it would serve no purpose. All he'd get was a faceful of knuckles.

The door at the top of the steps opened and two uniformed policemen came down.

'My tip-off was right, Davidson,' Parker said loudly as they surveyed the cellar. 'Looks like we got a cellar-rat here, and look at them tins. That has to be black market stuff.'

'Looks like it,' Davidson agreed.

Parker walked across to Harry, totally ignoring Jumbo in the opposite chair. 'Heinrich Schwarz, also known as Harry Black, I'm arresting you on suspicion of dealing in black market goods. You don't have to say anything, but anything you do say will be taken down in writing and given in evidence against you.'

He pulled Harry to his feet and, reaching for Jumbo's knife, cut the rope round his wrists, immediately replacing it with a pair of handcuffs.

'Resisting arrest, are we?' he snarled and pounded his fist into Harry's face. 'Owed you that,' he said. Harry fell back into the chair, his head singing, blood spurting from his nose. Parker then cut the rope around Harry's legs and between them, the two cops pushed him up the steps and out into the street. It was totally dark. No one saw them emerge from the house, no one saw Harry being pushed into a waiting police car, no one saw Jumbo depositing a box of tinned food into its boot. As he was driven to a police station some distance away, Harry wondered at them using a car, taking him so far.

Parker's station, he thought gloomily. Parker's station and Mikey's petrol.

Once again Harry found himself in a police cell for the weekend and on Monday morning he appeared in the police court. The box of tins was produced as evidence of what the police had found in the cellar. Charges of assaulting a policeman, resisting arrest, and theft of a valuable gold bracelet were also brought. He was sent down. Heinrich Schwarz, aka Harry Black, was once again in the clutches of the law. He simply disappeared into the system. PC Parker had earned his pay; he shared Mikey's bonus with PC Davidson and they had commendations on their records.

Jumbo, who was apparently entirely invisible during the arrest, had disappeared into the night. He was at Mikey's side in the morning and none of them gave Harry Black another thought.

Chapter Thirty-Seven

Charlotte waited all Saturday evening, but Harry didn't come.
'Why don't you go to Kemble Street again?' Caroline suggested on Sunday morning. 'See if there's anyone who knows where the Federmans have gone. One of the neighbours perhaps? It's Sunday, so there should be people around, perhaps people who're usually at work.'

Caroline thought it would give Charlotte something else to think about after the disappointment of the previous evening. She knew how much Charlotte had been looking forward to seeing Harry again, but when the little blighter hadn't turned up, with no warning and no explanation, Caroline could cheerfully have throttled him. Seven o'clock had come and gone. Charlotte waited in the children's sitting room, reading to some of the younger ones, one ear listening for the expected ring at the door, but it never came. By eight o'clock most of the children had gone to bed. Only a few older girls were still up, listening to the wireless in the sitting room as they helped with the mending. Charlotte helped too, but her mind wasn't on her work.

Caroline had come into the room to send the children to bed and found Charlotte sitting miserably, holding a half-mended sock and staring into space.

'He hasn't come, Miss Morrison,' she said. 'Harry hasn't come. He said we'd go dancing.'

Charlotte was desolate and Caroline furious. So the next morning she made her suggestion.

Charlotte hadn't wanted to bother, but urged by Caroline, she allowed herself to be persuaded. As she sat on the bus to Shoreditch, she was thinking more about finding Harry rather than finding the Federmans. She wondered, as she had for much of the night, why he hadn't come as promised, but she was no nearer an answer.

I might find him in Kemble Street, she thought with a tiny flicker of hope. It's where he was before. Maybe he'll be there again.

When she got off the bus and walked the last few hundred yards, she searched the faces of the people she passed, but there was no sign of Harry. She turned into Kemble Street, walking slowly passed the burned-out houses until she came to number sixty-five. Standing in the doorway, she called his name, but there was no answer. She went inside and on reaching the kitchen, she saw at once that the door to the cellar was open, leaning at a drunken angle against the wall. She edged her way across the room and peered down the cellar steps. She could see very little, but thinking that Harry might be down there, hurt? Ill? She went down a couple of steps and called his name again.

'Harry? Harry, are you there? It's me, Lisa.'

There was no reply from the darkness of the cellar and the silence of the house settled on her. Her fear of that cellar flooded through her and, suddenly losing her nerve, she ran back up the steps, scurrying through the kitchen and out into the sunlit street. Pale, her breath catching in her throat, she stood on the pavement, trying to quell her fear.

'I say, are you all right?'

Charlotte turned to find a woman who looked vaguely familiar, crossing the street towards her. Still struggling for breath, Charlotte couldn't answer.

'You look awfully queer, dear. Is anything wrong?'

'No.' Charlotte managed to force the word out. 'No, I'm fine.'

'What was you doing in that house?' asked the woman. 'You shouldn't go into derelicts, you know, they ain't safe.'

'I...' Charlotte hesitated, 'I was looking for someone.'

'Who was you looking for?' asked the woman. 'The Federmans don't live there no more.'

'The Federmans!' Charlotte focused on the woman properly for the first time. 'Do you know the Federmans?'

'I should do, they was my neighbours. I'm Shirley Newman. I used to live opposite.' She peered at Charlotte. 'Don't I know you?'

'Mrs Newman whose husband was a sailor?'

'That's me. Just back looking at the old house. We're going to try and have it repaired.' She looked at Charlotte again. 'What's your name?'

'Charlotte Smith.'

'Was it Mr and Mrs Federman you was looking for?' Shirley asked.

'No,' said Charlotte, for a moment thinking still of Harry. 'I mean, yes it was.'

'They're long gone,' Shirley said. 'Moved away more 'an eighteen months ago.'

Charlotte felt a surge of excitement. 'D'you know where they've gone?' she asked. 'Where they are now, I mean?' All thoughts of Harry fled as she realised Mrs Newman might be able to tell her where to find the Federmans.

'Yes, I know where they are, but who's asking?'

'Lisa. Lisa Becker. I used to live with them.'

'Thought you said your name was Charlotte something.' Shirley looked at her suspiciously.

'It is now; it wasn't.'

'So you're Lisa Becker, the German girl what was killed in the Blitz?'

'Yes, yes,' cried Charlotte.

'They think you're dead,' Shirley said accusingly. 'Where've you been all this time?'

'I lost my memory,' Charlotte said, 'but never mind that now. I came here to try and find them, to tell them I'm safe, but I don't know where they are. Tell me where they are, please tell me.'

Shirley Newman looked at the girl standing in front of her. She hadn't known Lisa properly when she'd been living with the Federmans. She hadn't liked the idea of living near a German; like so many when war broke out she'd felt an immediate antipathy to anyone from Germany, refugee or not. But she'd seen Lisa about and she'd lost her own home in that first raid of the Blitz, the night when Lisa had gone missing. She remembered Naomi's distress as she'd searched the hospitals and rescue centres, and now here was this Charlotte, claiming to be the missing girl, Lisa. She could be, Shirley supposed, but standing in front of her ruined home, she had even less reason to like Germans now and didn't really care.

'Won't you tell me where they are? Please?' Charlotte begged. 'Just give me their address so I can write and tell them I'm all right.'

'Tell you what I'll do,' Shirley said. 'Tell me your address and when I get back home, I'll tell them where you are. Then if they want to see you after all this time, they can come and find you.'

Charlotte told her the Livingston Road address. 'I should write it for you,' she said. 'Have you paper?'

'No,' said Shirley, 'but I'll remember.' And with that she turned away, back to the ruin of her own house.

Charlotte stared after her. Why wouldn't this woman, this neighbour, tell her where the Federmans had gone? She walked a little way down the road, looking at the other houses, wondering whom she could ask. The obvious place would have been the Duke, but that was long gone, only a patch of wilderness where the pub had once stood. Behind her she heard the sound of footsteps and looking round she saw Shirley Newman walking briskly away. On impulse, Charlotte followed her. Shirley had said, 'When I get home.' She must live near to the Federmans.

All I have to do, thought Charlotte in excitement, is follow her home.

Dropping back a little way so that Shirley wouldn't notice her if she turned round, Charlotte followed her through the streets. But Shirley didn't look round, she was in a hurry to catch her train. Even when she got on a bus, she was unaware of Charlotte jumping on just before the bus drew away.

When they reached Liverpool Street station and Charlotte realised that Shirley was going to catch a train, her heart sank. She had a little money for a ticket, but even if she followed Shirley aboard, she wouldn't know where to get off.

She saw Shirley accost a porter and moving closer heard his answer to her question.

'Feneton? Platform ten. Leaves in ten minutes.'

Feneton. He'd told her all she needed to know. Charlotte hurried to the ticket office, bought a ticket to Feneton and ran to platform ten. There was no sign of Shirley, but that didn't matter now. Now she knew where she was going she didn't need to keep her in sight until they got there. She sat in a corner seat and within moments the train started to move. It was only then that she thought of Caroline Morrison. She would soon be wondering where on earth Charlotte had got to. She sighed. Too late to worry about that now, she thought. When I get to this Feneton place I'll find a phone box and ring and tell Miss Morrison where I am.

When the train steamed into Feneton, only a few people got off. Charlotte hung back as Shirley strode out of the station. It was still early evening and daylight, so she followed at a distance, but Shirley, obviously busy with her own thoughts, walked briskly down the road without looking back. Charlotte followed, and as they passed the pub, the Feneton Arms, Shirley paused as if about to go in, then apparently thinking better of it walked on. Charlotte, who had ducked into a doorway, also paused when she reached the pub. Should she keep following Shirley? She didn't trust her to tell the Federmans anything about her. She would try to find them on her own, she decided, and where better to ask if anyone knew a family called Federman? Uncle Dan had always enjoyed a pint at the Duke, perhaps he was a regular here now. Taking a deep breath, Charlotte pushed open the door of the lounge bar and went inside.

The room wasn't busy, several RAF officers were standing, drinking at the bar, and a couple were seated at a table in the window. The woman behind the bar looked up and smiled as Charlotte paused in the doorway. Encouraged by her smile, Charlotte walked across to the bar.

'Can I help you, dear?' asked the woman. She could see that the girl who had just come in was too young to be buying a drink.

'I was wondering...' Charlotte began and hesitated.

'Yes?'

'I was wondering if you happen to know a Mr and Mrs Federman.' Charlotte felt the colour flood her cheeks.

'I might,' replied the barmaid. 'Who's asking?'

'I am Lisa. I am looking for Aunt Naomi and Uncle Dan.'

The woman stared at her and then saying, 'Wait here a minute,' disappeared through a door.

Charlotte waited, conscious of the interested eyes of the RAF men at the bar beside her.

Moments later the door behind the bar burst open again and another woman appeared. She stared at Charlotte and the colour drained from her face.

'Lisa?' she whispered. 'Lisa? Is it really you?' She raised the flap in the bar counter and came out beside Charlotte. 'Oh, my darling girl, where have you been? We thought you were dead. Oh, Lisa!' And with that she flung her arms round Charlotte and burst into tears. Charlotte was crying too, and the barmaid said, 'Take her upstairs, Naomi. I can manage here, we're not busy.'

Naomi took Charlotte's hand and led her out of the bar and upstairs. She pushed open a door and they went into a sitting room. A man, who was reading the paper, looked up as they came in.

'Hallo, love,' he said. 'Who's this?'

'Uncle Dan?' Charlotte said. 'It's me, Lisa.'

Dan started up from his chair and stared at her incredulously. 'Lisa? Our Lisa?' He held out a hand and she crossed the room to be gathered into the bear hug of his arms.

'Where have you been? What happened to you?'

'We thought you were dead...'

'I was injured in a raid and...'

They all spoke at once and all stopped again as shaky tears and laughter took over.

'Let's sit down,' Naomi said. 'Then we can talk properly. Oh, Lisa, I can't believe you're here.'

'I can't believe I found you at last,' Charlotte said. 'I wrote...'

They sat, the three of them, and as the daylight faded into dusk and darkness, told their stories. Charlotte of her lost memory and evacuation to Wynsdown, Naomi of her evacuation to Feneton and the birth of Nicholas, now asleep next door in the bedroom, and Dan of the night of the second Great Fire of London, followed by his permanent move to Feneton.

'But how did you find us now?' asked Naomi.

Charlotte explained about following Shirley. 'I didn't know where you were in the village, but I thought maybe someone in the pub would know.'

'Why on earth didn't the stupid woman simply tell you where we was?' demanded Dan. 'She knew we was desperate to find you.'

'She probably wanted to be the one to tell us,' Naomi said. 'Make her feel important.' She had no illusions about Shirley. She was grateful to her for bringing her to Feneton, but since she'd got to know her better, she knew that they'd never be real friends. Each had done a good turn for the other, and that was that.

'So, where did you say you was living now?' Dan asked and, as she began to explain about working at the Livingston Road children's home, Charlotte suddenly clapped her hand over her mouth.

'They don't know where I am now,' she cried. 'Miss Morrison will think I'm lost.'

'You must ring her, now,' Naomi said sharply. 'Come downstairs with me and you can phone her. It's dark and she'll be very worried about you.'

They went downstairs and when Naomi had explained, Jenny waved them to the phone. 'Help yourself.'

The relief tinged with anger in Caroline's voice when Charlotte was finally put through was clear to hear.

'Thank God, Charlotte, I thought you'd got lost. You shouldn't have gone off on your own like that. We've been worried sick.'

'I'm sorry, Miss Morrison, but I had to take the chance of finding Aunt Naomi and Uncle Dan while it was there.'

'I know,' agreed Caroline, but there was still an edge to her voice. 'When will you be coming back? I assume you will be coming back?'

'Yes, of course, I will catch the train tomorrow.'

'Have you got enough money?'

'I have enough,' Charlotte assured her, though she had no idea if it were true.

Their three minutes up, they said goodbye and Charlotte replaced the receiver.

'You can take the rest of the evening off,' Jenny told Naomi. 'We'll be closed at ten as it's Sunday. Jim and I can manage down here.' She smiled at Charlotte. 'I expect you've a lot to catch up on.'

Naomi thanked her and they went back upstairs where Dan was waiting in the living room. Beside him was a small suitcase.

'Thought you'd like this back,' he said.

Charlotte's eyes widened as she saw the little case she'd brought with her from Hanau. 'My things?' she whispered. She took the case and opened it and there, lying on the top, just as Naomi had intended, the first thing she saw was the letter from her mother. With a cry she picked it up and smoothing out the creases read once again the words her mother had written to her three years ago.

She glanced back at her foster parents, tears again in her eyes. 'I thought I'd lost my things, my letter from Mutti. But you kept them for me.'

That night Charlotte slept on the sofa in the living room. Naomi had heated up some soup on the gas ring in the corner and made cheese sandwiches to go with it, and as they ate the three of them continued to tell of the things that had happened since that fateful day two years earlier.

Charlotte wondered if she'd sleep at all, with all the emotions of the day, but as soon as she snuggled down under the blanket Naomi found for her, she slid, exhausted, into oblivion. She was awoken the next morning by a pair of hands pulling at her hair. She sat up with a start and found herself face to face with a toddling baby boy.

'Oh, Nicky, you naughty boy,' cried Naomi rushing into the room and scooping him up. 'I'm sorry, Lisa, I didn't mean him to wake you.' She smiled as Charlotte held out her arms to the child. 'This is your big sister, Lisa,' she told the boy as she passed him over. 'Can you say Lisa?' Nicky allowed himself to be settled on Charlotte's knee and inspected her face at close quarters.

'Lee?' he said.

'That's right, clever boy, Lisa.'

They all sat up to the table for a breakfast of porridge, toast and tea, and as they ate Charlotte looked round at her family, her London family, and once again tears slid down her cheeks.

'Lee cryin',' announced Nicky from his high chair.

'Yes,' agreed Charlotte, 'but with happiness.'

She caught the train back to Liverpool Street later that morning. Dan had had to go to work, but Naomi and Nicky accompanied her to the station, and Naomi bought her ticket.

'Now, you've got the phone number, haven't you?' she said as they waited on the platform. 'We can keep in touch by post now, but if there's anything urgent you can ring the pub.'

'And you can ring Livingston Road. Oh, Aunt Naomi, I can't believe I've found you!'

'Well, we ain't going to lose you again now, Lisa.'

The train steamed into the station and with a quick kiss to Naomi and Nicky, Charlotte scrambled aboard, once again carrying her small brown suitcase. Leaning out of the window, she called, 'I'll be back to see you again very soon, I promise.' The train started to move and they all waved until it rounded a bend and they were out of sight.

When she reached Livingston Road she went straight to Caroline's office.

'Oh, Miss Morrison,' she cried, 'I'm so sorry to have worried you.'

Caroline Morrison gave a weary sigh. 'It's all right, Charlotte, as long as you're all right. Now, tell me all about it.'

When Harry didn't reappear for another two weeks, Caroline decided it was time to tell Charlotte about her inheritance. She was spurred on to this by a call from Avril saying that the solicitor needed Charlotte to sign some papers. So that evening, when the home was at last quiet, she sat Charlotte down and told her about Miss Edie's will.

'She's left everything to you, Charlotte,' she explained. 'It's in trust until you're twenty-one, but the house is yours, you can live there if you want to, and you'll have a suitable income from the estate until it becomes yours absolutely.'

Charlotte stared at her, unable to take it all in.

'You mean everything she owned is now mine? All her things?'

'Yes, everything. But the financial side will be looked after by David Swanson and Mr Thompson. They're the trustees and they will manage your affairs until you're of age.'

'Miss Edie left me all this?'

'She did,' Caroline agreed with a smile. 'She loved you very much.'

Chapter Thirty-Eight

Charlotte travelled back to Wynsdown the following week. As the train chugged its way westward, she considered the amazing turn her life had taken in the last few weeks. She had found and lost Harry, she had found the Federmans and she had discovered that she now had property and money of her own.

The clothes that had been folded so neatly into her little suitcase by Naomi were far too small for her now and she gave them to Caroline to use for the children in the home. The letter from her mother, her passport, her other immigration documents, her old ration book and her original identity card were now safely in her handbag. She could now prove that she was who she said she was, and she found that very comforting.

'You'll come and stay with us,' Avril had said on the phone. 'We're all looking forward to seeing you.'

Charlotte had agreed. She certainly didn't want to stay by herself in Blackdown House and the vicarage would be overcrowded, but welcoming. Despite having been away for only a few months, Charlotte knew that she was a different person from the one who'd left Wynsdown.

'Someone'll meet you at the station,' Avril promised.

'Probably Dr Masters,' Caroline had said. 'He's the one with the extra petrol.'

It wasn't Dr Masters whom Charlotte found waiting outside the station, but Billy. For a moment she paused, unseen, clutching her suitcase, and then he turned and saw her. His face cracked into a huge grin and he crossed the few yards between them in two strides.

Taking her case from her and dumping it unceremoniously on the ground he gathered her into his arms and held her hard against him. He made no move to kiss her, but for a long moment they clung together before he gently put her from him and looked down into her face.

'Oh, Char,' he murmured. 'I have missed you!'

Charlotte didn't answer and he picked up her case and led the way to where the farm car was parked.

When they reached the car they were greeted by frantic barking and Bessie, confined to the back seat, erupted when Billy opened the door. She flung herself at Charlotte, a flurry of bouncing feet and wildly waving tail, and Charlotte, bending down, found her face being washed with an exuberant pink tongue.

'Bessie!' she cried. 'Oh Bessie, I have missed you.'

Billy, standing watching, thought sadly that Charlotte had given her dog a more enthusiastic welcome than she'd given him. His own fault, he knew, but things were different now and he was determined that, while she was in Wynsdown, even for a short time, he would woo her back to him.

She turned glowing eyes up to him now and said, 'Oh, Billy, thank you for bringing her. I have missed her so.' And the glow in her eyes made his heart turn over.

They put the excited dog back into the car and once he'd settled Charlotte into the passenger seat Billy went round to the front and swung the starting handle. The engine spluttered into life and he jumped into the driving seat and they set off up the familiar lanes towards the village. An awkward silence enclosed them for some time and neither of them seemed to know how to break it.

'How have you been?' Billy asked eventually.

'All right,' Charlotte replied. 'You?'

'Oh I'm fine,' Billy assured her. 'Busy on the farm, you know. How was London?'

'Big. Noisy.'

'Bombs?'

'No, children!'

They both laughed before the silence lapsed round them again.

'Thank you for looking after Bessie,' Charlotte said. 'I hope she's behaved herself.'

'She's fine. Training her up with Jet. She's an intelligent dog.'

'I wish I could take her back to London with me. The children in the home would love her.' She sighed. 'But I know she's better off down here in the country.'

'How long are you staying?' asked Billy.

'Not sure yet,' Charlotte answered. 'It depends on lots of things.'

'Mum's hoping you'll have time to come over to the farm one day and have your dinner with us.' He glanced across at her. 'You will, won't you, Char? We want to hear all about what you're doing in London.'

'Of course I will. I'd love to.' She turned to look him as she spoke, saw the shadow of his face in the dusky light, saw his hands strong and firm on the steering wheel and for the first time since she'd arrived she felt a rush of remembered affection for him.

'Thank you for coming to fetch me, Billy,' she said softly.

'No problem. I wanted you to myself, even if only for a little while. Everyone's waiting to welcome you at the vicarage.'

He was quite right. When he pulled up outside the vicarage gate, the door was flung open and Avril and David came out to greet them with cries of delight.

'Charlotte, my dear. You're looking well. Did you have a good journey?'

'What a long day you've had. Come on in and have something to eat. Only shepherd's pie, but I know it's one of your favourites.'

The Dawson children, dressed in pyjamas and ready for bed, were waiting indoors. Charlotte gave them each a hug. Billy had come into the house too and was invited to stay for the shepherd's pie, but he declined.

'Better get back,' he said. 'I'll come over tomorrow afternoon to see you, Charlotte. Perhaps we can walk the dogs together?'

Charlotte smiled at him and said, 'Yes, I'd like that.'

The following morning Mr Thompson came up from Cheddar. He, the vicar and Charlotte spent much of the morning in David's office, going over the terms of Miss Edie's will.

There was a bequest to the church but apart from that every-thing else was to come to Charlotte. Miss Edie had added an explanation of her bequest.

I have left everything to Liselotte Becker, also known as Charlotte Smith, so that after this dreadful war she will be able to live her life to the full. It is too precious to waste on regrets of what might have been. Look forward, Charlotte, not back. I wasted too much of my life doing that. Please don't do the same.

'I shall open a bank account for you, Charlotte,' said Mr Thompson, 'and each month we'll pay in an allowance, so that you have enough money for all you need.'

'But I don't need money,' Charlotte protested. 'I earn money at the home.'

'Yes, we know that,' said Mr Thompson. 'It won't be a large sum, ten pounds a month...'

Charlotte's eyes widened at the amount. It didn't sound like a small sum to her.

'... but,' he continued with a smile, 'it will give you a little extra if you need it. You can always save it up, if you don't use it.'

He explained that Blackdown House was hers and that the costs of its upkeep would be met by the trust.

'You don't have to worry about anything, my dear,' the vicar told her. 'It'll all be looked after until you're twenty-one. After that it'll be up to you, but Mr Thompson and I will always be here to advise you.'

That afternoon Charlotte went back to Blackdown House.

'Would you like me to come with you?' Avril had asked, but Charlotte shook her head.

'No, I think I'd rather go alone.'

'Of course,' Avril had agreed with a smile. But she had been a little worried. Charlotte was still only sixteen and though she had at once noticed the new maturity that Caroline had mentioned on the phone, Avril felt that recent events had given Charlotte much to bear.

Mr Thompson had given her the bunch of keys Miss Edie had always kept in her handbag and Charlotte let herself into the house. She wandered through the rooms, so still and quiet, each with its own memory. She sat on the window seat in her own bedroom and looked out across the fields at the view that had become so familiar to her. It was just as she'd remembered it, dressed in autumn colours, the bracken brown, the grass yellowing, the trees golden, red and orange and the hills sharp-edged against the pale blue October sky. So different, she thought, from the roof-scape that she saw from her attic window in Livingston Road, so peaceful compared with the continuous noise of the London streets.

She looked round the room, but there was nothing of hers left. She had taken everything with her in her flight to London. For flight it had been, she knew that now, as she sat in the haven of what had been her home. She had run from her misery.

Too late to come back, she thought. My life is in London now, working at Livingston Road. She thought about Harry and wondered yet again where he was. Since she had found Aunt Naomi and Uncle Dan again Harry had retreated to the back of her mind. But he was still there, reappearing occasionally when she least expected him, dropping in and out of her thoughts as he'd dropped in and out of her life. Charlotte swung from being angry with him to worrying about him and then back to anger again. He could at least have said he wasn't coming, rung the home or sent a message or something, so that she didn't look a fool in front of Miss Morrison and the others; all dressed up and nowhere to go. Maybe he'd put in another appearance when she got back to London. If he did, she wondered, how would she feel about it? Would she be pleased to see him? She didn't know. She would only know for sure if and when it happened.

With a sigh she pushed him to the back of her mind, got to her feet and crossed the landing into Miss Edie's room. It, too, had been left untouched, as if Miss Edie might return at any moment. Charlotte went over to the bedside table and picked up the photograph of Herbert. She looked down at his smiling face and found herself smiling back at him.

'I'll take you with me,' she said aloud. 'I won't leave you here to be thrown away.' She opened the bedside drawer and saw, beside a bottle of aspirin, lying on top of the hankies, the dog-eared telegram and a letter with an army postmark, addressed to Miss Edie. She picked them both up and put them and the photograph into her pocket. She would never read the letter or the telegram, she would burn those as soon as she had the opportunity, but the photo she would keep.

At last she came to the spare room, the room with the doorway into the attic.

'You may want to have a look at everything that's been stored in the loft,' Mr Thompson had said, 'before we have it cleared away. There may be things there that you'd like kept, but much of what's there will probably be Everard family possessions which'll mean nothing to you. I'll go through any papers in case they're important.'

The door had always been kept locked. Charlotte found the key on the bunch she'd been given, unlocked the door and went in. It was as it had always been. Neat bed, chest of drawers, wardrobe, and in the corner, the triangular door into the attic. Charlotte looked across at the wardrobe, which Miss Edie'd kept locked. She'd never mentioned why it was locked or what it contained, but Charlotte decided that she should be the one to open it now Miss Edie had gone. She looked at the various keys in her hand and selected one that looked hopeful. It fitted and, though stiff, she was able to turn it and open the wardrobe door. Inside hung a single garment. A white lace wedding dress. Charlotte stared at it, tears springing to her eyes. Miss Edie had already made her wedding dress before she heard that Herbert had been killed. She had kept it safe, locked away with her hopes and dreams, just in case the telegram had been wrong. Just in case Herbert came home.

Hearing a sound downstairs, Charlotte quickly closed and locked the wardrobe door.

'Who's there?' she called as she went to the top of the stairs.

'It's me,' called Billy. 'Mrs Swanson said you were here.'

Charlotte came back down the stairs. 'I was just looking round the house again,' she said. 'I've finished now.'

It had been suggested to her that it would be better to tell no one about Miss Edie's will. 'It's nobody's business but yours,' the vicar had said. 'Better if you're not to be the topic of village gossip.'

'It'll get out eventually,' he said to Avril later, 'but there's no need to subject the child to more comment.'

Charlotte had agreed to say nothing. She would be going back to London in a couple of days, anyway. Caroline already knew; there was no need to tell anyone else.

'I've brought the dogs with me,' Billy said as they went back into the garden and Charlotte locked up.

'Miss Edie'd be pleased with the garden,' she said, looking round at the tidy vegetable patch. 'Who's been looking after it, I wonder?'

Billy didn't answer and she looked across at him sharply. 'Was it you, Billy?'

'I helped,' he said casually. 'Thought we might go across towards the gorge, what do you think?'

It was a bright October day; the sun struck flashes of brilliance on the autumn trees. They walked along the track that led out of the village and up through the copse on to the open hillside beyond. As they walked past the observation post from where Billy and his father had watched the German plane crash, Charlotte said, 'Do you still come out here to watch for enemy planes?'

'Only if there's a warning,' Billy replied. 'We still get them even though the threat of invasion seems to have lessened now that Hitler's bogged down with the Russians. He'll have his work cut out there, but at least it means his attention's elsewhere.'

Billy was right. The threat of a German invasion had indeed decreased. Billy was still part of the auxiliaries; they still had everything in place in case the threat returned, but they all thought that the danger, once so imminent, had now diminished. For Billy the relief was more than the general lessening of tension felt by everyone else. It was an intense, personal relief. The Germans weren't coming and, if they weren't, the danger he'd feared for Charlotte, both as a refugee German and as the girlfriend of an auxiliary, was no longer a threat. He knew that he still couldn't explain his sudden coolness towards her after the midsummer dance, but he was determined to try and repair the damage it had caused between them. Getting their friendship back on its old, easy footing was the first step.

They let the dogs run as they came out on to the hilltop. The freshening breeze brought colour to Charlotte's cheeks and her spirits lifted as they walked the familiar pathway.

'I have missed all this,' she said, waving her arm to encompass the view. 'London is very shut in. The buildings all crowd round you and you can only see in straight lines.'

'Tell me about London,' Billy said. 'What was it like going back there after living here in the country for so long?'

'Difficult at first,' admitted Charlotte, 'but you get used to it. The noise, the bustle, the crowds of people. But it's a sad place with all the bomb damage. Empty spaces where houses once stood, ruined buildings waiting to be cleared.'

As they walked Charlotte told Billy about her visit to Kemble Street and the ruins she found there. She told him, with tears in her eyes, about Hilda. 'She and her family were so kind to me when I first came to London, and now she's dead. She was killed in the raid that injured me.' She told him about finding Aunt Naomi and Uncle Dan at last. 'They'd searched everywhere for me, but they thought I'd been with Hilda and that I was dead, too. They moved away from London when the house was destroyed.' As she talked it was as if a great burden was slipping from her shoulders. She'd had no one in whom she could confide her thoughts and fears since Miss Edie's death. Everyone had been very kind, but she had held on to her innermost feelings and shared them with no one. Somehow with Billy it was different and, almost without realising, she slipped back into their earlier, easy amity, and told him all about her life in London and her work in the children's home. The only person she didn't mention was Harry. Billy was not the person with whom to discuss Harry.

They sat down on a fallen tree trunk and Billy listened as she poured out what had happened to her since she'd left Wynsdown. 'When are you going back?' he asked. 'I assume you are.'

'In a couple of days,' Charlotte replied, 'three at the most. Miss Morrison has given me time off for a few days, but she needs me back up there. You have to remember it's my job now. I'm not just helping her, I'm earning my living.'

'You could come back here and earn your living,' suggested Billy. He took her hand. 'I miss you, you know.'

Charlotte let her hand rest in his, but smiling at him, shook her head. 'I miss you, too, Billy. But my place is in London now. The children in the home where I work need looking after. They've all lost their homes and lots of them their families too. That's all happened to me, so I know what that's like. Sometimes I can help them get through it.'

A breeze blew up and Charlotte shivered. 'We should be getting back,' she said, getting to her feet. 'I said I'd be back at the vicarage for early supper with the children.'

Billy whistled the dogs, which had been happily exploring a rabbit warren under a nearby hedge, and they turned their steps back towards the village, Charlotte with her hand tucked comfortably through Billy's arm. When they finally reached the village green, the sun had disappeared and the air was decidedly chilly.

'Will you come over to the farm tomorrow?' Billy asked her, looking up at her as he bent to clip leads to the dogs' collars. 'Have your dinner with us?'

Charlotte nodded. 'Yes, I'd love to. When shall I come?'

A smile spread over Billy's face and he said, 'Just come when you're ready. Ma'll be expecting you.'

The last couple of days went very quickly and suddenly Charlotte was on her way back to London. It was Billy who went with her on the bus to Cheddar to see her off at the station.

'How will you get back to the village?' she asked as they boarded the bus.

'Walk, of course,' Billy replied with a grin. ''Tisn't that far.'

As they waited on the platform, her case at her feet, Charlotte could feel tears pricking her eyes. She knew she had to return to London, but she was sorry to be leaving Wynsdown and all the people there who'd done their best to make her feel it was her home. As the train chugged round the corner, Billy put his arms round her and held her close.

'Look after yourself in London,' he said into her hair. 'Don't go getting lost again.'

Charlotte returned his hug and then broke free as the train snorted to a halt beside her.

Billy opened the door for her to get in and heaved her suitcase up into the rack. 'Take care,' he said as he jumped back down on to the platform. 'And you never know, I might just come up the Smoke to visit you.'

The guard blew his whistle and the train began to move. Billy jogged along the platform beside the open window and to his delight as the train drew away, Charlotte leaned out to wave and called back, 'Yes, Billy, do.'

As the train rounded the curve she pulled the window up and sat down on her seat. Blinking away the tears that had threatened to overflow, she thought about the day she'd spent at the farm. It had been a lovely day and she had spent the morning, as she had so often before, helping Billy's mother in the farmyard and in the kitchen till the men came in for their midday meal. As they were preparing the vegetables, Margaret Shepherd had said, 'It's lovely to have you back, Charlotte, if only for a few days. We've all missed you, Billy in particular, of course.'

'Has he?' Charlotte couldn't help letting a little bitterness creep into her voice as she remembered how her happiness of the midsummer dance had evaporated in the face of Billy's coolness towards her after the German plane had crashed. She had spoken in German, words of comfort to the injured pilot, words of comfort to an enemy.

'Of course he has,' Margaret chided her gently. 'You know how fond of you he is. I know he wasn't... well, quite himself for a while, but he was involved in sommat secret that was preying on his mind.'

'Secret?' echoed Charlotte. 'What sort of secret?'

Margaret shrugged. 'I don't know, my lover, he ain't said nothing to his dad nor me, but we know him and he were worriting about sommat for sure. Sommat to do with them trainings he went off to do.' She gave Charlotte a reassuring smile. 'But seems like it's over now. Our Billy's our Billy again.'

That afternoon they went round the farm with the dogs and she watched Billy training the two of them with a few sheep. The dogs were learning to work in tandem and, as she'd watched, Charlotte knew she could never take Bessie back to London with her. Her place was here in Wynsdown, even if her own wasn't.

They'd been back in time to help John Shepherd with the afternoon milking and then Billy had walked her back to the vicarage.

Avril had been pleased to see that their friendship had been rekindled. Billy Shepherd was a good solid man, no stranger to hard work, with a generous heart. She'd heard Caroline's misgivings about the young German refugee, Harry, who seemed to have some sort of hold on Charlotte.

'I don't think he's holding something over her,' Caroline had said, 'but there is a very special connection between them, they came on the same train from Germany. The thing is, I don't really trust him. I certainly didn't tell Charlotte about Miss Edie's will till I was pretty sure he wasn't coming back, but a letter has come for her. It's postmarked HMP Brixton.'

'You mean the prison?' exclaimed Avril.

'Yes. I think he's probably inside. He was arrested some months ago as an enemy alien, so perhaps he's been arrested again. The thing is, do I give her the letter, or do I simply forget about it?'

'Oh, Caro, I don't know,' Avril said. 'What do you think?'

'One minute I think I won't tell her about it and if he turns up again they'll just think it was another casualty of the wartime post, and then the next I think that's morally wrong. I shouldn't try and play God and decide what's best for her. I'd be furious if someone did that to me, wouldn't you?'

'Even if it was for your own good?'

'Who's to decide what's for her good? It's not up to me.' She sighed as the pips went. 'Time's up,' she said. 'I think I'll—' but before Avril could hear her decision, the line went dead and she didn't know what Caroline was intending to do.

Perhaps, she thought as she saw Billy help Charlotte on to the Cheddar bus the next day, with a bit of luck she'll forget the disappearing Harry and remember Billy, waiting for her here in Wynsdown.

Caroline was waiting up for Charlotte when she got back to Livingston Road.

'My dear girl, you must be so tired,' she cried as she hurried her into the warmth of the home's big kitchen and set some soup to heat on the stove. 'How did you get on? How was my sister? It must have been lovely to get out of London, even if only for a few days.'

She poured the hot soup into a bowl and, cutting the crust off a loaf and a wedge of cheese, she set the food down in front of Charlotte.

Charlotte was indeed feeling tired. Several times during the journey the train had been shunted into a siding to allow a more important train to pass by on the main line and it had finally arrived in London nearly three hours behind schedule. She was grateful for the food and as she ate the bread and drank the soup, she told Miss Morrison about her time in Wynsdown.

'Did you get everything sorted out with the solicitor?'

Charlotte explained the arrangements, both financial and about Blackdown House.

'Mr Thompson is going to look after the maintenance of the house,' she said. 'He thinks we should let it, furnished, for the time being. I've taken a few small things that I want and packed them into a trunk. Mrs Swanson's going to keep them for me until I have somewhere else to store them.' She thought again of the wedding dress she'd folded so carefully into the trunk, the veil which had hung with it. No one had seen them but her. Laid with them were Herbert's photo and both the letter and the telegram Miss Edie had kept all those years. Charlotte had planned to burn those, but at the last minute had slipped them in the trunk instead.

The only thing she had brought back to London with her was the piano music she'd been practising for her exam, before Miss Edie died. She had missed playing the piano more than she'd have thought possible. There was an old piano in the home at Livingston Road, but she'd had little time to do more than play simple tunes for the children to sing to.

If I really have a little money of my own now, she thought, I might try and find someone to teach me again.

So, she'd packed the music in her case and brought it back to London.

Apart from that she took nothing. She'd had no wish to go into the attic and search through the boxes and cases that were stored there. She simply told Avril Swanson that she could go through everything and take anything that would be of use to anyone in the parish.

'Of course, if I find anything of value,' Avril had said, 'I'll set it aside for you to look at. There may be things there that would fetch a fair price in an auction room.'

As Caroline listened, she was still struggling with her decision. Should she pass on the letter that she was sure had come from Harry, or not? She had been very tempted to open it, just to be sure it was from him; but who else could it be from? Who else would Charlotte know in Brixton prison? She had decided to hang on to the letter for a few days and see how Charlotte settled back into the Livingston Road routine. Then, if all was well, she would find a suitable time to give it to her.

'Have you told anyone about your legacy?' she asked now.

Charlotte shook her head. 'No, not yet. The vicar said it would be better if it wasn't generally known yet. It'd be round the village in no time.'

'Will you tell the Federmans?'

'I probably will,' Charlotte replied. 'I don't want them to think that they have to provide for me any more. They know I've got a job with you, but Uncle Dan was saying something about giving me a little extra so that I could go up and see them from time to time. With the allowance Mr Thompson is giving me, he certainly won't have to pay my fares when I visit them.'

Would she tell Harry? Caroline wondered. If she handed over the letter, would Charlotte tell Harry about her good fortune? Somehow, Caroline felt, if Harry discovered Charlotte had come into money, there would be cartoon pound signs whirling in his eyes.

Chapter Thirty-Nine

June 1944

Billy Shepherd got off the train that afternoon and caught a bus to Livingston Road. He had made the journey several times over the last eighteen months. Charlotte was still working at the children's home. She had not returned to Wynsdown, but when she got back to London she had written to Billy and, unlikely correspondent though he was, he had answered her letter by return. Their correspondence had continued until Christmas, when Billy took the train to London and spent the festive season with Charlotte and all the other inmates of the Livingston Road home. He had been a great favourite with the children, dressing up as Father Christmas on Christmas Day and handing out presents to everyone.

All of them were pleased enough to receive a special present and when Billy reappeared, minus red coat and white beard, he was greeted by an ecstatic Mary, one of the youngest children.

'Uncle Billy, Uncle Billy, Father Christmas was here!'

'No! Really?' he cried, looking amazed.

'He was! He was!' shrieked Mary. 'But oh, Uncle Billy,' her face fell, 'you missed him!'

Billy gave her a hug. 'Never mind, Mary, perhaps I'll see him next year.'

'But next year's so far away,' wailed the little girl. 'Can you wait that long?'

Billy smiled, and thinking of Charlotte, he replied, 'I can wait as long as it takes.'

The population of the home was continually changing, but all the children looked forward to Billy's visits. Charlotte did, too. She welcomed him with open arms and they always hugged each other fiercely, but Billy was treading carefully, and apart from a gentle kiss under the mistletoe at Christmas, he'd never moved for anything closer. He knew she was holding him at arm's length and though he wasn't sure why, he was afraid if he hurried her he would lose her altogether. Their friendship was firm and strong and, for the time being at least, he was prepared to settle for that.

Harry was the ghost. Harry still lingered in Charlotte's mind. He had disappeared from her life as suddenly as he'd come into it, but she couldn't forget him. He was the only one left from 'before'. But Billy knew nothing of Harry.

As Billy got off the bus, his heart beat faster at the thought of seeing her. Two minutes' walk and he'd be there. He paused at a news stand to buy a paper. Everyone was still buzzing with the news of the Normandy landings and the fact that the Allies were finally taking the war to the Germans, bringing the end of the conflict ever nearer.

Later that evening, he and Charlotte walked home, hand in hand, after a visit to the cinema. When Billy had arrived, Caroline had sent them off to the pictures for an evening's relaxation. Life in the home had suddenly become more hectic. Since the Allied landings in Normandy, just a couple of weeks ago, there had been a renewed bombardment of London, but now the bombs that came to deliver death and destruction carried no crew. They flew, pilot-less, out of the night, their engines whirring until the fatal moment when they cut out. Sometimes they dropped immediately, destroying whatever lay beneath them, others continued their flight, coasting silently through the air until they dived, unannounced, to explode on the homes of those below. Hundreds of people had been made homeless again, hundreds more had been killed or injured. The doodlebugs, as they'd become known, were taking Hitler's revenge.

Caroline had had to find room for more and more children, left homeless by this new onslaught. Her tiny staff were worked off their feet. They'd moved out of their own rooms to accommodate more refugee children. Four small girls were put in Caroline's room and she slept in her office. Charlotte had a camp bed in the living room along with some of the older girls, her tiny attic having been taken over by three boys, sleeping head to toe in a row on the floor. Until this renewed bombardment, whenever he'd been visiting, Billy had slept on a mattress in the small staff room, but that was now where Matron and Mrs Downs slept. This visit he was going to have to manage with a blanket on the scullery floor.

'You're going to be very uncomfortable with just a blanket,' Charlotte said as they strolled home.

'I'll be fine,' Billy assured her. 'It's summer after all.'

'Yes, but not a very warm one,' Charlotte said. She was right. The night was cool and although a half moon lighted their way through the streets, the air was chilly and there were few people about.

And then they heard it. The distinctive pulsing whir of an engine, high above them. Both looked up. There it was, a dark, lethal shape, against the ragged moonlit sky, and even as they looked, the whirring stopped.

'Doodlebug!' cried Billy and, grabbing Charlotte's hand, dragged her into a shop doorway, holding her close against him as they huddled in the illusory safety of the porch. There was a moment's silence and the doodlebug cruised on, then with a whoosh it hurtled out of the sky and exploded, the sound echoing down the narrow streets, the blast following, blowing in the windows and doors of the houses that lined the opposite side of the street. The noise of the explosion was followed by the sound of crashing masonry, shattering glass and screaming. Billy and Charlotte clung to each other, but the sheltering doorway had done its work. They were buffeted by the blast, but it had spent its force down the middle of the road, the flying glass had passed them by and they were uninjured. For a long moment they stood as if transfixed, then Billy said, 'You all right, Char?'

Charlotte nodded a little shakily. 'Yes,' she breathed, 'I think so.'

'Come on then,' Billy said, 'we'd better go and help.'

He took her hand and they stumbled out of the doorway and made their way back up the blasted street. There was rubble everywhere, broken glass, shards of timber, heaps of bricks. Following the shouts for help, they rounded the corner and saw to their horror that the doodlebug had taken out the cinema with a direct hit. All that remained of the building where they had spent their evening was a crater in the ground and a heap of rubble. The buildings round it leaned at crazy angles, tottering as if trying to regain their balance; some of them succeeded, others continued to crumble and then, giving up, crashed inward, floor upon floor folding in upon anyone left inside.

People were pouring out of the buildings that had survived. Many were injured, some superficially with no more than cuts and bruises, others with broken limbs or blood-soaked bodies, struggling to drag themselves clear. Everything, everyone, was covered in the dust that still swirled like smoke in the air.

Charlotte stared in horror at the scene before her. From the darkness, voices cried out for help, cries of pain, desperate calls from beneath the ruins. Lights were brought and rescuers began the frantic search through the rubble, looking for survivors.

Billy said, 'Wait here. I'll go and help.' And before she could answer he had hurried off towards a gaping hole that had once been the front door of a small block of flats. The top storey was missing, the roofless walls stark against the moonlit sky. He pushed his way in through the gap and, taking out the pocket torch he always carried with him, he shone it round inside. The ground was covered with chunks of fallen plaster, bricks and pieces of timber. Glass crunched beneath his feet and the dust filled his lungs, but the central staircase seemed to be intact, at least for the first flight up. He was about to creep up the stairs to see if anyone had survived on the floor above when he heard a woman calling.

'Help, help, we're under here.' The cry came from somewhere beneath the stairs. Billy edged his way through the fallen masonry and shone his torch into the darkness.

'I can hear you,' came the cry. 'Can you hear me? I can hear you. Please get us out. Get us out before the roof falls in.'

'I'm coming,' Billy called back. By the light of the torch he could
see that there was a door leading to a space under the stairs, but the
way to it was blocked by fallen debris.

'Your door is blocked,' he called. 'I'm going for help.' He went
back outside to try and find someone to help him clear the rubble,
but everyone in the street was working flat out to drag others from
the ruins. Billy was on his own. He'd have to try and move the debris
himself. He went back inside and, laying his torch on a pile of stone
began to pull the rubble away from the door. 'Don't worry,' he
called as he heaved at the broken bricks and concrete. 'I'm here. I'll
get you out. Who's in there? Anybody hurt?'

'No, it's just me and my baby.'

Billy felt a bubble of panic. A baby. There was a baby in there.
He had to get them out. 'OK,' he called. 'Hold on, I'm doing my
best.'

Suddenly he felt someone beside him and, glancing up gratefully,
he found Charlotte reaching for a piece of timber, pulling it free and
tossing it aside.

'Char,' he breathed, 'you shouldn't be in here, it's too
dangerous.'

'Not too dangerous for you,' she said as she pulled another piece
of wood out of the way. 'Two of us'll get it cleared in half the time.'

It had taken her every ounce of courage to follow Billy into the
depths of the pitch-black building. Her fear of dark, enclosed spaces
had flooded through her as she'd approached the gaping doorway,
but Billy was in there. She'd seen him come out once and look for
help, but there'd been none and so she knew she had to go in herself.
How could she stand out in the street, an onlooker, when there were
people trapped in the collapsed building? Billy was risking his life
trying to rescue them and though it was the stuff of her worst nightmares, Charlotte knew she had to confront her terror once and for
all and go inside to help him.

Together they pulled at the rubbled remains, using their bare
hands to shift the detritus away from the door. It seemed to take for
ever, but with both of them clearing the way it wasn't very long
before they had made a narrow passageway through to the door.

Not only had all the debris been blocking it, its lintel was aslant the top, wedging it in place.

'We're nearly there,' Billy called encouragingly to those trapped inside. 'Which way does the door open? In, towards you or outwards?'

'Outwards,' came the shaky reply. 'Oh, do hurry! There's bits of ceiling crumbling in on us here.'

Billy grasped the door handle and heaved, but the door remained jammed. 'I can't open the door,' he said. 'It's stuck. Can you stand clear of it? Is there room in there?'

'Not much, but I'm standing clear.'

'Right,' Billy said, trying to keep his voice calm. 'I'm going to try and break the door open.' He looked at Charlotte. 'Go outside and see if you can get someone to come and help,' he said. 'I'm not sure I've the strength to do this on my own.'

Charlotte nodded and hurried back out into the street. Everything was in chaos. People scurried in all directions, air raid wardens giving instructions, men hauling bricks away from a collapsed doorway, rescuers carrying away the wounded on makeshift stretchers, firemen further down the street, dousing a fire that had broken out in one of the damaged buildings. There seemed to be no one she could call to help Billy. Then she saw that one of the firemen had an axe and was clearing some debris away from the flames that still flickered within the building. She rushed over to him.

'Come quickly, oh, please come quickly!' she called. 'There's someone trapped in those flats over there. My boyfriend, Billy, is trying to get them out, but he can't break down the door.'

'Right-ho, love, show me where.'

She led the man back to the flats and in through the gaping doorway.

He took one look at the situation and swore under his breath. 'Christ almighty, this whole bloody lot could come down any time!' He turned to Charlotte. 'You wait outside, love,' he said firmly. 'We'll have them out in no time. Stand well clear.' He gave her a little shove towards the door and then turned his attention to the job in hand.

'Billy?'

'Yes, I'm here.'

'Better leave this to me, mate. I got an axe. Soon have that door open. Who's in there?'

'Don't know. A woman and a baby, I think.'

'Going to get you out, lady,' the fireman shouted through the door. 'Got to break the door down, so stand well clear if you can. Who's in there with you?'

'Just me and Josie.'

'All right. Just hang on tight and be ready to come out fast. I'm coming in.'

Billy stood aside, keeping his torch focused on the door as the fireman edged down the pathway they had cleared. He swung his axe and the blade bit into the wood of the door. There came a scream from inside.

'Hold on, lady,' commanded the fireman, and swung the axe again. The door shuddered but still it held firm.

'Oh, hurry, do hurry,' came the cry from inside. 'Stuff's falling on my head!'

The third swing of the axe produced a slit in the door and Billy, still shining his torch for the fireman, could see two frightened eyes peering out through the gap.

'Stand back!' bellowed the fireman and the eyes disappeared. He swung the axe yet again and this time the door disintegrated. He grabbed the broken pieces and pulling them free called, 'Out with you, lady.' The woman emerged through the hole, clutching the baby in her arms. As she did so there was a rumble above them. Billy grabbed at her and propelled her out into the street. About to follow, he glanced behind him to see the fireman crashing to the ground as a piece of falling stone struck him on the head. The ominous rumbling increased, but oblivious to its warning, Billy turned back to the prostrate fireman. As more debris began to shower round them, Billy managed to get his hands under the man's arms. Backing towards the doorway he half lifted, half dragged him towards the safety of the street. The fireman was no light-weight and though Billy was strong, he was struggling to move him. A sound like a gunshot made him look back. The staircase had cracked, its central pillar folding under the strain, and the ceiling above sagged, a spider's web of cracks snaking from one side to the other. It would only be moments before the whole lot collapsed in on them. With a super-human effort, Billy heaved the inert man through the door and staggered out into the night, dragging them both clear. With a final creak, the concrete ceiling crumbled and the floor above plunged to where they'd been standing. Someone was shouting as hands reached to pull them away from the disintegrating building. 'Look out! Look out, she's going. She's going!'

With a final rumble the remaining walls imploded and the building came crashing down, a cloud of dust and debris boiling round it.

Charlotte flung herself into the arms of the still-dazed Billy, clinging to him and crying, 'Billy, oh, Billy, I thought you were dead. Oh, thank God, thank God!'

For a moment they stood there, clinging to each other amid the tumult and the swirling dust, before they returned to the reality of the devastation around them and broke apart.

Billy looked down at the fireman who, still out cold, was being loaded on to a stretcher. One of the other firemen put a hand on Billy's shoulder.

'Thanks, mate. If you hadn't got him out he'd be under that lot.' He jerked his head at the flattened building. Sighing, he added, 'Doubt if anyone else from them flats has survived. No more we can do for them now.' He looked round at the general chaos left by the flying bomb. 'Not much we can do here for anyone, not till it's daylight and we can see the worst. I should take your girl home, now. You've both had enough by the looks of you.' He nodded towards Billy's face. 'You should go to a first aid post and have that cut looked at, too,' he advised. 'Looks like it needs a stitch to me.' He raised his hand in salute and turned away to oversee his mate being loaded, with other casualties, into an ambulance.

Billy put a hand to his forehead and felt it come away sticky with blood. He hadn't even realised that he'd been injured. He turned to find Charlotte trying to calm the woman they had rescued. She stood, clinging to her baby, with tears streaming down her face.

'What do I do?' She was almost incoherent. 'Where do I go?'

'Anyone else with you?' Charlotte asked.

'No, just Josie and me sleeping in the broom cupboard under the stairs.' She looked at the collapsed building. 'We've lost everything,' she wailed. 'Everything. We've got nothing left. What am I going to do? What am I going to do?'

'You'd better come home with me,' Charlotte said. 'I work in a children's home not far from here. You can stay there for tonight.' She turned to Billy. 'Come on, Billy, we've got get...' She turned back to the woman, 'What's your name?'

'Ethel, Ethel Shilton.'

'We've got to get Ethel and Josie back to the home.'

Together they led Ethel, with baby Josie in her arms, back through the streets to Livingston Road. The debris from the doodle-bug was extensive, with broken glass, fallen chimneys and blown-in doors for half a mile. When they reached the home and opened the front door, Caroline appeared, pale-faced, in the hallway.

'Charlotte, Billy, thank God!' she cried when she saw them. 'I was afraid you were somewhere near that bomb.' Then she took in their dust-covered clothes and faces and the cut on Billy's forehead. 'You were! Are you all right? Billy, that cut looks nasty, let me see.'

'Caroline,' Charlotte cut across her, addressing her by her Christian name for the first time, 'this is Ethel Shilton, with her baby, Josie. The bomb wrecked their home. Billy got them out, but they've nowhere to go, so I've brought them here.'

'Quite right, too,' Caroline said, wondering, even as she said it, where on earth she was going to find room for this woman and her baby. 'Come with me, Ethel, let's get you and Josie comfortable.' She turned back to Charlotte and Billy and said, 'You two better go into the kitchen and get cleaned up. The kettle's on the stove. We'll make some tea.' And with that, she and Ethel disappeared upstairs.

Charlotte took Billy's hand. 'Come on,' she said, 'let's wash that cut of yours. It looks nasty.' Once in the kitchen, Billy pushed the door shut behind him.

'Let me look at that cut,' Charlotte began, but Billy simply stepped towards her, took her in his arms and as she clung to him, he bent his head and kissed her. Kissed her as he had kissed her so long ago on that midsummer eve.

To his delight he felt her respond and when he finally lifted his head, he said, 'Oh, Charlotte, my darling Charlotte, I do love you.'

Chapter Forty

1945

Prison had not improved Harry. He had been held in Brixton while on remand, but once he'd been sentenced – three years for looting, resisting arrest, assaulting a police officer and selling goods on the black market – he was transferred to Gloucester gaol.

He had been allowed to write one letter and he'd written to Lisa, explaining what had happened to him, but he'd had no reply. He didn't know if she'd ever received the letter, but decided that if she had, she must have answered after he'd been transferred to Gloucester. Screws weren't in the business of forwarding mail.

When he'd been incarcerated on the Isle of Man, he'd been befriended by Alfred Muller. Eventually he had used his time to prepare himself for his release into the world outside. Alfred had saved him from himself and given him a real stake in his future. In Gloucester gaol he found a new mentor, but got a different sort of education.

His first night he'd had to fight off the attentions of his cell mate, Puggy Merton. Puggy was short and fat, with sagging breasts and a pudgy bottom. The moment Harry was put into the cell he looked at him with lustful eyes. He'd always had a penchant for young boys – indeed that was why he was languishing here at His Majesty's pleasure – but to have a sturdy young man delivered to his cell made him think that there might be a God after all. That night he'd slithered on to Harry's bunk, pushing him up against the wall and blocking his escape with his bulk.

'Now then, boy,' Puggy murmured, wriggling against him, 'we

can have a bit of fun. You play ball with me... balls with me...' he giggled, 'and I'll look after you.'

Running his hands along Harry's thighs he gripped his backside and made the mistake of trying to turn him over. Harry, awaiting his opportunity, had smashed his fist into Puggy's face and brought his knee up, hard and fast, into Puggy's flabby groin. With a gasp of pain Puggy rolled off the narrow bunk on to the floor, but before he could get up, Harry was upon him, his hands pinning Puggy's arms and his knee across his windpipe.

'Do that again, mate,' Harry hissed, 'and you're a dead man.'

Their third cell mate, Rick Richards, had been paying no attention to what was going down on the bunk below – he was used to Puggy – but when he realised that the new lad was in danger of murdering Puggy, he called down. 'Knock it off, young 'un, or you'll be in here for life and it'll be a short one.'

Harry had let Puggy go and got back on to his own bunk, but remembering the fear that Rolf's knife had instilled, he decided to try and arm himself. A few days later he managed to smuggle a knife out of the canteen. It wasn't particularly sharp and didn't look particularly fearsome, but he spent hours honing it against the rough stone wall of his cell. The next time Puggy tried Harry, begging him for a favour, Harry whipped out the knife and, holding it to Puggy's privates, threatened to emasculate him with it. He was only a lad, but it soon got round that he knew how to handle himself and he was left alone.

The godfather on his wing was an East End boss called Dennis Duncan, known to inmates and staff alike as Denny Dunc. He still had ten years of his sentence for grievous bodily harm to run, but Harry soon discovered that Denny Dunc had some sort of clout within the prison. What he said went. Even the screws knew better than to get on the wrong side of Denny Dunc.

'Get that lad Harry Black out of Puggy's cell,' Denny said. 'He can come in with me for a bit.'

Officer Roddick was surprised. 'What about Teddy Thomas?' Teddy was Denny's most loyal sidekick, who always shared his cell.

'Put him with Puggy.'

*

From then on it was clear to both inmates and staff that Harry was under Denny Dunc's protection.

His sentence had included hard labour, and for the first six months Harry had been taken out to a quarry and spent the day breaking up stones to be used in bomb damage repairs. It was indeed hard labour, but it built up his strength, and despite his small stature, few would take him on without serious thought.

As Alfred had done before, Denny took Harry's education in hand. 'It's a jungle out there, Harry boy. Dog eat dog. So, you got to be the bigger, stronger dog, know what I mean?'

Harry did. He knew he'd been set up by Mikey Sharp and was considering what revenge he could exact once he got out. He told Denny what had happened and Denny laughed.

'Well, what did you expect, Harry? That he'd welcome you with open arms and let you move in on his manor? I'd have done the same, boy, if you'd come nosing on my patch. You're lucky he only got you fingered and put away. I might have been less gentle. Done sommat more permanent. Get my drift?'

Harry did and grinned ruefully. 'It was stupid to think I could take him on, but I learn fast and I shan't make that mistake again.'

'Believe you,' said Denny. 'You'll do all right. What you going to do when you get out of here? Plans, have you? I could use a lad like you.'

'No.' Harry shook his head. 'Thanks, Denny, but when I'm out of here and this fucking war's over, I'm going to fetch my girl and we're going to go to Australia. Plenty of scope for a man of talent over there.'

'Got a girl, have you?'

'Sort of. Least she will be when I get out of here.'

'You realise the Aussies probably won't let you in now you've got a criminal record,' Denny said.

'How will they know?' said Harry. 'I'll change my name. I'm a refugee. Lost all my papers in my escape, didn't I?'

'You'll need new ones,' Denny said. 'You'll still have to provide them with something, ID card, ration book, something to prove that you're who you say you are.' He looked across at the younger man. 'You do me a couple of favours when you get out and I can get you set up with whatever you need, know what I mean?'

'Like what?'

'Birth certificate, ID card, driving licence, you name it.'

'No, I mean what favours?'

Denny grinned at him appreciatively. 'You're learning. Nothing much, just carry a couple of messages to some friends of mine when they let you out.'

'Messages?'

'Maybe a letter or two. Screws won't search you on the way out, I'll see to that.'

'And I get...?'

Denny Dunc smiled. 'You, my son, get a new identity.'

It worked as Denny Dunc had described. On the morning Harry was let out into the spring sunshine, having served just less than his three years, he was handed back his belongings, such as they were, and without further ado the heavy doors swung closed behind him. He was free, and concealed in the seat of his trousers were three letters, for delivery to three of Denny Dunc's 'associates'.

'They got stuff to arrange for me,' Denny said. 'When you've delivered them letters, go to the Crooked Billet down near the Isle of Dogs. Ask for Freddie. He'll be expecting you. He'll sort you out with a new ID, then you can disappear and turn up in Sydney or wherever. I might even join you down there. Don't plan on staying in here much longer.'

It wasn't hard to find Denny's associates and Harry delivered the letters. He was careful, as Denny had warned him to be, to make sure that he wasn't followed. Then he set off to find the Crooked Billet.

Freddie was indeed expecting him. 'Better come to my studio, later,' he said, glancing round nervously. He gave Harry an address. 'After dark come round the back and I'll let you in.'

Freddie took his photo and wrote down some details. 'Come back here next weekend,' he said, 'Sunday evening, 'bout nine. I'll have your stuff ready by then.'

Harry did as he was told and the following Sunday he returned to the studio. Freddie, waiting, opened the door before Harry had a chance to knock.

'Come in,' Freddie hissed and, with a quick glance out into the yard, hastily closed the door behind him. 'Here you are, all the things Denny Dunc asked me to do.' He handed Harry an envelope. Harry tipped the contents out on to the table and found he was a completely new person. A dog-eared ID card named him as Victor Merritt, as did the ration book with some of the coupons already clipped and the birth certificate, George Merritt, son of Doris and William Merritt, born in Hackney on 25 July 1925. Most important of all was a passport, Victor Merritt's passport complete with Harry's photograph. He could travel anywhere.

'Who's Victor Merritt?' he asked.

Freddie scowled at him. 'You are,' he said. 'The address on them papers was took out by a V2, so there shouldn't be any queries. You was bombed out, that's all.'

Harry nodded and scooped up the documents, sliding them back into the envelope.

'An' you tell Denny Dunc that I done a good job, eh?' Freddie looked at him anxiously. 'Tell him his are ready, too, when he wants them.'

'I'll tell him,' agreed Harry, knowing full well he'd never see Denny Dunc again. Now he'd got his new papers, Harry Black would disappear. Vic Merritt, merchant seaman, would soon be leaving for Australia and he planned to take Lisa with him.

Harry wanted to find Lisa, to talk to her, to explain his plans for them both, but he wanted to do it without that dragon woman Morrison being about. He knew she didn't trust him and thought she'd probably try and stop Lisa going away with him. He made his way to Livingston Road in the hope of seeing her. All round him excitement was in the air. The people in the streets were buzzing with unconfirmed reports of a German surrender. Germany had finally been defeated. The war was over.

*

Charlotte was busy inside the house. The children had all been sent home early from school, the talk of nothing but the supposed surrender.

'I can't really believe it's all over,' Matron said to Caroline as they settled the children down for tea. 'No more bombing, no more V2s pulverising us. Life can get back to normal.'

'Not official yet,' Caroline warned. 'We'll put the wireless on later and see what they say on the news.'

After supper Caroline had gathered all the inhabitants of the home into the sitting room and switched on the wireless. Even the youngest had stayed up to hear that war was over. A great cheer went up when the news was announced officially. The Germans had surrendered. Everyone hugged and kissed, all talking excitedly, laughing, singing. Only Charlotte couldn't quite join in the joy. She was pleased that the war seemed to be over, but she knew it wasn't over for her. Now she had to find out if any of her family had survived.

She helped as always, putting the younger children to bed, but somehow she couldn't summon up the joyfulness, the exhilaration felt by everyone else.

'You should be out celebrating, not hanging about here in the house,' Ethel Shilton told her. 'Why don't you go up west? That's where all the fun is.'

Ethel and her baby Josie had become fixtures in the Livingston Road home. Caroline had squeezed them in on the night they'd escaped the doodlebug attack and Ethel had stayed. She earned their keep helping in the home and Josie, the youngest in the house, had become the pet of everyone, toddling about and getting in the way.

'No, thanks, Ethel,' Charlotte said. 'I'm celebrating here with all of you.'

The next day, however, was entirely different. The whole of London seemed to have erupted on to the streets. Charlotte took some of the children to the park while Caroline organised a huge party for them in the street outside. There'd been a storm in the night, but it hadn't dampened anyone's spirits and now the sun had burst through it was turning into a beautifully warm summer's day. As the children walked in an excited crocodile to the park, they could hear bells from the surrounding churches ringing out for victory; a new and cheerful sound. There'd been no bells during the hostilities, they had been reserved as a warning of invasion, but now that threat was gone, they rang out loud and long. There were few cars on the streets, but people were gathering, heading into the town, and everywhere there was laughter, shouts of joy, dancing.

As they reached the park gates Charlotte let the children break croc and run to the playground. She stood and watched them for a moment before following more slowly to the children's area, fenced off in one corner of the park.

'Lisa!'

Charlotte spun round and there he was, Harry Black, grinning at her in his inimitable way. She stared at him for a moment and he said, 'Aren't you pleased to see me? I got out.'

'Out? Of course, I mean... I... where have you been, Harry?' Charlotte tried to pull her thoughts together.

'Inside,' he replied shortly.

'Inside?' Charlotte looked confused. 'Inside where?'

'In prison. Look, I'm out now and I've come to find you.'

'In prison? Why, I mean when... Oh, Harry, what did you do?'

'Nothing,' Harry said. 'Well, nothing that loads of other people weren't doing as well. But that doesn't matter any more, does it? I mean, I done my time and now I'm out again I came straight to find you. You been all right, have you?'

Charlotte nodded and then said, 'Oh, Harry, why didn't you let me know? I didn't know what had happened to you. You just disappeared.'

'Like you did,' Harry reminded her. 'Look, I did write, but maybe you didn't get my letter.'

'No, I didn't. You were going to come back the next Saturday and you never did.'

'Well, I got arrested. I wrote from Brixton, but maybe the screws don't post letters. I don't know.'

'Screws?'

'Prison officers. Pigs, they are. Still I'm here now so let's forget about them. Let's go up west and celebrate the end of fucking Hitler.'

'Maybe later,' Charlotte said, glancing over at the group of children she'd brought with her. 'I can't just up and leave leave them here. I've got to take them back to the party.'

'Party? What party?'

'There's a street party in Livingston Road. I've brought the kids out here to keep them out of the way while it's being got ready.'

'We'll go after that, then,' Harry said cheerfully, apparently unaware that she couldn't simply walk away from her job in the home when she wanted to. He grinned at her. 'You're looking great, Lisa,' he said and, reaching over, he pulled her roughly into his arms and began to kiss her. For a moment she felt his lips on hers, the remembered feel of his tongue dancing with her own, and then she broke away and, breathing heavily, flopped down on the grass. Harry dropped down beside her and reached for her hand.

'Sorry,' he said quickly, 'sorry, shouldn't be doing that in public, I know. Just that I missed you, Lisa. I been thinking about you all the time I was... away. Bet you were thinking about me, too, eh?'

'Sometimes,' Charlotte conceded, but didn't add, 'but not for months now'.

'I've got great plans for us,' Harry told her. 'Now this fu— dreadful war is over we can get out of this country. Told you I wanted to go to Australia, didn't I?' He didn't wait for her reply, but went on, 'Start again in a young country. We can do really well over there... we can—'

'Harry! Stop!'

'Stop what? It'll be you and me, doll, just like we always thought.'

'We didn't always think—' Charlotte broke in, but it was as if she hadn't spoken.

'We've survived it all, Lisa. Now we're entitled. You and me.'

'But I don't want to go to Australia, Harry.' Charlotte tried to keep her voice soft and reasonable, not allow the rising panic she felt to sound in her words.

'You do, you will, when you think about it. Look, forget it for now, eh? Let's just celebrate the end of the war. You and me. We've defeated Hitler because we've survived!'

Charlotte wasn't going to get into any discussions about what she was going to do now that Germany'd surrendered. Her first priority would be to find news of her family. She looked at her watch and, managing a smile for Harry said, 'We'd better get back.' She called to the children, scattered in the playground. 'Come on, everyone, time to go home for the party.'

'Is Uncle Billy coming?' asked Mary Beale. She was one of the children who'd been in the home for well over a year and always looked forward to Billy's occasional visits.

'No, not today,' replied Charlotte.

'Oh!' cried Mary. 'I wanted him to come to the party, didn't you, Miss Charlotte?'

'It would have been nice if he could have,' agreed Charlotte carefully, 'but he can't today.'

'Who's this Uncle Billy, then?' demanded Harry as the children paired up for the walk back to Livingston Road.

'Just a friend,' Charlotte said. 'Someone who comes and helps at the home sometimes.' She wondered, even as she said it, why she was lying, or at least concealing the truth from Harry. All she knew was that she didn't want him to know about Billy.

She hurried the children along and, as they reached the home, Caroline came out to meet them. When she saw Harry her heart sank. She recognised him at once and she didn't like the way he had a proprietorial hand on Charlotte's arm as they walked up the road. She schooled her face, however, and came towards them, extending a hand. 'Harry, isn't it?'

'He found us in the park,' Charlotte said by way of explanation. 'He's coming to the party.'

'Lovely,' said Caroline. 'You're more than welcome, Harry. We haven't seen you for some time. Now, Charlotte, will you take the children indoors to wash their hands and then we'll sit them down.'

Tables had been pushed together to form one long one, straight down the middle of the road, with places laid for the children down either side. Covered with white sheets, they were decorated with red, white and blue ribbons and there was a balloon tied to the back of each chair. The children stared in amazement at the food spread out, waiting for them. Few of them had ever seen so much. Other houses in the street had laid out tables as well and everyone seemed to joining in to one huge party. While Charlotte hurried the children inside, Harry spoke to Caroline.

'Lisa and I are going up west to join in all the celebrations, later,' he told her. 'When you don't need her here any more. It's a great day, isn't it?' Harry knew instinctively that Caroline didn't like him, or didn't trust him, or both. When he spoke to her he was very careful of his language and his accent. Thanks to Alfred he could speak fluent English, with perhaps the hint of a Birmingham accent, and Harry, being Harry, always spoke to suit his listener; he made sure there was nothing of East London in his voice now.

Caroline wasn't very happy about the outing, but felt she couldn't say no. Once the party was over and the children were back indoors, she could hardly pretend she needed Charlotte's help. And anyway, she thought, it can't do any harm. It would do Charlotte good to get away for a few hours and join in the celebrations.

'That sounds fun,' was all she said. She was about to turn away when Harry said, 'I didn't just do a bunk, you know. I was arrested again, some mix-up about still being an enemy alien. I did write to explain to Lisa, but she says she didn't get my letter.'

Caroline tried to keep her face neutral, but she could feel the colour creeping into her cheeks. She thought of the letter with the Brixton postmark still tucked into a drawer in her bureau. She had never given it to Charlotte. She'd hoped Harry was gone for good.

'I expect it got lost along the way,' she said rather weakly. 'So much post went astray, didn't it? Especially in London, what with the raids.'

'Yeah, probably.' Harry gave her a knowing look. Clearly he didn't believe her. Then his expression changed and he said brightly, 'Still, I'm back now, so it doesn't matter.'

The street party was a great success; the amount of food that had been conjured out of store cupboards and collected from the backs of larders and gathered from allotments was amazing. Mrs Downs had managed to make two cakes from precious stores she'd been saving and other families in the street all contributed preserved foods and hoarded stores, so that it was a feast worthy of the name. One man, further down the street, home on leave when the peace had been declared, produced an accordion and started to play. Someone started to sing and soon everyone joined in. Someone else produced a fiddle and, climbing on to a chair, began playing exuberant jigs and flings, so that grown-ups and children alike were tapping their feet and many of them jumped up to dance. Harry grabbed Charlotte into his arms and was soon spinning her around in a victory dance, while other couples did the same. The drink flowed, the merriment increased and the austerities of the war were forgotten as they celebrated the peace.

'Told your Miss Morrison we were going up west when this party's over,' Harry murmured as he held close for a moment or two.

'You asked her?'

'Nah,' Harry grinned. 'Told her!'

'Oh.' Charlotte tried to hide her dismay. She did want to go up to town and celebrate with the hundreds of others that were flocking to Buckingham Palace, Trafalgar Square, Piccadilly Circus, of course she did, but she didn't like the way Harry was taking charge.

'Go on, you two,' Caroline said as the tired children were shepherded indoors. 'Off you go and have a lovely time. Give my love to the king if you see him… and Mr Churchill!'

Charlotte collected her handbag and checked she had her purse with her. At least she had money of her own now and didn't have to rely on Harry. They took a bus to the West End and then joined the crowds in Trafalgar Square. People were singing and dancing. The gaiety was infectious and several times Charlotte found herself being spun round, arms linked with those of a laughing soldier or sailor, before Harry grabbed her back again, swinging her through the crowds that had gathered everywhere.

'I want to see the king,' Charlotte called to Harry.

'Whatever for?'

'Because he's the king!' she shouted, and pulled him towards The Mall. Harry shrugged and followed her, keeping a tight grip on her hand. It would be so easy to get separated in such a crush. Gradually they eased their way up The Mall until at last they were in the multitude crammed into the space around the Victoria Memorial. The crowd was heaving from side to side, those at the front almost crushed against the railings that protected the courtyard.

'We want the king! We want the king!' The chant was incessant, growing in volume. Charlotte chanted along with the rest. She longed to see the king and the queen. High above them she could see the balcony where they might appear. It was draped in red and gold ready for the king and his family to make another appearance.

'They come out earlier,' said the man beside her, a child perched on his shoulders. 'We didn't half cheer!'

'Do you think he'll come out again?' Charlotte asked.

The man laughed. 'Don't know, do I? 'Spect so.'

'We want the king!' Even Harry was shouting.

Suddenly the long windows to the balcony opened and the king and queen stepped out. They were greeted by a roar as the crowd cheered them and the princesses who followed them, cheered until they were hoarse. Moments later there was another movement behind them and Winston Churchill appeared on the balcony, standing between the king and queen. He waved and gave his famous V for victory salute and the massed crowds below called his name and cheered him to the skies.

When they'd all gone back into the palace, the long windows closing behind them, Harry pulled at Charlotte's hand and said, 'Come on, Lisa. You've seen the king now. Let's go somewhere else.'

A warm dusk was falling, but there were lights everywhere. They moved slowly through the sea of people and managed to get into Green Park where there was a little more space. Charlotte sat down on a grassy bank, kicked off her shoes and sighed.

'That was so exciting, seeing the king and queen... and Mr Churchill.'

'Yeah.' Harry sounded less than enthusiastic.

'Oh come on, Harry!' cried Charlotte. 'You were cheering like everyone else.'

'They mean nothing to me,' Harry said. 'Kings and queens. We don't need them.'

Charlotte was annoyed. 'Well, remember he's king of Australia, too. If you're going there.'

'What d'you mean *if* I'm going there,' Harry said. 'Course I'm going there. With you. You and me together.'

'Harry, I can't.'

'Why ever not? It'll be a great life out there.' He waved his hand expansively. 'A new, young country. A place with a future.'

'Firstly, I can't go anywhere yet. I have to discover what happened to my family.'

'Lisa,' Harry spoke gently, 'you know what happened to your family.'

'No,' she snapped, 'no, I don't. They may not be dead. They may just have had to move. They may have been kept prisoner somewhere and now they'll be released.'

'Oh come on, Lisa, you've heard what they've been finding over there, these camps. God, we even heard about them in Gloucester.'

'They may not have been in one of those.' Charlotte was almost shouting now. 'They may not have been in any camp. Harry, I have to find out. Don't you understand?'

'No, I don't. You have to be a realist, Lisa. You're on your own, now. Just like me. We have to stick together, and there's no point in staying in this godforsaken country. They aren't going to get over this war for years, and I don't intend to stay in such a grey, miserable place for a day longer than I have to.'

'It's the country that gave you safe haven,' Charlotte reminded him.

'It's the country that's locked me up for four of the six years I've been here,' Harry replied bitterly. 'It's got nothing to offer me. I can't wait to get out.'

'But I don't want to leave,' Charlotte said. 'I've got a home here.'

'What,' scoffed Harry, 'a bedroom in a children's home?'

'No,' answered Charlotte. 'In the country, where I was evacuated.'

'What with those Federman people? Did you trace them?'

'Yes, I did and I see them from time to time, but I didn't mean them. You know when I lost my memory I was evacuated to a village in Somerset.'

'Yeah. So you spent a couple of years in a village. Doesn't make it your home, does it? Just because you lived there for a bit. And anyway, you told me the old bird you lived with there died.'

'She did,' replied Charlotte, 'but she left me her house in her will, so you see I really do have a home here in England.'

'Left you her house?'

If Caroline had been with them, her worst fears about Harry would have been realised; she could almost have watched the pound signs whirling in his eyes.

'Yes.'

'But Lisa, that's fantastic,' Harry cried and flung his arms around her. 'You can sell it and then we'll have money to start our life together in Australia!'

'Harry, I told you, I'm not going to Australia. I have to find—'

'You have to find out about your family first, I quite understand that, Lisa, course I do, but when you have…' He cocked his head at her and grinned, but she didn't meet his eye.

'Come on, Lisa,' he protested, 'you owe it to me, the way I stood up for you, fought for you. I'll always be there to look after you, promise.'

'Like you've been these last two years?' Charlotte said, sarcasm in her voice.

'That's different,' Harry snapped. 'I couldn't help that, could I? An' I came to find you again the minute I could, didn't I?' He reached out and took her hand. 'Don't let's quarrel,' he said in a more conciliatory tone. 'You're my girl, Lisa. We belong together, you and me.'

Chapter Forty-One

Billy and his parents had listened to the news of the German surrender on the wireless the previous night and they had hugged each other with joy. Now they were all safe. Jane was still in Bristol, nursing, but in no more danger from the bombs.

'I'm going up to see Charlotte,' Billy cried. 'She's safe at last.' He thought of the V2 rockets that had been raining down on London and the south-east of England for the last nine months. Billy had seen what a V1 could do, but the anti-aircraft gunners had got quite good at shooting those down. As they had no pilot, once they were pinned by a searchlight, they could take no evasive action. But the V2s were an entirely different matter. Travelling faster than the speed of sound, they hurtled through space before nose-diving without warning on to an unsuspecting target below. Thousands of civilians in the last few months had been killed by these horrific weapons, rockets that exploded their destruction before the sound of their arrival caught up with them.

Every time Billy had left Charlotte in London, he had been terrified that she would become the victim of one of these attacks, the death throes of the Nazi regime. London was the target, fear and misery was the aim and the attacks had been successful in both.

'I'll go first thing in the morning,' Billy said.

John looked across at him. 'Cows still need milking even if Hitler's dead,' he said, smothering a smile. 'Not sure I can spare you at such short notice.'

'Oh, Dad, come on—' began Billy, but his mother interrupted.

'Take no notice of him, Billy,' she said. 'He's codding you. I'll do the milking with him. Anyway, if I know Wynsdown, there'll be no work done tomorrow. The whole place'll be one huge party.'

Margaret Shepherd was quite right. Wynsdown was celebrating VE day in typical Wynsdown style. Within minutes of the broadcast, Marjorie Bellinger was on the phone to Avril Swanson and they were planning the village jollifications. From dawn on the following morning people were up and about, stringing bunting across the trees, moving tables and more importantly preparing food for a feast. Jack Barrett set up a bar outside the Magpie. No one was thinking about licensing laws on such a wonderful day, and he'd started pulling pints for those who'd come to help set up before most people had had their breakfast.

Billy left them all to their joyful celebrations and rode his bike down the hill to the station. He didn't know how long it would take him to get to London, but he didn't care. He was determined to get there, to see Charlotte, and now that the war was over, to take the plunge and suggest they might have a future together.

Since the night of the V1 that had come so near to killing them, Charlotte had allowed him to draw a little closer. Billy knew he still needed to proceed slowly and gently. As Margaret had said once, when they had touched on the subject of Charlotte, 'You can't blame the girl for holding back, Billy. Think about it, son. Almost everyone she's loved has disappeared or died. She's afraid, so take things steady.'

Billy understood the wisdom of her words and on the two occasions since that he'd managed to snatch a couple of days at Livingston Road, he had held back. It was a V1 that had propelled her into his arms and he hoped there wouldn't have to be another of those before he could hold her that closely again, but as he sat on the train that wandered cross-country to take him to her, he wondered, since there would be no more V1s or V2s, if it was at last time to remind her how much he loved her.

He got off the train and found himself in a joyful crowd, swinging its way through the streets, celebrating and singing as it went. Captured by the mood, Billy found he was beaming, being clapped on the back by total strangers. The whole capital was swamped with people, gathering anywhere there was room for a crowd, many well-oiled, but mostly good-natured as they crammed together in Trafalgar Square, dancing the conga along Piccadilly and calling for the king outside Buckingham Palace. With some difficulty Billy managed to make his way to Livingston Road, walking much of it as buses were few and far between and those that did run were filled with celebrating Londoners.

When he turned into Livingston Road he found a street party there was just breaking up. The tables and chairs stood empty, surrounded by the debris of the feast. Further up the road families were still sitting outside their houses, glasses of alcohol clasped in their hands as they swapped and reswapped stories of what had happened to them 'in the war'. As Billy walked along the road more than one man pressed a glass into his hand and insisted that he drank a toast to the king and to victory.

When at last he reached the children's home dusk was beginning to fall. He went up to the front door and, finding it open, he went inside. The first person he saw was little Mary.

'Uncle Billy!' she shrieked with delight. 'Miss Charlotte said you weren't coming! You missed the party.'

'Oh, no! Did I? Was it a good party?'

'We had cake and balloons,' Mary informed him.

'Then it certainly was a good one,' Billy said. 'Is Miss Charlotte upstairs, Mary?'

'No,' replied the child. 'She's gone out. She's gone out with her friend, Harry.'

'Harry?' Billy felt as though he'd been douched with cold water. Who the hell was Harry?

'He came to the party,' Mary said. 'I didn't like him.'

Billy didn't like the *sound* of him. Harry? Was he about to lose Charlotte to someone he'd never even heard of?

At that moment Caroline Morrison emerged from her office. 'What are you doing still downstairs, Mary?' she scolded. 'Upstairs with you. We've had a lovely day, but now it's bedtime.'

Mary scuttled off up the stairs and Caroline held out her hand

461

to Billy. 'Isn't it wonderful,' she said with a smile. 'I can't believe it's all over.'

'Over for us,' Billy agreed. 'All we have to do now is see off the Japanese.'

'I know,' said Caroline sombrely, 'but at least the bombing's stopped here, so these children aren't in danger of being annihilated.'

'Is Charlotte here?' Billy asked, although he already knew the answer. Mary had supplied that, but not the answers to the other questions that now filled his mind.

'No,' replied Caroline. 'She's gone up to town to join in the celebrations.'

'By herself?' Billy imbued his question with surprise.

'No, with an old friend. Look, Billy, you'd better come into my office and I'll explain.' She led the way back into her office and closed the door behind them. Waving him to a chair she sat behind her desk. For a moment neither of them said anything, then Caroline said, 'When Charlotte first arrived in London, she was fostered with a couple in Shoreditch.'

'Yes, I know all that.'

'Well, as you might guess, as a German she wasn't popular with all her classmates at school and she was subjected to quite a lot of bullying.' Billy nodded – he'd seen the same happen to her in Wynsdown.

'But a lad who'd come from the same town as she had, on the same train I think, took on the bullies and after that they left her alone. His name was Heinrich Schwarz, but he soon changed it to Harry, Harry Black.'

'And she's gone into town with him?'

'There's a bit more to this story than that,' Caroline said and she outlined what had happened to Harry since. 'He came to see her soon after she moved up here,' she said. 'I think they met up at the house where Charlotte used to live with her foster parents. It was damaged in a raid.'

'Yes, I know, she told me all about that.'

'About meeting with Harry?'

'No, about the house being destroyed and how she's found her foster parents again, since.'

'Yes, that's right,' Caroline said. 'Well, after that one visit, Harry disappeared again and it turns out he's been in prison.'

'And you let him take Charlotte into town?' Billy was horrified. 'A gaol-bird?'

'I don't know the ins and outs of it,' Caroline said defensively. 'He only turned up again today and it was hardly a day for asking his intentions. Charlotte is fond of him and he's the only link with her life before the war, with her family. She was surprised to see him after so long, but she was pleased as well. If I'd known you were coming, Billy... if *she'd* known you were coming, I'm sure she'd have waited for you, so you could all three have gone together. But I didn't and she didn't, and I thought she'd earned herself the chance to celebrate the end of the war with everyone else.'

'And she didn't know where he was all that time when he didn't show up?' demanded Billy.

'No. Though I have to admit that I had a pretty good idea.'

'Why?'

Caroline sighed and told him about the letter from Brixton prison. 'I have to say that I don't like him and I don't trust him, but I felt if I tried to turn her against him, I'd be doing just the opposite and pushing her into his arms.'

'Have you still got the letter?' asked Billy

'No,' lied Caroline. 'I burned it.'

'Did you read it?'

'No, but I didn't want Charlotte to know I'd kept it from her.'

'You've told me about it,' Billy pointed out. 'I can tell her.'

'Of course you can,' conceded Caroline, 'but it won't change things. She now knows Harry has been in prison, and all it will do is stir things up.'

Billy sat and considered what Caroline had told him. 'Is she in love with him?' he asked at last.

'I don't know. I don't think so, but she does feel something for him; gratitude maybe, friendship, the bond of a shared past?'

'Has he got a some sort of hold over her?'

Caroline shrugged. 'Who can say? Not a hold as such, but I'd say he's a manipulator and perhaps he puts emotional pressure on her. He's certainly a survivor, and survivors have to be very good at looking after number one. He may not be too choosy about how he tries to get his own way.'

'And you've let her go into London with a man like that?' Billy's disgust was barely suppressed.

'Billy, I couldn't have stopped her. She's nineteen next month. She has to make her own decisions. I'll admit I wasn't keen on her going, but I couldn't stand in her way.'

'When'll she be back?'

'I don't know, Billy. Late, I imagine, with all the festivities the BBC tell us are going on in the West End. I don't think you need to worry about her safety. I don't think Harry'll harm her.' She got to her feet and said, 'Come on, you must be starving. Let me find you something to eat.' She smiled across at him. She was fond of Billy and hoped that one day he and Charlotte might make a go of it.

'At least you haven't got to sleep in the scullery this time,' she said as she led the way into the kitchen. 'Several of the children have moved on recently and we're all back in our own rooms for now. You can have the camp bed in the sitting room.'

Darkness fell and most of those in the home went to bed. Caroline and Billy sat in the sitting room and waited for Charlotte and Harry to come home. They could hear the sounds of continued celebration echoing in through the open window, the revellers' singing becoming increasingly tuneless as the beer still flowed.

It was past midnight when they heard the front door open and the sound of whispers in the hallway. Billy went straight out and saw Charlotte creeping in, shushing Harry who was hard on her heels. When she saw Billy she gave a little cry, her hand flying to her mouth to stifle the sound.

'Billy,' she whispered in delight and stepped towards him. Without a second's hesitation he enfolded her in his arms. All earlier caution gone, Billy bent his head and kissed her, long and deep. He was claiming her as his, determined to leave this Harry bloke in no doubt as to his claim.

'Billy,' she said, when she could say anything at all, 'I didn't know you were coming.'

Still with his arms round her, he smiled down at her. 'So I see,' he said. 'Never mind. I thought we should celebrate together and here I am.' He glanced across at Harry who stood in the door, his face like thunder. 'Who's this?' Billy asked, as if he didn't know already.

Before she could answer, Harry stepped forward and said, 'I'm Harry Black, an old friend of Lisa's. We go a long way back.'

'Lisa?'

'Lieselotte Becker, from Hanau... like me.'

Their voices had been getting louder and Caroline, who had followed Billy into the hall, said, 'Keep your voices down, or you'll wake the whole house. Come into the sitting room.' She led the way, closing the door firmly behind them. Harry glanced at the camp bed that was made up in one corner. Charlotte followed his gaze.

'Billy has a camp bed in a corner somewhere when the home is very full,' she said in explanation.

Harry grunted. 'Here a lot, is he? Surprised he ain't in the army.'

'It's late,' Caroline said, ignoring this remark. 'We've got to be up early in the morning as usual, so it's time you went now, Harry.' She turned back and opened the door.

Harry didn't move. 'Went?' he said. 'Went where? I haven't got anywhere to go.'

'Well, I'm sorry, Harry,' Caroline said firmly, 'but you can't stay here. We haven't any room.'

'You got room for him.' Harry jerked his head towards Billy. 'He don't live here, neither.'

If Caroline noticed the East End creeping into Harry's voice, she ignored it. 'Billy comes here from time to time,' she said. 'He's great with the children and we all love to have him.'

She walked into the hall and opened the front door. The sounds of revelry drifted in from further down the road, where for the first time in nearly six years the street lamps were on, casting pale green pools of light on the pavement. For the first time in nearly six years Caroline was able to stand in a lighted, open front door, a true sign that there was no more danger from the sky.

465

Harry stared, stony-faced, at Charlotte and Billy as they stood together, Billy's arm still round Charlotte's shoulders. No one spoke and then, with an exaggerated shrug he said, 'I'll be back in the morning, Lisa. We can make our plans then.' With that he slouched out of the room. He paused in the hallway where Caroline stood beside the open door.

'I'll be back tomorrow,' he said, 'and I'll be telling Lisa that you stole her letter. I know you did. I could see it in your face. You could be regretting that before too long, Miss High-and-Mighty Morrison. She'd never have given that bloke the time of day if she'd knowed I was coming back for her.'

'Goodnight, Harry,' said Caroline, and she closed the door behind him.

For a long moment Harry stared at the closed door. He wondered if Lisa would come after him and so he waited a little further down the street, but the front door remained closed and in the end he gave up and strode away. Since he'd come out of prison he'd actually been dossing down at a rescue centre, pretending to have been bombed out, with nowhere to stay. At least it had meant he had somewhere dry and warm to sleep. He'd been back to Kemble Street once, thinking he might be able to use the cellar again as temporary accommodation, but he found that the houses had been bulldozed. All that was left of number sixty-five and its neighbours was a cleared site waiting for the end of hostilities.

With his change of name, he'd had to move shelters and for the first time offered his new papers. He held his breath as the WVS volunteer glanced at them and looking at the address said, 'That block went weeks ago. Where've you been since then?'

Harry smiled at her sadly. 'Just got back,' he said. 'I was at sea at the time. Came home to find it gone, my home. Just a hole in the ground now.'

'Oh, poor you!' cried the woman, her eyes full of sympathy for this brave young man who'd lost his home while serving at sea. 'Don't worry, we'll find you somewhere very soon. In the meantime, Mr Merritt, you can stay here. There's only a men's dormitory, but I can find you a space in there.'

'That'll be fine,' Harry assured her. 'It's only till my leave's up.'

He wasn't the last to return to the centre that night. Although there was normally a curfew so that late comers didn't disturb those already in bed, tonight, VE night, no one cared and many of the beds in the dormitory remained empty as their occupants stayed out celebrating.

When Caroline closed the door behind Harry she went back into the sitting room. Billy was at the window, looking out into the street, but Charlotte was standing beside the cold fireplace. When she saw her expression on the girl's face Caroline knew that Harry's parting comments had been overheard.

'What letter?' Charlotte said without preamble. 'What letter was Harry talking about?'

Caroline sighed and looked across at Billy, but his face was impassive. 'Sit down, Charlotte,' she said. Charlotte did as she was told, perching on the front of an armchair as if about to leap to her feet again.

'That Saturday, when Harry didn't come as promised, you were so upset. I was furious with him for standing you up. Remember the next day I sent you back to Kemble Street to try and get news of the Federmans?'

Charlotte nodded, but made no reply.

'Well,' Caroline drew a deep breath, 'you found them and suddenly your world changed. You were so thrilled to find them again, to see the baby...'

'What about this letter?'

'I'm coming to that,' Caroline said. 'You seemed so much happier than I'd seen you for ages,' she went on. 'And then one morning, when you were down at Wynsdown seeing Mr Thompson, a letter came for you. It had an HMP Brixton postmark. The only person I could think of who might write to you from Brixton prison was Harry.'

'And what did the letter say?' asked Charlotte coldly.

'I don't know,' Caroline said quietly. 'I didn't open it.'

'You threw it away.'

'No, I didn't. I kept it. There were several times when I was about to give it to you, but you seemed to have taken control of your life and,' she glanced again across at Billy, 'I didn't want to stir every-thing up again.'

'You never liked Harry,' Charlotte said, her voice breaking as she spoke. 'You didn't want him to come back into my life, did you? But it was my life and I *did* want him back.'

Caroline could see the tears in Charlotte's eyes and she was filled with regret. Charlotte was right, she'd no right to have kept the letter from her, however good her motives had been.

Charlotte fought to keep her tears at bay. 'So where is it now?' she demanded, 'This letter?'

'It's in my bureau.'

Billy, standing a silent spectator as Caroline admitted what she'd done, started at this information. She had told him she'd destroyed the letter and hearing Charlotte's reaction he'd been feeling relief that she had. Now the inevitable was about to happen. Harry was staking his claim.

Caroline turned and went into her office, coming back holding a buff-coloured envelope and handing it to Charlotte. She took it and looked at it, addressed to her at Livingston Road. The postmark was smudged, the date unreadable, but the frank HMP Brixton, though faint, was there.

Without a word, or a look at either Caroline or Billy, she left the room and went upstairs to her own room, her refuge. She sat down on the bed and for a long time she looked at the envelope and then at last she slipped her finger under the flap. Opening it, she pulled out the single sheet it contained; a letter written in pencil on a sheet of lined paper.

Dear Lisa
I've been arrested and charged with lots of things. Most of them aren't true and it's a fit up. I don't know when they'll be letting me out again. I'm being tried next month some time. When I do get out I'll come and find you and we can get

*together again. I'll be here in Brixton for a while yet, so you
can write to me here. Can't believe I'm banged up again after
I'd just got out of the internment camp.*

Please write.

Love Harry

Charlotte read the letter through twice and at last allowed the
tears to spill down her cheeks. Harry had written to her, but because
Caroline had hidden the letter he thought she'd abandoned him. She
lay down on her bed, still fully dressed, and wept.

The next morning she woke, tired and miserable. Everything
about her life had seemed to be moving to some sort of resolution,
an equilibrium. The war was over, here in London anyway; she was
going to search for her family, she had a home if she wanted to move
back to Somerset, she knew Billy loved her and she'd come to believe
that it might be safe to love him in return. And now, because of this
letter, a letter she should have received nearly three years ago, everything had disintegrated round her. Her plans for searching for her
family seemed as stupid as Harry had told her they were. Her
reunion with the Federmans seemed far away. They were not
responsible for her any more, they had young Nicky, now four and
half. Her brother, they'd called him, but he wasn't and now it seemed
silly to pretend that he was. She and the Federmans would drift
apart as England picked itself up, dusted the war off its knees and
got on with life.

When she didn't appear for breakfast, Caroline sent Billy up to
see her. 'She certainly won't want to see me,' she said, 'but she loves
you, Billy. It's you who must be there to help her get through this.
You are her rock.'

Billy knocked on her door and when there was no answer he
turned the handle and went in. Charlotte was lying, still fully
clothed, on her bed, staring at the ceiling. He went over and sat
down on the bed beside her. She didn't look at him, but he took her
hand in his and stroking it gently said, 'Tell me about Harry.'

*

Harry woke early and having scrounged some breakfast at the centre, decided to go out and find some funds. The small handout he'd been given when he left Gloucester was fast dwindling and somehow he had to get enough money to buy his passage to Australia. His and Lisa's. He hadn't quite given up on her coming with him. When he saw her again and told her about the Morrison woman hiding his letter, she'd know that he'd been thinking about her all the time he was away. That clod-hopping bloke from the country would discover that he, Harry, was the one Lisa would choose. They belonged together.

He stuffed his new papers into his pocket – there was no way he was leaving those in the centre for some thieving bastard to nick – and set off to trawl the crowds still surging about the streets. One of the skills Denny Dunc had encouraged him to acquire, while in Gloucester, was the picking of pockets. An old lag, known as 'Dipper' for his talent in this direction, had taken Harry in hand and by the time he left, Harry was an accomplished pickpocket.

'Never know when you'll need a bob or two to tide you over,' Denny Dunc had said and Harry was about to try his luck. With the crowds still celebrating, many of them boozy and dozy with alcohol, it would, Harry thought as he made his way to Trafalgar Square, be easy pickings. He was just walking up The Strand when he felt a hand on his arm and turned to see Mick Derham, one of the men he'd taken Denny's message to.

'All right, 'Arry?' Mick said.

'Yeah, why? What's up?'

'Denny wants yer.'

'Denny does? He's inside.'

Mick gave him a gap-toothed grin. 'Not any more, 'e ain't. We got 'im out yesterday.'

'Out?' Harry couldn't take in what Mick was saying.

'Everyone else was busy celebratin',' grinned Mick. 'Seemed a good day to go for it. Anyhow,' he went on, 'you got to come with me. Denny wants yer.'

Harry was about to protest, but when he saw the steel in Mick's expression, it seemed a better idea to go with him. They turned back and Mick led him through a maze of side streets, glancing behind from time to time to make sure they weren't being followed.

'How did you know where to find me?' Harry asked.

Mick treated him to the same gap-toothed grin. 'Always knowed where to find you, mate. Denny knew he'd need you sooner or later. Part of the plan, you.'

At last they reached a tiny street down by the docks, narrow, hemmed in by tall buildings. Mick tapped on a door with brown, peeling paint and moments later it opened and they went inside. Another of Denny Dunc's henchmen led them upstairs to a small room overlooking the street and there they found the man himself, sitting in an armchair, a glass of whisky at his elbow.

'Harry, boy!' he cried as Harry came in. 'Good to see you, son.' He glanced at Mick and said, 'No trouble? Good. Give the lad a drink.' Mick slurped some whisky into a glass from an open bottle on the table and handed it to Harry.

'Sit down, Harry,' Denny said, suddenly serious, 'and I tell you what's going down. Surprised to see me, are you?'

Harry took a swig of whisky and nodded. 'Yeah, how'd you swing it?'

'Never mind how, Harry, it's been planned for months, just waiting for the right day. You played your part, now you get your reward.'

'My reward?' Harry wasn't sure he liked the sound of that.

'Coming to Australia, my son. Coming to Australia with me.'

Harry stared at him. 'Australia?'

'It's what you wanted, wasn't it? A clean record sheet. A passport. A new name. I gave you all those, Harry, or should I be calling you "Vic" now? Anyhow, it's all sorted.'

'What's all sorted, Denny?'

'Got a couple of berths on a merchant. *Maiden Lady*. Leaves tomorrow.'

'Tomorrow!'

'Not soon enough for you, Harry boy? Never mind, it's the best I can do.'

'But how...'

Denny gave him a self-satisfied grin. 'Money, boy. Money. Money'll buy you anything if you've got enough. All we have to do is be sure the rozzers don't find us before we go. They'll be on the lookout for you, because they'll know you had a hand in my escape.'

'But I didn't do anything,' gulped Harry.

'Course you did, son. Needed to get my messages out, didn't I? And once they break my tame screw, which they will, all will be revealed. So we have to be well clear before they work it all out. Lucky for us the rozzers ain't very bright. Should take them a while, but we can't take no risks, so it's indoors here for you and me, till we go on board tomorrow night.'

'Why me?' asked Harry, wondering how on earth he was going to get away.

'Cos you're clean, boy. Vic Merritt ain't got a record and you're Vic Merritt now, just like you wanted. Me? I'm George Merritt, your old dad. Travelling together to a new life now that we've been made homeless in London.'

'But... Lisa...' As he said her name, Harry knew he shouldn't have mentioned her.

Denny gave him such a fierce glare that his words trailed away. 'We know you've got a girl, Harry— Vic, I mean, got to get used to calling you that. We know about Lisa and where she is. If you still want her when we get there, Mick here can get her sent out, no trouble, can't you, Mick?'

Mick nodded. 'No trouble, boss.'

Harry thought of Lisa, so vulnerable, unaware that anyone knew about her or was watching her and he said, casually, 'No problem then, I can send for her when we're settled.'

He thought he saw the slightest relaxation in Denny's face, but it was gone as quickly as it came as he said, 'Knew you'd understand, son. Always problems once we involve the ladies... love 'em!' He heaved a sigh. 'My old lady's staying behind. Can't even visit her before I go, the rozzers'll be watching her place like hawks, hoping to nab me there. Still, she knows the score and she never goes without.'

They remained in the upstairs room until dusk the following day. Mick had brought in a paper that had a small piece about Denny's escape, but with the excitement of VE day, it was only half an inch at the bottom of the back page.

'So much the better,' Denny said when he saw it, but Harry had a sneaking suspicion that he was sorry that his escape hadn't made a bigger splash.

As dusk turned to dark, *Maiden Lady* slipped her mooring and slid off down the Thames. Harry stood on deck and watched the lights, now shining clearly along the shore, recede as they reached the sea. He was on his way to Australia; not quite as he planned with Lisa by his side but, he thought with a fatalistic shrug, he'd write to her when he got there and explain it wasn't his fault that he'd gone without her. Lisa would understand.

Chapter Forty-Two

The letter from Switzerland arrived a month later. Charlotte had looked up Nikolaus Becker's address and had written to him yet again. She'd heard nothing from him since he'd returned her letter to her parents back in 1940, but she was desperately hoping that was because the address he'd had for her no longer existed.

It had been a difficult month since VE day. Charlotte continued to work in Livingston Road, but there was a distinct coolness between her and Caroline. She had waited impatiently for Harry to come back as he'd promised, but when he did not, she gradually had to accept that he wasn't going to. It was no good blaming Caroline. She hadn't caused his disappearance and the longer Harry was gone the more Charlotte had to admit that Caroline had, though misguided, thought she was acting in Charlotte's best interests when she'd withheld his letter.

Billy had had to go home again, but not before Charlotte had told him all about Harry, how he'd befriended her, what he meant to her. Billy realised straight away that now was not the time to ask Charlotte to marry him as he'd been intending. Harry's arrival and disappearance were too raw. All his gentle approach, his wooing of Charlotte had been wasted, Billy thought bitterly, wiped out at a stroke by the return of Harry Black.

Charlotte had told him, however, about Miss Edie's bequest. It was still been a matter of conjecture in the village, but no one was really any the wiser. Charlotte had told no one else until she'd told Harry and now she felt it was only fair to tell Billy, too.

He'd stared at her for a moment before saying, 'You mean Blackdown House is yours?'

She nodded.

'But what about the Nicholsons who live there now?'

'They're tenants. They're just renting it for the duration of the war.'

'So you might come back and live there, now the war's over.' Billy tried to keep his voice even, so that the hope that leaped within him didn't sound in his words.

'I don't know, Billy. It all depends.'

Depends on what? Billy wanted to ask, but all he said was, 'Does Harry know?'

It seemed to him that everything related back to Harry. He was glad that Harry hadn't put in an appearance since VE day, but Billy was afraid that he might simply be biding his time until he, Billy, went home again.

'Yes, I told him when I saw him.'

Billy was dying to ask what Harry's reaction had been, but he wanted all thoughts of Harry to fade as fast as possible, so he said nothing.

The day the letter arrived, Charlotte was out with some of the children in the park. She sat and watched them playing on the swings and remembered how Harry had found her there. She glanced round, half expecting to see him coming up behind her, but instead, to her surprise, she saw Caroline hurrying towards her.

'Caroline? What's the matter?'

'You've got a letter, I thought you'd want to see it straight away.'

Charlotte's thoughts flew to Harry, but when she took the letter she saw that the stamps were foreign... Swiss.

'I'll look after the children,' Caroline said. 'You go home and read it in peace.'

Charlotte needed no second bidding. On the back of the envelope, scrawled in the small pointy writing she'd seen before, was the name Nikolaus Becker and an address in Zurich. She almost ran back to the house and went straight up to her room. Nikolaus had answered her letter at last. She sat on the bed and as she had when she'd been given Harry's letter, she looked at the envelope for a long time before having the courage to open it. She assumed it had news of her family, but would it be the news she'd been awaiting so long? Harry had said they would all have vanished into the Nazi killing machine. Was he going to be proved right?

Slowly she opened the envelope and pulled out the letter. It was dated ten days ago.

My Dear Lieselotte
I am so glad you have contacted me again with a new address. I have written to you before at the old one but received no reply. I managed to contact Bloomsbury House and found to my dismay that you were reported killed in September 1940. They had no record of your survival.

Now that the hostilities are over in Europe many hundreds of survivors of the Nazi camps have been found and some have been connected with their relatives through the American hospitals and the Red Cross. I am delighted to tell you your mother is one of them. She has been in an American army hospital since she was rescued from some labour camp, I don't know where, but she remembered me and the Red Cross made contact. I have arranged for her to come to Zurich. I am sorry to say that there is no sign of your brother or father. Names are being published daily of those who have perished, but so far no news good or bad of them. I don't know how your mother managed to survive, but she has, though she is extremely weak. I don't know much of your circumstances now, but if you were able to come to Zurich I know it would make her very happy. She is in no state to travel to England to see you. To be honest with you, I'm not sure she will ever be well again. Perhaps, with good nursing here in Switzerland, she may recover to some extent, but if you can come I think it should be as soon as possible. I include my telephone number, but it may be impossible to speak to me. As you can imagine, with the end of the war, things are in chaos and even our neutral Switzerland is badly affected.

*If you are able to come and visit, my wife, Anna, and I
would be delighted if you would stay with us for a few days.*

*Please write your intentions to me soon, so that if you are
able to come, we can make arrangements for your stay.*

Yours,

Nikolaus Becker

Charlotte felt a sudden surge of joy. Mutti was alive and had
been moved to a hospital in Switzerland. There was no news of Papa
or Martin, but that didn't mean they were dead, just not found yet.
Mutti was alive and Mutti needed her. Charlotte leaped to her feet
and ran downstairs to find Caroline. She had to share her great
news with someone. As she reached the hall, Caroline was returning
with the children from the park. She saw the joy on Charlotte's face,
and all animosity between them died as she flung herself into
Caroline's arms.

'She's alive!' she cried as the tears streamed down her face. 'My
mother's alive.'

Caroline hugged her tight, her own tears mingling with
Charlotte's. 'That's wonderful news, just wonderful,' she said. 'Oh,
Charlotte, my dearest, I'm so pleased for you.'

A little later when they had the chance to sit down with a cup of
tea, she asked, 'So, what are you going to do?'

'I've thought it all through,' Charlotte told her. 'I'm going down
to Somerset tomorrow to see Mr Thompson and the vicar. I need
money from my trust to pay my fare to Zurich.'

'But how will you get there?'

'Boat, train, whatever way I can.'

Caroline, seeing that Charlotte was determined and anxious to
repair the damage her withholding Harry's letter had done between
them, said, 'We shall miss you while you're away, but things are a
little easier just now and Ethel has been a godsend.'

Charlotte left for Somerset the next day. She had phoned the
Swansons to say she was coming and Avril had sounded delighted.

'How lovely,' she cried. 'We can't wait to see you. Someone'll
meet you at the station. How long can you stay?'

'Just a flying visit, I'm afraid. I have to see the vicar and Mr Thompson, but,' Charlotte promised, 'I'll tell you all about it when I see you.' Then the pips went and she said goodbye.

Billy was waiting at the station, standing on the platform when Charlotte got off the train. They hugged and Billy kissed her briefly on the mouth before leading her out to John Shepherd's car.

'This is a sudden visit,' Billy said as they drove up the hill to Wynsdown. 'Has something happened?' As soon as he'd heard that Charlotte was coming down for a few days, he'd begun to worry that Harry had reappeared. Charlotte's reply, 'I'll tell you all about it when we've got a chance to talk properly, Billy,' did little to reassure him.

The Swansons greeted Charlotte with delight.

'Charlotte, my dear girl, it's so lovely to see you,' Avril said as she hugged her. 'We can't wait to hear how things are in London.' She was indeed agog. Caroline had hinted that there was something important that Charlotte wanted to discuss with her trustees, but she'd learned her lesson and would say no more. There was no way that she was going to interfere in Charlotte's life again.

'Hold on, Avril,' laughed the vicar as he, too, gave Charlotte a hug. 'The poor girl's only just walked in the door. Feed her first, then we can chat.'

'Yes, yes, of course,' Avril said. She glanced across at Billy, standing in the doorway. 'You'll stay for supper, Billy?'

After they'd finished the meal, they sat round the familiar kitchen table and listened to what she had to say.

'So you see,' Charlotte finished, 'I need some of my money so that I can go to Zurich and find my mother.'

'By yourself?' Avril sounded alarmed.

'Of course not,' said Billy. 'I'm going with her.'

Charlotte turned and stared at him. 'Billy, you can't.'

'Why not? Why can't I?'

'It's so far. I don't know what I'm going to find there. I don't know long I'm going to be.'

'I know,' Billy replied. 'That's why I'm coming with you.'

'I – I don't know...' Charlotte began, hope and uncertainty in her eyes.

'I do,' said Billy firmly. He reached across the table and took her hand. 'You can't think I'd let you go on your own, Char. No buts, I'm coming.'

'Then we'll need to release enough money to get you both there and back,' David said. 'I'll speak to Thompson in the morning and we'll get it all arranged.'

That night Charlotte lay in bed in the vicarage and thought about the journey ahead. It wouldn't be easy crossing war-torn France and though she'd been determined to go, the thought of having Billy with her had lifted a burden she hadn't realised she'd been carrying.

Next morning they all met with Mr Thompson and the two trustees agreed to release the money Charlotte and Billy would need for their journey. They left Wynsdown together on the afternoon train.

They crossed over to France and took a train to Paris. The French railways were still running and they managed to catch a late-night train to Strasbourg on the next leg of their journey. As they sat together in the compartment, surrounded by people dozing to the movement of the train, Charlotte curled up against Billy, her head on his shoulder, his arms holding her close. They, too, nodded from time to time, but Charlotte was too strung up to sleep properly. She had no idea of what state her mother was in, just that she'd been in hospital and was frail.

They finally reached Zurich three days after they had left Wynsdown. Tired and hungry, having eaten nothing but the sandwiches they'd brought for the journey, they found a café in the station and had some sort of soup and some crusty bread and cheese before setting out to find Nikolaus. There were taxis waiting outside the station and Charlotte gave the driver Nikolaus Becker's address.

'Seems an extravagance taking a taxi,' she said as they drove through the city, clean and bright and undefaced by the ravages of war, 'but I don't know how else we'll find him.'

Billy squeezed her hand. 'You're right,' he said. 'And that's the quickest way to find your mother.'

Nikolaus Becker lived in an apartment block in a side street, not far from the business district. The taxi deposited them outside and Charlotte looked at the row of bells beside the communal front door. There it was, Becker N. She gave Billy a nervous smile and pressed the bell. Would Cousin Nikolaus be expecting her? She had tried to phone as soon as she'd got his letter, but it was impossible to get a line to Zurich, so she had written to tell him she was on her way, but she had no idea whether or not he would have received her letter yet. The door opened with a buzz and they went in. Stairs led upwards and there was a cage lift. They took the stairs.

There seemed to be two apartments on each floor, each with a name and a bell outside. The Beckers lived on the second floor.

When Charlotte pressed their bell the door opened almost immediately and a maid in a black uniform stood there. 'Yes?'

'Lieselotte Becker to see Herr Becker.' Charlotte spoke in German, though the words sounded odd even to her own ears. She hadn't spoken German since the night she'd comforted Dieter Karhausen.

The maid stood aside and let them into a wide hallway. 'Wait here please,' she said, 'I'll see if Herr Becker is at home.'

Nikolaus Becker appeared moments later, peering at the couple who waited in his front hall. 'Lieselotte?' he said. 'Is it really you?'

Charlotte assured him it was and introduced Billy, who, speaking no German simply smiled and shook hands. Nikolaus led them into a large drawing room that looked out on to the street below. As they entered a woman got up from a chair by the window and Nikolaus introduced her as his wife, Anna. She was tall, taller than her husband, elegantly dressed with her silver hair swept up into a chignon.

'Lisa,' she drawled, 'we're *so* glad you came. We were hoping you would.'

'I did write,' Charlotte said, 'but maybe I've got here before my letter. How's my mother?'

'And who is this?' Anna didn't answer her question, but looked at Billy with interest.

'This is my friend, Billy Shepherd,' Charlotte said. She had no time to go into the ins and outs of her relationship with Billy. 'How's my mother? Where is she?'

'She's in a nursing home,' replied Anna. 'We couldn't look after her here.'

Charlotte, who had just sat down, got at once to her feet. 'Can you take me to see her?'

'Of course,' Anna said smoothly, 'but surely you'll take a little refreshment first?'

'No, thank you,' Charlotte said. 'We've had something. Please, can you take us to the nursing home?'

Anna smiled. 'Of course, Nikolaus'll take you. Where were you planning to stay?'

Billy could see that Charlotte was getting agitated and said softly, 'What's going on, Char?'

'Nothing, Mr Shepherd, I do assure you,' Anna said in perfect English. 'I was just asking where you were planning to stay during your visit. Lisa is, of course, most welcome to stay here with us, but since you are with her, you'd probably be more comfortable in an hotel.'

Billy gave a polite smile, but Charlotte could see he was angry. 'Of course,' he replied. 'Don't worry about us. We shall find a hotel once Charlotte's seen her mother.'

'Charlotte?'

'Lisa. Lisa's mother.'

'I see, well, perhaps you'd like to wash your hands, freshen up a little while Nikolaus fetches the car.' She showed them across the hall where there was a large bathroom. Charlotte went in first, and when she'd closed the door behind her, peered into the mirror above the basin. Staring back at her was a pale-faced girl, with huge tired eyes. They'd come so far and she'd thought for a moment that her mother would be waiting here in this apartment when she arrived. She should have known, she supposed that Mutti would need proper nursing care, but as she'd walked into the opulent apartment, she'd been glad that her mother was in such pleasant surroundings.

Nikolaus drove them the three or four miles to the nursing home. He seemed more relaxed now that there were just the three of them and he spoke more easily.

'Your poor mother made contact with us through the Red Cross just before the surrender,' he said. 'We'd heard nothing of any of them before that. I arranged for her to be brought here, but she was in a far worse state than I'd expected.' He sighed. 'We couldn't look after her at home, Lisa. Anna, my wife....' His voice faltered to embarrassed silence.

'I'm know you did all you could,' Charlotte assured him. 'Thank you for taking care of her and for sending for me.'

'I'm afraid you'll find her very changed,' Nikolaus said sadly.

'Did she say anything about Papa or Martin?' Charlotte asked. 'Does she know where they are?'

Nikolaus sighed again. 'I will tell you what she said.' He pulled up into the car park of a large house, cut the engine and turned to face her. 'It is not good news, I'm afraid. Franz was arrested and we have no news of him. Martin lived with your mother for a while and then they came and took him away. Because he was blind they sent him to a home for the handicapped somewhere in Bavaria, but he died.'

'How?' whispered Charlotte.

'We don't know. Your mother simply got a card saying he was dead.'

'What did she do? Where did she go?'

'She was helped by one of your father's old patients. He had saved the life of her son after the Great War, and she'd never forgotten. She wasn't Jewish, but she took your mother in and hid her. She kept her hidden until someone betrayed them to the Gestapo. They were both arrested and sent to a camp. I don't know what happened to the other woman, but your mother managed to survive until the Americans came.' Nikolaus fell silent for a moment and then added, 'I thought you should know all these things before you see her. Those that survived the camps... It explains how she is.' He gestured to the house. 'Go in and ask for her. I will wait for you here.'

They had been speaking German and Billy had listened to the flow of conversation without understanding it, not the words, but he understood the import, from their voices and the way the colour drained from Charlotte's face and her jaw set as she battled with unshed tears. He was holding her hand and her grip had tightened as she sat, ramrod-straight in the back of the car, and listened to what Nikolaus was telling her.

When at last he fell silent, the air in the car seemed stifling. Charlotte opened the door and got out. Billy followed her and waited as she leaned back into the car and said something else. Then she said, 'Come on, Billy. She's in here.' And turning, she walked resolutely up to the front door and rang the bell.

A nurse led them along a corridor and stopped outside one of the doors. 'She's in here. She's a little weak, today.' She opened the door and said brightly, 'Now then, Marta. Here's your daughter come to see you.'

'I'll wait outside,' Billy said, but Charlotte shook her head.

'No,' she said. 'Come in with me. Please?'

Together they walked into the room. It was small, but it was filled with sunlight that streamed through a window overlooking the garden. The bed stood in the middle, a chair on either side, and on it lay an emaciated figure, scarcely bigger than a child. If Charlotte hadn't known it was her mother, she wouldn't have recognised her. Her limbs were skeletal, her face no more than a skin-covered skull. Wisps of thin grey hair clung to her head and her eyes, though open, were glazed and unseeing.

Charlotte stared at her for a long moment, stunned by what she saw, unable to take it in. Cousin Nikolaus had warned her that her mother was ill, but she wasn't prepared for this. Tears sprang to her eyes, but she blinked them away. She had to be strong. She'd found her mother and she had to be strong for her.

She moved to the bedside and reached for the bony hand that lay above the covers.

'Mutti?' she whispered. 'Mutti? It's me, Lisa.' Sitting down on the chair, she stroked her mother's hand. There was no reaction from the tiny figure on the bed, but Lisa continued to speak to her,

her voice soft and gentle. 'Mutti, I'm here. It's Lisa. I've come from London to find you and when you're better, I'll take you home.'

She continued to talk to her, just in case Mutti was somewhere inside this husk of a woman and could hear her. Softly, she told her about her life in England, about the Federmans, how they'd looked after her, how she'd been evacuated to Wynsdown, about Miss Edie's kindness, how she was working in a children's home. Once, just once, she felt a returning pressure from the hand she held. She looked into her mother's face and saw a flicker behind the eyes.

'Billy's here with me,' Charlotte told her. 'He's come all the way with me, to see you.' She glanced across at Billy, who was standing by the window, the sun striking his fair hair, creating a halo round his head. 'He's been my good angel, Mutti.'

There was a movement from the bed and Charlotte looked back, just in time to see a moment of lucidity in her mother's eyes and to hear the breathed word, 'Lisa!' And then the light went out. Marta Becker was gone.

Charlotte knew at once. Her mother had recognised her, and knowing she was alive, had simply let go, slipping away into merciful oblivion. Charlotte saw Marta's face relax, the pain smoothed away in death, and caught a glimpse of the mother she'd last seen over six years ago. She sat dry-eyed, still holding Mutti's hand for a long while before she gently released it and stood up. She held out her arms to Billy, standing so silently by the window, and he gathered her to him, his face resting against her hair.

The sun still streamed through the window, bathing the silent room in light and warmth, and for a long moment they stood together, before Charlotte looked up into Billy's face and said, 'Let's go, Billy. It's time to go home.'

Epilogue

The whole village had turned out to see them, to help celebrate the first Wynsdown wedding since the end of the war. The church, brilliant with dahlias and chrysanthemums, was full of excited, happy people. The autumn sun shone through the stained glass, casting patterns on the flagged floor, and there was an excited buzz of conversation in the congregation.

Billy stood nervously beside his best man, Malcolm, waiting for Charlotte to arrive. Behind him sat his parents and Jane. His mother beamed at everyone from under the brim of her new straw hat, his father, crammed rather uncomfortably into a suit, ran his finger round the collar of his new shirt and wished he didn't have to wear a tie, but both were proud as Punch of their tall, handsome son, standing, waiting for his bride.

There was a stir at the back of the church as Naomi Federman came in, walking down the aisle to take her place in the front pew. Everyone wanted to see Charlotte's foster mother, come all the way from Suffolk. As mother of the bride, she had been at Blackdown House, helping Charlotte into her wedding dress, the wedding dress Miss Edie had made so lovingly over twenty-five years earlier.

When she'd come down to Wynsdown on her return from Switzerland, Charlotte had unpacked it from the trunk and tried it on, and with a few alterations it fitted her perfectly.

'Do you think she'd mind me wearing it?' she'd asked Avril anxiously. 'Miss Edie?'

'No,' Avril assured her with a smile. 'I think she'd be delighted.'

'You are lucky,' Clare said enviously as she helped Naomi to arrange the veil over her dark hair. 'No one has proper wedding dresses these days.'

'You look beautiful, Lisa,' Naomi said, tears in her eyes. 'We're all so proud of you. Your parents and Miss Edie would be, too. Your Billy's a lucky man.'

Charlotte walked into the church on the arm of her foster father, Uncle Dan. As she paused at the door to greet the vicar, Clare straightened the skirt of her dress and, taking Nicky's hand stood him in front of Charlotte.

'Remember,' she whispered, 'just walk in front of Charlotte... Lisa, I mean... till she gets to the steps and then go and sit with your mum.'

Nicky nodded seriously, conscious of his special part in Lisa's wedding. He was a page and that made him special. He'd even had new shoes for the occasion. He looked down at them, brown shining sandals on his feet, and beamed with delight.

The organ began to play and Billy turned to see his Charlotte walking slowly down the aisle on her uncle Dan's arm, coming to be married, to him. Tears of joy filled his eyes and as Charlotte reached him and threw back her veil, he saw his own joy reflected in her face. Charlotte handed her bouquet to Clare, then turning back to Billy, she took his outstretched hand and they both stepped forward, ready to begin their life together.